HOME ON THE RANCH:
REDEMPTION

——————— ⚒ ———————

LAURA MARIE ALTOM
New York Times **Bestselling Author**
CATHY McDAVID

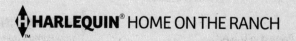

HARLEQUIN® HOME ON THE RANCH

ISBN-13: 978-1-335-50708-2

First published as The Cowboy SEAL
by Harlequin Books in 2014 and
Her Rodeo Man by Harlequin Books in 2015.

Home on the Ranch: Redemption
Copyright © 2018 by Harlequin Books S.A.

The publisher acknowledges the copyright
holders of the individual works as follows:

The Cowboy SEAL
Copyright © 2014 by Laura Marie Altom

Her Rodeo Man
Copyright © 2015 by Cathy McDavid

Recycling programs
for this product may
not exist in your area.

Printed in U.S.A.

www.Harlequin.com

CONTENTS

Laura Marie Altom is a bestselling and award-winning author who has penned nearly fifty books. After college (go, Hogs!), Laura Marie did a brief stint as an interior designer before becoming a stay-at-home mom to boy-girl twins and a bonus son. Always an avid romance reader, she knew it was time to try her hand at writing when she found herself replotting the afternoon soaps.

When not immersed in her next story, Laura plays video games, tackles Mount Laundry and, of course, reads romance!

Laura loves hearing from readers at either PO Box 2074, Tulsa, OK 74101, or by email, balipalm@aol.com.

Love winning fun stuff? Check out lauramariealtom.com.

Books by Laura Marie Altom

Harlequin Western Romance

Cowboy SEALs

The SEAL's Miracle Baby
The Baby and the Cowboy SEAL
The SEAL's Second Chance Baby
The Cowboy SEAL's Jingle Bell Baby
The Cowboy SEAL's Christmas Baby

Visit the Author Profile page at Harlequin.com for more titles.

THE COWBOY SEAL

LAURA MARIE ALTOM

This story is dedicated to Dr. Keith L. Stanley and Dr. Brent C. Nossaman, as well as the nurses and staff of Tulsa Bone & Joint. Thank you for giving me back my hand!

Chapter 1

"Hey there, cowboy."

From his stool at Tipsea's crowded bar, Navy SEAL Cooper Hansen cast a sideways glance at the stacked brunette who'd slipped her arm around his shoulders.

"Buy a lady a drink?"

"Be happy to…" After tipping the brim of his raggedy straw Stetson, he nodded to the bartender. "Only I'm gonna need you to finish it over there."

When he pointed to the opposite side of the most popular squid hangout in town—her expression morphed from confusion to anger. "I should've known better than to chase after a no-good cowboy in a SEAL bar. Obviously, you don't have a clue what it's like to be a *real* man."

"Guess not." Rather than watch her go, he swigged his longneck brew, intent on enjoying his few remaining hours of freedom for what he feared could be a good, long while.

His pal and team member, Grady Matthews, took the stool alongside him. Everyone called him Sheikh due to the fact that on any given night of the week, he was surrounded by his own personal harem of beauties. "You do know the object of hitting a bar is to go home with the pretty girl, not to run her off, right?"

After taking another deep pull, Cooper snorted. "Thanks for the advice, but given my current dark-ass mood, the only place any sane woman would want me is far away."

"There you are, Cowboy!" Another longtime friend and team member, Heath Stone, wandered up. "Everyone's looking for you. The whole point of this gathering was to give you a night so good, you don't forget to hurry back."

"I appreciate it, man—" Cooper patted his friend's shoulder "—but knowing what's ahead of me, any hellhole on the planet looks better than where I'm headed."

"Which is where? Sorry, I only paid attention to the guys'-night portion of the email." He gave him a wink and an elbow nudge. "Not that I'm complaining, but I can't remember the last time I've been out of the house. Libby keeps me on a tight leash."

"And if you don't kiss me, I'll give that leash a good, hard tug." Heath's wife, Libby, snuck up behind him to nuzzle his neck. Cooper was no expert on the whole love thing, but if he was a betting man, he'd say his friend was a goner.

While the two indulged in giggling and good, old-fashioned necking, Cooper discreetly looked away. The bar was dim and Pearl Jam loud. Tipsea's was a legend in Norfolk, and since another team member's wife purchased it, SEALs always drank free—a perk Cooper would very much miss. The grunge rock? Not so much. He was more of an old-school Hank Williams kind of guy.

His pals meant well by hosting this shindig, but the God's honest truth was that he'd just as soon get on with things. No amount of beer or pretty women would sugarcoat the fact that what he had waiting for him back home in Brewer's Falls, Colorado, was good, old-fashioned hell.

"How's Clint doing?" Millie Hansen looked up from the stack of bills she'd been arranging in order of importance. The electric company's blaze-orange shut-off notice took precedence over the two late-payment credit card notices.

"Finally asleep." As she was near to sleepwalking herself, Millie's heart went out to her sister-in-law, Peg.

"I can't thank you enough for your help. Since Jim died…" She removed her reading glasses, blotting her eyes with her sweater sleeve—who could afford genuine tissues?

"He's my dad. Where else would I be?" She arched her head back and closed her eyes.

At 10:00 p.m. on a blustery January Monday, the old Queen Anne home shuddered from the force of the Colorado plain's wind. The desk's banker's lamp provided the office's only light. Both kids were blessedly in their rooms—Millie didn't fool herself by believing the older one was actually sleeping. Eleven-year-old LeeAnn was probably reading with the aid of a flashlight beneath her covers. J.J.—age seven—had crashed before Millie finished tucking him in.

She set her reading glasses atop her open, ledger-style checkbook. "Hate to bring up a sore subject, but did you ever hear from Cooper?"

Peg sighed. "Left a half-dozen messages. Does hearing his gruff voice mail recording count as contact?"

"What're we going to do?" During the long days spent cooking and doing the dozens of other daily chores it took to keep the ranch running, Millie didn't have time to worry, much less spare a thought for her absentee brother-in-law, Cooper. But at night, fears crept in, slithering into every vulnerable part of her soul, reminding her just how bad the past few years had been and how much worse her future could get. If they lost the ranch that'd been in the Hansen family for over a hundred years, she didn't know what they'd do—where they'd even go.

"I ask myself that question every night when I'm up pacing, because worry won't let me sleep."

"Will we make it to spring?"

Shrugging, Peg leaned forward, resting her elbows on her knees. "You know I'd stay if I could, but my savings is dwindling, and I still have a mortgage back in Denver. The hospital won't give me more leave. Come Monday, I'm expected back."

Millie swallowed the knot in her throat and nodded. "I understand."

"Dad's stable enough that I've arranged for a series of nurses and therapists to keep up with his rehabilitation here at home. His speech therapist said Dad's making all the right sounds, so with work, in between official therapy sessions, you and I should be able to help him make the right connections. Hopefully, a few neighbors will step in to help with his general care during the day."

And at night? Caring for a stroke victim was an around-the-clock job. Getting the Black Angus herd that would be their salvation come spring through what was feeling like a never-ending winter wasn't exactly your average nine-to-fiver. Then there were her kids, whom Millie already spent precious little time with. The weight of her responsibilities bore down on her shoulders, making them ache. "Lynette mentioned she'd be willing to come over anytime we need her. I'll give her a call." Lynette was Millie's best friend since kindergarten. She'd been a godsend after Jim died.

"Good. Maybe Wilma could help out some, too? I'll drive up every weekend." Wilma was a widowed neighbor who used to be in a quilting circle with the woman who would've been Millie's mother-in-law—that is, if Kay Hansen had lived long enough to see her youngest son marry. Her death was never spoken of. Her passing had launched the beginning of the Hansen family's unraveling.

Exhaustion from the twenty-seven-hour drive did nothing to ease the acid churning in Cooper's stomach. The cold, cloudy morning cast a gray pall over his already dreary hometown.

In the twelve years since he'd been gone, nothing about Brewer's Falls had changed. Same bedraggled downtown with the century-old brick bank that also served as the post office and drugstore. Besides the feed store, Elmer's Grocery, the diner, bar and community center, no other businesses lined the only road. The few kids were bused the two-hour round trip to attend school in Wilmington.

The half-block stretch of sidewalks was weed-choked and cracked, and the few trees were bare. Hanging baskets filled with the brown ghosts of summer's bounty swung from the diner's porch.

In all of a minute's time, he'd left town to turn onto the dirt road leading to his family's ranch. He'd forgotten the plain's stark beauty, and yet he'd joined the Navy with the express purpose of finding that same beauty at sea.

The ugly-ass town with its homely jumble of buildings had no redeeming qualities other than, he supposed, the good people who lived there. A few old-timers. His little brother's widow and her kids—the nephew and niece that due to his father's hatred, Cooper had never even met.

If anything, the lonely town served as a blight upon the otherwise beautiful land. Hell, Brewer's Falls didn't even have a waterfall. The town's founder—Hawthorne Brewer—thought the idyllic name might draw in folks wanting a quieter way of life.

The road was in even worse shape than he remembered, which served his purpose well, considering the rock-strewn surface forced him to slow his pace.

The school bus passed.

Were his niece and nephew on board?

For a moment, the passing vehicle's dust cloud impeded his view, but when the dust settled, the life he'd spent years trying to forget came roaring into view.

At first, the two-story home, outbuildings and the cottonwoods his grandparents had planted were a distant speck. As they grew, so did his dread.

You're not my son, but a murderer....

Bile rose in his throat while his palms sweat and his pulse uncomfortably raced.

The Black Angus cattle that, for as long as Cooper could remember had been the ranch's lifeblood, huddled near the south pasture feeding station. The livestock's breath fogged in the cold morning air. How many mornings just like this had he ridden out at dawn to check on them?

It seemed inconceivable that he'd once felt more at ease on the back of his horse than he now did at a depth of a hundred feet.

The closer the house loomed, the more evident it became that the ranch and its occupants had fallen on hard times. His big sister, Peg—an ICU nurse who'd long since moved to Denver—was the only family he talked to. She'd told him that after his brother's death, his father had for all practical purposes shut down. Cooper had offered to return then, but Peg reported having broached the topic with their dad only to find him not just unreceptive, but downright hostile.

And so Cooper had continued his exile.

He pulled onto the house's dirt drive, holding his breath when passing the spot where basically, his life had ended. Sure, he'd worked hard and made a new family with his SEAL team, but it was his old one he mourned.

The one he'd literally and figuratively killed.

He put his truck in park, letting it idle for a minute before cutting the engine. He braced his forearms against the wheel, resting his chin atop them, staring at the house that in his mind's eye had once been the most wondrous place on earth. Now the front porch gutter sagged and over a decade's worth of summer sun had faded his mother's favorite shade of yellow paint to dirty white. Weeds choked her flower garden, and the branch holding his childhood tire swing had broken.

A dozen memories knotted his throat—cruel reminders that this was no longer his home. Per his sister's repeated requests, he'd help until his dad got back on his feet, but after that, Cooper would retreat to the haven the Navy had become.

Forcing a deep breath, he knew he could no longer put off the inevitable. From the sounds of it, his dad was in such bad shape, he wouldn't even realize his son had stepped foot in the house. By the time he did, Cooper would've worked up his courage enough to face him.

Out of his ride, he grabbed his ditty bag from the truck bed, slinging it over his shoulder.

Feet leaden, heart heavier still, he crossed the mostly dirt yard to mount steps he'd last tread upon when he'd essentially been a boy. The Navy had honed him into a man, but confronting his past eroded his training like ocean waves ripping apart a fragile shore.

It all came rushing back.

That god-awful night when he'd done the unthinkable. His sister's screams. His brother's and father's stoic stares. The funeral. The guilt that clung tight to this day.

"Cooper?"

He looked up to find his sister-in-law, his little brother's high school sweetheart, clutching her tattered blue robe closed at the throat.

He removed his hat, pinning it to his chest. "Hey…"

"What're you doing here? I thought— I'm sorry.

Where are my manners?" She held open the front door. "Get in here before you catch your death of cold."

He brushed past her, hyperaware of the light floral fragrance she'd worn since her sixteenth birthday when his brother had gifted it to her, declaring her to be the prettiest girl he knew. Millie was no longer pretty, but beautiful. Her hair a deep chestnut, and her haunted gaze as blue as a spring sky, despite dark circles shadowing her eyes. He couldn't help but stare. Catching himself, hating that his face grew warm, he sharply looked away.

The contrast of the front room's warmth to the outside chill caused him to shiver. He'd forgotten a real winter's bite.

"I—I can't believe you're here." She'd backed onto the sofa arm—the same sofa he used to catch her and Jim making out on. She fussed with her hair, looking at him, then away. "Peg tried calling so many times…."

"Sorry." He set his ditty bag on the wood floor, then shrugged out of his Navy-issued pea jacket to hang it on the rack near the door. He'd have felt a damn sight better with his hat back on, but his mother had never allowed hats in the house, so he hung it alongside his coat. "I've been out of town." Syria had been *lovely* this time of year. "Guess I should've called, but…"

"It's okay. I understand."

Did she? Did she have a clue what it had been like for him to one day belong to a loving, complete family and the next to have accidentally committed an act so heinous, his own father never spoke to him again?

"You're here now, and that's what matters."

"Yeah…" Unsure what to do with his hands, he crammed them into his pockets.

"I imagine you want to see your dad?"

He sharply exhaled. "No. Hell, no."

"Then why did you come?"

"Peg said you need me."

She chewed on that for a moment, then shook her head. "I needed you when Jim died, too. Where were you then?"

"Aw, come on, Mill… You know this is complicated." Skimming his hands over his buzz-cut hair, he turned away from her and sighed. "Got any coffee?"

"Sure."

He followed her into the kitchen, momentarily distracted by the womanly sway of her hips. Two kids had changed her body, but for the better. He liked her with a little meat on her bones—not that it was his place to assess such a thing. She'd always been—would always be—his brother's girl.

She handed him a steaming mug.

He took a sip, only to blanch. "You always did make awful coffee. Good to see that hasn't changed."

Her faint smile didn't reach blue eyes glistening with unshed tears. "I can't believe you're really here."

"In the flesh."

"How long are you staying?"

"Long as you need me." Or at least until his dad regained his faculties enough to kick him out again. To this day, his father's hatred still burned, but the worst part of all was that Cooper didn't blame him. Hell, the whole reason he worked himself so damned hard during the day was so exhaustion granted some small measure of peace at night.

"You haven't changed a bit," she noted from behind

her own mug. "I always could see the gears working in your mind."

"Yeah?" He dumped his coffee down the drain then started making a fresh pot. "Tell me, swami, what am I thinking?"

"About her." She crept up behind him, killing him when she slipped her arms around his waist for a desperately needed, but undeserved hug. Her kindness made it impossible to breathe, to think, to understand that after all this time, why he was even here. "It's okay, Coop." She rested her forehead between his shoulder blades. Her warm exhalations sent shock waves through his T-shirt then radiating across his back. "I mean, obviously it's not okay, but you have to let it go. Your mom was so kind. She'd hate seeing you this way."

A dozen years' grief and anger and heartache balled inside him, threatening to shatter. Why was Millie being nice? Why didn't she yell or condemn him for staying away? Why didn't she do anything other than give him the comfort he'd so desperately craved?

"Coop, look at me...." Her small hands tugged him around to face her, and when she used those hands to cup his cheeks while her gaze locked with his, he couldn't for a second longer hold in his pain. What was he doing here? No matter what Peg said, he never should've come. "Honey, yes, what happened was awful, but it was an accident. Everyone knows that. No one blames you."

A sarcastic laugh escaped him. "Have you met my father?"

"When your mom died, he was out of his mind with grief. He didn't know what he was saying or doing. I'll bet if you two talked now, then—"

"How are we going to do that? The man suffered a stroke."

"That doesn't mean he can't listen. At least give it a try. You owe yourself that much."

How could she say that after what he'd done? The world—let alone his father—didn't owe him shit. "Coming here—it was a mistake. I never should've—"

"You're wrong, Cooper. Your dad may not admit it, but he needs you. I need you." She stepped back to gesture to the dilapidated kitchen with its outdated appliances, faded wallpaper and torn linoleum floor. "This place needs you."

He slammed the filter drawer shut on the ancient Mr. Coffee. "More than you could ever know, I appreciate your kind words, Mill, but seriously? What does anyone need with a guy who killed his own mother?"

Chapter 2

Millie's mind still reeled from the fact that her husband's brother was even in the room, let alone the fact that he was here to stay awhile. His mere presence was a godsend. While she considered the tragedy that'd caused his mother's death to be ancient history, for him it seemed time had stood still. Had he even begun to process the fact Jim was gone, too?

Before the coffee finished brewing, he pulled out the glass pot, replacing it with his mug. With it only half-full, he replaced the pot.

"Better?" she found the wherewithal to ask after he'd downed a good portion of the brew.

"Much." His faint smile reminded her so much of her lost love that her heart skipped a beat. It'd been three years since she'd lost Jim, and while she thought of him often—would never forget him—in the time he'd been gone, more urgent matters occupied the space grief had once filled in her heart.

"Hungry?" she asked. "The kids got oatmeal, but if you want, I'll cook you up something more substantial." Busying her flighty hands, she rummaged through the fridge. "There's a little bacon. We always have plenty of eggs. Pancakes? Do you still like them?"

"Coffee's fine," he said with a wag of his mug. He looked her up and down, then politely aimed his stare out the kitchen window. "Judging by your outfit, you haven't done any of the outside chores?"

She reddened, clutching the robe close at her throat.

"I assume the routine hasn't changed?"

"No, but you're probably tired from your drive. Why don't you nap for a bit, and after I check on your dad, I'll head outside."

"No need. Fresh air will do me good."

"You do know you're eventually going to have to see him."

"Dad?"

"The Easter Bunny…"

He finished his coffee then put the mug in the sink. "Not if I can help it." He nodded to the tan Carhartt hanging on a hook by the back door. "Mind if I borrow that?"

"Help yourself." The duster-style coat had belonged to Jim. Sometimes when she felt particularly overwhelmed, she wore it to remind her of him. It used to smell of him—the trace of the tobacco he'd chewed. How many times had she scolded him to quit, afraid of losing him to cancer when instead he'd passed from a hunting accident?

"Was this my brother's?"

Swallowing the knot in her throat, she nodded.

She wanted to rail on him for not having had the common decency—the respect—to attend Jim's funeral, but she lacked the strength to argue.

"About that…"

"J-just go, Cooper." She didn't want to hear what he had to say, because no mere explanation would ever be good enough. No matter what, a man didn't miss his own brother's funeral. Just didn't happen.

The set of his stubbled square jaw was grim, but then so was the inside of her battered heart. Peg might've told him what the past few years without her husband had been like for Millie, but he didn't really know. Beyond the financial toll Jim's death had taken, emotionally, she felt as if a spring twister had uprooted every aspect of her and her kids' lives. And speaking of her kids, they'd never even had the pleasure of meeting their uncle Cooper.

"Okay…" he mumbled.

Never-ending seconds stretched between them. Her watering eyes refused to quit stinging, and her frayed nerves itched for a fight.

"Thanks for the coffee. Guess I'll head outside."

Only after he'd gone, leaving her with just the wall of brutal January air to prove he'd ever even been in the room, did Millie dare exhale.

From a workload standpoint, having Cooper back on the ranch might be a godsend, but would it be worth the emotional toll?

"Hey, girl…" Cooper approached Sassy, the sorrel mare he'd been given for his eighteenth birthday. At the time, working this ranch, finding a good woman, having kids, had been all he'd ever wanted from life. Strange how even though he'd accomplished and seen more than he ever could've dreamed, he still felt like that kid who'd been run off in shame. "Long time, no see, huh?"

He stroked her nose and was rewarded by a warm, breathy snort against his palm. For this weather, he should've worn gloves and a hat, but pride won over common sense when he'd scurried for the barn's safety.

Regardless of where things stood with his father, Cooper knew damn well he'd done wrong by his brother and sweet Millie.

It'd been ages since he'd saddled a horse, and it took a while to get his bearings. Having followed the routine since he'd been a kid, he knew the drill, just had to reacquaint himself with where everything was stored. He found leather work gloves that'd seen better days and a hat that looked like a horse had stomped it to death before it'd wrestled with a tractor. Regardless, he slapped it on his head, thankful for the warmth, but wishing the simple work didn't leave his mind with so much space to wander.

Millie wasn't flashy.

Hell, back in Virginia Beach, she wasn't the sort of woman to whom he'd have given a second glance. Funny thing was, back at Tipsea's, he'd only been on the prowl for one thing, and it sure wouldn't have made his momma proud. A woman like Millie, who was as at home in a big country kitchen as she was out on the range, was the kind of catch a man could be proud to escort to a Grange Hall dance.

His brother had been damned lucky to have found someone like Millie so young. Little good it'd done him, though, seeing how he'd gone and died way before his time. What'd Jim been thinking, shooting from a moving four-wheeler? Had disaster written all over it.

Yeah? How many shots you taken from a Mark V at fifty knots, yet you're still ticking?

Jim may have been hot-dogging, but it wasn't a stunt Cooper hadn't tried himself. Only difference was that Cooper had gone fast enough for the devil not to catch up.

Even when they'd been kids, Millie had been a feisty little thing. He couldn't even imagine the fury she'd had with her husband for putting himself in that position. With two kids, he should've known better.

But then who was Cooper to talk?

His entire adult life had been based on a split-second nightmare from which he still hadn't awoken.

"How are you this morning?" Millie asked her father-in-law, even though she knew he couldn't respond.

He replied with a snarling growl.

To say Clint was having a tough time adjusting to his new reality was putting it mildly. Poor guy had been a powerhouse all his life. He was making progress in his recovery, but it was far too slow for his liking.

Millie hustled through the personal-hygiene routine Peg taught her to follow. The nurse would handle his primary bathing, but no matter how much her father-in-law clearly resented Millie invading his personal space, for his own well-being, the job needed to be done.

"You should've seen your naughty granddaughter trying to get out of school this morning." While brushing Clint's teeth, she kept up a line of running chatter. She couldn't tell if her attempt at levity had any effect on the patient, but it at least helped calm her nerves. "It's cold enough out there, we might have to break the smoke off the chimney."

All her good cheer earned was another grunt.

"Your new therapist should be here after a while. I think she'll be working on speech today. Peg's got a whole slew of folks coming out to help." She tidied his bedding. "It's gonna be a regular Grand Central Station 'round here."

More grumbling erupted from Clint, but she ignored him in favor of slipping his small whiteboard around his neck, along with the attached dry-erase marker. It was a struggle for him to smoothly move his right arm and hand, but as with the rest of his recovery, with each passing day he grew more adept at the skill.

"Now that you're all cleaned up, I'm going to make your breakfast then be right back."

She prepared a light meal of scrambled eggs with cheese and pureed peaches. Clint loved coffee, so she filled a lidded mug with the steaming liquid then added a few ice cubes before sealing the top and adding a straw. Would he notice it wasn't her usual awful brew?

Peg said Clint's hearing was fine.

Had he heard Cooper enter the house?

Millie didn't have long to wait for an answer. She entered Clint's room only to find he'd already been practicing his writing. On his board were the barely legible letters: *C-O-O-P?*

His bloodshot eyes begged for an answer that left her wishing they'd found a way to install Clint's hospital-style bed in the upstairs master bedroom as opposed to Kay's old sewing room.

How much had Clint heard?

With an extra cantankerous growl, he waved the board hard enough to send the attached marker flying on its string. The writing instrument landed smack dab in the center of Clint's eggs, which only made him roar louder.

Jerking the marker back as if it were on a yo-yo string, he drew a line through his former word to painstakingly write: *O-U-T!*

"Who are you?"

After a long day of checking the well-being of not just the cattle, but fencing and the overall state of the land, as well, Cooper had just finished brushing his horse when a pretty, freckle-faced girl, whose braids reminded him an awful lot of Millie's back when she'd been a kid, raised her chin and scowled.

"Mom doesn't like strangers messing with our livestock."

The fire flashing behind her sky-blue eyes also reminded him of her momma. "You must be LeeAnn?"

"Yeah?" Eyes narrowed, she asked, "Who are you, and how do you know my name?"

A boy peeked out from behind the partially closed door. He had the same red hair Jim had had when he'd been about that age. Jim Junior? Or J.J., as Peg more often called him. Through emails, Cooper had seen the kids' pictures, but they hadn't done them justice.

His throat grew uncomfortably tight.

How proud his brother must've been of these two, which only made his actions all the more undecipherable. If Cooper possessed such treasure, he'd be so careful....

But then he'd treasured his mother and look what'd happened to her.

Cooper pulled himself together, removed his right glove, then cautiously approached his niece, holding out his hand for her to shake. "LeeAnn, J.J., sorry it's taken me so long to finally meet you. I'm your uncle Cooper."

"The Navy SEAL?" Seven-year-old J.J. found his courage and bolted out from his hiding spot. "Dad said you blow up ships and scuba dive and other cool stuff."

Judging by LeeAnn's prepubescent scowl, she wasn't impressed. "Mom said you abandoned your family when we needed you most."

How did he respond? Millie had only spoken the truth.

From behind him, Sassy snorted.

"You didn't ride her, did you?" His pint-size nemesis followed him on his trek to the feed bin. "Because if you did, don't *ever* do it again. Sassy's *mine*."

"Interesting…" He scooped grain into a bucket. The faint earthy-sweet smell brought him back to a time when he'd been LeeAnn and J.J.'s age. Everything had been so simple then. Do his chores, his homework, play with the dog. Speaking of which, he hadn't seen their mutt, Marvel. Not a good sign. "Because Sassy was a birthday present for me."

"You've gotta be like a hundred," his nephew noted.

Most days, I feel like it. "Only seventy-five."

"That's still pretty old…."

His niece narrowed her eyes. "That's not true. I heard Mom talking to Aunt Peg about Grandpa, and she said he was in his seventies. That means you can't be that old—probably just like fifty."

Cooper laughed. "Yeah, that's closer."

LeeAnn wrenched the feed bucket from him. "Since she's my horse, I'll take care of her."

"Be my guest." Cooper backed away. "But since I'll be here awhile, do you think we might work out a deal?"

"Like what?" She stroked the horse's nose.

"Sassy's allowed to help me with the cattle while you're at school, then she's all yours once you get home?"

"Sounds good to me." J.J. took an apple from his backpack and sat on a hay bale to eat it, all the while watching the negotiation with rapt interest.

The girl nibbled her lower lip. Another trait she'd inherited from her mom. "I'll think about it."

"Fair enough."

"LeeAnn! J.J.!" Millie called from the house.

"Bye!" Jim's son bolted.

His sister chased after him.

Cooper gave Sassy one last pat, made sure the three other horses had plenty of food and water, then closed up the barn for the night. As the day had wound on, the weather had only grown more ugly. At five, clouds were so heavy that it was almost dark. Sleet pelted his nose and cheeks on his walk across the yard.

As miserably cold as the day had been and night now was, Cooper would've preferred to spend the evening in his truck rather than go back into the house. He didn't belong there. At least in Virginia, he'd been part of a well-oiled team.

On the ranch, he wasn't sure what he was. No-good son. Disrespectful brother. Forgotten uncle.

"Coop?"

He glanced out from beneath his hat brim to find Millie hollering at him from the back porch. Much like she had with her robe, she now clutched the lapels of a chunky brown sweater. Wind whipped her long hair, and when she drew it back, she looked so lovely in the golden light spilling from the house that his breath caught in his throat.

Lord, what was wrong with him? Appraising his brother's wife? There was a special place in hell for men like him.

"Hurry, before your feet freeze to the yard!"

He did hurry, but only because he didn't want her hanging around outside waiting for him.

"Thanks." He brushed past her, hating that he once again noticed her sweet floral smell. He removed his hat and stood there for a sec, adjusting to not only the kitchen's warmth, but also the sight of the space filled with industrious bodies.

J.J. sat at the round oak table, frowning at an open math book. LeeAnn sat alongside him, making an unholy mess with an ugly papier-mâché mountain.

Millie had left him and now stood at the sink, washing broccoli. "Pardon the clutter. LeeAnn's volcano is due soon, and J.J. has a math test tomorrow. I heard you all formally met in the barn?"

"Yes, ma'am." What else should he say? That she'd raised a couple of fine-looking kids? That he was an ass and coward for not meeting them before now? Instead, he glanced back to the table and said the first stupid thing that popped into his head. "That's supposed to be a volcano?"

The second he asked the question, he regretted it. His few hastily spoken words ruined the bucolic family scene.

His pretty niece leaped up from the table, then dashed from the room.

"It's an *awesome* volcano!" J.J. declared before throwing his pencil at Cooper, then also leaving the room.

"I realize you've probably never been around kids," Millie said, "but you might try digging around in your big, tough Army Guy head to look for a sensitivity gene. LeeAnn's worked really hard on her science project. You didn't have to tear her down." Having delivered his tongue-lashing, Millie chased after her brood.

From upstairs came the sound of a door slamming, then muffled tears.

Son of a biscuit…

He slapped his hat onto the back-door rack and shrugged out of his brother's coat, hanging it up, too. Then he just stood there, woefully unsure what to do with his frozen hands or confused heart.

"For the record," he said under his breath, "I'm a Navy Guy."

Chapter 3

Millie held her arms around her sobbing daughter, rocking her side to side from where they sat on the edge of the bed. "Honey, he didn't mean it. You're going to have the best volcano your school's ever seen."

"I'll help, Lee." Sweet-tempered J.J. cozied up to his sister's other side. Since their father died, both kids had grown infinitely more sensitive. Millie knew one of these days she'd need to toughen them to the ways of the world, but not quite yet. They'd already been through enough. She couldn't even comprehend what would happen if they also lost their grandpa or the only home they'd ever known.

A knock sounded on the door frame.

She glanced in that direction to find Cooper taking up far too much room. He was not only tall, but his shoulders were broad, too. Back when they'd been teens, he'd been a cocky, self-assured hothead who'd never lacked for the company of a blonde, brunette or redhead. When he'd spent weekends calf-roping, rodeo buckle bunnies swarmed him like hummingbirds to nectar. She'd far preferred her even-tempered Jim. Cooper had always been just a little too *wild*.

"Make him go away," LeeAnn mumbled into Millie's shoulder.

"Look…" Cooper rammed his hands into his jeans pockets. "I'm awfully sorry about hurting your feelings."

"No, you're not!"

"LeeAnn…" Millie scolded. While she certainly didn't agree with her brother-in-law's ham-handed actions, she didn't for a moment believe him deliberately cruel. He spent all his time around mercenary types. She honestly wasn't even sure what a Navy SEAL did. Regardless, she was reasonably certain he hadn't spent a lot of time around kids.

"I really am sorry." The farther he ventured into the ultragirly room with its pink-floral walls, brass bed piled with stuffed animals and antique dressing table and bench Millie had picked up for a song at a barn auction, the more out of his element Cooper looked. "Ever heard of Pompeii?"

"I saw a movie on it," J.J. said.

"Cool." Cooper's warm, sad, unsure smile touched Millie's heart. He was trying to be a good uncle, but that was kind of hard when jumping in this late in the game. He took his phone from his back pocket then a few seconds later, handed it to her son. "This pic is of me and a few friends. We had some downtime and toured through the ruins."

"Whoa…" J.J.'s eyes widened. "That's awesome! You really were there."

"Doesn't make him like some kind of volcano expert," LeeAnn noted.

"I've always wanted to see Pompeii…" Millie couldn't help but stare in wonder at the photo. Beyond the three smiling men stretched a weathered street frozen in time. Snow-capped Mount Vesuvius towered in the background. The scene was all at once chilling, yet intriguing. The place seemed inconceivably far from Brewer's Falls.

"It was amazing but also sad." He flipped through more pics, some taken of the former citizens who had turned to stone. "Anyway… LeeAnn, you're right, I'm not even close to being a volcano expert, but if you wouldn't mind, I'd love lending a hand with your project. I wire a mean explosive and between the two of us, we could probably muster some impressive concussive force."

While both kids stared, Millie pressed her lips tight. *Concussive force?* He did realize the science fair was being held in an elementary school gym and not Afghanistan? Still, she appreciated his willingness to at least try helping her daughter. Lord knew, her own volcano-building skills were lacking. "That sounds nice," she said to her brother-in-law, "only you might scale down the eruption."

"Gotcha." He half smiled. "Small eruptions."

For only an instant, their gazes locked, but that was long enough to leave her knowing he still unnerved her in a womanly way. It'd been three long years since she'd lost her husband, and as much as she'd told herself—and her matchmaking friend, Lynette—she had no interest in dating, something about Cooper had always exuded raw sex appeal. It wasn't anything deliberate on his part, it just *was*. Had always been. Because she'd been happy with Jim, she'd studied Cooper's escapades from afar. But here, now, something about the way his lips stroked the perfectly innocuous word, *eruptions,* sent her lonely, yearning body straight to the gutter.

Her mind, on the other hand, stayed strong. If she ever decided to start dating, she'd steer far clear of anyone remotely like her brother-in-law!

"J.J., hon," the boy's mother asked an hour later from across the kitchen table, "will you say grace?"

"Yes, ma'am." He bowed his head. "God is great, God is good…"

While the boy finished, Cooper discreetly put down his fork, pretending he hadn't already nabbed a bite. The last time he'd prayed before a meal had been the last night he'd been in this house.

He looked up just as J.J. muttered *Amen,* to find Millie staring. Damn, she'd grown into a fine-looking woman. And damn, how he hated even noticing the fact.

Conversation flowed into a river of avoidance, meandering past dangerous topics such as his brother or father. Meatloaf passing and the weather took on inordinate levels of importance.

This suited Cooper just fine. He had no interest in rehashing the past and lacked the courage to wander too far into the future. His only plan was to keep things casual then head back to Virginia ASAP to rejoin his SEAL team.

"Uncle Cooper?" J.J. asked. The kid sported a seriously cute milk mustache.

"Yeah?"

"How come you didn't visit Grandpa with us tonight while he ate his dinner?"

Whoosh. Just like that, his lazy river turned into a raging waterfall, culminating in a pool of boiling indigestion. He messed with his broccoli. "I, ah, needed to clean up before your mom's tasty dinner."

"Okay." Apparently satisfied with Cooper's answer, the child reached across the table for a third roll.

His niece wasn't about to take his answer at face value. "I heard Aunt Peg and Mom talking about how much you *hate* Grandpa and he *hates* you."

"LeeAnn!" Millie set her iced tea glass on the table hard enough to rattle the serving platters. "Apologize to your uncle."

"Wh-why do you hate Grandpa?" J.J. asked, voice cracking as he looked from his uncle to his mom. "I love him a whole lot."

Son of a biscuit...

"Millie..." Cooper set his fork by his plate and pushed back his chair. "Thanks for this fine meal, but I've got to run into town. Please leave the dishes for me, and I'll wash 'em later."

"What's he gonna do in town?" LeeAnn asked, carrying on with her meal as if nothing had even happened. "Everything's closed."

Cooper had already left out the front door.

Millie covered her face with her hands. At this time of night, there was only one thing a man could do in Brewer's Falls—drink.

"Mom?" J.J. pressed. "What's Uncle Cooper gonna do? And why does he hate Grandpa?"

At that moment, Millie was the one hating Cooper for running out on her yet again. But then wait—during her initial crisis after she'd first lost Jim, he hadn't even bothered to show up.

"Mom?"

"J.J., *hush!*" She never snapped at her kids, but this was one time she needed space to think, breathe. She got up from the table and delivered a hasty apology before running for the stairs.

In her room, she tossed herself across the foot of the bed she and Jim had shared. Never had she needed him more. His quiet strength and logic and calm in the face of any storm.

She wanted—needed—so badly to cry, but tears wouldn't come.

Frustration for her situation balled in her stomach, punching with pain. If she had a lick of sense, she'd do the adult thing—pull herself together and join her children downstairs. She needed to play a game with them and clean the kitchen. Do research on how to build a science-fair volcano. Play mix and match with which bills she could afford to pay. Check on Clint to see if he needed anything.

While she *needed* to do all of that, what she *wanted* was an indulgent soak in the hall bathroom's claw-foot tub.

Cooper sauntered into the smoky bar, taking a seat on a counter stool. In all the years he'd lived in the one-horse town, he'd never been in the old place. Not much to look at with twenty or so country-type patrons, dim lighting, honky-tonk-blaring jukebox, a few ratty pool tables and neon beer signs decorating the walls. But as long as the liquor bit, that'd get the job of escaping—even for a moment—done. After a few drinks, he probably wouldn't even mind the yeast scent of a quarter-century's worth of stale beer that'd sloshed onto the red industrial-style carpet.

He said to the guy behind the bar, "Shot of Jim Beam, please."

"I'll be damned… Cooper?"

"Mr. Walker?" *Seriously?* Talk about jumping from the frying pan into the fire. The grizzled cowboy not only happened to be one of his father's best friends, but owned the land adjoining the Hansen ranch.

He extended his hand for Cooper to shake. "Please, call me Mack. Figure if you're old enough to drink and serve our country, you're old enough for us to be on a first-name basis." He poured Cooper's shot then one for himself. Raising it, he said, "About time you came home."

"Only temporarily…" Cooper downed the fiery elixir. "I'll head back to my base just as soon as things get settled."

"By *things,* I assume you're talking about your father? Damn shame. Everyone's just sick about the run of bad luck your family's been having."

In no mood to hash over the past or present, Cooper wagged his glass. "Another."

Mack obligingly poured. "Things that bad out there, huh?"

Cooper winced from the liquor's bite.

"I told your father he was a damned fool for running you off. What happened with your momma… Straight-up accident that could've happened to any one of us. I know deep in his heart Clint agrees, but he's too damned stubborn to tell anyone—let alone his firstborn—any different."

The tears stinging Cooper's eyes hurt worse than the liquor burning his throat.

"He needs you. Millie needs you. Hell, even those ragtag kids of hers need you. Yep…" He smacked the wood counter. "'Bout damned time you came home."

Nice sentiment, but for his own sanity, Cooper knew he was only passing through. A long time ago he'd lost his home, his way, and for a messed-up guy like him, there was no such thing as second chances.

"Where've you been?" Millie warmed her hands in front of the living room's woodstove, wishing she hadn't been on edge ever since Cooper had run off, vowing she wouldn't lower herself to even turn around and look at him. She thought her lazy, twenty-minute soak would make her feel better, but all it had done was given her the privacy needed to think—not good for a woman in her condition. Hot water, plus loneliness, plus closing her eyes to envision the first handsome face she'd seen in years had proven anything but relaxing. Especially when that face belonged to her dead husband's brother!

"Where do you think?"

She knew exactly where he'd been. She shouldn't have wasted the breath needed to ask. "It was a serious dick move for you to walk out like that. You owe your niece and nephew an explanation."

"*Dick move?* Talk to your momma with that mouth?"

She spun around to face him, only to find him unnervingly close. "You know better than most anyone I don't even have a mom, so you can put that sass back in your pocket."

"Sorry." He held up his hands in surrender, and her stupid, confused heart skipped a beat. The only reason she even found him attractive was the endearing similarities he'd shared with his brother. Mossy-green eyes and the faint rise in the bridge of his nose. The way his lips looked pouty when he said his m's. The way he made her wistful and achy and irrationally mad about how perfect her life had once been and no longer was. "You're right. I shouldn't have taken off, but honestly?" He shook his head, and his crooked smile further lessened her anger's hold. "I was scared." He removed his battered straw cowboy hat, crossing the room to hang it on the rack by the door. Even with his buzz cut, he sported a wicked case of hat hair and damn if it didn't look good. "Those kids of yours asked tough questions. I don't even know the answers for myself."

"I get that, but they're kids. They weren't even born when your mom died, and they take it personally when their only uncle never even had the decency to send them a birthday card. They're smart, Coop. Their little ears pick up more than I'd like, and as much as Peg loves you, she's also that exasperated by your disappearing act."

"I didn't just—"

"Shh!" she admonished when he'd gotten too loud. "Do you want to wake J.J. and LeeAnn? Even worse— your dad?"

"Sorry," he said in a softer tone. He sat hard on the sofa, cradling his forehead in his hands. "But you know damn well I didn't just *disappear*. When you run down your mother with a truck, then your father tells you to, and I quote—*Get the hell out of my house and don't* ever *come back*—it tends to linger on a man's soul." When he looked up, even by the light of the room's only lamp, she could tell his eyes had welled. She hated to see him hurting, but she'd hurt, too. They all had. They all were, still. He didn't own the rights to pain.

"Look…" With every part of her being, she wanted to go to him. Sit beside him and slip her arm around his shoulders, but she physically couldn't. Her feet literally wouldn't move. Outside, sleet pelted century-old windows. The weatherman out of Denver said they could have six inches of snow by morning. "I smoothed things over with the kids by giving them an abridged version of what happened with their grandmother. But for your own well-being, you have to once and for all get it through your thick head that the only one who blames you for the accident is your father—well, aside from yourself. Why did your mom even go out there? She knew better."

A laugh as cold as the wind rattling the shutters escaped him. "Her dying words were that she'd run outside to give me a piece of her mind for drinking and staying out so late. She then told me if she'd had a lick of sense, she'd have gone to bed early in case she needed to bail me out of the county jail come morning."

"There you go. So see? She admitted she was partially to blame. Do you honestly think that just because of your cantankerous father she'd have expected you to carry this ache inside you for all these—"

A crash of metal erupted from the back bedroom where Clint was supposed to be sleeping. Then came a gut-wrenching growl.

"What was that?" Cooper asked, already on his feet, heading in that direction.

Her stomach knotted. "I would imagine, *that* was your father...."

Chapter 4

"Go see him," Millie said. "You can't avoid Clint forever."

Cooper knew she was right. Sooner or later he'd have to make peace with his father. Or at the very least, for Millie and her kids' sake, forge some semblance of civility between them. But how did he start? It wasn't as if the walls of grief standing between them could be broken with a mere apology.

Another growl rose above the stove's crackling fire and wind rattling the shutters.

"Cooper..." His sister-in-law's condemning stare made him feel all of twelve. He'd felt more comfortable staring down a shark. Her intense stare conveyed more than a day's worth of words. It told him loud and clear that until he at least spoke with his father, she wouldn't grant him a moment's peace.

"Aw, hell…" He brushed past her, hating the cramped space forcing them together. His arm didn't stop tingling from where they'd touched till he reached the end of the hall.

Cooper forced a deep breath then knocked on the closed door of his mom's old sewing room—the only possible downstairs place where Millie and his sister could have stashed his ailing father.

Rather than wait for an answer, his pulse taking the cadence of a rapid-fire machine gun, Cooper thrust open the door. He'd literally dreaded this moment for the past twelve years. "You still got a problem with me, old man?"

Clint launched a new series of growls then pitiful, racking coughs.

"You've got to calm down," Millie said, already tidying the mess her patient had made by toppling his rolling metal tray. "I meant to tell you earlier that Cooper had come for a visit, but it must've slipped my mind."

The cantankerous old man thrashed as best he could then settled when Millie took a plastic water cup from the nightstand and held the straw to his dried and cracked lips.

Cooper had readied himself for a fight with the man he used to know. The barrel-chested, ham-fisted, mean-as-a-cornered-rattler father who'd sent him packing. What he faced was a pathetic shadow of Cooper's memories. Make no mistake, judging by his scowl and dark glare, Clint still wasn't a teddy bear. But he had lost a good fifty pounds, and his complexion was as pale as the threadbare sheets and quilts covering his bed.

Clint's current condition left Cooper's eyes stinging. He'd steeled himself for battle with a lion, not a lamb.

"There you go," Millie soothed. "It's medicine time, and I'll bet you thought I forgot you." After kissing the old man's forehead, she fished three tablets from three different prescription bottles, patiently helping Clint one at a time down them all with more water. When he signaled that he had drunk his fill, she covered his lips with ointment. "Feel better?"

The old man had his dry-erase board slung around his neck. With his good hand he wrote *O-U-T* then underlined it twice before pointing in Cooper's general direction.

Instantaneously, Cooper's anger was replaced by profound sadness. And a jolt of something he never in a million years would've expected—a fierce longing to make things right with this man he'd once so deeply loved. His mind's eye no longer replayed their last night together, but flashes of Clint patiently teaching him to change his truck's oil or beaming with pride when Cooper won his first rodeo. Then came a myriad of shared holidays and ordinary Tuesday-night suppers and racing his brother, Jim, off the school bus, both of them running as fast as they could to find out what their father had been up to in the barn. His dad had taught Cooper how to shoot a rifle, smoke cigars and treat women. What Clint hadn't done was prepare his son for how to let him go.

Which meant that in addition to saving this ragtag old ranch, Cooper now felt responsible for saving his dad.

He felt obligated to say as much, but instead, clung to the room's shadows. Gratitude for Millie knotted his throat while she fussed with his father's pillows and blankets. Cooper should've helped her. After all, the patient was his dad. But his boots felt nailed to the wood floor.

Millie asked, "What did you do with the remote to your TV?"

Cooper had only just noticed the ancient model set atop the dresser. The volume had been turned all the way down on The Weather Channel's forecaster. Another pleasant memory accosted him when he thought back to the time he and Jim had helped Clint with their first satellite dish. Exciting didn't begin to cover how awesome it'd been to have hundreds of channels—not that their mom ever let them and Peg watch as much TV as they'd have liked.

"What're you smiling about?" Millie asked, on her knees, using a towel to sop water from his father's spilled plastic pitcher.

Cooper knelt to help, taking the towel from her. "Remember when we got MTV?"

She sat back on her haunches and frowned. "How could I forget? That was around the same time you asked why my boobs were smaller than everyone else's."

Cooper winced. "Wasn't it enough retribution for you that because of that comment, Mom made me scrub baseboards for a week?"

"No."

By the time they finished cleaning, Clint had drifted off to sleep and softly snored.

"Looks like his meds finally kicked in." Millie fished the TV remote from where it had fallen under the bed.

"Yeah…" Cooper stood there like a dope, holding the damp towel they'd used for the floor, watching Millie as she finished cleaning the last of his old man's mess.

The past bore down on Cooper's shoulders, making

every inch of him ache—not just his body, but soul. He'd lost so much. His mom. Jim. And now, for all practical purposes, his dad.

That sting was back behind his eyes.

Cooper couldn't remember the last time he'd broken down—maybe not since that long ago awful night. "I—I've gotta get out of here."

Planning an escape to the barn, he pitched the towel on the kitchen table before making a beeline for the back door. But before he could get it open, Millie was there, wrapping her arms around him, holding strong through his emotional fall.

His tears were ugly and all-consuming, making his muscles seize. Though he had no right, Cooper clung to Millie, breathing her in. She smelled good and familiar. Of everything he'd left and tried so hard to forget, but clearly had not yet succeeded.

"I—I'm sorry," he managed after finally getting ahold of himself. "Shit…" He released her to rake his fingers through his hair. "I'm not even sure what just happened."

"Something that probably needed to happen back when your mom died? And again, for your brother?" She rubbed her hand along his upper arm. "Plus, it can't have been easy—finding your dad in that condition."

"Stop making excuses." Not wanting her to see him, he turned to the wall, planting his palms flat against the cool plaster, then his forehead.

She stepped behind him. He knew, because he sensed her. Felt her heat. When she kneaded his shoulders, he closed his eyes and groaned. "Lord, that feels good."

"I'm glad."

"You should stop."

"Why?" She worked her thumbs between his shoulder blades.

"Because I don't deserve your comfort any more than you've deserved to be stuck here on your own with this mess."

"This *mess* you refer to happens to be your father. The man who taught me to cook a mean elk steak and nursed me through losing my husband." She stopped giving Cooper pleasure to instead urge him around. Her pained expression, the unshed tears shining in her eyes, made the whiskey lingering in his gut catch fire.

He winced from the sudden pang.

Something in her expression darkened to the point he hardly recognized her. She took a step back and crossed her arms. "Mess, huh? You honestly think of your own dad having had a stroke so callously?"

"Come on, Mill, it was just an expression. I didn't—"

"Hush." For what felt like eternity, she stood hugging herself, lips pressed tight, eyes luminous from tears threatening to spill. "For a second I actually felt sorry for you." She laughed before conking her forehead with her palm. "But now I realize who I'm dealing with—the guy your brother called *Cold Coop,* aka The Human Iceberg. Jim hated you for leaving like you did, but I always made excuses. I told him you were hurting. When our daughter was born, and you couldn't be bothered to meet her, I told him you were an integral part of our country's security, and that I was sure you'd come just as soon as you got leave. When our son was born, and you still didn't show…" She shook her head and chuckled. "Despite the fact that Peg had told you our happy news on the phone, I assured Jim you must not have received the official birth announcement, oth-

erwise nothing could've kept you away. When Jim died, and you still didn't come home, well, that I chalked up to you being wrapped up in your own grief. But how could you bear knowing all of us were here falling apart? How could you just carry on as if your brother and niece and nephew and father didn't even matter?"

By this time, Cooper had fully regained his emotions, while Millie seemed to be teetering on the edge. She didn't bother hiding her tears, and as usual, according to her capsulated version of the past decade and then some, he didn't bother to care. He sure didn't extend one iota of effort to provide her the comfort she obviously not only needed, but also deserved.

The woman was a saint, but after his meltdown, he felt empty inside. Like a shell. And so he just stood there. Stoic and still as if she'd been a drill sergeant giving him hell for not shining his shoes.

"What's wrong with you?" she shrieked. "You're like a machine—only instead of working, someone flipped your *off* switch. Peg needed you! *I* needed you, but you weren't there!" When she stepped deep into his personal space, pummeling his chest, he stood there and took it. He deserved the worst she could dish out and then some.

"I'm sorry," he finally said. And he was. But what did she want him to do? Sure, he'd help with his dad and the ranch, but he had no means with which to magically repair their mutually broken past. "Really sorry."

"S-sorry?" She laughed through her tears then raised her hand to slap him, only he caught her wrist and pulled her close, instinct screaming at him to hold on to her and never let go. This woman was a lifeline to all he'd once held dear. Every bad thing she'd said about him had been true. He was the worst of the worst.

Lower than pond scum. For the past twelve years, she'd carried his world, and he'd callously, cruelly let her.

That stopped now.

He had to get a grip. But to do that, he'd need her help.

"I hate you," she said into his chest while keeping such a tight grip on his T-shirt that it pulled against his back.

"I know…" *I hate me.* He kissed the crown of her head. "I'm sorry. So crazy, freakin' sorry. But I'm back, and everything's going to be okay. I promise." *With every breath of my being, I promise, Millie.*

"I want to believe you." She sagged against him until he held the bulk of her weight just to keep her from crumpling to the floor. "But…"

She didn't have to finish her sentence for him to know what she'd been about to say. That of course she wanted to believe him, but when it came to his family, he'd dropped the proverbial ball so many times, it'd shattered.

Chapter 5

"Mom? Are you alive?"

Millie cautiously opened her tear-swollen eyes to find her son standing at the head of her bed. Though J.J.'s expression read concerned, his red snowsuit and Power Ranger hat and gloves read Snow Day.

"Cool! Since you are alive, can I go build a fort?"

She groaned. "Honey, what time is it? And did you do your chores?" On weekends and any other time they didn't have school, the kids were in charge of egg collecting and cleaning the litter box—not that they often saw the orange tabby named Cheetah, who mostly preferred hiding behind the dining room's half-dead ficus.

"Me and LeeAnn tried doing chores, but Uncle Coop already did 'em."

She sat up in the bed. "Even the cat box?"

"Well…" J.J. dropped his gaze in the telltale sign

of a fib. "Since he made breakfast for me and Lee and Grandpa, I bet he did that and checked on the chickens, too."

"Uh-huh…" She grabbed her robe from the foot of the bed, then slipped her feet out from under the covers and into house shoes. The home had been built in 1905, meaning the woodstove and a few space heaters were all they had for heat. On many mornings, she'd woken to air cold enough to see her breath. Thankfully, this wasn't one. "Come on," she said to her son after switching off the valiantly humming space heater then shrugging into her robe and cinching the belt. "Let's see what's going on."

"Okay—" J.J. took her hand "—but we'd have more fun if we just went outside and built a fort."

"Why's that?" she asked with trepidation. To say the previous night had been rocky would be the understatement of the century. She and Cooper's uncomfortable scene had ended with her dashing upstairs and slamming her door. Not only had she been saddened and infuriated by her brother-in-law, but the fact that she'd then sought comfort from him as well had all been too much to bear. For the first time in recent memory, she'd cried herself to sleep. But she didn't have time for such folly. She had Clint and her children to care for—not to mention this godforsaken ranch. Most winter mornings, she woke wishing herself a million miles away. Then came spring, and along with the first daffodils, up rose her indefatigable hope.

"Well—" on the way down the stairs, J.J. wiped his runny nose on his coat sleeve "—Lee's having a fight with Uncle Cooper, and Grandpa's been making a *lot* of scary noises."

Swell…

From the base of the stairs, raised voices could clearly be heard.

"Grandpa doesn't like you! Leave him alone!"

"Doesn't matter if he likes me or not. He just needs to quit being a stubborn old mule and eat."

Never had Millie more understood the meaning of being careful what she wished for. She'd long believed Cooper's return would be the answer to her every prayer, but apparently, she couldn't have been more wrong.

She hastened her pace only to find herself in the middle of even more chaos than the night before.

Cooper sat calmly on the edge of his father's bed, doing an admirable job of trying to feed him what she guessed from the beige splatters dotting his quilts, the floor and walls was oatmeal. With each new spoonful, he used his good arm to swat at his son.

"Gwet aut!" Clint hollered.

Initially, the shock of his volume took Millie aback, but then the significance of what'd just happened sank in. "Clint, you spoke!" She approached the bed and gestured for Cooper to hand her the oatmeal bowl. "That was awesome. Your speech therapist will be thrilled."

"I'm happy for you, Grandpa!" J.J. hugged Clint's clean arm.

"See, Dad?" Cooper took a damp dishrag from the rolling tray table and wiped cereal clumps from his father's red flannel pajama top. "No matter how much you hate me being here, I'm technically good for you."

"Arggghh!"

"What?" Cooper prompted his father. "I didn't quite catch that. Mind repeating?"

"Mom, make him stop," LeeAnn begged from the foot of the bed.

"Aigh ate uuu!"

"Mom, *please...*"

"What's that, old man?" Cooper taunted. "You hate me? Good, because right about now, I'm not exactly feeling warm and fuzzy toward you." He tapped his temple. "Even after all this time, though I can rationalize in my head that what happened to Mom was an accident, in here—" he patted his chest "—the way you treated me—the way you made your pal, the sheriff, keep me from attending my own mother's funeral? What the hell? Who does that? The whole thing still keeps me up at night."

"Stop!" LeeAnn cried to Cooper. "I don't blame Grandpa for hating you! You're the devil!"

"Lee!" Millie set the bowl on the nightstand in favor of going to her daughter. "Honey, please take J.J. outside to gather the eggs and make sure the heat lamp's still on."

"But, Mom, I—"

"Lee, just go." Millie hated being short with the girl, but felt at least temporarily removing her kids from this toxic environment was best for all involved. Deep down, as tough as this father-son duel was to witness, she suspected it was doing them both good.

"Fine." LeeAnn held out her hand to her brother. "Come on, brat."

"You're a brat!"

"Both of you, knock it off!" Millie snapped. What a difference a day made. She'd grown accustomed to constant worry, but this added a whole new dimension to family fun.

When the kids were outside, Millie drew Cooper into the hall, shutting Clint's door behind her. "Look, I think I get what you've been trying to do with your dad—the whole tough-love routine—but maybe adding stress to an already difficult situation isn't the best course."

"I wasn't *trying* to do anything. I heard him banging around in there, and since you were still sleeping and your friend Lynette called and said because her car won't start, she won't be able to make it today, I figured I'd give you a hand. Turns out the old bastard didn't want breakfast, but to give me a hard time."

"Cooper... You belittling him makes me uncomfortable."

"Sorry." Outside, the wind howled. In the cramped hall, he paced, his expression every bit as tormented as the storm. "At the moment, his very existence isn't doing much for me."

"You don't mean that."

"No, I don't, but honestly?" His pinched expression broke her heart. No—what really broke her heart was the way so much time had passed, yet everything between father and son had not only stayed the same, but maybe even grown worse. "I've been here just shy of twenty-four hours and feel like I'm going batshit crazy. I know my dad's going through a rough patch, but we're all in this together now."

She winced at his language, though mirrored the sentiment.

"If you don't mind taking over in there—" he gestured toward his dad's room "—I need to check the cattle."

Though he was yet again retreating, Millie knew that this time it was only temporary and for a noble cause.

Their prized herd did need to be checked, and the fact that she wouldn't be the one making the long ride out to the south pasture in these treacherous conditions made her heart swell with gratitude.

"Thank you."

"You're welcome." His gaze met hers and locked.

His intensity startled her to the point that she had to look away. Her pulse raced, and she wasn't sure what to do with her hands, so she fussed with her robe's belt, feeling all of thirteen upon realizing that Cooper was still the most handsome cowboy in town. Don't get her wrong—she'd loved her husband with every ounce of her being, but Jim had been a kind soul. Cooper? Well, even back in high school his downright sinful sooty-lashed stare had made rodeo queens swoon and female teachers forgive missing homework.

From the kitchen came the sound of the back door crashing open. "Mom!" LeeAnn hollered. "Come quick!"

Covering her suddenly flushed face with her hands, Millie found herself actually welcoming whatever emergency her daughter had brought inside. At least it would distract her from Cooper's mossy-green gaze.

The rooster's crow coming from the kitchen was her first clue that she should abandon all hope of finding peace that morning.

"Mom, the heat lamp's not on and the chickens were shivering. We're bringing them inside."

Millie pressed her lips tight while J.J. set his favorite golden wyandotte on the kitchen floor. She fussed a bit, fluffing her feathers and preening, then made a beeline for the cat food.

Cooper cut her off at the pass to set the food bowl

on the counter. "Mill, before we get the house full of feathers and chicken shit, do you have a spare bulb for the lamp in case it's an easy fix?"

J.J. gaped. "Uncle Cooper, you're not allowed to say that word."

"Sorry." He had the good grace to actually redden.

"Apology accepted." Millie was embarrassed to admit she didn't have spare anything. The bulbs had been on her shopping list for ages, but with barely enough money to pay for food, let alone heat, what was the point of even having a list? "And no, I don't have an extra."

"Okay…" He covered his face with his hands, then sighed. "J.J., how about you help your mom build some kind of pen, and I'll help your sister bring the chickens inside—"

LeeAnn shuffled through the back door, carrying a hen under each arm. "It's freezing out there, and a branch knocked a hole in the roof."

Millie groaned, looking heavenward to ask, "Really? Our plates aren't already full enough?"

"Relax." Behind her, Cooper lightly rubbed her shoulders. "We'll keep the chickens inside until the storm passes, then, after our next supply run, I'll rig a lamp for them in one of the empty horse stalls in the barn. Hopefully, the coop shouldn't take but a day or two to fix."

"Sure. Thanks." She didn't want to find comfort in his take-charge demeanor and especially not from his touch, but how could she not when it felt as if she'd been running uphill ever since Clint's stroke? To now have a man around to do the stereotypically manly chores made her feel as if her uphill charge had, at least for the time being, transitioned to a stroll through a nice, flat meadow. Call her old-fashioned, but when it came to gender roles, she missed doing mostly so-called woman's work. "J.J., hon, do me a favor and run out to get some firewood. Pretend it's giant Lincoln Logs and build a little fence."

"Cool! That sounds fun!" He dashed outside.

LeeAnn had placed the ladder-backed table chairs in front of the living room and hall pass-throughs. She was such a good girl. Always eager to help. It broke Millie's heart to see her always so blue—even more so ever since Cooper had shown up. Would she eventually cut him some slack?

Millie glanced his way to find him bundled up, once again wearing Jim's duster. He'd slapped his hat on, and the mere sight of him took her breath away. She wanted to stay mad at him for having left all those years ago, but she lacked the energy to fight.

"I'll bring in the rest of the hens then check on the cattle."

"Thank you," she said to him, then again to her daughter, who'd cleaned poo with a damp paper towel.

Cold air lingered when Cooper left. It smelled crisp and clean. Of cautious hope.

"He's awful," LeeAnn said after Cooper had closed the door. "I wish he'd stayed away."

"I'm sorry about what you saw between him and Grandpa. When your grandma died, things were..." Where did she start in explaining to her little girl just how terrible Clint's grief had actually been? True, what'd happened to Kay had been an accident, but Clint had treated his elder son as if the tragedy had been no less than murder. The uglier details weren't the sort of matter she cared to casually discuss with her daughter. "Well… Things were really hard. And Grandpa and your uncle… They didn't get along. Your uncle didn't leave because he wanted to, but because Grandpa made him."

LeeAnn furrowed her brows. "Grandpa Clint wouldn't do that. He's nice."

"Sure, he is. But, honey, remember that this all happened a long time ago. Way before you were even born. Your uncle has a right to be upset. So does Grandpa. The two of them have a lot of talking to do, but that's kind of hard with Grandpa not being able to talk." Millie would be lying if she didn't admit to also harboring a deep well of resentment toward her husband's brother. But acting on that now wouldn't get the chickens in from the cold or make sure the cattle were okay or perform Clint's morning bathing routine.

"Mom?" LeeAnn picked up a chicken, stroking her neck until the creature happily cooed. Millie thought it was Cluck—the kids had them all named, but she couldn't keep them straight. "Do you still miss Daddy?"

The question caught Millie off guard and raised a lump in her throat. "Of course. I think about him every day."

"Good." She set down the chicken to hug Millie. "I didn't like it when Uncle Cooper rubbed your shoulders the way Daddy used to. My friend Julie's mom and dad got divorced, and now her mom married some new guy who Julie doesn't like. I don't want you to be with anyone else."

"Honey, where is all of this coming from?" Millie tipped up LeeAnn's chin, searching her dear features. "Your father meant the world to me. He always will."

"Promise?"

Millie had just nodded when J.J. and Cooper laughed their way through the back door. Both carried squawking hens and were red-cheeked and coated in a dusting of snow. The vision of her smiley son warmed her more efficiently than a roaring fire. As for the fire in her belly Cooper's whisker-stubbled jaw evoked, well, she just wasn't going there.

"You should see it, Mom!" J.J.'s nose ran, so she handed him a paper towel to use to wipe it. "That tree smooshed the chicken coop like Godzilla! *Bam! Rwaar!*"

"It's that bad?" she asked Cooper.

"'Fraid so." His expression was grim. "It's a wonder none of the *occupants* were hurt."

A series of muffled growls erupted from Clint's room.

Millie punctuated those with her own groan.

"Want me to check on him?" Cooper offered.

"Thanks, but the mom in me thinks you two should be grounded from each other."

Judging by Cooper's scowl, he disagreed with her judgment. "Whatever. J.J.? Wanna check the cattle with me?"

"Yeah!" His supersize grin faded. "But I need to build the chicken fence first. Can you wait?"

"I'll do you one better—while you work on the fence, I'll grab some plywood and straw from the barn. We'll use it to protect your mom's floor until we rig a heat lamp in the barn."

"Okay!" J.J. dashed outside for more wood.

"Cooper…" Millie's mind reeled. Too much was happening too fast. LeeAnn making her promise to never love another man besides Jim. Chickens in her kitchen. J.J.'s instant connection with his uncle. LeeAnn's instant hatred of him. Toss Clint and way too much snow into the mix and Millie's plate wasn't just full, but spilling over onto her now filthy kitchen floor. "Do you think it's wise to take J.J. out to check the cattle?"

"Why wouldn't it be? He's already bundled up. I assume he can ride?"

"Well, sure. Jim had him on horseback practically since he learned to walk."

Cooper sighed. "Then what's the problem?"

Where did she start? Her son was beyond precious to her. Along with his sister, the duo had been her reason for living ever since Jim died. As much as one part of her appreciated Cooper riding in on his white horse disguised as a ratty old pickup, another part of her resented his very presence. She and Clint had managed on their own for all these years and didn't need Cooper showing up, thinking he had all the answers. Only the joke was on her, because at the moment, as overwhelmed as she was—he did.

A fact that scared her to her core.

Because Cooper might be a dependable, stand-up guy in the Navy. But when it came to his track record on being around when his family needed him most? His stats were an abysmal 1-288-0. A single, early-morning chicken rescue hardly made him a trustworthy man.

Chapter 6

Cooper gritted his teeth against the icy assault that had him pulling his hat brim lower and his coat collar higher. Clouds may have cleared, making way for blinding sun, but the wind had only grown stronger, driving the dry twelve inches of snow into an otherworldly landscape of towering drifts and bare earth.

"Sorry, girl." He leaned forward, stroking Sassy's mane.

It was a good thing he hadn't dragged his nephew out here—though if the kid planned on making his living off the land he would soon enough have to learn how much fun it was working in less than ideal conditions.

Cooper would've given his left nut for his SEAL cold-weather gear right about now. He was a damn fool for thinking Jim's duster and his straw hat could handle what had to be a wind chill well into negative digits.

A thirty-minute ride landed him in the heart of the herd. They'd strayed a good mile from the feed station, so after driving them all in that direction, he broke the stock tank's ice, then headed back to the barn.

With the wind at his back, the trek wasn't quite as miserable, but damn near close.

He got Sassy settled in her stall then loaded his truck bed with hay bales and range cubes before heading back out to the herd. He considered himself a die-hard traditionalist, much preferring to check cattle on horseback, but years and missions had battered his body, and the cold combined with being back in a saddle made him ache in places he'd forgotten he had.

With the heater blasting and staticky Hank Williams playing on the radio, Cooper's mind was no longer preoccupied with the cold, but considering he now had the luxury of allowing his mind to wander while zigzagging between drifts, that wasn't necessarily a good thing.

When he refused to think about his cantankerous old man, or the laser beams of hate his niece blasted him with, his thoughts drifted to the forbidden—Millie in her robe. The way it'd hung open at her throat, showing far too much collarbone than he'd been comfortable seeing.

He'd always had a thing for that particular spot on a woman. But Millie wasn't just any woman. Their shared history made his most complex missions look like a cakewalk. She'd been his brother's wife, for God's sake. Some things were sacred between brothers and that was one. *Thou shall not covet thy brother's wife.*

Didn't matter that Jim was long gone.

It was a matter of principle.

Cooper had thankfully reached the herd, squelching

the whole issue by busting up hay bales then spreading range cubes. Bellows and snorts accompanied his surprisingly satisfying work.

Though Cooper was usually outside, he couldn't remember the last time he'd been around animals. He'd missed it. The work's simple grace. No one shot at him. No one's life was at stake if he forgot any of a mission's minutiae. Don't get him wrong—he loved his job, but this…

He breathed deeply of the lung-searing cold air, but instead of it bothering him, he found it invigorating. He hadn't realized how much he'd missed this place. How much this land was still a part of him.

Like Millie?

Yeah… He wasn't going there.

He finished counting cattle, only to come up one short of the seventy-six Peg had told him they had.

Shit.

Considering that this stretch of the family land was pancake flat for as far as the eye could see, and the Black Angus contrasted sharply against the winter grass and snow, this meant the stray was hidden behind a drift, either lost or hurt.

It took an hour of meandering through the drifts, but he finally found her, only to have his stomach knot with concern. Why hadn't Millie or Peg told him they had a momma due to deliver a winter calf? Never failed, they always somehow managed to come in a storm.

The cow had found a slight dip in the land, and in the few minutes he'd been watching, she'd already gotten up and down only to get back up again. Judging by the half-frozen fluid on her hind legs, her water sack had recently broken, only her teats were slick and shiny—

usually an indication that she'd already had her calf and it had fed. Most cows safely delivered their calves without incident, and they usually didn't appreciate a crowd. Judging by the momma's level of agitation, it looked like this was the case here.

Despite this fact, with the temps so low, he'd feel a lot better at least seeing the calf to make sure it seemed healthy.

He approached the cow nice and slow, only to get a surprise. "I'll be damned…" Tucked in between drifts was one cleaned, contented-looking calf and another looking forlorn and shivering. "Looks like someone had twins."

Didn't happen often, but when it did, one of the calves ran the risk of being rejected.

Cooper removed his coat, wrapped it around the shivering calf, then settled it in the truck bed. His hope was that the cow would see her calf and follow with the other, but no such luck. Just as he'd feared, she'd rejected her second born, which meant it would be up to Cooper to bottle feed it milk and colostrum.

Back when he'd helped out on a daily basis, Cooper remembered Clint having kept some frozen—just in case. If not, Cooper would put in a call to the vet.

He looked back to find the cow's firstborn on her feet and nursing—a great sign that all was well where they were concerned. But the little one he moved to the truck's front seat wasn't yet out of the woods.

"Let's get you warmed up."

The poor little thing still shivered.

Cooper revved the engine, then turned the heater knob to high.

Since he knew the way through the snowdrift maze,

the trip to the barn took under ten minutes—only now that the calf had stopped shivering, Cooper was reluctant to put the little darlin' back outside without a heat lamp.

What would Millie say about having chickens and a calf in her kitchen? The thought of her pretty face all scrunched into a frown made him smile. But what really warmed him through and through was the certainty that even though she might temporarily be caught off guard by their houseguest, she'd care for it as well as she did every other creature in the house.

He admired the hell out of her. She understandably didn't think much of him. Would that ever change? Would she ever again think of herself not just as his sister-in-law, but as his friend?

"Sorry, Peg, but I've gotta go." Millie pressed the off button on the phone then stared at Cooper and what he'd brought through the back door. "*Really?* Helga couldn't have held on a little longer?" For a split second, Millie indulged in feeling sorry for herself at having a calf added to her kitchen menagerie, but then she surged into action. The only guarantee her life had ever come with was that what could go wrong, would. This was just another one of those occasions.

"Helga?" Cooper shifted his weight from one leg to the other. The calf was woefully small, but Millie guessed him to still weigh between sixty and seventy pounds. "You couldn't have come up with a better name?"

"Cool!" J.J. bounded into the kitchen. "Does this mean we have a pet cow?"

"Only until we get a heating lamp rigged in the

barn." Millie tugged Cooper by his coat sleeve to follow her onto the heated back porch. She fit the drain plug in the oversize utility sink, then ran warm water. "Let's get him clean and warmed up."

Cooper gingerly nestled the calf into the big sink. It was a tight squeeze—probably the bathtub would've been a better fit—but for now, this would do.

What wouldn't do? The awkward awareness stemming from working alongside Cooper—especially when every so often his elbow accidentally grazed her breasts. In an effort to keep her mind on the calf's welfare, as opposed to her jittery hands and inability to even hold the mild pet shampoo, she asked, "I'm assuming the little guy's momma rejected him. Got any clue why?"

"*Helga* had twins. Her firstborn's fat and happy. My guess is she was as surprised by this one as we are."

"Twins… Never saw that coming." With her hands sudsy, Millie nudged hair from her cheek with her shoulder, but that only landed the escaped curl on her mouth.

"Let me help…" Cooper swept the lock over her cheek, tucking it behind her ear. His finger was warm and wet and blazed a trail she could feel, but didn't want to.

"Thanks—not just for that, but you know…bringing in this guy."

He nodded, but then graced her with a slow grin that did funny things to her stomach. "No problem. I'm not a total deadbeat, you know."

"Yeah…" *I do.*

Time slowed as she drank him in, remembering the many good times she and Jim and Cooper had shared. But she couldn't just flip a switch and make all those years she'd hated and resented him for not being there go away. Even before they'd been in-laws, they'd been friends. Good, lifelong friends. She'd never known her dad, and her mom had virtually abandoned her to be raised by her maternal grandparents. The Hansens had been like a second family to her. It'd been inconceivable how Cooper had lived with himself for not having come home.

But he's home now. Shouldn't that count for something?

"Dad still keep colostrum in the deep freeze?"

"There should be some in there."

"Good. When we finish, I'll make a bottle."

"Thanks. I'll find you the powdered formula."

"I'd appreciate it."

What changed? Why the stilted formality?

She finished scrubbing the calf then let the water drain before rinsing him with the sprayer. Under Cooper's appraisal, her every movement felt stiff and labored—as if she were under water.

A growl followed by metallic clanking came from the general direction of Clint's room.

"Want me to check on Grandpa?" The whole time Millie had stood hyperaware of Cooper, LeeAnn and J.J. had hovered near the kitchen pass-through. What did that say about her state of mind that she hadn't even noticed her kids had been in the room?

"I'll do it," she said.

Cooper asked, "What do you want me to do about this guy?"

"Lee, please grab a couple of old quilts—you know, the ones I put over the garden for frost?"

The girl nodded.

"Pile them in the corner by the fridge. It should be nice and warm."

"Yes, ma'am."

"J.J.—" Millie knelt to his level "—I need you to run down to the basement and get the feeder bottles we used when we had those two calves with scours. They should be somewhere on the shelves by my flowerpots."

"Okay." Her son bit his lower lip while his eyes filled with tears. "Is the baby going to be all right? He's so tiny."

She pulled J.J. into a hug. Her son had already witnessed too many hardships during his short life. She couldn't bear for him to have one more. "He will if I have anything to say about it."

With the calf nestled in a cozy quilt nest, Cooper ducked his head while taking the ninety-degree turn on the basement stairs. He'd conked his head on the damned rafter so many times as a gangly teen that even his long absence couldn't make him forget.

J.J. clomped behind him as they descended into the cool, damp cavernous space. "Did you know my dad?"

"Sure did." Cooper swept aside a low-hanging cobweb.

"Are you like him?"

Not really. Jim had always been the better of the two of them. Kinder. The sort who volunteered to stay home from a weekend bender to help an elderly neighbor plant her garden. "I suppose we looked a little alike. He was my brother."

"Like Lee's my sister?"

"Right." Cooper opened the freezer lid, welcoming the blast of cold air on his heated cheeks. Made him uncomfortable thinking about what a selfish prick he used to be.

The kid took a scooter that'd been leaned against a wall and rode it across the stone floor. "I'd rather have a brother. Lee's grumpy all the time. And did you know she talks to *boys?*"

Cooper looked up from the freezer. "How old is she?"

"She's in fifth grade. My friend Cayden said he saw her kiss a kid who's in sixth grade. Isn't that gross?"

Actually, yes.

Just a guess, but Cooper didn't think his brother would be on board with this kind of information. As the girl's uncle, had he been there for her since Jim's death, Cooper would've felt right at home giving her a stern lecture on staying the hell away from boys until she was thirty.

"Do you know what sex is? Cayden said his biggest brother got caught having sex on their couch."

Though Cooper already had the colostrum, he stuck his head back in the chest-style freezer just to escape the kid's questioning stare.

"Well?" J.J. unfortunately persisted. "Do you know what sex is?"

Cooper coughed. What kind of kids was Millie raising? "Actually, I do know what it is—bad. Very, very bad, and it's not anything you need to be talking about till you're thirty." *Would that fall under the* do as I say, not as I do *form of parenting?* Cooper lost his virginity at sixteen to a nineteen-year-old dental hygienist in the bed of her truck.

"Oh." J.J. stopped riding. "Okay, well, I won't do it, then."

"Excellent. Glad to hear it."

"Do you remember what I was s'posed to be getting?"

"These?" Cooper had spied three plastic feeder bottles exactly where Millie had described and grabbed them.

"Yeah! Bottles!"

Eager to not only escape the gloomy basement, but also his nephew's questions, Cooper headed back up the stairs, figuring the kid would follow. Only he didn't. "Aren't you coming?"

"Do you want me to?"

"I guess." Cooper furrowed his eyebrows. What did that mean? Was this some kind of trick question? "I mean, your mom told you to help, right?"

He nodded.

"Okay, then, come on…" He pressed against the wall, urging J.J. to pass him on the stairs.

"Cool!" The kid bolted as if he was on springs. "Do you think the calf's gonna live or die like my dad?"

Cooper inwardly groaned. If having rugrats always involved this many awkward questions, he wanted no part of ever having a child of his own.

Chapter 7

By the time the kids had been put to bed and Clint's evening care had been completed, Millie collapsed onto the sofa, setting the baby monitor she used to make sure he didn't need her in the night on the coffee table. Every inch of her ached from the exertion of their action-packed day.

Cheetah, the cat, slinked out from behind the recliner to dart into the kitchen.

"I don't even know why I feed you," she said to the inhospitable creature.

When the phone rang, she contemplated letting the machine pick up, but on the chance it was one of Clint's home-health therapists, she mustered the energy to fish the phone from the couch cushions—the spot where LeeAnn typically left it. "Hello?"

"Well? How's it going? You were supposed to call me back."

Peg. Millie had forgotten she'd been on the phone with Cooper's sister right before he'd shown up with the calf.

"What happened?"

Since the upstairs shower was still running, Millie gave her sister-in-law the short version of the chaotic day's events.

"Wait—so why do you still have a calf and chickens in the kitchen?"

"Because of the storm, the feed store had a run on heat-lamp bulbs. Ernest won't have more in till he can make a supply run to Denver."

"Good grief." Peg groaned. "I'm working twelve-hour shifts, so I can have long weekends off. Want me to pick one up for you before I head your way?"

"Thanks for the offer, but the even worse news is that one of the biggest limbs on the cottonwood out back fell on the coop. It's a total loss. Your brother said he can rebuild it, but who knows how long that'll take."

"You can't have chickens in your house indefinitely…."

"I know…" Millie drew the afghan from the sofa back to tuck it around her legs. "Cooper's rigging a temporary fix in the barn. Since the kids have school tomorrow, we're driving into Denver for the parts he needs."

"Who's staying with Dad?"

"Lynette. Plus, the traveling nurse should be here." After they found chicken-coop supplies, they'd grocery shop.

"Good. You need a break."

"Agreed. Only…" She wrapped one of the afghan's frayed strands around her pinkie finger tight enough for her nail to turn white.

"What's the problem?"

Upstairs, the shower turned off.

The thought of Cooper standing there buck naked struck her as disconcerting. The old house only had one and a half baths, meaning...

Her cheeks flamed.

"The problem," she said to her sister-in-law in an effort to get her wandering mind back on topic, "is your brother. He's everywhere. I can't think around him. He's just—"

Back on her feet, she fished behind a row of Jim's dusty old civil war history tomes for the Oreos she kept hidden in a Ziploc bag. It wasn't that she begrudged the kids' cookies—she made them all the time. But Oreos were her thing. Her grandmother had always laughed about the baking gene having skipped her generation. She'd filled their cookie jar with store-bought fare. Millie hadn't complained. All these years later, the same treat that'd gotten her through her rocky early childhood was still her go-to food security blanket.

A creak on the stairs had her chewing faster, before tucking the bag back in its hiding place.

"What're you stashing?"

Hand to her chest, she willed her racing pulse to slow. "Cooper. You scared me half to death."

"Good thing it was only halfway," he teased without smiling.

"Yeah..." Back in school, they used to be friends, so why now did she find herself wishing he'd just stay in his room?

From the phone she'd cradled between her breasts, Peg's tinny voice asked, "Millie? Millie, are you there?"

"That my sister?"

She nodded.

He reached for the phone.

During the hand-off, their fingers brushed, which only flustered her further. What was it about him that had her feeling like she'd returned to seventh grade?

"Hey, girl. When do I get to see you?"

Cheetah returned to do a figure-eight around Cooper's ankles. *Traitor.*

While Cooper and his sister talked, Millie checked to make sure Clint's meds had kicked in then wandered into the kitchen with the intent to unload the dishwasher. But when she flicked on the lights, it woke the menagerie, and the rooster quite literally flew his makeshift coop. Having always considered herself a reasonably intelligent person, why hadn't she thought earlier about devising a way to keep her flock from flying?

She'd hoped catching Barry would be easy, but he'd landed atop the fridge.

"When I do catch you," she said in a singsong voice while easing one of the kitchen table chairs in his direction, "I'm going to fry you."

She stood on the chair, slowly reaching for the stupid bird.

"Need help?"

Upon hearing Cooper's voice, Barry was back on the move, finally resting on the rim of LeeAnn's lopsided volcano that she'd left on the table.

"I nearly had him, if you'd stop skulking."

"Skulking?" He crept toward the bird, and in a ridiculously fast move, had him captured and tucked under his arm.

"You know what I mean." What a mess. Everything was just such an awful mess—and she wasn't just talking about her kitchen, which would have to be fumigated once the chickens and calf got to their temporary home in the barn. She feared the truest source of disarray was her own heart. Having her brother-in-law back in the mix was all at once a godsend and a curse. "You're always so sneaky."

"Mill…" He stroked the side of the bird's head. And damn Barry for closing his eyes and cooing. "All I did was walk into the room. No sneaking or skulking. Just walking." He took the phone from the waistband of his black warm-up pants, returning it to the charging stand.

Whatever! Just stop!

Like a doofus, she still stood on the chair in front of the fridge and stared at him. Mouth dry, pulse haywire, she felt on the edge of a breakdown and had no idea why! His being there should've made everything easier. He'd certainly lightened her workload. So why did everything suddenly seem so hard?

Maybe because he wore no shirt, and his chest and abs formed a muscular wall?

"Need help?" he asked.

"With what?" Flighty hand to her mouth, she nibbled the tip of her pinkie finger.

"Getting down? Wiping all those Oreo crumbs off your T-shirt? Rigging something to keep old Barry here from another flight?"

"H-how do you know his name?"

"Your son told me. He's a good kid."

"The best." Why was her mouth so dry? Why did her right eye keep twitching every time she looked Cooper's way? And how did he know she'd been eating Oreos? And why did just thinking about him looking at her chest cause her nipples to harden? Lord, she was a bona fide Texas twister of a disaster!

"Help?" He now stood beside her. Even with the benefit of her chair, she was only a few inches taller.

"Thanks, but I can do it." After scrambling down, she shoved the chair back under the table then brushed crumbs from her chest.

He took a step back, raising his hands in surrender. "Want me to handle tucking in our escapee?"

"W-would you mind?" Because honestly, after their hectic day, Millie had more than she could handle with just being in the same close space as Cooper. "I—I'm ready for bed."

She retrieved Clint's monitor from the living room then made her own escape up the stairs.

The dimly lit kitchen was too intimate.

It brought back memories of all the nights she and Jim sat at the table over cups of steaming cocoa, plotting and planning the rest of their lives. Whether to sign J.J. up for baseball or steer him toward rodeo. Whether they should let LeeAnn enroll in that hoity-toity Denver art class her second-grade teacher had recommended. When Jim had been alive, everything had seemed so simple. He and Clint ran the ranch, and she cared for them, their children and home.

Now?

She wore so many hats that if she sprouted eight extra heads, she still couldn't wear them all.

After brushing her teeth in the bathroom, which still smelled rich from Cooper's musky shampoo, she checked on J.J. to find him sleeping.

She took the toy truck out from under his flannel

pajama-clad legs then tugged the covers up to his chin. She kissed his forehead, whispering, "I love you."

From behind LeeAnn's door came a girly giggle. *"You're crazy..."*

Millie didn't bother knocking, and upon entering the room, she held out her hand. She and her daughter had done this dance before. "Phone."

LeeAnn sighed with majestic preteen aplomb. "God, Mom, I'm almost twelve, and everyone on the planet has a cell but me."

"Gosh, Lee, you may be right, but that doesn't give you permission to take my cell from my purse. You know we only have it for emergencies, and those minutes are expensive."

"I hate you, and I hate being poor!" Back in bed, her daughter finished her performance by tugging the covers over her head.

This probably should've been the moment when Millie nipped that sass by grounding LeeAnn for the rest of her life, but she didn't have the strength. After perching on the bed's edge, she ran her hand along her daughter's side. "Know what? I'm kind of sick of being poor myself, only you might find this hard to believe, but hon, we're actually pretty rich—and blessed. We have a nice, solid roof over our heads and plenty of food in our bellies. We have each other and love and—"

"Stop!" LeeAnn sat up, letting the quilts fall around her waist. "You say we're so rich and blessed? Then how come Daddy died and Grandpa had a stroke? And our barn's so crappy that the chickens have to live in our kitchen?"

"Lee..." Millie's throat tightened. She'd asked herself the same questions countless times, and was fresh out of fortifying platitudes. "Look, since you're *sooo* old, I'll be straight with you. No one's more tired of our temporary cash *shortage* than me, but it is what it is. I wasn't raised to be a quitter and neither were you. When times are tough, we just have to dig in our heels and fight harder. We—"

"Mom, seriously, *please* stop. Our life sucks. Everything sucks, and sometimes I just want to run away!" She was crying, and the sound of her child's sobs shattered what little remained of Millie's heart.

"Okay, yes—" she drew LeeAnn into a hug "—at the moment, there's not a whole lot to be happy about, but you know what?"

"What?" Sniff, sniff.

"On the bright side, things can't get much worse, right?"

Millie kissed the crown of her daughter's head, then tucked her in, longing for simpler times back when Jim had been here to coparent. J.J. she could still handle, but with her daughter, Millie felt about as in control as if she were juggling boiling water.

In the hall, she'd just shut LeeAnn's door and turned for her own room when Cooper reached the top of the stairs.

When their eyes locked, she stopped breathing.

Had she really just noted that things couldn't get worse?

"Everything all right?" he asked.

She wagged the cell. "Just putting on my sheriff hat. Guess I'm not ready for her to be acting this old so soon. When we were her age, no one had phones."

"True. But then to her way of thinking, we probably seem old enough to have been riding dinosaurs to school." He cracked a smile. "Pretty sure your old Chevette could've technically been from the Stone Age. That thing was nasty."

"Oh—" she raised her eyebrows "—like your truck was much better?"

"At least it was a Ford."

"Watch it…" Lord, Cooper and Jim used to battle for hours over the merits of Ford versus Chevy trucks. She'd forgotten. In the hall's chill, her throat knotted under the guilty weight of how much else of her husband's daily quirks she'd forgotten.

Outside, the wind had once again picked up and rattled the shutters.

"I really am sorry about Jim. I would've come to the funeral, but didn't even know he'd died until a month after he'd been gone. By then…" He shrugged. Rammed his hands into his pockets. "Well, I couldn't."

"Sure. I understand." But she didn't. Which was no doubt a big part of the reason why she found it so difficult being around him.

Cooper hid out from Millie until she'd shut herself into her room for the night.

Once the coast was clear, he handled the half-dozen chores still needing to be addressed, then was too keyed up to sleep. He tried boning up on the latest deep-dive recs, but his job felt a million miles away. What he really needed to think about, but didn't want to, was the mess he'd made of things here.

He sat on the sofa, leaning forward to cradle his forehead in his hands.

In the short run, he'd soon enough get the ranch in ship-shape order, but what about long-term? Would

Millie and he ever again be on friendly terms? Would he grow as close to his niece and nephew as an uncle rightfully should?

Then there was Clint...

Cooper rose, heading toward his father's room, careful to avoid the creakiest spots in the old wood floor.

In the moonlight, his dad looked frail. His breathing was labored, and the cantankerous old goat had worked off all of his covers.

Quietly and efficiently, Cooper straightened Clint's linens, tucking them in hopes that they'd stay put through the night.

His feelings where his dad was concerned were all over the map. Of course Cooper loved him, but that love was tainted by the alienation Clint had caused. But then was it fair to blame his father for their estrangement, when if Cooper hadn't hurt his mother, nothing in any of their lives would've even changed?

Millie woke earlier than she would've liked. At five-thirty, it was still dark and the wind still blew. Not up to dealing with chickens and the calf in her robe, she pulled on jeans and a hoodie, topping her thick socks with her most comfortable pair of pink cowboy boots.

Jim had bought them for her as a first wedding anniversary present. She'd been so proud. They were decadent and impractical, and she still loved them as much as she did him. Only he was long gone, and over the years she'd found her remembered love changing. Sometimes, she loved him as a wife. Other times, almost in a mothering capacity when she wished she could scold him for having been so reckless with his precious life. Like his mom, he hadn't had to die. If she'd stayed on the porch. If he'd stayed in his seat, both would've still been alive today.

In the kitchen, she was surprised to find a few much-needed fortifications to their makeshift pens. Hay bales now formed a sturdier wall for the chickens, and a tent had been made from purple-striped disposable table-cloths left over from LeeAnn's last birthday. She peeked under to find Barry and his harem still sleeping.

"How are you?" she asked the tiny calf, stroking the top of his soft head.

He also had a new hay bale enclosure, and while the width made the kitchen feel smaller, she was glad to know there wouldn't soon be a stampede.

When had Cooper done all of this? He'd never been so conscientious as a teen.

"You probably need a bottle, huh? It's been a while since your last feeding." For optimum health, he'd need to be fed every twelve hours for the next three months. How many changes would've happened by then? Would Clint be walking or talking? Would the new chicken coop be done? Would she feel comfortable being in the same space as her brother-in-law? "Hard to believe it'll be almost Easter when we get you back with the herd."

He looked up at her with his big, dark eyes, and she melted.

"How could your mother not love you?"

She rubbed his nose, smiling when his warm exhalations tickled her palm.

By the time she finished warming the calf's milk and feeding him his bottle, the chickens were waking with throaty gurgles. She was just about to launch a search for feed in the coop's ruin when she noticed the bag leaning against the wall. The scoop was even inside.

Cooper had thought of everything. Right down to bringing in the water and feeder bowls—she'd made do with a paper plate and plastic mixing bowl.

She should be grateful toward him, so why the flash of resentment?

Since Clint's stroke, she'd single-handedly cared for the house and ranch. In her head she knew her brother-in-law was a godsend, but her heart told another story. For her, his mere presence was an admission that she couldn't cope. Which honestly? Okay, was true. But her stubborn streak didn't want to admit it—especially to of all people, Cooper.

Scowling, she bypassed coffee in favor of her private cookie stash.

In the dark living room, guided by moonlight reflecting off snow, she took her bag to the sofa. Only just as she was about to sit, something beneath the afghan moved!

Chapter 8

"Unless you want things to get awkward real fast," Cooper said from the sofa, "you might want to sit somewhere else."

"There you go again…" Breathing heavy, Millie clutched her cookie bag to her chest. In the pale moonlight, she looked fragile. Still pretty, but dangerously thin and pale. "Skulking."

Groaning, he rubbed his hands over his whisker-stubbled face. "You try sitting on me, and yet I'm the bad guy?"

"I didn't say—" she dropped one of her contraband half-eaten cookies back in the bag "—never mind. What're you even doing here? Why weren't you sleeping in your old room?"

"Funny…" He eased upright. It'd been a long time since he'd done manual labor, and his body felt every hay bale and feed sack he'd lifted. Back on base, he worked out religiously, but lifting weights and swimming had nothing on the whole ranch routine. He felt every one of his thirty years and then some. "Ever since setting foot back on this land, I've worked my ass off to make things easier on you, but all you've done is complain. If you don't want me here, why did you ask me to come?"

"Point of fact?" She sat on his dad's recliner, but far from leaning back to relax, she remained as straight and unwelcoming as a fence post. "I wasn't the one asking you to come home. That was your sister."

"Want me to leave?"

Yes! "No. Of course not. I just… Well, maybe we could establish a few ground rules as to where you'll be and when?"

"Ground rules?" Had she lost her ever-lovin' mind? "As in, I shouldn't leave my room between the hours of 6:00 p.m and 6:00 a.m.?"

"Exactly." He'd meant the question to be sarcastic, but judging by her eager nod, she'd totally missed his point. "The less time you spend with the kids and me, the better. I thought we could somehow recapture our old *happy family* vibe, but…" She shook her head. "Your dad's expected to make a full recovery, so once he's back on his horse, you should—"

"Climb back on mine and ride the hell out of town?"

She blanched. "I didn't mean it like that."

He leaned forward, resting his elbows on his knees. "I'll bite. Go ahead, Mill, explain to me how else you—"

"Mommy?"

Cooper glanced over his shoulder to find sleepy,

messy-haired J.J. The kid was crazy cute. Smart. Jim would be damned proud.

"Hey, hon." She went to her son, pulling him against her for a hug. "You're up early."

"I know. I was excited to see if we have another snow day."

"Gosh, I forgot to check. Let's turn on the TV and see."

She scooped up her little boy and carried him to the recliner, settling him on her lap.

J.J. took the remote from a side table and soon had the room filled with a cooking segment on making snow ice cream. School closings scrolled across the bottom of the screen.

How many mornings had Cooper sat in that same chair, holding his breath with his fingers crossed to see Wilmington Public Schools.

The scroll restarted with the statement that *Aurora Public Schools will be in session.* Wilmington hadn't been listed.

"Aw, man…" Wearing a mighty pout, J.J. crossed his arms. "I wanted to help build the new chicken coop."

"Trust me," Cooper said, "probably for the next week or even two, I'll need plenty of help."

"Okay…" He scrambled from his mom's lap. "Guess I'll eat cereal and pet the calf."

"Sounds like a great plan," Millie said.

"I like him…" Cooper hadn't meant to give the thought voice, and now that he had, in light of his sister-in-law flat out telling him she didn't want him being around her kids, he couldn't figure out why. What would forging a relationship with them hurt? Especially with their father gone.

He looked up to find Millie staring.

For a split second, their gazes locked, but then she turned away. "Think about what I said. I don't mean you should literally stay in your room whenever the kids are home, but you might think about heading out to the barn or maybe looking up old friends."

When a clang and growl erupted from his father's room, Millie bolted toward that direction.

Cooper leaned forward, cradling his face in his hands. Why was he even here? He wasn't wanted.

But you are clearly needed.

For now, that would have to be enough. He'd spent his entire adult life helping others in need, and he wasn't about to stop now—no matter what Millie said.

"Relax. Clint will be fine."

Millie hugged her longtime friend and neighbor, Lynette, whispering in her ear, "It's not him I'm worried about. How am I going to last an entire day being alone with Cooper?"

After checking to make sure Cooper was outside, Lynette said, "Sweetie, only in my dreams am I alone with a man as fine as him. Zane and I have been together so long, I feel like we've grown relationship barnacles."

"Oh, stop. You two are adorable." Like Jim and her, they'd met in high school and married right after graduating.

"He's so boring. And have you seen his beer belly? He looks fifteen months pregnant. Now, if I had a man like Coop…" She whistled. "What I could do alone with him in a closet for five minutes."

"Lynette!" Millie laughed, but couldn't help but be

a bit jealous of her friend. Zane might've gained a few pounds, but at least he was alive.

"All I'm saying is that Jim's been gone awhile. If you and Coop gravitated together, well—"

"Stop right there."

"Valentine's Day is right around the corner. Mack Walker's planning a big shindig at his bar. My mom said he's trying to impress Wilma. There's even going to be champagne and a chocolate fountain. Doesn't get much fancier than that."

"I suppose not..." Would Cooper even go? If he did, what kind of woman would he take?

Speaking of the cowboy devil, he honked his truck's horn.

An hour earlier, the kids had gotten on the school bus. While she'd fed and bathed Clint, her brother-in-law had checked the horses and driven out for a quick look at the cattle.

"You know—" Lynette tapped her chin "—back in the day, wouldn't propriety have demanded Cooper not only watch over you, but marry you? Pretty sure it's even in the Bible."

"You're being ridiculous—not about the Bible—but your matchmaking." Millie shrugged on her red wool coat. "I don't even like Cooper."

"But even you have to admit he's as hot as July sun?"

Or possibly hotter.

Cooper again honked the horn.

Millie gave her friend one last hug and kissed her cheek. "Thanks for watching Clint. Hopefully, we'll be back before the kids get home."

"Go ahead and ignore me," Lynette shouted behind her as she walked out the door. "Mark my words, despite your sourpuss expression, the two of you are going to have a great day together!"

"Buh-bye!" Millie gave her well-intentioned but delusional friend a backward wave.

Twenty minutes into the supply trip to Denver, Cooper had had just about all he could take of Millie's silent treatment. He got it. She wasn't buying what he was selling—only to his way of thinking, he wasn't offering her anything other than hard work and friendship.

"Warm enough?" He nudged the heat higher. Though the cold was still brutal, the wind had died and the sun shone.

"Sure."

"I felt bad for J.J. Poor little guy. Nothing worse than not getting a snow day you're expecting."

"Uh-huh." She stared out the passenger window as if the view was as riveting as a UFO landing.

"LeeAnn, on the other hand, looked happy about getting to school."

Millie sighed.

Cooper didn't care. They'd once been close. He might not deserve her forgiveness, but for some unfathomable reason, he craved it. And so if his chitchat already had him in hot water, he figured what did he have to lose by jumping right into a roiling-hot sulphur spring? "I've got a confession to make."

"Oh?"

"Or maybe not? You might already know." He glanced her way to find her gaze now tightly focused on the straight, lonely road ahead. The high plains landscape was gorgeous in its simplicity. The snow-peaked front range rose in front of them like a majestic dream.

"Jim said he wouldn't tell you, but you two were probably close enough that he told you everything, huh?"

"Oh, for pity's sake…"

"What?" He hazarded another glance in her direction, only to lock head-on with her sparkling sky-blue gaze.

"Spit it out already."

"Okay…" He forced a deep breath. "Remember when Jim went hunting for a week in Wyoming?"

"What about it? He went hunting all the time."

"Yeah, well, that week he wasn't hunting, but with me."

"In Wyoming?" Her eyes widened.

"Norfolk. He crashed at my apartment. Seeing him again…" Cooper's throat knotted. Seeing his brother again had been surreal. And bittersweet. Jim had left with essentially nothing having been fixed. His little brother had told him to man up and make the first move toward repairing his relationship with his father. Cooper promised he would—soon. Just not soon enough, as Jim died two months later. If he had gone back then, would he have prevented both his dad's stroke and Jim's death? "Seeing him again was nice."

"Nice?" Millie's voice had taken on a shrill tone. "How very Cooper of you to drop a bomb like this then leave it sitting between us undetonated. You're such an ass."

"I'm not trying to be. I thought you'd want to know."

"That my husband lied to me? Apparently didn't trust me enough to tell me he was going to see his brother? Why would he lie about something like that when he knew no one pushed for a reconciliation for all of you harder than me? *Argh!*" She slammed the side window with the heel of her fist.

"Look, the last thing I wanted was to get you all riled up." The silent tears streaming down her cheeks made him feel all the more helpless, so he focused on the road and driving—apparently the only thing he could do without royally screwing it up. "I thought knowing might somehow help."

"Shut up, Cooper. I wish you'd never come home." *Me, too....*

Millie's fury was the only thing keeping her upright during the endless day of errands needing to be run. Story of her life. Putting out fires with never enough water—meaning, cash.

In this case, she and Cooper were at Lowe's, standing side by side while looking at ready-to-assemble shed kits that could be used to replace the chicken coop.

"These are so far out my budget," Millie mumbled, shrugging deeper into her coat to ward off the wind's bite. "I might as well be buying a chicken Taj Mahal."

"Then let me take care of it," Cooper offered. "And since I'm not up on my Indian architecture, would you settle for a nice Victorian?"

Teeth chattering, she shot him a sideways glare.

He tossed her his keys. "See that Red Lobster?"

Maybe a couple hundred yards away in the next parking lot over sat the restaurant Millie hadn't before noticed. "Yeah. What about it?"

"Grab us a table. I'll make arrangements to get what we need delivered and meet you there."

"Don't be ridiculous. Do you know how much lunch

out would cost? If you're hungry, I've got granola bars in my purse."

His jaw hardened—which should've made her dislike him all the more for growing impatient with her. But that steely determination he'd wielded at the farm supply store and now here, only made him more disgustingly attractive. Did he have any idea how much she hated conceding even that one point to him? That even with his whisker-stubbled cheeks ruddy from wind, he was still one of the finest-looking men she'd ever known? "You do realize that every second you keep us out here arguing is only making us both colder?"

Lord, how she hated to admit it, but he had a point. And it'd literally been years since she'd had buttery seafood. What the heck? If he was buying… After the bombshell he'd dropped on her that morning, the very least he owed her was a free meal.

"Fine," she said from between gritted teeth—they were chattering from the cold. "Want me to get you anything to drink?"

"Spiked coffee."

Twenty-five minutes later, Millie sat in a toasty booth, sipping from her own sinfully rich Bailey's and coffee. If only for a moment, she closed her eyes and slowly exhaled.

Everything would be okay.

She wasn't sure how, but she'd come too far to give up now. She and the kids and Clint had survived—even if not thrived, exactly—on their own, and despite Cooper's presence, she'd continue the tradition. She was a strong, capable woman and—

From the restaurant's entry, she watched Cooper approach.

Her mouth went dry and her pulse raced.

For a man to look so good ought to be criminal. Beneath his battered cowboy hat, even with his lips pressed into a thin, cranky line, he looked just as good back when she'd worshipped him in their high school cafeteria as he did now.

"Damn…" He eased into the booth and took off his hat to set beside him. "I'll bet the temp dropped twenty degrees just in the time it took me to walk across the parking lot. This mine?" He eyed his still-steaming mug.

She nodded.

He took a sip and groaned. The way he'd arched his head back and closed his eyes left her squirming. Did he have to make plain old coffee-drinking look obscene?

The waitress came and went, and while Cooper ate his weight in Cheddar Bay Biscuits, Millie picked at her Caesar salad.

"Something wrong with your food?"

"Not at all." Unless she paid attention to how much female consideration her brother-in-law unwittingly garnished. While he focused on food, at least a dozen hungry-eyed ladies apparently craved him! A fact that shouldn't have even bothered her, but did. Chalk it up to just one more reason why the sooner Cooper returned to his self-imposed exile, the better off they'd all be.

After a fortifying sip of her coffee, she picked up where they'd last left off on their meaningful conversation. "Did Jim tell you why?"

Cooper paused midbite. "You mean why he didn't tell you about his trip?"

She nodded while curling her finger around her mug's handle.

"Simple answer?" He dropped his biscuit on a saucer. "One that basically makes me feel like an even bigger pile of crap?"

Works for me…

"He said he would've rather spent the money on a trip for you and the kids, but—"

"I get it." And she did. How many times had she and Jim daydreamed about taking LeeAnn and J.J. to Disney? Yes, that money could've gone toward a once-in-a-lifetime trip—even better, been used to make house or barn repairs. But honestly? Now that she'd had a few hours to mull it over, her anger's edge had dulled. "I really do. And you know, as miffed as I am that he didn't trust me not to flip out at him over the money, it makes me feel…" Her eyes welled before she could complete her thought.

She glanced up to find Cooper's eyes shining.

He shocked her by reaching across the table to cover her hand. No—*shocked* would be too tame of a word. His tender, sweet touch *devastated* her. She wanted—needed—to hate him, but what was the point? The adult in her could rationalize that they were both the walking wounded. Granted, for different reasons, but Cooper had to be every bit as raw on the inside as she was. His guilt couldn't be any easier to bear than her grief.

They sat like that forever.

The restaurant's canned, easy-listening music and ambient conversations and clatter faded until all Millie heard was the thunder of her own heart.

It'd been three endless years since she'd been touched. *Really* touched. Sure, she hugged the kids and Peg and her friends, but that wasn't the same. This… This was indescribably good and maybe a little thrill-

ing and made her long to just snuggle up against someone and release a long, slow exhale. Only when it came
down to it, truthfully, she didn't want to be held by just
anyone, but Cooper—the only guy she'd ever been attracted to besides her husband.

How twisted was that?

Wrong on every level, but she couldn't help how
she felt.

She lifted her gaze only to collide with his. He looked
all at once apologetic and yet determined. But for what?
Did he feel as flustered around her as she did him?

"Here you go." The waitress startled Millie back
to reality—only, she didn't want to go. "An Admiral's
Feast for you, sir. And, ma'am, your grilled shrimp
skewer."

"Thanks," Cooper said.

"Need anything else?" the too-chipper, twentysomething blonde asked.

"We're good." Thank heavens her brother-in-law answered, because Millie didn't think she could.

Cooper withdrew his hand.

Losing not only his heat, but also his strength, felt
akin to her bones having turned to jelly. No matter how
deeply she'd resented his help that morning, deep down,
she knew she needed him. He wasn't the enemy. Just
another soul lost to what was beginning to feel like an
almost insurmountable string of Hansen family trage-
dies. How would rejecting him, holding on to her frustration with him, make anything better?

They ate in silence.

Returned to the car with only polite chitchat.

She had to fix this, but wasn't sure how. "Thanks
for lunch. It was delicious—but way too expensive."

"Stop."

"What?" She climbed into the truck beside him.

"Okay, it's like this…" A muscle ticking in his jaw, he stared at the busy street in front of where she'd parked. His profile was hard. Weary. Make no mistake, he was still one of the most handsome men she'd ever known, but his gaze used to hold an internal glow that'd gone out. Was any of the old Cooper left? Was she partly to blame for his now looking so downtrodden? "I'm a grown man. Don't tell me what to spend, or where to sleep, or how long I'm allowed to stay in the public areas of the house where I spent the first eighteen years of my life. For the hundredth time—sorry I hurt you. Sorry I never took the time to really get to know J.J. and Lee, but I'm trying… And if you'd just—"

Not thinking, just doing, Millie unfastened her seat belt and leaned across the truck's cab to kiss Cooper's cheek. But then he turned, and her lips grazed his. And her heart took off on a runaway canter fueled by sheer panic.

That kiss had been a total accident, so why were her lips tingling and a much lower heat pooling and her mouth turning dry and…

"Son of a biscuit, Mill, what was that?" Not only did Cooper cover his mouth, but as if she were a dangerously thorny cactus, he jerked a foot away.

Chapter 9

Millie retreated to the relative safety of her side of the truck. "*That* was supposed to have been a platonic thanks-for-lunch kiss to your cheek, but you had to ruin it by turning."

"How have I ruined anything—I mean, at least, lately? Ever since showing up, I've worked my ass off and spent a bundle. You're the one putting on the big chill."

"I just kissed you!"

"That's my point—why the hell would you *ever* kiss me? You're my brother's wife. Kissing you doesn't—"

"Wait—you think I *for real* meant to kiss you? No, no, no…" She covered her face with her hands. "You totally misread the situation." But had he? Sure, she'd meant to kiss him on the cheek, only her body traitorously wasn't concerned about the mix-up. It'd been years since she'd kissed a man, and apparently, judging by her still-galloping pulse, she'd liked it!

What kind of horrible woman was she? Who kissed their brother-in-law? A straight-up harlot, that's who!

He started the truck.

"Don't you think we should talk more about this?"

Backed out of their parking space.

"It *really* was an accident."

Maneuvered the vehicle through the bustling lot.

"Cooper?"

Only after making a right onto the busy main traffic artery did he ask, "We still need to run by a grocery store?"

"No. Let's just get home." She crossed her arms. Fine. He wanted to keep up the silent treatment? Two could play that game.

A short while later, he pulled into the King Soopers in Thornton. Parked the car and killed the engine.

"I told you I wanted to go straight home."

His sideways half smile played teeter-totter with her heart. Not only did he bring back shadows of his brother, but more. He reminded her of the girl she'd been before taking her friendship with Jim to another level. Before then, she'd been Team Cooper all the way, worshipping him from the anonymity of crowded school hallways and rodeo stands. Her body seemed all tense and confused about the fact that she wasn't a lovesick teen anymore, and Cooper was no longer her crush.

After taking the key from the ignition, he said, "Only one problem with me taking you straight home."

She gulped. "What's that?"

"I got a hankering for something sweet last night, and, well…" His already wind-chapped cheeks further reddened. "I, ah, ate the rest of your private stash of Oreos."

The way he said *private stash* made it sound like her cookies were porn!

Now her cheeks superheated. "You're awful." And not just for eating her secret treats, but for making her feel all flustered and as if she'd lost control of her own body. Before he'd shown up, things like kissing and hugging and fornicating hadn't even been on her radar. Most days, she forgot she was even a woman. Now? Cooper had unwittingly made her crave something far more than cookies. And that fact shamed her to her core.

"Uncle Cooper! Look what I made at school!"

Cooper looked up from his job of hanging heat lamps by chains from the barn's lower rafters to find J.J. charging his way, holding a shoe box under his arm.

It'd been two days since what he now called the *Denver Incident,* and his primary mission had become keeping a safe distance from his sister-in-law. Her cute son and daughter were another matter. Although LeeAnn wanted nothing to do with him, J.J. stuck to him like peanut butter on a cracker. The goofy kid was about as nutty, too. But in a good way.

"We've been learning about the ocean and stuff, and since my friend Cayden says Navy guys like you are swimming all the time, I thought you might miss the beach, so I made you this!" Out of breath from his long-winded speech, the kid finally stopped talking to grin. Lord, he was a cutie. Looked just like the pics of his dad at that age.

Cooper climbed down from the ladder to check out J.J.'s creation. For once, the weather wasn't half-bad,

Temps in the fifties with no wind. "All right, buddy—" he ruffled the boy's hair "—show me what you've got."

J.J. lifted the box's lid to reveal a crude diorama of a beach scene. Though the sand contained scraps of paper and yarn, the water was made of blue construction paper, and a reef was constructed with painted rocks, Cooper's throat knotted upon seeing a green plastic army guy on top of the water. What he assumed was a scuba suit had been drawn on with a marker. "Is that me?"

"Uh-huh," his nephew said, "and that gray blob is a shark you were gonna save me from, but one of the coral rocks smashed it on the bus. Do you still like it?"

"Buddy, it's the most amazing thing I've ever seen. Thank you." With reverence, Cooper set the box on a ladder rung to give the boy a hug. "I love it."

"I love you, Uncle Cooper. I'm glad you live with us."

The words and resulting emotion struck Cooper like a punch. How could this kid *love* him? He hardly even knew him. But then maybe that was the magic of being a kid. They don't carry around a decade of regrets to use when judging a man's character.

To say Cooper was gobsmacked by J.J.'s affection was an understatement. He was also honored—and afraid. He didn't live with J.J. and his mom and sister and grandpa. As soon as Clint was back on his feet, Cooper was gone. What would his nephew think about him then?

"I, ah, love you, too, bud." What else could Cooper say? They were blood relations. Of course he loved him. But he also was unsure what that even meant. When Cooper returned to the Navy, as fast as J.J. had declared his affection, would he take it away?

J.J. squirmed from Cooper's hold and ran over to the calf's new enclosure. "Aw, you got his house made!" He opened the pen door and sat alongside the resting animal. J.J. hugged him. "You're so cute! I love you!"

Okay, wait… The calf was also getting J.J.'s love?

What did that mean in the grand scheme of things? Was the *L* word no big deal to kids? How was Cooper supposed to know? He'd talk to Millie about it, but after the kissing incident, he didn't trust himself to be anywhere near her.

Regardless of whether the kiss was accidental or not, it'd resulted in heat rocketing through him with the speed of a cracked whip. Not cool, considering who she was.

Their trek through the grocery store and the endless ride home had been torture. How did he begin to process the fact that by doing something as innocuous as turning his head, he'd changed everything? He'd always been aware of Millie. How sweet and kind and pretty she was. But now that kiss had added a shocking twist to her repertoire. It'd made him see her as not just his sister-in-law, or the friend she'd been back in school, but as a woman.

A desirable woman.

Even if his dad healed faster than anyone expected, it would still take a long time before he fully recovered. Cooper could potentially be stuck out here on the prairie for months. Not good.

Especially when he glanced toward his nephew still hugging the calf. That precious sight squeezed a long-forgotten place in his heart that was reserved for all things innocent and good.

In his line of work, he mostly saw darkness. The cumulative effects of which had fundamentally changed him. Left him doubting whether anything good was even left in this world. But looking at his nephew and the calf proved innocence was still possible.

But fleeting. Fragile. For the calf would grow and be sold. J.J. would grow and leave this lonely place. Cooper wouldn't be around long enough to witness either. By the time Cooper came inside for the night, supper had come and gone, and LeeAnn had taken over the kitchen table with her volcano construction. J.J. had finished his homework and was upstairs, playing his Xbox.

The harlot in Millie who'd enjoyed that kiss was glad Cooper had spent most of the past forty-eight hours in the barn. The nice person in her feared that in his attempt to steer clear of her, he'd work himself to death.

"Finished?" she asked while he hung his hat and coat on the back-door pegs.

"Yeah. The chickens and calf are toasty, and I'm sure the horses aren't minding the heat wave. I'll get to work on the new coop in the morning."

"Mill-eeee!"

"Duty calls." She looked toward Clint's room. "I made you a dinner plate. It's in the oven."

"Thanks. Smells good."

The whole time she helped Clint get ready for bed, she couldn't get her mind off his son. Did Cooper like her new pork chop recipe? Were he and LeeAnn sharing the table? After he ate, would he go to bed or share her TV time with her? Part of her wished he'd stay in his room. Another part wondered what it might be like for them to share a civilized adult conversation.

And more adult kisses?

Her cheeks blazed.

Clint tapped his whiteboard. It read *Where is he?*

"I assume in the kitchen, just now eating supper." The traveling nurse, a speech therapist and physical therapist had all visited. A change in Clint's meds had him less drowsy, more cantankerous and speaking a smidge more clearly. "He's always working."

Clint grunted.

"Don't believe me?" She outlined all that Cooper had recently done. And how now that her kitchen had been sanitized and spit-shined, she found herself missing the chickens and calf.

Clint wrote *Don't trust him!*

She sighed. "I don't mean to be disrespectful, but knock it off. He's done more around here in a few days than I could've in a month. You should be grateful to him. I know I am." Despite the tension between them that was as plain as summer heat on shimmering blacktop, not for a second would she discount Cooper's value to the ranch.

That kiss meant nothing. It'd been a split-second mistake to add to her ever-growing mountain.

Clint was back to tapping on his whiteboard. *He's the devil!*

"Oh, stop. You hating your son isn't going to bring your wife back. Do you think she'd approve of this feud? If anything, she'd be ashamed of you for not insisting Cooper come home years ago. Did you know Jim even secretly tried mending fences?" Whereas she'd initially been mad at Jim for lying to her, after letting the fact sink in, she now saw it as brave. When Clint was at full strength, he'd been a force to contend with. No one dared cross him.

Her father-in-law growled.

She gave him a dirty look. "Like it or not, Clint Hansen, things are changing around here for the better."

After giving him his meds, she made sure his lightweight plastic pitcher was filled with fresh water, and that his TV remote was on the nightstand in case he woke in the middle of the night. The physical therapist had mentioned that in the coming weeks, he wanted Clint upright for a portion of his days. He also had simple exercises to do for regaining his strength.

"That should do it," she said after tidying his quilts.

"Thwank oooh."

She kissed his leathery cheek. "You're welcome. I love you. Now go to sleep and wake up less cantankerous."

In the kitchen, Millie expected to find Cooper at the table, but there was no sign of him.

"Where's your uncle?" she asked her daughter, trying to strike a casual, conversational tone as if his whereabouts didn't really matter. Which they didn't. She just wanted to know if he liked her pork chops. Because no way had she actually missed him the past couple of days.

LeeAnn shrugged. "Beats me. Do you think this is tall enough?"

After peeking in the oven to see if Cooper had even taken his plate—he had—she told her daughter, "Looks good to me. Maybe even it out on the back side?"

She sighed. "That's gonna take forever. God, this is so boring!"

"Sorry. Maybe you should've picked another project." Millie wanted to find Cooper, but instead joined her daughter in slapping more of the goopy papier-mâché strips onto her volcano.

What was it about him that had her craving his company? And why had she made that ridiculous speech about his staying away? If she hadn't, he might be in the kitchen, helping with this admitted snooze fest of a project. Was she a bad mom for hating the annual science fair? "How much do you have left to do after you paint your mountain?"

"Not much. The pop bottle eruption part seems super easy. Then I have to write the paper. And make the backboard. Oh—and find pictures for the backboard. Think Uncle Cooper would let me use a couple of his from Pompeii?"

"Probably. Does that mean you two are now friends?"

LeeAnn made a preteen look of disgust. "Eew, no. But his pictures were pretty cool."

"True…" Millie couldn't wrap her mind around how far away Pompeii actually was. She'd barely been out of the state. Would Cooper mind talking about his travels? What other pictures did he have? Was he one of those Navy guys with a woman in every port? If so, were they like girlfriends to him or just lovers?

Her cheeks flamed.

"Mom, are you okay?" LeeAnn froze with her hands in the glue and water mixture.

"Sure. Why?"

"You don't look so hot. Or I mean you do look hot— but all red and blotchy."

Thanks. *Just what every woman wants to hear…*

Millie helped LeeAnn finish, then they carried the volcano to the porch, setting it on top of the washing machine to dry.

"Mom, could I *please* use your cell to call Kara?"

Millie sighed. "Hon, we've been over this before. What's wrong with the house phone?"

"She's having boy problems and I need privacy. The house phone gets staticky in my room."

"Tell you what—" she kissed LeeAnn's forehead "—since I'm headed upstairs for a nice, long soak in the tub, that leaves the phone down here nice and private for you—although I'm worried about what you and Kara have going on that's so bad I can't hear about it."

"Mom..." Millie's child wielded preteen sarcasm like a burr under her saddle. It wasn't quite disrespectful enough to warrant punishment, but nonetheless annoying.

"All right, I'm leaving, but watch your sass."

Exhaustion clung to Millie's shoulders, weighing her down and making her movements sluggish. She lacked the energy to fish her cookies from out of hiding, and every stair felt like a mountain.

Cooper's bedroom door was thankfully closed.

Gunfire erupted from J.J.'s lair, meaning he was still playing one of those too-violent video games she hated. Jim had loved them all, and even as a toddler, J.J. enjoyed sitting on his dad's lap, helping shoot monsters. He had so few memories of his father, Millie didn't have the heart to take this one. She did at least limit his killing to dinosaurs and aliens.

"You about ready for bed?" she asked on her way into his room.

"Nope," J.J. said, "but Uncle Cooper is. He snores *really* loud."

Sure enough, big, strong Cooper had stretched out on a beanbag chair, using a pile of stuffed animals for a pillow.

Cheetah had stretched across his lap and actually purred!

In sleep, Cooper's expression looked softer. The concentration line between his brows all but vanished save for a thin line. His long lashes swept his whisker-stubbled cheeks. He truly was far too handsome for his own good.

Back in school, the girls who hadn't yet had their turn with him, loved him. The girls who'd loved and lost hated him. Since she'd been with Jim, that had landed Millie in the neutral zone in regard to feeling anything about Cooper. Now, with Jim's memory so distant, she'd forgotten his smell or even what it'd felt like waking up to him holding her. Where did that currently leave her status with Cooper? How many lovers had he left hating him all over the globe?

On the floor beside him was an empty plate. Did this mean he had liked her pork chops?

She put her hands to her yet-again flaming cheeks.

What was wrong with her? Why was her mind constantly in the gutter? Regardless of whether Cooper had eaten her chops or suddenly declared her the most fascinating woman in the world, the fact remained that he was her brother-in-law. Period. End of discussion.

"How about you turn off your game, brush your teeth and let me tuck you in."

"Mo-om..."

"Wrong answer. How about *yes, ma'am?*"

"Yes, ma'am. Just let me save."

Cooper stirred. "Sorry...didn't mean to drift off on you, bud. Did you get through Raptor Valley?"

Cheetah hopped down, only to vanish beneath J.J.'s bed.

All Millie could think was, *How come I don't look that hot when first waking?*

"Not yet, and Mom won't let me stay up."

Laughing, Cooper said, "When I was your age, I never wanted to sleep. Now that's all I want to do."

Fanning herself, Millie couldn't help but smile and nod. "True."

"Yeah, but you two are *really* old." J.J. turned off his game.

"I forgot." On his feet, Cooper stretched, which made him seem even larger beside her. He stood six-two. She knew, because Jim had been six foot even and complained about his big brother being taller.

"Your dinner was tasty." Cooper knelt to pick up his plate.

"Thanks." With her mouth curiously dry, Millie licked her lips. "Glad you liked it. The recipe was new." What in the world had possessed her to tag on that last bit?

"I liked the fennel."

What was she supposed to do with her hands? "You know about fennel?"

"In Pakistan, the locals roast it and chew it after dinner."

J.J.'s eyes widened. "You've been to Pakistan?"

"Sure have." Cooper fished his phone from his pocket and a moment later showed his nephew pictures of snow-capped mountains and an exotic-looking white building. "The temple is in Karachi. My friends and I were there looking for a bad guy."

"*Whoa...* That's cool! Did you find him?" J.J. asked.

"Sure did."

"Did you shoot him?"

"J.J.!" Millie gripped her son's shoulders, aiming him toward the bathroom. "Brush your teeth."

"Yes, ma'am…" If he pouted any harder, his bottom lip would touch the back porch stairs.

"Sorry about that," Millie said with her son out of earshot. "He's the product of too many video games."

"It's all right." With his phone back in his pocket, Cooper's usual unreadable expression had slipped back into place. "He's a good kid."

"Thanks." Curiosity ate away at her—not to mention the fact that she craved hearing more of his story. Was there anywhere he hadn't been? Was he mostly working when he traveled, or did he often get a chance to do tourist things like he had in Pompeii? "Well? What did you do with the bad guy?"

The faint smile he cast in her direction ignited fireflies in her stomach.

"If I told you, I'd have to kill you."

Now her eyes widened. "It's *that* bad?"

He laughed. "I'm kidding. Honestly, I'm not sure what happened. After my team and I caught him, CIA spooks took over from there."

"Sounds dangerous." Millie nibbled her lower lip. While his stories fascinated her, she didn't like thinking of him in peril. Which was why she next blurted, "How many times have you been shot at?"

Wincing, he said, "More than I'd like to remember."

"Which means? Five? Ten? A hundred?"

He sat on the edge of J.J.'s bed. "For the most part, SEALs like to be phantoms—in and out of a place before anyone even knows we've been there. Every so often, plans go to shit—pardon my French—and then all hell breaks loose. Couldn't give you any hard facts on how often it happens. It's just part of the job."

"Getting shot at doesn't bother you?"

He shrugged. "Haven't much thought about it."

"But you could die…" And all of a sudden, that knowledge trampled the lightning bugs dancing in her tummy.

"Don't take this personally, but honestly? Since losing Mom, and then Jim—" he bowed his head, gripping the plate hard enough for his knuckles to whiten "—I haven't had all that much reason to live."

Chapter 10

Cooper normally wasn't so chatty, and he sure as hell didn't know what'd possessed him to start up now.

"I—I'm sorry you feel that way."

"Is what it is," he said in his most matter-of-fact tone.

J.J. bounded into the room, dive-bombing the bed so hard that Cooper damn near lost his balance.

"Slow down, mister. I'm guessing your mom would rather tuck you in the bed, than scrape you off the wall."

The kid thought about that for a second, then busted out laughing. "Eeeew, gross! My pillow would be all full of guts and stuff!"

"J.J.!" Millie scolded. "Settle down and get under the covers."

What was up with that? Her always being so up-tight with her kids? Had his mom been that way? Or had it been so long since her death that he couldn't re-

member standard operating procedure when it came
to parenting?

When Millie approached her son, Cooper's senses
went haywire. Only because he'd been so long without a
woman, he found every inch of her attractive, from the
way she smelled like the daffodils he used to pick out on
the old Walker homestead to the faint rasp in her voice.

His nephew had scrambled under the covers. Minty-
smelling toothpaste clung to the corners of his grin.
"Can Uncle Cooper read me a story and tuck me in?"

"Honey, let's not bother him. He's—"

"I'd love to, bud. What do you want me to read?"
While J.J. practically bounced from the bed to the book-
shelf, Cooper tried deciphering Millie's dour look and
failed. They used to be friends, but now he wasn't sure
where they stood. He knew she didn't want him getting close to her kids, but even he could tell his nephew
was desperate for a father figure. Jim had been gone a
while. Had she ever thought of remarrying?

The thought of her hooking up with some random
guy down at Mack's bar didn't sit so well.

"You about done?" Cooper asked.

"How about this one?" The human ball of energy
was back in bed, tugging the quilts to his chin. "It's
my favorite!"

"Captain Underpants?"

"It's really awesome," J.J. assured him.

Cooper looked to Millie for her endorsement.

She nodded. "It's a little out there, but all in good fun."

"Well, in that case…" Cooper couldn't resist giving J.J. a few tickles to his ribs, which sent the kid into
a fit of giggles. "Let's start reading. This place could
use some fun."

* * *

Fun.

An hour later, soaking up to her neck in the tub's steaming water, Millie tried focusing on what'd been the sweet sound of her son's laughter, as opposed to the man causing J.J.'s smile. Cooper had been spot-on about there having been no fun in the house for a good, long while, but what was she supposed to do about it?

Ever since Clint's stroke, there was so much work that even when Peg had been staying with them, Millie never felt caught up enough to indulge in lighthearted banter with her kids. Lately, it seemed like all she ever did was harp.

Brush your teeth. Do your homework and chores.

Far from being the fun, vibrant mom she'd always intended to be, most days she felt like an old biddy, constantly nagging.

How was it that Cooper hadn't even been in residence a week, and yet he was already the popular parent—and he wasn't even a parent, but an uncle!

It wasn't fair.

A knock on the bathroom door startled her. "Mill?"

She crossed her legs and covered her breasts with her hands. Her nipples instantly hardened. Damn, Cooper. "Wh-what?"

"Dad's hungry. What should I give him?"

A tranquilizer dart!

The moment the hateful thought struck, she tamped it out. What precious private time she found, she treasured, but she didn't have to take her annoyance at this intrusion out on poor Clint.

"Um… There's pudding in Tupperware tubs on the second shelf in the fridge."

"Thanks."

The hall floor was creaky, and she didn't hear him leaving. But then to be fair, she hadn't heard him approach. If he was still standing there, what was he doing? Was he as hot and bothered about her nakedness as she was? That pathetically thin door and a hundred-year-old skeleton-key lock were the only things keeping them apart. Well—those, and the fact that he was her brother-in-law, for heaven's sake!

"Mill?" he asked in a muffled tone.

"Y-yes?" Why had her breath hitched? Why did her breasts ache?

"Thanks again for dinner. You make a mean chop."

Before she could tell him he was welcome, the telltale creaky plank floor told her he'd already headed for the stairs.

Meanwhile, his praise for her cooking ignited a slow-burning fuse that led straight to an old-fashioned powder keg of irrational excitement.

What was wrong with her? Why did she feel like she'd gone back in time to their high school chemistry lab where, instead of focusing on her experiments, she'd studied the way the sun had perpetually tanned his neck? Back then, she and Jim had been friends, but not yet *more*.

Cooper didn't know it, but one of the biggest reasons she'd fallen for his brother was because of the time Jim had saved her from certain humiliation almost brought on by his big brother. She'd just worked up the courage to ask him to their school's annual Sadie Hawkin's dance when Jim strongly hinted that Cooper was hoping Bethany asked him. Sure enough, the two had not only gone together, but ended up dating for a couple months. If Millie had asked Cooper to the dance and he'd turned her down, she'd have been mortified. Millie had never forgotten Jim's act of kindness in giving her a heads-up regarding his brother's affections, even though years later, he'd admitted his reasoning hadn't been entirely altruistic since he'd wanted her to ask him to the dance! She had, and that first date had blossomed into a warm fulfillment that'd made her bone-deep content for all the years of their marriage.

Yeah? So what's got you so discontented now?
Millie scowled.

How come every time she saw Cooper, her mind dove straight to the gutter? Like back to that kiss.

Eyes closed, she couldn't help wondering what it would be like if he'd kissed her intentionally instead of just by accident? And then what if that accidental kissing had led to his becoming all rough and ready, dragging her across his truck seat to straddle him? And what if she'd been wearing a tank top, cowboy boots and her favorite long prairie skirt that just happened to hitch up? Exposing her bare thighs? And if she'd had on her good white-lace panties and her soft inner thighs rubbed against Cooper's rough, sun-faded jeans? He'd press his fingers into the back of her head, pulling her to him for a kiss that left her dizzy-punch-drunk and gasping. And then he'd rake his lips lower, down her throat and collarbone, all the while grazing his hands lower, too, until they weren't just on her lower back, but easing under her panties where her butt met the backs of her thighs.

He'd give her a teasing squeeze, and the erotic jolt might damn near make her faint. *"Darlin', you trying to do me in?"*

She'd giggle—no, deliver a sultry vixen laugh. *"Yes-sir. Is my scandalous plan workin'?"*

He'd groan, slipping those roving fingers of his—

Eyes wide open, splashing upright, Millie was mortified to find that she'd slid her fingers perilously close to giving herself a happy ending!

First thing in the morning, she'd start seeing about hiring an extra hand—just until Clint was back on his feet. Because for her own sanity, Cooper needed to go.

"I d-don't want it fr-from y-you!"

Cooper forced a deep breath. "Seeing how Saint Millie's upstairs in the tub, I'm your only choice in nurses. Now, you going to be a cantankerous old mule, or hush up and eat the damned pudding?"

Clint growled.

"I feel the same, Dad, but—" Tears stung Cooper's eyes. Frustration balled inside him, manifesting in him smacking the heel of his hand against the door frame.

His old man reared back in shock or maybe just surprise. Regardless, in that moment, he looked so frail that shame cloaked Cooper in sadness. How much time had been lost on this grudge?

"I h-h-hate you!"

"I know, Dad." Instead of moving away from his father, he moved closer. And then he pulled his too-thin frame into a hug.

At first, Clint fought him, but then the old man fell limp, and then with what little strength he had, he hugged back. Even immediately after his mom's death, Cooper had never heard his father cry, but he did now. The sobs were ugly and heartbreaking, yet strangely cleansing.

The harder Clint cried, the closer Cooper held him. And remembered the good times. And was so very grateful they weren't too late to start over.

"I'm sorry," he said.

His father issued his own garbled apology, and even though anyone else listening might not have understood, Cooper did. The sentiment meant the world to him, as he'd been waiting a decade for not only his father's forgiveness, but also to come home.

Only Millie had made it clear this was no longer his home, but hers.

"Did you find the pudding?" Millie stood outside the still-steamy bathroom, holding a towel sarong-style around her breasts. She thought Cooper had still been downstairs, which was why she'd thought it safe to make a dash for her bedroom. Wrong.

"Sure did." His eyes were red. And teary. Had he been crying?

In the moment, his strangely sad expression trumped her awkwardness over her state of undress. "Everything okay?"

Though he nodded, she couldn't have said she believed him.

"Clint let you feed him without any complaining?"

His lips curved into a ghostly smile. "I wouldn't go that far, but yeah… He got the whole cup down."

"Great…" She shivered. Water droplets evaporated between her shoulder blades, but that didn't cool the heat pooling low in her belly. One look at Cooper's lips brought her all-too-rich fantasy of the two of them roaring to life. If she hadn't needed her hands to hold up her towel, she'd have clasped her flaming cheeks. "I should probably get dressed."

"Sure." He stepped aside, but she tried anticipating his direction and failed.

"Sorry," she said when they collided, wishing her every nerve didn't tingle with an exhilarating rush. Was she losing her mind? This was Cooper of all people. "I'm just gonna…"

They sidestepped each other two more times before she'd almost managed to reach the safety of her room.

"Hey," he said before she had the chance to step all the way in and close the door. "Mind if we talk a sec— that is, once you…" He gestured toward her electrified body, which only reminded her of her fantasy and how good his rough fingers had felt gliding along her—

No. Talking to him, looking at him, thinking about him was totally out of the question. "Sorry, but I'm really tired. In the morning—we'll talk then. Okay?"

He looked crestfallen. "Sure."

What did he even want to talk about? Cattle? J.J.? His father? What if it'd been something important?

"Good night."

"'Night." Her mouth went dry. Was he feeling odd, too? This curious sense of confusion whenever they shared the same space? "Cooper?"

"Yeah?" He'd turned away but now looked back. When their gazes locked, the air thickened, making it hard to think or breathe.

"Was it anything important?"

He shook his head. "Nothing that can't wait."

"Okay, well…" Why wouldn't her legs move? She wanted to stay here on her room's threshold with him, but also didn't. Her traitorous imagination just kept re-playing him leaning in for a kiss. "Good night."

His eyes narrowed. "We've already been through that."

"Right." Beyond flustered, she bolted all the way into her room, shut the door and threw herself across the foot of her bed. What was wrong with her? She was a mom. A caregiver. A widow.

She was far too sensible for crushes, and even if she did have one, Cooper was the last man on earth she'd be attracted to—well, scratch that. Any woman in her right mind would be *attracted* to him, but that was different. She wasn't talking about something as shallow as finding him *hot*.

Then what are you talking about? her conscience nudged.

Even more to the point, what was she fantasizing about? Because her vision of him—*them*—had crossed every sane person's acceptable behavior boundary.

Come first light, Cooper downed black coffee and instant oatmeal, checked on his dad to find him lightly snoring then fixed a bottle for the calf before shrug-ging on his brother's coat and heading out to the barn.

"Hey, fella…" he said to the little guy who stood in his pen, excited to see him—as opposed to the wide-eyed, startled-doe look he typically got from Millie. "Hungry?"

Cooper removed his gloves, resting them on the lip of a feed bucket. He liked the feel of the calf's warm, breathy snorts against his palm. He'd forgotten the sim-ple pleasures of being in the barn when the sun rises. The way dust motes swirled in the sunbeams piercing through holes in the wood-plank walls. The rich scents of hay and leather. The sound of a light breeze whistling high in the rafters.

He took a deep breath, slowly exhaling.

"Had a big night," he said to his bovine pal. "Not sure how, but Dad and I turned a corner." He'd wanted so badly to share the miracle with Millie, but as usual, she'd treated him like a pariah.

What was she doing now?

Still snoozing until time to wake her kiddos? Or standing at the kitchen counter, looking sleepy-pretty in her fluffy pink robe? Lord, she'd grown into a fine-looking woman.

"Wanna hear a confession?" he asked the greedily suckling calf. "Yeah? Okay, well, true story—I'm a sucker for a woman in the morning." Messy hair and smudged mascara only heightened his pleasure. "I've always been a little jealous of my married friends." They were the lucky ones, waking up alongside their beauties every day—at least when they weren't out on missions.

Cooper sighed.

He could count on one hand the number of mornings he'd rolled over to be greeted by a welcoming smile. Sure, he'd been with his fair share of women, but precious few he'd cared enough about to spend the night.

Since his mother's death, Cooper had only lived half a life. On the job, he was all in and then some, but when it came to personal stuff, he was lost.

The barn door creaked open.

He glanced in that direction, expecting to see J.J. bounding in to feed the chickens. Instead, he saw Millie decked out in her pink robe and cowboy boots. Backlit by the sun, her tumble of hair formed a long halo. Her unaffected beauty quite literally took his breath away.

"There you are." Closing the door behind her, she hustled over to the calf, petting him, then warming her hands beneath his heat lamp. "Brr. It's chillier out here than I thought."

"Which raises the question—" he scooped feed for the chickens, sprinkling it on the floor of their pen "—why are you out here?"

She used the toe of her boot to shift straw. "I felt bad."

"'Bout what?" He carried the chickens' water dish to the spigot.

"Last night. You wanted to talk, and I—"

"Forget about it." Because by the light of day, he no longer had the courage to open up to anyone—let alone Millie—about what had transpired with his father. Right after it happened, in the heat of the moment, he couldn't wait to share. But now he realized what a mistake opening up to Millie would be.

He already had a tough enough time physically staying away from her. If he ever let her emotionally inside? He'd be a goner.

Chapter 11

"**M**om, eew!" Acting as if it were filled with worms, LeeAnn tossed her lunch sack to the counter. "You put J.J.'s gross bologna sandwich in my bag instead of my peanut butter."

"Sorry," Millie said in a not exactly sympathetic tone. *What was Cooper's problem?* She'd gone to the barn carrying an olive branch and come back with her arm a bloody stump. "Ever think you might be old enough to fix your own lunch?"

"I would," her daughter sassed, "but you always say I dawdle."

"You do." Millie switched the sandwiches, and even though she knew her daughter should be doing more around the house, she instantly regretted her sharp words. The kids had been through so much. What could it hurt for her to coddle them a little while longer? Besides, it wasn't LeeAnn she was upset with, but her uncle.

She felt like a darned fool. What had possessed her to traipse out to the barn like that?

"Mom?" J.J. wore his Transformers T-shirt inside out, and he hadn't even tried brushing his hair. "Have you seen my sneakers?"

"No, sweetie, but let's find 'em soon. The bus will be here any minute."

Ten minutes later, Millie had successfully gotten both kids on the bus, and now sat on the sofa holding an Oreo in each hand.

With a morning like this, what did that forecast about the rest of her day?

As if on cue, Clint hollered for her attention.

"Hold your horses," she hollered right back.

She'd already made most of his breakfast—just needed to add butter and sugar to his oatmeal.

She leisurely finished her cookies then trudged back to the kitchen to fix Clint's plate.

While she bustled around, Cheetah gave himself a bath on top of the fridge. She stuck out her tongue at the traitorous fur ball.

"Here you go," she said to Clint a short while later in his room.

Her smile felt forced. Most mornings, she enjoyed seeing the kids off to school and caring for Clint, but on this day, she'd have rather taken her entire bag of cookies upstairs to hide with under the covers.

Her father-in-law tapped his marker board. It read: *Where's my son?*

His son? This was a new development. Since when did Clint claim Cooper? "Last I saw him, he was in the barn." She stirred the melting pat of butter into the oatmeal. "By now, he's probably out checking the cattle."

"T-take m-me."

"To look after the cattle? We'll have to ask Peg about that. She'll be here tomorrow for the weekend."

He nodded, then pointed to his bowl, motioning that he'd like to take the spoon.

"You're not just eating your oats this morning, but feeling them."

He lurched for the spoon, managed to grab hold, but then spilled his first bite, which launched a tantrum.

"Simmer down." She wiped the mess from his pajama top with a warm, damp cloth. "This time, let me guide you, and we'll see if we can manage together."

He scowled.

"You don't like that idea?"

"D-do my-myself."

"I know you can, and I love that you're wanting to try, but—" He grabbed hold of her latest spoonful and flung it.

"Dad!" Cooper barked. "Knock it off."

Feeling as if she'd walked in on a movie that had already started, Millie was beyond confused by the sight of Cooper calmly curling his father's fingers around the oversize spoon his physical therapist had provided, then helping him guide it to his mouth.

"There you go…" Cooper's voice was gentle and patient, and certainly not from the same man she usually saw at Clint's bedside. "That's it, slow and steady. We'll get you back to normal in no time."

Millie stood on the sidelines until Clint had finished his entire meal—toward the end, even feeding himself for a couple bites. The change in not just his physical abilities, but also his attitude, was profound. Something had to have happened between the last time she'd tucked him in and now.

Millie tried helping Clint with his usual bathing routine, but he wasn't having it, and wanted only Cooper to help.

That afternoon, by the time her father-in-law's speech therapist arrived, Millie stood at the kitchen sink, washing lunch dishes—or at least trying to. What she mostly focused on was Cooper. He was out back, wielding a chain saw to clear the remains of fallen cottonwood branches.

Before he could start on the chicken coop, the debris had to be cleared. It was a big job. The kind of thing she might've helped Jim and Clint tackle. Part of her thought she should head outside to lend a hand, but tensions between them had been running so high, what if he didn't want her anywhere near him? Besides, he was clearly capable of handling even this large of a task on his own.

It was already one on the gorgeous sunny day, and the temperature had apparently grown warm enough to warrant Cooper removing his shirt.

While the running faucet overflowed the mixing bowl she'd set in the sink, she couldn't help but visually drink the man in. The breadth of his chest. The definition of his abs. The way his faded jeans hung low on his hips and how he'd half-assed tucked his pant legs into his cowboy boots.

In raising the saw, his biceps flexed.

What would it feel like for him to hold me?

The moment the thought struck, Millie banished it. Clearly, the next time Lynette nagged her about dating, she might need to at least entertain the possibility. She and her husband had shared a healthy physical relationship, and she missed that aspect of her life. The only thing driving these inappropriate thoughts were basic needs for closeness and companionship. Plain and simple. No great mysterious longings for specifically Cooper, but essentially any man.

He'd cut quite a pile of limbs and turned off the saw. The sudden peace was welcome, but not as much as when he bent to gather logs for the woodpile. In the process, he offered mesmerizing views of his strong back, narrow waist and mouthwatering derriere.

She licked her lips.

"Holy mother of all that's good in this world…" Clint's speech therapist, Stacie, nudged Millie aside to fill his water pitcher from the tap. "A man that good-looking ought to be criminal."

"He's not so special…" Millie managed to say, though her mouth had grown painfully dry. *Liar!*

The pretty twentysomething female therapist whistled. "If you say so. Is he single?"

"*Cooper?* I suppose."

"How long's he going to be in town?"

Millie started to speak, but bit her tongue. Wincing, she raised her hands to her mouth.

"You okay?"

Millie nodded. "I'm fine. Thanks. And for the record, I'm not sure when my brother-in-law's leaving. I suppose as soon as his dad's back on his feet."

The therapist smiled. "Hmm… That gives me at least a couple months to get something going. And Valentine's Day is almost here. Mack's dating Wilma Meadows, and he's asking everyone to spread the word about a big party he's throwing at the bar. Know if he goes for my type—Cooper, not Mack?" Petite? Blonde? Flawless hair, makeup and nails?

Probably. "Gosh, I wouldn't have a clue."

"Need help?"

"Sure." Cooper set a trio of fresh logs on the woodpile against the side of the house. "At this point, all there is left to do is haul the rest of what I cut. Looks like the coop's foundation is intact, so building a new one shouldn't be a big deal."

"That's good." They soon set into a rhythm. "I once saw a fancy chicken coop in that *Oprah Magazine.* Looked like a tiny Victorian mansion."

"That a hint?" His sideways grin gave wing to the butterflies that'd taken up residence low in her belly.

"Not at all. Just making small talk to pass the time." He nodded.

"While I've got you, that was some miracle you worked with your dad."

His shrug did little to satisfy her curiosity.

"Did something happen? You know, like a breakthrough between you two?"

He placed his latest load of wood on the pile, then stretched, cradling the small of his back. "Why do you care?"

"Excuse me?" Before she could set her logs, he took them from her, in the process brushing against her in that maddeningly innocent way he had of driving her beyond distraction without having really done anything at all.

"You heard me…" He left her to get more wood.

"Wait—" Dawning was slow to come, but when it

did, she chased after him. "Is this about last night? When you asked me to talk?"

"Drop it, okay?"

"Don't be like that."

"Mill…"

Upon his arrival, the last thing she'd wanted was for them to constantly be at odds. So why were they? Knowing guilt knotted her stomach. She innately knew the reason they never got along, and the responsibility rested solely on her conscience. She was prickly around him, because of her physical attraction. It made as little sense in her head as it did in her heart. Nonetheless, that was the truth, and she'd never been the type to shy from blame.

"Coop?"

"What?" His terse tone made her wince.

"Just guessing, but when I made that ground-rules speech, I think you may have taken it a smidge more literally than I'd intended."

"How else was I supposed to take it? You pretty much made it plain that I'm not wanted. That said, even a blind pig could see you might not want me, but you damn well need me."

She cringed. *If you only knew…*

"You're right," she said. "I can't tell you how much I appreciate what you've already done." *And from now on, I promise not to let my apparent physical cravings interfere with common courtesy.* "I'm sorry about my earlier attitude."

"I don't need an apology. As soon as Dad's back on his feet, your problem will be solved when I'm gone."

Her throat knotted. Because of her harsh words, he viewed himself as a problem? If she was dead honest with herself, she knew nothing could be further from the truth. "Don't be silly. I appreciate your help more than you'll ever know. In fact, you've already made a transformation with your dad. What if you and I did the same?"

She met and held his gaze, wishing things could be different between them. That they could turn back the clock and be back in school, cracking a joke in chemistry class. Instead, she felt—

"Millie?" Stacie flounced out of the house in all her cute, young, disgustingly perky glory. "I'm all done! Clint did great!" She crossed the yard, holding out his monitor. "Thought you might need this."

"Thanks." Millie grit her teeth in annoyance. Couldn't Miss Perky Pants have stayed inside a few minutes longer? Or, better yet, left out the front door?

Stacie cinched her black satchel strap higher on her shoulder then crossed the short distance to Cooper, holding out her hand. "You must be Clint's son. I'm Stacie, his speech therapist."

"Good to meet you." After sharing his name, Cooper pulled the patented cowboy move of shaking her hand while tipping his hat. Lord, he looked good. And it made Millie sick that she couldn't help but notice! "Thanks for all you've been doing with my dad."

"Oh, it's my pleasure. How long will you be in town?"

"Just long enough, I s'pose." Classic infuriating cowboy response—long enough to be polite, but not convey any actual information.

Stacie didn't seem the least bit put off. If anything, his shortness only spurred her on. "Well, in that case, guess that means you'll be here for the big Valentine's Day party down at Mack's?"

"I'll be here," he said, his gaze roving off toward the south pasture. "But I'm not the party type."

"Well, you'd be doing me a *huge* favor if you switched that up." Big grin. Bat, bat of her lashes. "My creep boyfriend cheated on me with Allison—she's a waitress over at Maude's in Greenbriar. Anyway, the two of them are now an item, and since they'll be there, I wanted to show off my own shiny new toy."

A muscle ticked in his jaw. "Sorry, ma'am, but I'm not really the *boy toy* type, either."

"Oh, come on." She gave him an elbow nudge. "Millie, help me out here. How about both of you come? Peg's supposed to be here that weekend, right? I'll bet she wouldn't mind staying with Clint and the kids."

"Stacie…" Millie sighed. "This sort of thing just isn't me."

Miss Perky Pants pouted. "It'll be fun. You'll know everyone there. And who knows? Maybe you'll even find a cowboy all your own."

That suggestion raised Millie's hackles. First, if she wanted a man, she could darn well find one without Stacie's assistance. And second—well, she was too darn mad to even think of a second reason, but she was sure it was there somewhere. "You know what? I think I will go. And Cooper, you should go with Stacie."

The look he shot her way was darker than a spring thunderhead. "I. Said. I. Don't. Party."

"I know for a fact you drink beer *and* save people, so look on the event as an altruistic way to both save poor Stacie and down a few longnecks."

"Yaaaay!" Stacie said with a giggly leap, entwining

her arm with Cooper's. "It's a date. And since I live all the way out by the county line, I'll just be here around seven that Saturday night. That way, we can ride together." Wink, wink. "We're gonna have a ball."

"What the hell did you do that for?" Cooper asked Millie the second his *date* drove off.

"Do what?" she asked, all innocent, as if she didn't know exactly what he was talking about.

"You know *what*. I'm not going to be here much longer, and even if I were, dating a teenager is hardly on my agenda."

Millie grabbed an armful of logs. "Stacie's at least old enough to have graduated college. Besides, her suggestion that I couldn't find my own man really ticked me off."

"When did she say that?"

Men. "She just did. If you didn't get her undertone, then you must have earwax."

"Regardless, why'd you have to drag me into it? And since when are you on the prowl?"

"On the prowl?" She pitched her logs to their growing pile with a little more force than was probably necessary. "Jim's been gone three very long years. If I want to enjoy a little male company, I fail to see what business it is of yours."

Why did he get the feeling Millie was speaking a foreign language? "I never said it was…my business. Just that I didn't know you were interested in seeing anyone." *Because if I had—*

What? Would he have thought about asking her out himself? No. No way. He'd already caused his family enough shame. Putting moves on his brother's wife wouldn't exactly spit-shine his tarnished reputation. But then there was that accidental kiss. And the way last night, in the dimly lit hall, he'd wanted to press his fingertips to the water droplets glistening like diamonds on her collarbone. Don't even get him started on the way his body reacted to imagining her damp towel dropping to the floor. "If you are—ready to date, then sure. You should. It's not like you need my permission."

"I know." Why did her lips drop the slightest bit at the corners? Almost as if she was disappointed by his declaration.

"All right, then."

"Okay." Why was she all of a sudden breathing heavy? Why was he doing the same?

"If you can handle the rest of this—" she thumbed toward the back porch "—I need to do laundry then fix supper."

"Sure. Go ahead." *And when you're done doing that, how about explaining to me why the real reason I'm on edge is because if I asked any woman to be my Valentine, I'd want her to be you....*

Chapter 12

"I've been thinking..." Cooper said to Clint. It was a sunny Thursday afternoon, and for once, the temperature hovered in the low sixties and there wasn't a breath of wind. "How about the two of us ride out to the catfish pond?"

His dad grunted, which Cooper would take as an affirmative.

"You want to wear your pj's, or one of those swanky new sweatsuits Peg brought for you?"

"R-real c-clothes."

Cooper laughed. "If by real clothes, you mean a nice, worn-in pair of Wranglers, sorry, but Peg would have my hide."

"R-real!" his old man roared.

"Okay... Let me see what I can find."

Since Millie was busy with the laundry, Cooper took

the stairs two at a time to reach his father's old room. Opening the door was like opening a tomb, then stepping back in time. Nothing had changed since he'd last been there, kissing his mom goodbye before running out the door on that fateful night.

She'd sat at her dressing table, brushing her long hair. Every night, she'd faithfully counted one hundred strokes, then braided it before going to bed. Thinking of her only made his heart ache, so Cooper did what he'd grown best at—compartmentalizing his pain. He next fished through his dad's dresser for a pair of jeans and a red, plaid flannel shirt. Next came socks and his work boots. He spotted his dad's worn black-leather Stetson hanging on the back of the door, so he grabbed that, too.

Arms laden with Clint's duds, he damn near ran into Millie as she dashed up the stairs with a load of folded towels.

"What're you doing?" she asked.

"Man stuff."

"That doesn't sound good."

He shrugged. "It's a nice day. I figured Dad could use some fresh air."

"Probably." Her expression was unreadable as she rose a step higher than him. In the process, she accidentally brushed the length of her body against his. The sensation jolted his system. He wanted her. He couldn't have her. End of story.

Had she felt it, too? She stood staring, her kissable mouth partially open, eyes wide, breathing halted.

He had to get away from her before he went and did something stupid like tossing the damned towels down the stairs then pushing her up against the wall and kissing her till she begged for more—or maybe that would be him doing the begging? Either way, it couldn't happen, so he mumbled a goodbye, then carried on with his mission.

Back in his dad's room, he found Clint struggling to sit up, but in the process was coming dangerously close to falling out of bed.

"Whoa... Slow it down." Cooper raced over to help. "At the rate you're going, you're only going to get hurt, and then Peg's going to hurt me."

"H-help..." Clint had spotted the clothes Cooper had piled on the foot of the bed.

It took twenty minutes of tugging and wrangling to get his father dressed. The process was no doubt embarrassing for Clint and humbling for Cooper. All his life, he'd been not afraid of his dad, but intimidated—no, that wasn't even the right word. Maybe it'd been more a case of unquestioning respect. No matter what Clint did, Cooper had been in awe. Only with his mother's death, that'd changed. He'd no longer viewed his dad as someone to respect, but hate. Only hate was also a complicated thing, as it implied a degree of passion fueled by love.

Once his dad was fully clothed, Cooper lifted him into his wheelchair, rolled him out to the old work truck, again lifted him into the passenger seat then repeated the whole process to get him back in his chair and onto the catfish pond's dock.

Once the task was done, and Clint sat at the end of the dock, tipping his face back to catch the sun, a profound sense of gratitude swept over Cooper. He was so glad to be home, back on his family's land. Back with his father he'd always loved, but had lost. "Dad?"

Clint grunted.

"You do know how sorry I am about Mom, right? And everything that happened after?" He knelt alongside his father's chair, staring at the ripples a light breeze stirred on the water.

His father held out his good hand, and Cooper took it. Clint gave him a squeeze.

The simple motion conveyed so much without his father having to say a word.

"Boy, am I glad to see you." The Friday before Valentine's Day, Millie gave her sister-in-law an extra-fierce hug.

"Uh-oh, has Dad been grouchy?" Peg unwrapped her scarf to hang it on the wall peg in the front entry. The sun shone, but blustery wind stole any warmth.

"Clint's doing great." Millie swallowed a lump of guilt. She wouldn't be admitting to Peg that the real reason she was happy for the visit had more to do with Cooper than her father. Millie welcomed the role of human buffer Cooper's sister would play.

"Then what's the prob—" Peg's smile faded. "Don't tell me my brother's been causing you trouble?"

Not in the way you probably think. "Cooper's been, ah, a huge help. Can't I just miss you?"

"Aw…" Peg ambushed her with another hug. "I missed you, too. So where is Coop?"

"Probably out in the barn. We had a tiff over Saturday night, and he hasn't said two words since."

Peg hung her coat alongside her scarf. "What's going on Saturday night?"

"Valentine's Day?"

"Geez, I totally forgot." Peg headed toward her dad's room. "But what's that got to do with you and Cooper?"

Millie gave her the abridged version. "I don't even want to go, but Stacie made me so darned mad, I felt possessed."

"What do you care if she goes out with my brother?"

Cheeks blazing, Millie was grateful her sister-in-law couldn't hear her galloping heart. "I don't. I just—"

"Wait just a minute…" Peg stopped Millie just outside her father's closed door. "You don't have a thing for Cooper, do you?"

"Of course not!" If her sister-in-law guessed Millie's dirty secret, was there any way Cooper could know? "I loved Jim very much."

"Who said you didn't? But, hon…" Millie's heart ached when Peg cupped her hand to her forearm. Millie didn't deserve her kindness, but she craved it every bit as much as her Oreos. "…Jim's been gone a long time. You're allowed to—" she elbowed Millie's ribs, then winked "—*you know.*"

Oh, did Millie know! How many times had she imagined what being with Cooper might be like? Only Peg wasn't talking about that particular scenario.

"In fact, I think this is a great idea—you getting out. You might even have fun."

Outlook doubtful.

"Thanks, Aunt Peg! I love it!" Saturday morning, LeeAnn leaped from her seat at the kitchen table to give her aunt a hug for the fuzzy pink sweater she'd given her.

"You're welcome. You're going to look even prettier than you already are."

"Oh, wow!" J.J. was next to crush his aunt in a hug

for the Matchbox cars she'd given him. "You're like the best aunt *ever!*"

"Hope so—" Peg tweaked his nose "—especially since I'm your only aunt."

J.J. laughed.

Cooper felt strangely disconnected from the family scene. On a lark, he'd bought the kids gifts the last run he'd made to town. Walmart had had a big Valentine's display, and a sentimental streak tugged his heartstrings. How many birthdays and Christmases had he missed? Once he left, how many more would he miss again? What would it hurt to now spoil his niece and nephew on a minor holiday?

The cat brushed against his leg, so he knelt down to pet it. The little guy had started sleeping with him, which made Cooper at least feel somewhat wanted.

Millie made a special Valentine's breakfast of strawberry pancakes and chocolate cherry muffins.

"Why don't you come over and join the party?" Peg stood next to him at the kitchen counter.

"I will." He smiled, but his sister's pained gaze quickly made it fade.

"I've missed you so much." Her voice cracked. "Thank you for coming. I don't know what we—especially Millie—would've done without you."

"It's no big deal." How could he accept her gratitude when, if he were a real man, he'd have returned home years earlier? He'd have stood up to his old man and for however long it'd taken, worked to regain his trust, respect and love.

"Yes, it is. And now that you're here…" She wiped silent tears and sniffed before enfolding him in a hug that conveyed more than words ever could. "Well, I'm just glad."

"Me, too."

"Uncle Cooper?"

He looked down to see J.J. "What's up, bud?"

"Who're those presents for?" He pointed to the sack filled with crudely wrapped gifts that sat at Cooper's feet.

"What presents?" He grabbed the boy under his arms, swooping him high, loving his shrieking giggle.

The cat bolted off.

"You mean those?"

"Uh-huh," J.J. said when Cooper set him back on his feet.

Cooper lifted the sack onto the counter, drawing out two boxes of chocolate turtles. "These are for your mom and aunt." He presented them with a flourish.

"You shouldn't have," Peg said, already tearing open the plastic wrapping, "but I'm sure glad you did."

Millie held her box over her heart. Her eyes shone. Had her last Valentine come from his brother? "Thank you," she softly said. "These are my favorite."

I know. One long-ago night when they'd both been in middle school, they'd been at a fall carnival, playing bingo and eating pizza when she'd won. She'd had her pick of prizes. Gift certificates and video games and even lift tickets for Copper Mountain. What had she picked? Turtles. "I'm glad you like them."

She nodded, then looked away, ending the moment— if there'd ever even been one.

"Is there anything in that bag for me?" J.J. jumped while asking.

"Maybe," Cooper teased. "But ladies first. Here, LeeAnn…"

Never having been his biggest fan, she eyed the poorly wrapped box with suspicion but then cautiously tore the red, cupid-sprinkled paper. He held his breath when she removed the stuffed pink teddy bear that held a silver heart necklace and matching earrings, as well as a mini-iPod. Her smile was swift but then faded, almost as if she was forcing herself not to show emotion. Cooper's heart ached. How long until she accepted him like her brother already had?

"Thank you," she said. "The bear's super cute and I love the jewelry and iPod."

"There's an iTunes card in there, too." Cooper wasn't sure what to do with his hands. He'd never been awkward around the fairer sex, but LeeAnn and her mother were a tough crowd. "Figured you'd need it to buy songs."

LeeAnn looked at him as if she wanted to say more, but didn't.

"Want me to help you put on your necklace?" Millie asked.

LeeAnn shook her head before putting all of Cooper's gifts back in the box. "I don't have time. Remember? Kara's mom's picking me up. We're going to an IMAX in Denver then for pizza and a sleepover. You already said I could like a week ago."

"I remember," Millie said. "Sorry. Just slipped my mind."

"Since she's having a sleepover," J.J. asked, vrooming one of his cars across the table, "can Cayden spend the night here?"

Millie opened her mouth, but Peg beat her to the

punch. "Since I'm in charge tonight, how about Cayden comes *and* we have something extra special for dinner?"

"Like popcorn and candy bars?"

Peg laughed. "Sounds perfect."

Millie said, "How about at least adding a banana and glass of milk?"

J.J. pouted. "Okay…"

Though Cooper hardly felt part of the cozy holiday scene, he wanted to be. After clearing his throat, he said to his nephew, "Bud, there's one more present in my bag. Bet it's for you."

"Yaaaay!" Hyped up on three sugary muffins and the couple of pieces of candy he'd already pilfered from his aunt, the kid hopped to accept Cooper's gift. "What is it?"

"Why don't you unwrap it and find out?" Millie suggested before glancing Cooper's way. Had he imagined it, or had her expression softened?

J.J. tore into his gift, then went haywire. "Oh, my gosh! It's a Wii! It's a Wii! I gotta call Cayden!"

"Slow down." Millie snagged his arm before he got to the phone. "Isn't there something you need to do first?"

"Brush my teeth?" He'd scrunched his freckled face in confusion.

"How about thank your uncle?"

"Oh, yeah! But he already knows I love him. I told him the other day." J.J. gave him a fast hug. "Thank you, Uncle Cooper! This is like the best present I ever got in my whole life! You're awesome!"

"You're welcome, bud. Glad you like it." He ruffled the kid's hair, trying to play it cool when he felt like bawling. LeeAnn and J.J. weren't just random kids, but his family. His blood. Every once in a while, when he looked at LeeAnn, she reminded him of his mom. And J.J. had all of the Hansen men's green eyes. Cooper had many great friends back in Virginia, but they weren't family. As much as he respected and admired them, their smiles had never tugged at his heart. "Go on," he said to J.J., "call your friend."

Honestly, Cooper needed the space. He wasn't sure how to cope with all this touchy-feely stuff. He'd been trained to stifle his emotions. So how come now he felt like the walking emotionally wounded?

His natural instinct was to hide out in his room.

Instead, he went to sit with his father. Over the past few days, he'd been reading to him. Cooper's SEAL friend, Grady, had gotten him hooked on vintage sea stories, so he'd started Thor Heyerdahl's *Kon-Tiki*. "Feel like listening to me ramble?"

His dad scribbled on his whiteboard: *Do I have a choice?*

The words might've been harsh, but his old man's eyes were smiling. Cooper took that as a good sign.

He grabbed the book from on top of the dresser, opened it to page seventy-eight then settled into the corner armchair to start reading.

"I think we have you to thank for this."

"What do you mean?" Cooper asked his sister after they'd shut the door to his father's room. Clint had eaten double his usual portion—mostly accomplished under his own steam—and Peg's awful jokes had even coaxed a few smiles. Once his night meds kicked in, though, he was out.

"Dad's improved more in the time you've been here than he did in all the weeks before you'd arrived."

Cooper shrugged. "I wouldn't put too much into it. He's got a lot of good people in and out of here all the time, helping him."

"Don't sell yourself short. Millie told me that at first, things between you and Dad were plenty tense, but then something changed. What happened?"

They'd moved into the entry hall and Peg sat on the third stair.

"Guess it's hard to pinpoint. One night, I think he came to the realization that I wasn't going anywhere, and meant him no harm. I apologized for Mom—at least, as best as I could." He bowed his head. "But we both know, no mere apology is ever going to make that right."

She rose to place a comforting hand on his arm. "Just so happens, I've had a few years to ponder the issue, and as simplistic as this might sound, I think that apology of yours wasn't even necessary. It was implied, you know? Of course you were sorry for what happened. We all were—are. But when it came down to it, Dad wanted you here to use as a verbal punching bag, and now he wants you back as his son—to try to put the pieces back together."

Cooper pulled away from her to peer out one of the front door sidelights. "But I'm not back. I'm not even capable of being the son he wants me to be."

"How do you know you're not already? Have you seen the scrapbook he keeps of you? The Navy sent announcements for every step of your journey. He might not have come right out and said it, but he's proud of you, Coop. So am I. Everything's gonna be all right. You'll see."

He happened to look up.

Millie stood at the top of the stairs. She wore a tight-bodiced, flare-skirted red dress with red cowboy boots. She'd left her hair down—long and wavy. Just the sort of style he'd like to run his hands through while kissing her thoroughly out behind the barn. She looked beautiful. The perfect Valentine jewel. Only the joke was on him, because she wasn't his—would never be his. Even if she wasn't his sister-in-law, she deserved the kind of sage, family man who'd stick around. Someone like Jim—a saint of the sort Cooper would never be.

His sister must've caught him ogling, as she followed his gaze. "Oh, Millie… You look gorgeous!"

"You think?" Millie asked with a twirl. "Are the boots too much?"

"It's Valentine's Day. Anything goes as long as it's red or pink."

"Oh—well, in that case, maybe I should add a feather boa?" Millie's laugh did funny things to Cooper's stomach. He didn't want Stacie to show up. He wanted to take Millie and her red dress and boots out for a nice steak dinner, then maybe go for a few slow turns with her around a dance floor. She peered down at him and frowned. "Cooper, you haven't even had a shower? Your date's going to be here in ten minutes."

"For the last time," Cooper said, "she's *not* my date."

Hands on her hips, she gave him a cocked-head sigh. "Whatever you're calling her, Stacie's arriving in ten minutes. We're meeting Lynette and Zane twenty minutes after that."

"Yes, sir, Master Chief." Mounting the steps, he saluted her on his way past, wishing she'd skipped the pretty floral perfume that made him crave doing more with her than dancing.

"Could she be any more obvious?" Millie wasn't normally the judgmental type, but the way Stacie had the audacity to squeeze Cooper's buns while they were two-stepping made her want to hurl.

"Who?" Lynette was too busy ferreting M&Ms out of the snack mix in a bowl on the table to be bothered with looking up.

"Who do you think? Stacie's done nothing but grope Cooper ever since she showed up at the front door. And don't even get me started on her cleavage. J.J. had a friend over, and I felt like locking the two boys in J.J.'s room until *Boobs on Parade* left the house."

Lynette laughed hard enough to choke on her beer, which resulted in much coughing and a trek to the crowded restroom. By the time they got back to the table, Mack's new girlfriend, Wilma, had cleared the dance floor and given the homegrown country band a break.

Wilma wore a red gingham square-dancing dress, and her platinum hair was tall enough that Millie guessed she prescribed to the old adage: *the higher a woman wore her hair, the closer she was to the Lord.*

"How y'all doin'?" Wilma had hijacked Mack's party, and sashayed up the two steps leading to the stage as though she owned the place. She took the microphone. "Havin' fun?"

"Yeah!" the crowd cried in a chorus of raised beers and some hard stuff.

Millie clamped her lips shut.

Stacie had Cooper pinned alongside the jukebox and put on a show of laughing at every little thing he said. Personally, Millie had never found the man to be funny or a particularly scintillating conversationalist.

Liar...

Lynnette set down her third beer and said, "Stare any harder, and you'll set the poor girl on fire."

"What're you talking about?"

Zane returned with a metal bucket filled with more brews. "There's quite a line at the bar. But never fear, ladies, your prince has returned. Drink up."

"Quit hamming and kiss me!" Lynette had had just enough to drink that she was apparently feeling frisky.

Millie still nursed her first longneck bottle. She wanted her wits about her to keep tabs on Stacie.

While Wilma rambled on about the upcoming couples-only dance, Millie glanced wistfully at her best friend, currently engaged in a sweet-spirited make-out session that made her jealous clear to her toes. Even in the center of the big crowd, loneliness consumed her. Since Jim's passing, who had she become? She was still a mom and a daughter-in-law, but no longer fully a woman—not in the way that mattered on this night dedicated to romance.

"Now that y'all know the rules," Wilma prattled on, "I want *only* couples out on this dance floor. Midway through the song, my fiancé..." The crowd took a minute to soak in the fact that Wilma wagged her diamond-clad ring finger for all to see.

A cheer broke out, then plenty of congratulations to Mack and his bride-to-be. At least the fact that she seemed to have assumed hostess duties of what was supposed to have been Mack's party now made sense.

Millie couldn't have felt lower than a mouse in a snake's belly. Making matters worse was Stacie, pushing Cooper onto the dance floor already crowded with couples. Apparently, he'd had just enough to drink to go along with her request.

"Thank you, thank you," Wilma gushed, "but let's get some other couples in the mood for love. Now, whoever Mack picks as most romantic couple on the dance floor is gonna win a free bucket of beer! Any questions?"

Chet Myers shouted from the bar, "Why can't us single guys win beer?"

Wilma dismissed Chet's comment. "Seriously, folks, we've got great games coming up for any singles who wanna find romance, but for now, this dance is for our couples. Remember, let's keep it clean, but most important, get romantic for Valentine's Day!"

The rowdy crowd erupted in a round of wolf whistles and cheers.

"Here we go…" Wilma signaled the band to start playing, and couples twirled round and round.

Stacie and Cooper stood close enough that a piece of straw wouldn't have fit between them.

Millie swigged her beer.

The two of them were disgusting. And cheaters! How did they technically qualify as a couple when this was their first date?

The crowd went wild when Mack hammed it up, gesturing for the crowd to choose which couples were their favorites.

Of course, Stacie and Cooper drew a big round of applause.

Millie's cheeks felt hot enough to be catsup-red.

Could Stacie be any more obvious? What the woman did with her hips was obscene!

The band started in with a nice and slow country love song.

Wilma shouted, "Think we have some lovers in this bunch?"

More drunken hollers raised the roof.

As much as Millie was tempted to run home to hide under her covers, all it took to convince her to stay was one look at Stacie with her hands in Cooper's hair and him not looking like he minded. Well, she'd show him a thing or two about flirting!

She pasted on her brightest smile before grabbing Buck Evans by his right arm. They'd gone to school together, and he used to be married, but his wife left him to launch her Vegas dancing career. Word had it she was a stripper, but Buck referred to her as a show-girl. "Wanna dance?"

"Ah, sure. I guess."

"Great. Come on." She couldn't get out on that dance floor fast enough. Two could play this game.

"I'm not a very good dancer," Buck said.

"That's okay," she assured him.

"Looks like we have a late entry!" Wilma shouted from the bandstand. "What do you think, y'all? Do they make a good-looking couple?"

Cheers erupted.

After a few more minutes of twirling, the music stopped, and along with it, Millie's heart.

Cooper stood right next to her, looking so stupid-handsome she could cry. What was it about him that made it impossible for her to even think of any other men? She didn't want him, but she sure didn't want Stacie fawning all over him, either.

Mack joined his fiancée on stage.

"Mack, hon," Wilma said, "who do you think deserves our first free bucket of Valentine's Day beer?"

Above her pounding pulse, Millie heard expected wolf whistles and few off-color comments.

What she didn't expect was to feel physically ill when Mack pointed at Stacie and Cooper then said, "Sorry to the rest of you folks, but those two look like they have what it takes to go the distance. Good luck to our happy couple!"

"Sorry we didn't win," Buck said. "If you want, I'll buy you a beer."

"That's okay." She delivered a warm pat to his arm. She shouldn't have used him like that. It was childish and beneath her. "You go on and have fun."

"You, too, Millie." He tipped his cowboy hat. Now, see? Why couldn't she be attracted to a nice, courteous guy like Buck? Why was her taboo brother-in-law the only man since Jim who'd made her heart beat faster?

While accepting their prize, along with a whole lot of smooching, the couple was gifted with cheap plastic crowns proclaiming them Romance King and Queen. When Stacie got a little too excited, dropping her crown onto her cleavage then staring expectantly at Cooper as if he should retrieve it, Millie felt like throwing up. Knowing she couldn't take too much more, she turned her back on the happy couple and aimed for the bar. Screw beer. She needed tequila!

She'd just downed her second shot when a familiar voice behind her said, "Thank God I found you. Please help."

Cooper had sidled alongside her—or he could've been a tequila-induced mirage. But she didn't think she'd had *that* much to drink.

"I need you to dance with me—you know, pretend we're an item so Stacie leaves me alone. You might even throw in a kiss for good measure—might look more convincing."

She wrinkled her nose. "Mr. Romance, why would I want to dance with or kiss you when you've clearly found your soul mate?"

He scowled. "Cut the sarcasm. I was playing along with this whole damned thing just to be polite, but now that she's getting serious, I need an escape route, and pretending to be interested in you is my only logical path. Are you in?"

Gee, that had to be the most romantic proposition she'd ever had—*not!* Still, if it got Cooper away from Stacie, Millie was all for trying. While Millie didn't want to be with him romantically, she was certain Stacie was no good. Why, she couldn't say right at that moment. Regardless, as Cooper's sister-in-law, she'd be doing not just him, but her entire family, a favor in sheltering him from Stacie's wicked ways.

"Come on, Mill, give me an answer. She's headed this way."

Stacie fluffed her hair as she walked, then adjusted her push-up bra for maximum cleavage. She wore enough lip gloss that if she went in for a kiss, poor Cooper would see his reflection.

His expression turned desperate. "Screw the dance. You know what desperate times call for, and this is one of those occasions." He slipped his arms loose around Millie's hips.

"Wh-what're you doing?" she asked, wishing his touch didn't feel so darned good.

"Leaning in to kiss you. *Please,* just go with it."

Terror struck until Cooper's warm, yeasty breath melded with hers. At first, his kiss was soft, testing. But then he increased his pressure until lightning bugs took up residence clear from her chest to her toes.

When he stopped, he whispered, "Think it worked?"

Millie peeked around his shoulder to find Stacie with her hands on her hips, looking madder than a racked bull.

In the meantime, Millie's lips still tingled from Cooper's kiss—even more alarming was the fact that she craved more. The walls closed in around her. The smoky, too-warm air. All the people. The smells. Cologne and perfume. Beer and whiskey and cheeseburgers.

The band had started playing again, and Stacie was kicking up a fuss about Cooper, and how he was supposed to have been kissing her.

A low, tight knot formed at the back of Millie's throat, and she feared the only way to find release would be an ugly round of tears. Not only was she embarrassed, but ashamed, too. No matter what the reason, she'd had no business kissing her brother-in-law. Period.

Millie pushed through the crowd, running for the bar's rear exit.

She pushed open the door only to gulp in fresh night air. The cold came as a welcome relief to the suffocating warmth inside.

When her sobs hit, they weren't pretty, and she hid between the Dumpster and a couple of old trash barrels.

"Mill? You out here?"

Great. Her Valentine had stepped outside for a visit—no doubt to laugh at her just like everyone else in the crowd. The last person on earth she wanted to see was Cooper. He was smart enough that he should have known she'd want nothing to do with him.

"Go away," she snapped.

"There you are…" He'd carried his pea jacket and now slipped it over her shoulders.

She welcomed the warmth, but most of all, her body traitorously craved his masculine smell. The leather and musky citrus she'd grown to recognize as being uniquely his. "Thanks."

"You're welcome. Mind telling me what you're doing out here?"

"Isn't it obvious?"

"Not entirely…"

She sighed. "To spell it out, I'm mad at you for making a fool out of me in front of damn near the whole town. You never should've asked me to kiss you. And I never should've agreed. No matter how compelling your excuse may have been, I should've been strong enough to deny you. Most of all, I'm mad at myself for ever being goaded into leaving the house in the first pla—"

Before she could finish her rant, he cupped her face between his big, rough hands, silencing her with another kiss. This one slower and sweeter, transforming the cruel February night into a balmy summer in her heart. Only Cooper had no business being anywhere near her heart, which was why she pushed him away. "Stop."

"Sorry. Must've been the beer."

Just when she thought she couldn't have sunk lower, he'd had to go and blame kissing her not once, but twice, on being drunk?

Millie raised her hand to slap his damned handsome face, but he caught her wrist on the way up, leaned in to kiss her again then tossed her the truck keys. "Once you've sobered up, mind giving Stacie a lift back to the house? I'll find my own ride."

Chapter 13

"He did what?" Peg whispered so as not to wake the boys, who'd made a fort in J.J.'s room. Half of it hung out in the hall, so they couldn't shut J.J.'s door. Cheetah seemed fascinated by it, and sat under the ragged sheet canopy. "Start over from the beginning."

She and Millie sat cross-legged on Millie's bed, holding the bag of Oreos between them. Millie told her about the dance contest, and how Cooper wanted her to serve as a dating decoy for Stacie, but left out the part about him kissing her again behind the bar. "You can't imagine how awkward it was when I had to tell Stacie he'd taken off—God only knows where. Plus, I had his coat. For all I know, he could be frozen in a ditch."

Peg snorted. "He's a Navy SEAL. Pretty sure he'd find a way to survive in Antarctica with tooth floss and a napkin."

"Still…" Millie sniffed. "It was a horrible night. Lynette's mad at me for leaving. Zane's mad at me because I got Lynette upset—the whole thing was a start-to-finish disaster."

"Okay, wait—go back to the part about the kiss." She took another cookie from the bag. "Out of morbid curiosity, how was it?"

Millie's eyes widened in panic. She couldn't very well say it'd been as sweet as downing a hundred bags of Oreos, so she forced a deep breath, crossed her fingers and lied. "The kiss? Um, it was okay."

"Just okay, huh? Show me your hands."

The heat in Millie's traitorous cheeks rose twenty degrees. "Why?"

"Because I have a feeling that behind your back, you're crossing your fingers. It's okay if you liked kissing him. I know you loved Jim, but sweetie, it's been a long time since he passed. He wouldn't want you to spend the rest of your life pining."

"True, but he also would never want me to forge a new life with his brother of all people—not that such an option is even on the table."

"I can see that…." Peg fussed with the cookie bag's Ziploc. "But this morning, when he gave Lee and J.J. their gifts, I saw the way you looked at him—the way J.J. looked at him. You feel something. J.J. clearly thinks Cooper hung the moon."

Millie interjected with, "LeeAnn can't stand him."

Peg laughed. "Lee can't stand anyone. Goes with the age."

"True." Millie couldn't help but laugh, too. But then her throat knotted. She had enjoyed Cooper's kiss. Too much. She could have kissed him all night and deep into the next morning, but at what cost? She was already financially broken. When Cooper left for Virginia, was she emotionally stable enough to suffer a second broken heart, as well? Of course, she didn't officially feel anything romantic toward him now, but as much as she'd already grown to crave his company, she had a sneaking suspicion that he'd be all too easy to love.

Cooper jogged the first ten miles to the house then cut across the pasture once he'd reached family land. Anyone outside of his SEAL team would probably think him nuts, but the run felt good. He was used to driving his body hard, and he'd run greater distances, in far colder temps while soaking wet. As he was dressed in a T-shirt, chunky sweater, jeans and deck shoes, this trek was a cakewalk. Hell, he didn't even have his heavy-ass backpack to worry about.

Unfortunately, by the time he reached the barn—he wasn't yet ready to go in the house and face his sister or Millie—he realized that while he may not have physical worries, he did have a fair amount of explaining to do.

Truth was, all night long he'd secretly hoped to kiss Millie. He didn't give a shit that it'd been in front of practically everyone he'd ever known outside of the Navy. Maybe deep down he'd wanted it that way? Just to get everything out on the table in a one-stop, efficient manner. But had that been fair to her?

Moreover, what was the point in declaring his intentions toward her when he wouldn't even be sticking around?

He groaned.

Sassy released a soft snort.

"How's it going, girl?" When he rubbed the horse's

nose, she leaned into his touch. "What I wouldn't give if all women were as uncomplicated as you."

The calf and chickens were down for the night, content beneath their respective heat lamps.

Now that the mess left by the fallen tree had been cleared, that meant he was good to go on assembling the new chicken coop. He hadn't mentioned it to Millie, but he'd remembered her saying how she'd once seen a fancy chicken coop and thought it was cool, so that was exactly what he planned to give her.

She deserved so much.

Only a fraction of which he was equipped to deliver.

Had the night gone the way she'd deserved, that kiss wouldn't have been an excuse for ditching Stacie, but so much more. As much as it pained him to admit, what she'd really deserved was a surprise kiss from a real man—maybe even that guy Buck, whom she'd danced with. She needed the sort of man who'd care for not only the ranch, but her and the kids, as well. He'd be a worthy son for Clint.

In short, Millie deserved a man who was everything Cooper wasn't.

"What're you still doing up?"

"What's it look like?" Millie hadn't meant to be sharp with Cooper. Or maybe she had.

He closed the back door behind him.

She shivered from the burst of cold air.

"Let me rephrase my question." He drew out the chair across from her, spun it around then straddled it. He was tall enough to rest his forearms on the chair's back. His cheeks were ruddy from the cold and his grown-out hair adorably mussed. Couldn't he at least have the decency to look bad? "Why are you up at 1:00 a.m. painting Lee-Ann's volcano?"

"The science fair is next Friday. She needed me to put a coat on for her this afternoon so it'd be dry enough tomorrow for her to start adding trees, but with all the party planning, my day got away from me."

"You outshone every woman in that bar."

"Hush." If her heart beat any faster, she'd pass out, doing a face-plant in the ugly brown paint.

"I mean it. I'm sorry I ran out on you, but I'm not sorry I kissed you."

"Cooper Hansen, I'm about two seconds from pitching this paint in your face. Do you have any idea how humiliated I was to not only go back into that bar alone, but having to explain to Stacie that you'd left her, too?"

"She get home okay?" He at least had the decency to bow his head.

"Well, gee, I wouldn't exactly know, seeing how about two seconds after I told her you'd left, she took off with some other guy and told me she'd find her own way back to her car."

He had the gall to grin, and he looked damned sexy doing it. "Guess since her car's not in the drive, my question was irrelevant."

"You think?"

"Ouch." He was back to grinning.

Millie wanted to slug him. Trouble was, she also wanted to kiss him. Instead, she fished one of the Oreos from her nearby Ziploc bag.

"I told you I didn't want to go out with her." He shrugged. "To my way of thinking, right from the start, that makes this whole mess your fault."

That's it—she put down her half-eaten cookie to dredge her paint brush across the paper plate then flick it at him. Unfortunately, more of the washable poster board paint landed on the table than him, but he had gained a few awkward-size freckles on his chin. This dating disaster was *all* his fault for always looking so damned good—even with paint freckles.

"Nice, Mill." He took a napkin from the holder she kept on the table. "Real mature."

"Oh—like you leaving me to deal with your date was mature?"

"For the last time, she wasn't my date. I only went along with this whole thing on the off chance I might get to spend more time with you."

"Please, don't do that."

"What?" Her heart fluttered just to witness a flash of his slow grin.

"Act like you care, when you obviously don't."

He leisurely rose, sauntering toward her with cowboy swagger.

Dear Lord...

"My problem—" he knelt alongside her, manhandling her chair until turning her far enough to face him "—is that I care too much. From the second I stepped back into this house, you've been all I can think of. I keep seeing flashes of you when we were kids and then older, in high school—back before you and Jim were even an item. How had I never noticed you? How had I let him get to you first? But then what kind of lowlife does that make me? If Jim were alive, he'd owe me an ass-kicking."

She licked her lips, willing her runaway pulse to slow. "That's the thing—he's not here. But we are. And that's got me so confused." *I want you more than I've ever wanted anything in my whole life.* But was that just her body talking? Or something more? How was she supposed to know?

He rose just high enough to kiss her, resting his hands on her thighs, singeing her tender flesh through her robe. "You taste so damned good."

He urged her mouth open, sweeping her tongue with his. An erotic jolt slammed through her, colliding flaming desire into an icy wall of guilt. Despite her speech, she still knew what they were doing was wrong, but that fact didn't even remotely slow them down.

When he took her hands, urging her from her chair, she let him, and when he dipped his kisses deep into her robe's open vee, she didn't offer the slightest protest. All that mattered was the velvety warmth centered between her legs and spreading like wicked syrup throughout every inch of her fevered body.

The house was quiet save for the clock ticking over the stove. Everyone had been sleeping for hours, which was why when Cooper untied her robe, instead of fighting him, she only held her breath, praying for release of the forbidden tension that'd been building ever since he'd come home.

He was kneeling again, worshipping her abdomen with kisses, skimming his hands along her hips, dragging down her panties until the room's chill touched her hot core.

Back to her lips, he kissed the breath from her, dizzying her from his urgency that surprisingly matched her own.

His slipping his finger inside her seemed the most natural thing in the world, as did his nipping her rock-

hard nipple through her bra. He set a rhythm that left
her alternately gasping and moaning, twining her arms
round his neck for support, kissing him, kissing him
until he made her come, moaning her pleasure into his
mouth.

"More…" she begged. She was no longer a mom or
widow, but a woman. A woman desperate to once again
feel alive in every sense of the word.

"Sure?"

Cheek pressed to the warm wall of his chest, she
nodded.

And then he was shoving aside the paint and volcano to ease her back, leaving her for only the instant
it took him to unfasten his jeans. He'd just touched his
tip inside her, when he stopped.

"Wh-what's wrong?" she managed to say. He needed
to keep going before she lost her nerve.

"I don't have protection."

"I don't care." And in the moment, she truly didn't.

It'd been so long, that the first few thrusts were painful. Tears sprung to her eyes, but then he slowed and
kissed pain away, and then pleasure was once again
building and spreading into a lavish labyrinth of stunning heat and joy and spiraling, ever-climbing, raw sensation. This man had somehow become her moon and
stars and everything in between.

With his every thrust, she gripped his biceps harder,
raising her hips, urging him deeper, deeper until she
came again in a glorious Technicolor dream.

He rested on top of her, showering her with ador-
ing kisses that only made her want him again. Was this
normal? It'd been so long since she'd been with a man,

she couldn't even remember. All she knew was that she wasn't sorry. Not one bit.

Though she probably would be in the morning…

Sunday morning, Cooper volunteered to help his dad eat breakfast. Considering what'd gone down in the kitchen the previous night, he wasn't sure he could ever again look at the table with a straight face.

"How are you?" Cooper asked, mixing butter and sugar into the oatmeal.

"T-tired."

"Me, too." He fed Clint his first bite. "I went on a date with your therapist. What's her name? Sandy? Sissy?"

"St-Stacie…"

"Yeah, that's it. Anyway, it was a rough night. She's a sweet girl, but not really my type. I guess when it comes down to it, if I ever settle down, I'd want a woman more like Millie. Someone who's not afraid to get her hands dirty, and isn't into all the fancy hair and makeup. I like an earthy girl, you know?"

His dad grunted then swallowed his latest bite.

"Truth is, I couldn't sleep a wink. Just thinking about things. Makes me crazy when that happens." He helped his dad with a few more spoonfuls then a few sips of coffee. "How come you couldn't sleep?"

Clint gestured for Cooper to hand over his white-board. He then wrote: *Too damned noisy!*

Cooper's stomach tightened. Did that mean what he thought it did? That his father hadn't been *out* when…

His cheeks felt hot enough to fry an egg. No, no, no.

"Too noisy, huh? What? Did you have an owl outside your window? Coyotes?"

Clint erased the board with his elbow, then wrote: *All that rutting!*

Cooper gulped. Okay, no biggie. No need to panic. He'd been trained in crisis management and thinking on his feet in the often-fluid situation of battle. "Geez, Dad, I'm sorry. I'll bet you overheard the movie I was watching. Parts were pretty racy—if you know what I mean."

His father didn't look all that convinced.

"Why does my volcano look splotchy?"

Late Sunday morning, Millie took a sheet of oatmeal cookies from the oven, pretending she hadn't heard her daughter's embarrassing question.

"Mom? Did you hear me?"

Mortification didn't begin describing how awful Millie felt about not only the odd paint pattern on LeeAnn's science-fair project, but also for her own downright scandalous behavior. What had she been thinking? "I heard you, okay? I don't know how it happened. Maybe Cheetah's been on the table?"

As traitorous as that cat was, he deserved the blame!

"Yeah, I'll bet he did it…"

"Have fun at your party?" *Wish I hadn't had quite so much fun at mine.*

"Yeah, but Kara and Finleigh kept calling boys, and the boy I wanted to talk to was at his grandparents' and couldn't talk. I wish I knew if he liked me."

"What boy?" Since when had her baby girl even known boys existed?

"His name's Damon. He's in sixth grade, and his eyes are all dreamy, but I don't want him using them to look at any other girls."

Back up the truck. Though Millie would like nothing more than to dissect every possible meaning behind what'd transpired after she and Cooper had—well, fornicated, for lack of a better word—it sounded like her daughter needed her more.

"Honey…" She used a spatula to transfer the cookies from the sheet to a plate. "Don't you think you're a little young for boys?"

"No. God, Mom, Kara's had a boyfriend for like three months."

"Okay, first—when you say boyfriend, what exactly are we talking? Like you just talk at recess? And second—do Kara's parents know about this guy?"

LeeAnn rolled her eyes. "You're so lame."

"And you're a little too mouthy. And way too young to be even thinking about boys."

"What do you know about them? It's not like you ever date."

Touché. "How about you take a nice, long time-out up in your room."

"I have to work on my volcano."

"Write on the research paper that goes along with it."

As luck would have it, Cooper chose that moment to stroll through the back door. He wore faded work jeans, boots, an old, red flannel shirt and his raggedy straw hat. Despite all of that, he looked so handsome, Millie dropped a cookie on the floor. And then her mind's eye recalled what'd happened right there on the kitchen table, and she wanted to dissolve into a confused puddle.

LeeAnn shot her uncle a preteen stony glare then stomped off toward the hall.

Cheetah shot out from under the table, dragging the cookie to the utility porch. Weird, traitorous cat who apparently thought he was a dog.

"What's she in a snit about?" Peg asked on her way into the kitchen from doing Clint's physical therapy.

"Can you believe it? Boys." Millie glanced up to catch Cooper's mossy-green gaze. Just thinking about what they'd done made her nipples harden. It'd been filthy! But then afterward, he'd been so sweet, and then strangely distant—as if nothing had even happened.

"She's too young for that."

"Exactly." To avoid looking at Cooper, Millie focused on spooning dough onto the cookie sheet.

"Mom!" J.J. called from the living room, where they were watching a movie. "When are the cookies gonna be done? Me and Cayden are starving!"

"Just a minute!" Why, on the one morning when she really needed private time with Cooper to dissect what'd transpired between them was all hell-a-poppin' in the Hansen home?

Chapter 14

"Pretty day, isn't it?"

"Yep." Cooper kept right on hammering. He didn't pause to admire how well Millie filled out her jeans, or how the sun glinted off the few red streaks in her hair. When he'd been in the kitchen—the scene of his crime—with her that morning, he couldn't escape fast enough.

Millie hung clothes on the line.

If not for the jet overhead bound for Denver International, they could have been in another century. Part of him wished they were. Lord knew, things would be less complicated. But then would they? All things being relative, nothing would change. He'd still have carried a wagonload of emotional baggage, and she'd still be his brother's widow.

"Looks like you're making good progress on the coop." She hung up a pint-size pair of jeans.

"Yep." He kept right on framing by fitting in a 2x4.

"You planning on avoiding me forever?"

Yep. "There's not much to say other than it shouldn't have happened. I shouldn't have let it."

"Did it ever occur to you that I'm half of this equation and wanted it to happen?"

He sighed. "Yeah, well, you shouldn't have. I'm no good, and you're like a saint. Raising two great kids, looking after my dad and the ranch. You're my brother's *wife.*"

"Correction…" She hung a tiny T-shirt. And another and another until her motions looked frantic. "I *was* Jim's wife, but he left me. He was stupid—so stupid, to die like he did. It was a useless, senseless death that still makes me furious." Now she was crying, and the racking sobs shredded Cooper's heart. "How could he be so careless with his life?"

He set down his hammer and went to her—not caring who saw.

"I'm sorry." He kissed the crown of her head.

She pushed him away. "No. I don't want pity. I want you to view me not as Jim's wife, your sister-in-law, but as me—*Millie.* The girl who watched you at rodeos and thought you were the wildest thing I'd ever seen. Jim was wonderfully safe, he was my rock, but you were—are…"

Her teary smile rocked his world.

"*Amazing.* And I don't just mean—you know. I'm talking about how you've swept in here and made everything better. I could've maintained the status quo, but by you taking the ranch duties off my hands, I feel like I can breathe again. I can't thank you enough for that."

He tucked his hands in his pockets. "You're welcome, but about last night… It can't happen again."

"Because you're not attracted to me?" The tears streaming down her cheeks glistened in the sun. And that felt wrong. No one should be crying on such a gift of a February day—especially not a woman as gorgeous as Millie.

"Seriously?" He drew her back into his arms for a kiss, then tucked flyaway strands of her hair behind her ears. "Never doubt your beauty. You're stunning."

"No, I'm not. My nails are a mess and my hair's never done. I saw the girls you dated in high school, and I would never have been one of them."

"Are we in high school?" He brushed his thumb over her full lower lip then leaned in for a nibble. "I sure as hell hope not, because then I wouldn't be able to do this…" He kissed her nice and slow, knowing the whole while he shouldn't, but what kind of man would he be to let a woman as perfect as she was spend one more moment crying?

Her breathy mew made him hard as hell. "Thought we weren't doing this anymore?"

"We're not. This really is the last time, okay?"

She returned his kiss, this time with a bad-girl hint of tongue. "Yes. That's probably best."

"No more insecurities, okay?" He tucked his hand under her chin, directing her gaze to his. "Promise?"

She nodded.

"Good girl." He kissed her forehead. The tip of her nose. He wanted to journey farther, but held strong in his resolve to keep his roving hands to himself. Their table *tango* never should've happened. She deserved better than that, than him.

Sunday afternoon, Millie stood alongside Peg's compact car while she rearranged the contents of her over-stuffed trunk in an attempt to close it. "Why don't you take out your toiletry case and put it in the backseat?"

"Because I've got all my quilting gear there. I finished a whole section while you and my brother were off partying."

"Whoa—don't you mean your brother and Stacie?" Because it was the God's honest truth that Millie hadn't enjoyed a lick of what'd gone on down at Mack's. And after? There went the annoying heat in her cheeks. Well, after had been a whole other story.

"Cut the act. I saw you two kissing out back today."

"You were spying on us?"

"I was washing dishes and happened to look out the window behind the sink. What if it'd been LeeAnn or J.J. who saw? Spill it. What's going on between you two?"

"We kissed, but it was no big deal. We both agreed it was a mistake. End of story."

"I don't think so. Do you feel something special for him? If so, when did you know? Is he quitting the Navy to stay here or still leaving, because I can't imagine you and the kids following him."

"Peg, stop." Millie looked over her shoulder to make sure they were still alone. "Even if I knew the answers to all of those questions, I don't think I'd tell you. Whatever's going on is complicated and—I'm sure in the grand scheme of things—nothing important. Just two lonely people sharing a moment."

"You two don't just have shared moments, Mill, but a long history. Think about it. You crushed on Cooper long before realizing Jim was the more stable of the two Hansen boys."

"Ha!" Millie hugged herself in twilight's growing chill. "What a crock that turned out to be. Hopefully, even Cooper's not stupid enough to stand up on a moving four-wheeler while shooting."

Peg sighed. "You ever going to forgive him?"

Millie crossed her arms. "Nope."

"Okay, well, for the record, I think you could do worse in men than Cooper. I'm beyond thrilled to see him and Dad getting along. Would it really be so awful for you to end up with another Hansen man?"

"Okay, wait—we shared a kiss, and already you're marrying us off?"

"Think about it. He's a ready-made dad and ranch hand. You could—and have—gone years without meeting another candidate as suitable as him." Peg tossed the toiletry bag on top of her quilting gear then slammed the trunk closed. "Just sayin'."

Thursday afternoon while cutting trash bags to protect LeeAnn's volcano from the light snow, Millie still couldn't get Peg's words out of her head.

Last week at this time, if someone had told her she'd have used a man for his body, she'd have laughed them out of the county, but in hindsight, had that essentially been what happened between her and Cooper? If Peg knew the whole truth, she'd freak.

Every time Millie relived what she and Cooper had done on this very table, her stomach flipped—only in a good way—wishing she had the courage to do it again.

"Mom?" LeeAnn asked. "Have you seen my report?"

"It's in your blue folder on top of the printer."

"Thanks."

"Can I have ice cream for dinner?" J.J. asked from in front of the freezer.

"No. Once we help your sister set up her project, we might have time to go out for dinner during the judging. We'll have to play it by ear."

"But I thought the science fair was tomorrow?"

"It is, but judges go through tonight to decide who won. Then tomorrow, all the people visiting the fair will be able to see the winners."

J.J. cocked his head. "I don't get it."

"Me, neither, bud." Cooper sauntered in from Clint's room, where he'd been helping his father eat.

No matter how many times Millie told herself she was over him, his striking profile never failed to send her pulse into a gallop.

Cooper grabbed a banana from the counter fruit bowl, snapped it in half, and gave part to her son. He then took a piece of bologna from the fridge, ate three-quarters and fed the rest to Cheetah, who rubbed against his ankles. Maybe that's how he got the cat to like him. Bribes! "How about we let your mom and LeeAnn just tell us where we need to be and when?"

"Yeah, that sounds good." J.J. looked to Cooper in awe.

"If I'm in charge—" Millie duct-taped the last trash bag in place "—then how about you two put on clean shirts? And one of you probably needs to wash your face."

"Oops, that's me," Cooper teased.

Even if it was meant for her son, Millie couldn't get

enough of her brother-in-law's smile. Since their talk in the backyard, though she wouldn't even try denying the sexual tension, there'd also been a lightness between them she found irresistible. He was also getting along great with J.J. and Clint. LeeAnn, however, still merely tolerated him—even after he'd printed his Mount Vesuvius and Pompeii pictures for her and helped with her project's eruption.

What if Peg was right? That Cooper truly was the guy she was meant to rebuild her life with? Only her insecurities and doubts caused them to miss their opportunity?

The question haunted her while loading everyone and LeeAnn's volcano into the truck, and more still while thanking Lynette for watching Clint while they'd be gone.

By the time Cooper had driven them to town, her mind felt messy. Once they'd all made two treks from the truck into the school through heavy snow with the various parts of LeeAnn's project, while J.J. ran around with found friends, Millie led Cooper to a seat on the gym's bleachers.

"Shouldn't we be helping her assemble everything?" he asked.

"Nope. She'd be disqualified."

"What if she doesn't remember where to put all the tubing?"

Millie cast him a sideways smile. "Relax. And welcome to being an uncle."

"Thanks." After returning her smile, he nudged her shoulder with his. He'd no doubt meant the gesture as friendly, so why did her whole body tingle? "All the uncle manuals skip this part—about wanting your niece to beat the crap out of every other kid in a purely scientific manner."

"Oh, of course." She laughed and nodded.

Other parents joined them in the stands until the school principal herded them all into the cafeteria to await the announcement of the winners.

"You know," Cooper said between bites of the chocolate cake the PTA moms had provided—turned out there hadn't been time for dinner, "though I saw a few other volcanoes, Lee clearly had the most complex."

"Absolutely."

Was it wrong that she found so much joy in once again coparenting? Cooper might technically only be her children's uncle, but she remembered Jim being every bit as competitive when it came to their kids' winning.

Even better? Not standing around alone while groups of moms and dads gathered. She'd grown weary of always being on her own. Before his stroke, Clint had tagged along whenever he could, but it'd never been the same.

Forty minutes and three pieces of cake later, Cooper asked, "How long does it take to determine Lee's the winner?"

"In my experience, whether you're waiting for a riding lesson to end or tutoring or Little League, it always takes around ten minutes longer than you feel you can stand waiting without a mental breakdown."

"Good to know," he said with a nod. "I'm damn near there."

Twenty minutes later, winners were finally named.

When LeeAnn came in third in her age group to a

robot that dunked cookies in milk and a tsunami machine, Cooper was outraged.

"What the hell?" he asked under his breath. "There's no way that scrawny kid made that robotic arm all on his own. Look at the way his dad's beaming—clear case of cheating to me. That guy probably works for NASA."

Millie grimaced. "Maybe, but another *uncling* tip for you is that despite how much you want to pitch a fit about any number of injustices toward one's child, we must always be gracious and follow the adage of catching more flies with honey than vinegar."

"That's bullshit."

She elbowed him. "Another rule? Even though you're a grown-up, you still can't cuss at school."

Sighing, he shook his head. "No wonder I was glad to get out of this place. Too damned many rules."

He got it again with her elbow. "I'm starving. Let's find the kids and get out of here."

"Yes, ma'am. Want to divide and conquer? I'll grab the munchkin and you find Lee?"

"Sounds like a plan." Yet another benefit of coparenting—not having to track down both kids by herself.

Watching Cooper's broad shoulders easily part through the crowd, Millie fully realized just how weary she'd grown of being a single parent. But that realization was a long way from promoting Cooper from uncle to dad.

J.J. still slept with a night-light, so Cooper couldn't help but wonder why he'd ventured so far down a dark school hall.

A metallic clang, then giggle, came from about fifty feet in front of Cooper's current location, and he was guessing by the sounds' slight diffusion, down another hall to the left. Sure enough, he soon had to make another turn into a new addition that hadn't been here when he'd attended this school.

He heard another giggle.

Saw a couple kissing in the faint light eking in from the snow-covered parking lot.

Cooper cleared his throat. "Excuse me. Either one of you seen— Are you freakin' kidding me?" His eyes narrowed. "LeeAnn?"

"Don't tell Mom."

"You—" Cooper pointed to the boy "—get the hell away from my niece."

The kid took one look at the same game face Cooper used when taking down terrorists and shot off toward the cafeteria.

"God—" LeeAnn straightened her long pigtails "—did you have to be so scary?"

"You're both lucky I didn't do worse. Your mom, on the other hand, is going to blow bigger than your volcano."

"*Please,* don't tell her."

Arms crossed, he asked, "Give me one good reason why I shouldn't."

"With Grandpa Clint's stroke and all the bills she's always worrying about, I don't want her worrying about me. I promise, I'll never kiss Damon again."

Damon? Coincidence that the kid's name was only one letter off from demon? Though Cooper hated to admit it, his niece had made a valid point. Millie did have a lot on her plate—considering what'd gone down Saturday night, even more than her daughter knew. Besides, since LeeAnn promised not to kiss the kid again, if Cooper did let it slide, then would she maybe cut him some slack and quit avoiding him like he had an infectious disease?

"Please, Uncle Cooper. I pinkie swear I won't even talk to him again. *Please,* don't tell Mom."

"All right," he said, "but I never want to catch you with that kid again."

By the time all four of them trudged back out to Cooper's truck, three inches of snow coated the windshield.

Millie hoped the roads would be clear enough by the next afternoon for Peg to make her usual weekend trip to see Clint.

Her evening with Cooper had been alarmingly pleasant, and she looked forward to his sister being around to chaperone, because honestly? As charming as he'd been tonight, she didn't trust herself to keep her hands off him.

He started the engine, then said to J.J., "Bud, you wanna help me clear windows?"

"I can't reach."

"That's what I'm for..."

"Cool! Piggyback me, Uncle Cooper!"

After her son bounced his way out of the truck, Millie angled on the front seat to get a better view of her daughter. "I'm proud of you. There were a lot of great projects."

LeeAnn shrugged. "I did okay, but only the first two in each category go to the regional science fair."

Millie patted LeeAnn's forearm. "Whenever that's supposed to be, we'll go do something fun. Next year, we won't make just a robotic arm, but a whole robot, okay?"

LeeAnn nodded, but still seemed down.

"Sweetie, don't sweat it. I'm super impressed by how hard you've worked. You should be proud, too."

J.J. banged on the window. *"Mom! Look at me!"*

Cooper had set him on the hood, where he was now standing while brushing snow from the windshield.

"Get him down from there!" Millie waved to get Cooper's attention, but it wouldn't have mattered, as he'd already done her bidding, and the two guys were climbing back in the truck.

"That was fun!" J.J. was still bouncing.

"How much cake did you eat?" she asked her son.

"I dunno. I think lots!"

"Sounds about right…"

Because of the snow, they opted to skip going out for dinner in favor of driving straight home. By the time they reached the house, at least another couple of inches of snow had fallen.

J.J. was asleep, so Cooper carried him in.

LeeAnn bounded past Millie to beat all of them to the front door. Once inside, she hollered good-night, then darted up the stairs to her room.

"Poor thing." Millie hung her coat and hat on the hook by the door. "She's really taking her loss hard."

"She'll get over it." For him to be the same guy who was angered by the fact that LeeAnn's project hadn't placed higher, Cooper didn't seem all that upset.

"I suppose."

"Want me to put him to bed?" Cooper kissed J.J.'s temple.

"Yes, please." His simple, sweet gesture toward her son tightened Millie's chest, making it hard to breathe. More every day, she cherished Cooper's connection to her kids. Tonight, he'd even somehow managed to find LeeAnn before her.

"Hey…" Lynette wandered in from the living room. "I was starting to worry about you guys. It's looking bad out there."

"We got behind a plow on the main road, so it wasn't too dicey. You'll probably want to be in four-wheel-drive for your trip home, though."

"I figured as much." She put a bookmark in the paperback she'd been reading.

"Want Cooper to drive you?"

"Thanks, but I've been dealing with this crap for a while. I'll be fine." Her friend waved off her concern much the way she had when Millie had taken off mad on Valentine's Day. They'd been friends since grade school, and no matter the tussle, it never took long for them to repair any damage.

Lynette agreed to call when she was safely home, then Millie saw her out the front door.

Cooper strode back down the stairs. "I'm going to check on Dad."

"Okay. You hungry? I was thinking about scrambling some eggs."

"Sounds good." He paused with his hand on the newel post.

"You all right?"

"Sure. Fine." His dour expression didn't match his words.

She eyed him for a few long seconds. "Lee's loss is weighing heavy on you, too, huh?"

He ducked his gaze. "I guess so."

"It's all right." Though she knew better than to touch him, she smoothed her hand up and down his back. His wool pea jacket was damp from snow, but this close and personal, she caught a whiff of his leathery aftershave and nearly drowned in contentment. Did he have to be so perfect in darn near every way? "Now that you're back in the kids' lives, there will be plenty more science fairs. You're more than welcome to help with every single one."

His faint smile faded. "Wish I'd be here, but from Virginia to Colorado is an awfully long ride."

"True," she conceded, "but we're worth it, don't you think?" The moment the words left her mouth, she regretted them.

The last thing she wanted was for him to for one second believe she wanted him to stay, because knowing Cooper and his newfound sense of family duty, he might just do it out of obligation.

When—*if*—she ever did enter into another committed relationship, she wanted it to be because he loved her, not because he felt sorry for her.

Chapter 15

A week later, Cooper was glad for Zane's help in raising the walls and putting the roof joists on Millie's chicken coop. Right now it was just a shell, but he remembered what she'd told him about wanting her birds to live in a fancy abode. Ever since, Cooper had been stuck on the idea of making her wildest chicken coop fantasy come true.

If only I could work on a few of her other fantasies....

It was nice being around his old school friend and rodeo buddy. The two of them had shared good times. Plus, having company helped Cooper's mind from straying to Millie and the alarming amount of moments he spent wishing they could be together.

By the time they'd installed the fourth and final roof brace, Zane collapsed onto the hard-packed ground.

"Are you trying to kill me? How the hell do you have so much energy?"

Cooper laughed. "Clean living, my friend."

"Bullshit. When we meet up at Mack's, you put a beer back just as fast as the rest of our old crew. Come on, what's your secret?"

"If I had to guess, I'd say it's my workout."

"Where are you hitting a gym around here?"

Cooper laughed. "You don't need a gym, man. It's all in here." He tapped his temple. "Run, do a few dozen pull-ups from one of the lower barn rafters. No big deal. If you want, meet me in the morning around five. I'll take you through my drill."

March 1, Millie sat in the home office, staring at a fresh pile of bills. So much around the place had changed, yet still more hadn't. She didn't tell Cooper about their financial problems, not because they were embarrassing, but because she knew once they culled the herd in late May, that they'd make enough to pay almost everything. In the meantime, she'd just have to keep juggling her available funds.

The kids got Jim's social security check, but that barely covered the basics. Clint also had social security, but his money had all been funneled into paying for his medical costs.

Cooper knocked on the open door. "Are you using the computer?"

"No. Go ahead." She scooped up her bill pile and set them on a side table across the room. "What are you going to do?"

"Since Dad and J.J. are finally occupied with a movie, I thought I'd answer a few emails and research my project." He winked. "My iPad's dead, and on the charger."

"Sure. Sounds good." She fought to maintain her composure. Ever since what he now called their *lapse in judgment,* he'd grown faultlessly, disgustingly polite. She missed their sometimes heated banter. Even more, she missed their few stolen kisses.

His project was rebuilding the chicken coop, but he was being so hush-hush about it that he'd gone so far as to string sheets across part of the yard so she couldn't see the structure from the kitchen sink window. He spent so much time out there, she couldn't imagine what it would look like. She'd told him about once admiring a fancy coop. Had he listened and was now breathing life into what she'd only meant as a casual statement?

The fact that he'd truly listened to her bit of small talk warmed her through and through. It had to be significant, right?

"Need me to get you anything?" she asked.

"No, thank you." He'd already opened an email.

"Okay, well, I'll leave you to it." What was wrong with him? How could he stand them being in the same room and not at least sharing a touch?

In a perfect world, he'd have entered the room and kissed her, maybe given her knotted shoulders a rub. They'd have shared their days and maybe wandered into the kitchen for cocoa and a slice of the cherry pie she'd made for that night's dessert.

"You all right?" He stopped typing to glance her way. Just the sight of his mossy-green stare was enough to make her knees weak. How did he maintain his composure? Or, like she suspected, was he just not that into her and his polite speech out by the clothesline had been his way of letting her down easy? "You look washed out."

"Thanks. That's the nicest thing anyone's said to me all week."

"Aw, I didn't mean it in a bad way. Just that you look tired. Why don't you have a nice long soak, then go to bed. I'll make sure everyone else is tucked in."

"You'd do that?" As much as she cherished bedtime rituals with J.J. and LeeAnn, the thought of letting Cooper assume all of her duties while she essentially pampered herself was too good of an opportunity to pass up.

"Sure. It's no problem." He didn't even look up from reading his letter. But then what had she expected? For him to sweep her into his arms, making her promise to add extra rose oil to her bathwater so her skin smelled nice when he snuggled alongside her in bed?

Her traitorous pulse raced at the possibilities of what else they might do in her bed.

"Go on," he said. "You're wasting valuable tub time."

Mouth dry from holding back all the things she wanted to say to him, but shouldn't, Millie visually drank him in once more then trudged upstairs to draw her water.

Once she'd submerged herself beneath fragrant bubbles and closed her eyes, she'd anticipated peace.

What she got were memories of their wild night in the kitchen that were hot enough to bring her bath water to a boil!

Next Wednesday, Cooper parked at the feed store's side door, killed the truck's engine then sighed. Millie sat alongside him. More than anything, he wanted to kiss her, but he fought the temptation.

The sky was gray, snow tumbled in halfhearted flurries and the temperature was a balmy ten degrees. As if checking the herd in this weather hadn't been enough fun, before she'd left for school, he'd caught LeeAnn on her mom's cell with that Damon kid—he knew, because he'd redialed the number. What was the protocol on this sort of thing? His niece had promised to never kiss the kid again, but should Cooper have extended that promise to include cutting all contact? But then how was that even possible when they'd see each other at school?

He asked, "Doesn't this town depress the hell out of you?"

"Wait until spring. Everything will look better."

"How?" The same planters filled with dead plants still hung from the street's ornamental light posts, and more storefronts were empty than filled. Weeds grew through sidewalk cracks, and there were more mounds of dirty snow than cars.

"What do you mean? You don't remember spring? The way everything greens up and the blue sky looks big enough for you to fly right into—" she grinned "—assuming you had wings."

"Right. There is that." *Lord, I want to kiss you.*

"You know what I mean. Yes, this winter has been especially nasty, but you'll see. Once May rolls around, this place is going to be looking mighty tempting. So tempting in fact, you might never want to leave."

He snorted. "You been sniffing J.J.'s school paste?" *The sooner I hit the road, the better.* Being around her was dangerous. She made him want the family he didn't deserve.

She answered his question with a dirty look. "In all

seriousness, before you came, I didn't hold out much hope for this place. I figured by spring we'd have lost the ranch and moved into a Denver apartment. Now..." Her wide-eyed look of gratitude made up for what the hiding sun couldn't. "For the first time in forever— knock on wood—I think everything might be okay."

Cooper wished he shared her optimism, but even if they made a boatload of cash at the cattle auction, he wasn't naive, and had seen her bills. They could sell the entire herd, and it wouldn't be enough to put the ranch on the solid foundation he wanted for her, his dad and the kids.

"Come outside. And close your eyes." Since both kids were still at school, Cooper took Millie's hand to guide her out to the backyard on the deceptively sunny mid-March day. Though it was bright, the air still held a nip from the previous night's sleet, meaning the sheet he'd hung to stop Millie from eyeing her surprise through the kitchen window had been frozen to the clothesline. "Oh—and put this on."

He took her long sweater from the back-door hook, holding it out for her to slip her arms through, wishing that when their arms accidentally brushed, his attraction for her hadn't felt more like pain. But then what was the point in lying? He honestly wanted her so bad, it hurt.

"How am I going to see?"

He took her hand. "Let me guide you."

Ever since learning of her wish for a fancy home in which to house her chickens, he'd been consumed with the idea to surprise her. For weeks, he'd toiled to make every part perfect, right down to planting pansies in the wide front porch's flower boxes.

During their morning workouts, Zane had come straight out and told him he was crazy for putting so much time, money and energy into this kind of nutty venture, but Cooper didn't care. He was crazy, all right.

Crazy about his brother's wife.

He'd do damn near anything for her. Anything, but tie her down to a misfit like himself.

"Are we almost there?" She tripped over an exposed tree root, but he caught her. Touching her and not kissing her proved a lesson in restraint.

"A little farther." The phrase also applied to how much he alternately looked forward to and dreaded leaving. His dad grew stronger by the day, which meant Cooper's time on the ranch was almost done. He led Millie past the clothesline and around the cottonwood. Upon reaching their destination, he forced a deep breath, wishing her reaction to his big reveal didn't mean so much. "Okay, open your eyes."

She gasped then covered her mouth with her hands. "Cooper, it's…" Her eyes welled.

"What's that mean? Are you happy? Sad?" If she didn't like what he'd done, though it might sound silly to anyone else, he'd be crushed. He'd poured himself into this project, heart and soul. What emotion he couldn't give to her, he'd given to the damn chickens. Stupid, but there it was.

"I'm…" She laughed through tears then damn near toppled him with a hug. "I'm so happy! This is stunning—you really did build me the Taj Mahal of chicken coops."

He sharply exhaled. *She likes it.*

Gratitude flowed through him, making him feel like a second-grader basking in his teacher's approval. But over the past couple of months, Millie had come to mean the world to him. Her opinion mattered.

"I'm in awe…" She gingerly stepped onto the front porch, laughing when she tried out the swing. Every inch of the coop had been covered in Victorian-era swag he'd painted in a half-dozen purple shades, ranging from lavender to deep violet.

"How can I ever thank you?"

You already did with your smile. "I'm good."

She opened the door slowly and with reverence. The inside smelled of new lumber, straw and grain. Under the heat lamps' glow, Millie's chickens gurgled and clucked in contentment. Golden sun warmed the floor through a skylight.

"This is almost too nice for just the chickens." She wiped tears from her cheeks. "It's amazing. Better than I'd even imagined."

"Good. Mission accomplished." But if that was truly the case, why was he already feeling empty inside? Like he needed another grand gesture to make Millie see how much he cared?

March passed, and then somehow it was Easter Sunday in late April. Just as Millie had predicted to Cooper on that frigid day in March, the high prairie had sprung back to life—much like her, only in a way she couldn't in a million years have predicted.

She was pregnant.

The fact alternately terrified and thrilled her.

On the terror side, right along with wondering how they'd ever financially manage with another mouth to feed and what her friends and neighbors would think of her having an unplanned baby she'd conceived with her brother-in-law, came the bonus worry of when she should tell Cooper her news.

By now, she knew him well enough to guess that once he learned he'd soon be a dad, he'd go all noble cowboy on her, demanding they march down to the courthouse for a wedding. But was that what she really wanted?

Make no mistake, with every part of her being, she wished he'd stay, but not out of a sense of obligation— because he felt trapped. Sure, tongues would wag, but gossips would soon enough find something else to occupy their chatter.

On the bright side, just as she'd never felt more healthy and vibrantly alive than when carrying Lee-Ann and J.J., this pregnancy was proving the same. Colors and smells seemed more vivid, and her heart swelled with an overall sense of well-being. This baby was a gift. Her proof that even after suffering through her loss of Jim, life didn't just have to soldier on, but sometimes it skipped while humming a happy tune.

While putting the finishing touches on the lamb cake she'd made for their annual after-church picnic, Millie allowed herself to daydream of Cooper's reaction to learning her news. Would he be elated? Confess his love and then pamper her right up to holding her hand through the delivery? Or would he feel bitter and trapped, wishing he'd never set foot back in his hometown?

The last thought made her queasy, so she downed a few saltines and ginger ale.

"You look pretty."

"Thanks." She glanced up to find Cooper leaning against the kitchen pass-through. He was so handsome, he took her breath away. If he wasn't happy about their baby, she wasn't sure how she'd cope. She guessed the same way she always had, dowsing her dreams with the hard work and even harder realities of living as a single mom on a working ranch.

Tell him, her heart urged, but her dry mouth strangely failed to work.

"Where is everyone?" His hair was still damp from a shower. Even from ten feet away, she smelled his leathery aftershave and wanted to rest her cheek against his chest, just breathing him in.

"Peg's outside with the kids, setting up tables in the yard. Thanks to the wheelchair ramp you built, Clint's with them—no doubt, barking orders."

Cooper laughed.

Since it wasn't a sound she heard often, Millie relished the moment.

"It's good seeing him up. His physical therapist said he should be walking under his own steam with just a cane by the end of the month."

"Thank goodness. His mood sure has improved since he's not always stuck in bed."

"Can you blame him?" Cooper sat at the table. The same table Millie still couldn't look at without blushing. "This is off topic, but I know you plan on culling the herd in the next month or two, and I did some research and found a company that does live internet auctions. That saves the stress on our stock of having to travel— except to their new home."

"Okay…" Since her pregnancy test had turned out positive, Millie hadn't even thought about the auction. But she needed to. The bills wouldn't pay themselves.

"Want me to set something up?"

"For when?" Because to her, culling the herd was synonymous with Cooper leaving.

"I was thinking about this time next month. That sound all right to you? Dad should be well enough to drive his four-wheeler by then. Plus, I'll move the rest of the herd to the north pasture. It's the closest and has easy access."

She only nodded, because she wasn't capable of more. So this was it? He had his escape plan in place and was good to go?

"If you think that's too soon, say the word and we can put it off. But my CO's wanting me back on base, and I'm sure you and the kids are ready to get the house back to yourselves."

Tell him! "Yep. You've got that right."

"Then I'll set everything up. You won't have to do anything but cash the check."

And raise our child and nurse my broken heart.

Cooper knew he was chewing Easter ham, but it tasted more like cardboard than brown-sugar glaze and cloves. He didn't fault the cook, but his own dour mood.

It didn't matter that the sun was shining and the temperature was T-shirt warm. Or that seated around this table was all of the family he had left in the world. Clint, Millie, J.J. and LeeAnn. His longtime friends Lynette and Zane. Even their closest neighbor, Mack, and his new bride, Wilma.

With his dad well on the way to a full recovery, all should've been right in Cooper's world. Even the calf he'd rescued had been weaned and now fit right in with the rest of the herd. Life should've been good. So how come ever since his talk with Millie about the cattle auction, he'd gotten the impression that she'd just as soon spit on him than look at him?

"Millie, d-dear, you d-did a fine job, but I'd like to say an ex-tra blessing." Though shaky, with Peg's help, Clint stood. His words spilled too fast and slurred, but he was unrecognizable from the broken man he'd been when Cooper had first arrived. "Th-thank you, Lord, for r-restoring my health, and f-for bringing home my son. A-men."

"Amen," all assembled said in unison.

Last year at this time, Cooper had been en route to Afghanistan. Back then, he never would've dreamed he'd hear his dad actually thank God for his being there, but now that he had, the thought of once again leaving brought on a mixed bag of emotions.

More than anything, he wanted to leave, but not for a logical reason. The truth was that the emotional bonds he'd formed with Millie and her kids and re-newed with his father were still too fragile and new to trust. Were they even real? Now that Clint's crisis had passed, would he morph back into the belligerent son of a bitch he'd been when he kicked Cooper off the family land?

"Uncle Cooper, look! I'm a walrus!" J.J. held a couple of asparagus *tusks* to his mouth.

Cooper feigned lurching back in fright. "You're scary, bud. Don't bite me."

J.J. growled and chomped until Millie scolded him to mind his manners.

After the meal, while the kids played with Nerf guns the Easter bunny had brought along with too much chocolate, Peg, Wilma and Lynette talked about *The*

Young and the Restless, and Clint, Zane and Mack recalled their favorite elk-hunting stories.

Cooper excused himself from the crowd, finding Millie on the front porch swing. "Care for company?"

She scooted over.

"You were awfully quiet at dinner."

"I could say the same about you."

"I s'pose." A soft, warm breeze rustled the tree leaves and tall grasses at the yard's edge.

Their thighs and hips and shoulders touched on the cramped swing. The resulting hum of attraction made it hard for him to think. Couldn't she feel it, too?

After a few minutes of shared silence, Millie asked, "Does it look like Zane has lost weight to you?"

"Yeah. He's looking good." Their morning workouts were paying off so well that a couple of their other old high school friends were following what Zane called his SEAL Sessions.

"Coop?" She angled to face him. "What do you think about kids?"

"You mean your kids, or kids in general?"

"In general."

He furrowed his forehead. "Well, the couples I know with babies always look exhausted, and the ones with school-age kids don't fare much better. I shudder to think how much trouble teens would be. The whole parenting thing sounds like a nightmare—not that J.J. and Lee aren't great, because they are. But with them, you and Jim already did the heavy lifting. I imagine starting from scratch would be a bitch."

She winced.

"I'm not sure how you and Jim did it."

"Yeah… It was rough." Her complexion paled.

"What's with the questions? Someone you know expecting?"

Chapter 16

That night, Millie sat on her bedroom's window seat, munching Oreos and trying to read, only her eyes didn't see to focus through tears.

Could Cooper have made himself any more clear? He didn't want a baby. And she just happened to be having his. Where did that leave her? What was she supposed to do?

She'd come close to confiding in Lynette and Peg, but couldn't. If her past pregnancies were any indication, by this time next month, she'd already be showing. She could play it off as a stress-eating weight gain for a little while, but eventually, the truth was literally going to pop out.

Millie put down her book to pace, but someone knocked on her closed door.

"Come in," she said, expecting LeeAnn or J.J.

"Hey." Cooper popped his head through the open door. "You decent?"

"Why wouldn't I be?"

"You never know. You being one of those quiet, good-girl types, your closet might be filled with male strippers." The fact that he said this with a straight face made her blood boil.

"Why are you here?" *Standing at my bedroom door, in my house, in my state?*

"Since your light was still on, I wanted to tell you how much I enjoyed your potato salad."

"My *potato salad?*" This whole conversation struck her as absurd. *I'm pregnant with your baby!* she wanted to scream. Instead, she demurely swept flyaway curls back into her ponytail. "Want the recipe?"

He furrowed his eyebrows. "What would I do with that? You know I don't cook."

"Just like you don't do kids?" The statement was petty and beneath her. So why had she said it? Maybe because she wanted so desperately to tell him about their baby, but was so afraid he'd have a negative reaction that she didn't dare.

"What's that supposed to mean?"

"Nothing. I'm sorry."

"No—you said it, so explain it." He shut the door, in the process, stealing all the oxygen from the room. It didn't matter that the night was warm and her window was open to a light breeze. He stood there larger than life, making her heart and mind spin like a child's top.

"I was referring to the comments you made when we were out on the porch swing. You made it plain you have no desire to be a father."

"So what? Why would that affect you?" Great question. One she had a very good answer for. *Tell him!*

"It doesn't, all right? Sorry I said anything."

Eyes narrowed, he asked, "What's going on with you, Mill? I thought we were in a good place. Am I missing something?"

Only everything! "I'm really tired. Do we have to do this now?"

"As far as I'm concerned, we don't have to do it ever. After the auction, I'll be gone. Your life will be back to normal, just as if I'd never even been here."

Only he had. And even though his time with them had been short, she remembered everything. Living with the chickens in the kitchen and bathing their newborn calf. The accidental kiss in the Red Lobster parking lot. Sharing intimate family moments like their special Valentine's Day breakfast. Being part of Clint's battle to regain his faculties. The wondrous chicken coop he'd built. Memories upon memories dulled her focus. She needed to remain strong in her resolve to not make him feel trapped into staying. If they were to ever share a true relationship based upon mutual love and respect, he had to come to her of his own free will—not a sense of obligation.

Tuesday, Cooper sat at the end of the old pond dock he and Jim had built with their father back when they'd both been in grade school. The day was fine with endless blue sky and a dazzling front range view.

He'd set up Clint in an outdoor canvas chair, handing him an already-baited, old-school cane pole that allowed for minimum work and maximum relaxation.

"I never thought I'd fish a-again…."

"I'm glad you're okay. You gave me a scare."

His dad grunted. "I scared m-myself."

The spring-fed pond's surface was glassy, giving them a clear view of the rocky bottom. The warm weather had brought out mayflies that flew in lazy patterns, every so often gliding too close to the water, only to then become fish food.

"I've missed this," Cooper said after dropping his own line in the water. There was so much left unsaid between them, but Clint had never been a big talker. Maybe it was a guy thing, but most of Cooper's favorite times with his father had been when they were alone, somehow speaking volumes without saying anything at all.

"You g-gonna marry her?"

"Huh?" Where had that come from? "You talking about Millie?"

His old man nodded. "Sh-she's a good g-girl."

"I think so, too, but that doesn't mean I'd marry her. Where in the world would you get an idea like that?" A beauty of a rainbow trout nibbled at his line, but darted away.

"S-seen you two t-together. Look g-good."

"Thanks, but that doesn't mean we're marriage material." Bedroom material? That was a whole other story. They might've only shared one night, but it'd been beyond hot. What he wouldn't give to try again—only this time in a proper bed.

"Th-think about it."

"I will," Cooper said, "but don't you think that'd be a little odd? Me picking up where Jim left off?"

"Sh-she needs a good man. Th-that's what you have b-become."

Cooper's eyes stung.

How long had he craved hearing exactly that from his father? But when it came to the chemistry he shared with Millie, her opinion was the only one that mattered. Lately, they'd gotten along about as well as a pillowcase filled with wet cats. He didn't know what he'd done to piss her off, but apparently, it must've been major.

"Wait—could you please say that again? I'm sure I didn't hear you right. There's probably a bad connection." Friday afternoon, Millie stood in the kitchen on the phone with the principal of LeeAnn's school, glaring at her gorgeous chicken coop, wishing anyone but Cooper had built it for her. That way, she wouldn't have to think nice things about him every time she gathered eggs.

"Mrs. Hansen, your daughter was caught in a compromising situation with a fellow student. We have rules against this, and she's received a week's worth of after-school detention. Because she rides the bus, that means you'll need to pick her up each day."

Holding her free hand to her suddenly pounding forehead, Millie forced a deep breath. "You must be mistaken. LeeAnn doesn't even talk to boys. I'll of course leave right away to pick her up, but this just can't be right."

"I realize news of this nature must be difficult to hear, Mrs. Hansen, but our security guard has video footage. Your daughter's identity is unmistakable."

After hanging up, Millie was so scattered, she couldn't even find her keys.

"What's up?" Cooper asked when she continued her

search in the office. He sat at the computer, answering emails.

Clint napped in a nearby armchair with his feet up on the matching ottoman.

"I just got the craziest call from LeeAnn's school, and it has me rattled. The principal said she was caught in a compromising position with a boy. What does that even mean?" She looked under a magazine pile with no luck. "LeeAnn doesn't even talk to boys, but he said they've got video proof. Anyway, I have to get over to the school to pick her up and get this whole thing straightened out."

"Go w-with her," a groggy Clint barked from his corner.

Millie shook her head. "Cooper, you should stay here in case your father needs anything. Plus, someone needs to be here when J.J. gets home."

"*I* can w-watch him," Clint said. "Not *in-val-id.*"

"I know," she said to her father-in-law, "but if you're watching J.J., who's going to watch you?"

"She makes a good point." Cooper shut down the desktop unit.

"G-go w-with her," Clint insisted. "M-Millie too upset to d-drive."

"Mill?" Cooper asked from his perch on the edge of the desk. "What do you think?"

She pressed her fingers to her pounding temples. Though she'd never needed Cooper more, in light of her pregnancy, she didn't want to lean on him. She needed to be strong enough that when he left, she felt capable of carrying on. That said, he wasn't gone yet. Would it be so awful to accept his help one last time?

"All right," she finally answered, but mostly because

she feared that without another adult present, if it turned out her precious baby girl truly had done what the principal accused her of, then Millie just might lose what little remained of her cool.

Seated in the principal's office alongside Cooper, never had Millie been more grateful for his presence. He'd been a rock for her on the long trip into town, repeatedly assuring her everything would be okay until she'd almost believed he was right.

But that had been before Principal Conroy turned his computer monitor around so they could all see the alleged event.

The more that unfolded onscreen, the more LeeAnn kissed some boy Millie had never even seen, then laughed and thrust out her rapidly developing breasts, the sicker Millie grew.

Acting on autopilot, she reached to Cooper for support, clasping his hand and appreciating his hearty squeeze of hers.

"Mrs. Hansen, I understand you're upset, but I'll need you to sign this document, stating that you've seen the evidence and accept LeeAnn's punishment."

"Of course…" Her hand shook so badly, that she had trouble writing her name.

"I can tell this is a shock to you, but sadly, it's not as uncommon as you might think. Now, I'm not suggesting there's a problem in your home, but I know LeeAnn lost her father at an impressionable age, which can sometimes lead to this sort of reaching out for male attention. The statistics on teen pregnancy are sobering, so you'll want to do everything you can to nip this behavior—"

"Stop right there," Cooper said. "LeeAnn kissed a

boy. I think we're a bit premature in declaring her a teenage mom."

While Cooper waged battle on her daughter's behalf, Millie couldn't help but think how ironic it was that she would soon become an unwed mother.

"I'm sorry you feel that way," the principal said in regard to one of Cooper's comments. Millie had been so deep into her own thoughts, she hadn't paid attention to the growing rift between the two men. "Mrs. Hansen, LeeAnn must be present in after-school detention each day next week or face expulsion. You'll be able to pick her up promptly at four thirty-five."

Cooper led the two ladies in his life to the truck.

They hadn't even had time to put their seat belts on when Millie lit into her daughter. "What do you think you were doing? You're too young for kissing— let alone, kissing at school."

Her daughter had the gall to roll her eyes. "God, Mom, I'm almost twelve."

"Yeah, well, if you plan on making it to the ripe old age of thirteen, you'd better cut that sass."

Cooper reversed out of their parking spot and headed home.

"You're so lame," LeeAnn fired back. "Uncle Cooper knew I made out with Damon, and he didn't care."

Cooper tightened his grip on the wheel. Did his niece seriously just rat him out?

"What?" Millie swung her attention back to him. "Is that true?"

"Yes and no. It's complicated, and she promised she'd never do it again."

"She *promised?* Lee's eleven! Didn't you ever lie to

your parents to get out of trouble? Only, that's right, you're not her parent, are you?"

"No…" Because Millie was understandably upset, he'd give her a pass on scolding him. He was more pissed at himself and his niece.

"Then if you caught my daughter doing something she shouldn't have been, why didn't you tell me?"

"Truth? I wanted her to like me."

Millie covered her face with her hands. "A parent doesn't have that luxury, Cooper."

"Guys, please stop fighting." LeeAnn had started crying, but Cooper suspected they were crocodile tears. "Mom, Uncle Cooper did yell at me when he caught me in the hall kissing Damon."

"When?" Millie inquired.

"The night of the science fair. Damon asked me to be his girlfriend, and said I had to kiss him."

"Cooper," Millie asked, "from the start, tell me what you know that I don't."

He sighed while zigzagging through traffic. "Look, that night, when we separated to find the kids, I stumbled across Lee and this punk. They were kissing, and I told her quite clearly to knock it off. She promised she'd never do it again. End of story."

"See, Mom?" LeeAnn braced her arms over the extended cab's front seat. "He didn't even care."

Millie snapped, "Sit back and put on your seat belt."

"Oh—I cared, all right," Cooper said to LeeAnn. "The only reason I didn't tell your mom was because she's already stressed enough. If you'd held up your end of the bargain, no one ever needed to know."

"Now you're stooping so low as to bargain with an eleven-year-old?"

"It wasn't like that," he said. Only seeing the incident now through Millie's eyes, he saw that it was. If he'd practiced full disclosure back in February, they wouldn't be fighting now. "I told her to stop, and never kiss again."

"Sure." Millie crossed her arms. "That makes about as much sense as if your father had told you to never drink again after you'd run down your mother. How could I be so stupid as to think you're even half the man your brother was? Jim might not have been flashy, but he was good. He knew better than to turn a blind eye to an eleven-year-old making out!"

On that dirty note, Cooper whipped her truck onto the busy highway's shoulder and killed the engine. "Did you honestly just go there? What happened with my mom has nothing to do with this. But you know what, Mill? If due to my lack of expert parental judgment, you're uncomfortable with me being around your kids, I'll be happy to take off first thing in the morning— that is, assuming you're okay with a screwup like me staying the night?"

"Sorry to barge in like this," Millie said to Lynette a little over an hour later. "I didn't know where else to turn."

"Of course." Lynette drew her into the simple ranch house she shared with Zane. "You know you're welcome here anytime."

Millie nodded while making her way to the sofa. Even though she'd delivered her big speech to Cooper, she'd been so upset that the moment he'd parked, she'd run off, leaving him to watch Clint and the kids. She was such a hypocrite, accusing him of being a rotten uncle when she wasn't exactly Mother of the Year. "I told you the basics of our fight over the phone, but I kind of left off the reason why Cooper and Lee's secret hit me so hard."

"Okay…" Her friend sat beside her.

"Is Zane in the house?"

"Nope. Can you believe it? He's out for a run. He's getting pretty buff." Lynette fanned herself. "God bless Cooper and his SEAL Session workout."

Millie rolled her eyes. She was not in the mood for singing Cooper's praises.

"So? What did you need to talk about? We have the house to ourselves and I'm all ears."

Where do I start?

Chapter 17

"C-calm down." Clint sat in the straight-backed chair next to Cooper's dresser. How his father had even gotten up the stairs was beyond him, but stubborn had always been Clint's middle name. "M-Millie didn't mean it. G-girl's got a w-wicked temper. S-stay."

"Love to, Dad, but I can't. I needed to be back on base a month ago." But more important, if he had to spend one more day around Millie, pretending he felt nothing for her but platonic affection, he'd go freakin' mad.

He felt awful about what had gone down with Lee-Ann. Millie was clearly right in that he had no business being around kids. The crazy thing was, though, the more he'd been around his niece and nephew, the more he craved being with them.

He'd miss them when he was gone.

"M-marry her."

"Dad…" Clint scooped the meager contents from his sock drawer into his duffel.

"I m-mean it. Worth a t-try."

"When—if—I ever get married, I don't want to just try, but really make it work. I want what Jim and Millie used to have. The perfect family."

His dad shook his head. "N-no such thing as p-perfect. All m-marriage is w-work."

"I don't know… You and Mom looked pretty good."

Clint smiled. "Your m-mom was a s-saint. I was the p-problem. S-stay. Give M-Millie—yourself—time. She looks at you l-like your m-mom once looked at m-me."

Cooper wished he could believe that, but he knew better.

Millie didn't want him, but to recreate what she'd shared with his brother. Unfortunately, as she'd been all too happy to point out, he'd never be half the man his brother had been.

"Whoa…" Lynette finished her wine in one big gulp. "I never saw this one coming. You and Cooper on the kitchen table? That's hot stuff…" She refilled her glass and took another deep swig. "You have to tell him about the baby, Mill. Like, now."

"But how? Especially after he came right out and said he doesn't have any interest in becoming a dad. And what about this thing with LeeAnn? He should've come to me right away about something that important."

"Agreed, but, sweetie, you have to understand that he hasn't been around kids since he was a kid himself. You can't expect him to right out of the gate be *WonderDad*."

"I know, but—"

"No—there's nothing more for you to say. You have to tell him. March your butt straight home and admit you've been scared about how he'd take the news, but that you're sorry, and would like to have an adult conversation about how the two of you plan to raise this child."

Millie nibbled her pinkie fingernail. "You do know you sound like a female *Dr. Phil?*"

"Good. You need some sense drilled into you, and since he's not available for consultation, guess I'll have to do." She stood, taking Millie by her hands to force her from the couch then push her toward the door. "Tell him. *Now.*"

"But why do you have to go?" J.J. asked once Cooper had loaded his truck and was ready to hit the highway. "I love you."

"I love you, too, bud." He knelt, wrapping his nephew in a hug.

J.J. tossed his chubby little arms around Cooper's neck and wouldn't let go. "Please, don't leave us. I thought you were going to be our dad."

"Sorry, dude, but you already had a great dad. I'm just your uncle. I promise I'll come visit, but you don't really need me to stay. You've got Grandpa Clint and your mom and sister and friends. Trust me, you'll hardly even notice I'm gone." Still holding J.J., Cooper stood then pushed open the screen door.

"Yes, I will…" The sniffling boy held on tighter.

Clint and LeeAnn followed them outside.

Seemed like just yesterday when Cooper had returned on that blustery January morning. The earth had felt as dead as he had. Everything had been cold and brown and dull. Now, on this night, crickets chirped, the temperature was downright balmy and, just as Millie promised back in March, everything in their world was green and fresh and new. Everything, that is, except for him. He was leaving this ranch feeling as defeated as when he'd come.

LeeAnn asked, "Uncle Cooper, are you leaving because of me?" The girl's question shredded what little remained of his heart.

"Lord, angel, no. I need to get back to the Navy. I know you and your mom will work all of this out. Just please try not to grow up so fast, okay? Promise, you'll have plenty of time for boys once you hit high school. But even then, I'll expect you to shoot me an email about them—you know, just so I can run a background check and make sure they're okay."

As moths danced in the porch lights' glow, she laughed through tears—this time, genuine.

Cooper's eyes stung, and if he hadn't had such a tight hold on his precious nephew, he'd have wiped them. As it was, he just let his tears fall. "I love you guys, so much. Be good for your mom, okay?"

"I will," J.J. said when Cooper set him down.

"C-call when you get there safe." Clint moved in for a hug. "I l-love you, son."

"Love you, too, Dad."

"P-please come home s-soon."

"I will. First chance I get leave." He had to cut this off. He'd seen enough of his SEAL buddies leaving their families to know long goodbyes only dragged out the inevitable. "All right, guys…" He gave all of them one last hug. "I should get going. Talk to you soon."

He walked to his truck on wooden legs. He didn't

want to go. The whole time he'd been on the ranch, he'd kept a part of himself back in Virginia. But now? He'd give anything if he and Millie could've worked past their issues and made a go at being a couple. He would've taken it slow. He would do anything for her—including leaving, because she'd told him that was what she wanted.

The sound of tires crunching on gravel alerted him to there being another vehicle on the drive. He glanced that way to see Millie behind her truck's wheel.

Damn. He'd hoped to have been gone before she got home.

She parked alongside him, her expression startled when she looked in the truck bed to find his duffel, ditty bag and a few boxes of mementos he wanted with him. The beach diorama J.J. had made for him was precious cargo, so it rode on the front seat.

"Are you leaving tonight? Now?" she asked.

J.J. bounded down the front porch stairs. "Mommy, please make him stay! *Please.*"

She hefted her crying son into her arms. "Honey, I wish I could, but Uncle Cooper has a very important job. The whole country needs him—not just us."

If only for a second he thought that was true—that Millie needed him, wanted him—dynamite couldn't have pried Cooper from this place.

"I don't care…" J.J. grew inconsolable.

"LeeAnn, could you please take your brother." Millie set J.J. down, kissing both of his tearstained cheeks, before aiming him toward the house. "Clint, I need a minute alone with Cooper. If you all have said your goodbyes, do you think you could watch the kids for a few minutes while I say mine?"

"W-will do." Clint ushered the kids inside.

"What do you want?" Cooper asked. He was sorry if his sharp words came off as cruel, but she hadn't exactly been a sweetheart to him—more like a lipstick-wearing rattler.

"We need to talk. I thought you weren't leaving till the morning?"

"Plans change."

"Coop…"

"What, Millie? I can't think of another thing you could say to me that hasn't already been said." Unless she wanted to admit she did feel something for him, and that she was as tired of pretending she didn't as he was. Otherwise, he was done.

"Well…" She licked her lips. "I'm not sure where to start."

"Then let's leave it at that."

Her eyes pooled. She opened her mouth, but no words came out, only a strangled sob.

He took it as his sign to go. Didn't she have any idea how crazy he was about her? If she'd given the faintest green light, he'd have retired from the Navy to stay. But she hadn't, and he'd grown weary of trying to please her when clearly, in her eyes, nothing he could ever do would be right.

"Goodbye, Millie." Before his own tears fell, he climbed in the truck. He refused to give her the satisfaction of seeing him fall apart.

But he did—fall apart, cry and punch the damn wheel.

He mourned not only the people he was leaving behind, but also his future that no longer held the slightest appeal. He'd joined the Navy looking for an escape, but all he wanted now was to be found.

Brewer's Falls—Millie, J.J., LeeAnn and his dad— were his home.

Driving through town, he now saw the appeal. Like him, with the changing seasons, it'd been reborn. Cascading flower baskets hung from every light post, and empty shop fronts had been filled with flea-market-style booths of seasonal wares. Potted flowers lined the sidewalks. Mack's bar and the restaurant had set out picnic tables—all currently filled by couples and families dining under the stars.

Cooper wanted so badly to once again be part of this place, but it just wasn't meant to be. And so he sped up, hoping the more miles he put between him and his pain, the better off he'd feel.

After the glow from Cooper's truck's taillights had faded, Millie didn't seek the comfort of her children or father-in-law to cry out her frustration. Instead, she went to the one place where she felt most connected to Cooper—the chicken palace he'd created.

She sat sideways on the swing, barefoot with her knees drawn to her chest.

Why hadn't she told him? She knew Cooper. One hint about her pregnancy would've kept him on the ranch. But what then? Would he marry her? Only to live out the rest of their lives resenting each other for being saddled in a loveless match? She deserved better. She demanded better.

Trouble was, only with the finality of watching him drive away did she realize she did love him—with every breath of her being. He was the first thing she thought of in the morning, and the last thing at night. Of course her kids meant the world to her, but somehow Cooper had also earned his way inside their world, only he didn't seem to know it.

She cupped her hands to her belly, connecting with the tiny life inside. Would she tell Cooper before or after their child's birth? She assumed once she did tell him that he'd want to be part of their baby's future, but what if deep down he didn't? He'd told her parenting sounded like a nightmare. Did she really want a man with that kind of attitude around her newborn?

Eyes closed, she prayed for peace, but her stomach kept churning with the phrase *I should've told him.*

The next day Cooper made it to St. Louis before needing a nap.

He'd always been fascinated by the Arch, so he pulled off I-70 to crash in the grassy park. To say his mood was dark would be an understatement. Judging by the amount of hyper kids and chasing parents, he'd have been better off at a grungy truck stop.

After finding a shady spot under a tree, he tried shutting his eyes, but his mind kept replaying J.J.'s crying plea for him to stay. Or the way LeeAnn had assumed her wrongdoing had been the cause for his leaving when nothing could be further from the truth.

He wanted the responsibility for his hasty departure solely on Millie, but that wouldn't be true.

When they'd made love, everything changed. They'd unleashed a genie that couldn't be put back in its bottle.

Even if he'd wanted to, he couldn't stop wanting her. But no—there was more to it than that. What he felt went deeper, with an infinite number of layers. He could be furious with her one moment, but still crave talking with her the next. He loved everything about her, from her hair to her laugh and smile. The way she smelled all flowery with a hint of sweet. He loved her kids and her house that'd once been his. And damn, did he love her kisses…

What did all of that add up to? Was he losing his mind, or could he possibly be *in love* with her?

That thought forced him upright.

Bracing his hands behind him, he stared out at the Mississippi River, breathing in the rich, musky smell.

I love Millie.

The solution to his every problem was so simple, he felt stupid for not having seen it before. But there it was. His entire adult life, he'd been trained to handle any situation with maximum efficiency and minimum effort, so why couldn't he apply those same ideals to a mule-stubborn woman?

On his feet, he strode to his truck with new purpose.

He had a lot of miles to go, but once he reached his destination, if his plan went the way he hoped, he might not travel again for a nice, long while.

It'd been ages since Millie had checked the cattle on horseback, but with Cooper gone, Sassy needed the exercise, and she needed fresh air to help her forget his leaving. It'd barely been twenty-four hours since he'd been gone, but she still couldn't seem to swallow past the knot in her throat.

It didn't help that she'd been up half the night, trying to console J.J. He didn't understand how the man he'd grown to love could leave him. Millie tried explaining about Cooper's job, but he was too young to understand.

LeeAnn hadn't fared much better.

And then there was poor Clint. The only time Millie had seen him cry since losing Jim was after Cooper drove away.

Millie had needed to be strong for her family, but how could she with Cooper's son or daughter growing inside? She should've told him. He deserved to know. But pride had gotten in the way. She couldn't bear begging for his affection.

The day was beautiful, with the temperature near eighty. The sky kissed the snow-capped Rockies, and a light breeze swayed the rolling prairie's tall grasses. She should've been tipping her head back, drinking in the sun. Instead, she focused on reaching the herd. She carefully counted heads then checked that they all looked healthy. This time of year, there was plenty of grass for them to graze on, and they drank from the spring-fed ponds.

With her work done, she sat back in the saddle, taking in the view.

How different would her life be if she had told Cooper about the baby? Would he be here with her now?

From this part of the family land, she had a clear view of their dirt road. A dust cloud rose at the end nearest town. Was the vehicle a neighbor approaching, or maybe the FedEx man—feeding Lynette's catalog addiction?

Millie began the short ride back to the barn, keeping an eye on the vehicle as it approached, glad for the distraction of getting her mind off Cooper and her sense of loss. She hadn't realized how much she'd appreciated his compliments about her cooking or appearance. Then there were those sexy, slow grins. He wasn't just handsome, but kind—not only to her, but her kids.

From her vantage, still a good half mile from the house, it looked as if the vehicle on the road had turned into their drive.

Once the dust settled, a black Ford truck that looked an awful lot like Cooper's sat parked in his usual spot.

Her chest tightened. Was she seeing a mirage?

Though the doctor told her riding should be safe as long as she didn't try anything fancy, Millie quickened Sassy's pace not quite to a gallop, but at least faster than her casual mosey.

Could it really be him?

If so, why? Had he forgotten something?

The ten-minute ride seemed to take forever, but when she finally reached the barn, she was gifted by an incredible sight.

There stood Cooper in all his glory—faded jeans, black T-shirt and his beat-up straw hat, which, to his credit, he removed when she approached.

"Hey," he said, taking Sassy's reins.

Millie gingerly climbed off her ride. "Hey, yourself. Forget something?"

He took a step forward, and then another until before Millie had time to process what was happening, Cooper cupped her cheek and kissed her. "Hell, yeah, I forgot something—you. I love you. And before you go and throw out some excuse why we shouldn't be together, I want to tell you why we should. You're beautiful and you and J.J. and Lee make me so happy. I said I didn't want kids, but I lied. I want dozens—but only if they're yours and mine—*ours.*"

Was this really happening? Millie's eyes welled and

the tension that had caused a constant knot in her stomach vanished. "You love me?"

"Yes." He took a step back, adopting a defensive posture. Hands out, as if welcoming a fight, he said, "Come on, I'm sure you have an argument all loaded up to shoot, but I'm not having it. We're going to get married and that's that. I'm not taking no for an answer."

Millie's emotions had gotten the best of her, and all she felt capable of doing was crying.

"Well? What do you have to say?"

So much. But nothing seemed to matter other than kissing him again. Even though she hadn't gone anywhere, pressing her lips against him felt akin to coming home. In only a few short months, he'd come to mean the world to her, but then hadn't he always in one way or another? For as long as she could remember, they'd always been friends. Now, they'd just change their status to friends with benefits and kids.

"That was nice," he said when they paused for air, "but you still haven't answered my question."

She bowed her head. "First, there's something you need to know. For weeks, I've tried finding the right way to say this, but I kept flubbing it up. Anyway…" After forcing a deep breath, she blurted, "I'm pregnant."

For a second he looked pale, but then his color returned along with a broad smile. "For real?"

She nodded. "Is that okay?" Such a stupid question. Even if it wasn't—okay—there wasn't a whole lot they could do about it now.

"Oh, sugar, it's way more than okay…" Dropping Sassy's reins, Cooper hugged her, lifting her feet off the ground to spin her in a slow circle, all the while kissing her till she wasn't sure how she'd ever lived without this man's love. After setting her to her feet, he tossed his hat high and let out a whoop. "I'm gonna be a daddy!"

Hands pressed to her flushed cheeks, Millie wasn't sure whether to laugh, cry or both. "I was so afraid to tell you. The last thing I wanted was for you to feel trapped. You've got your career back in Virginia. What're you going to do?"

"I've put about twelve hours of thought into that and I want to run something past you. That cattle auction I scheduled should bring in a pretty penny, but not enough to get the ranch totally out of the red. Plus, we'll have some lean years while we rebuild the herd. What would you think if I retire from the Navy so we can open a sideline business?"

"What were you thinking? Teaching riding lessons?"

"Bigger." He grinned. "You know how I've been helping Zane and some of our other friends work off their beer bellies?"

She nodded.

"Okay, picture this—we'll build a bunkhouse, and an obstacle course, and then run weekend retreats for guys—and gals—who want to push themselves hard enough to see if they have what it takes to be a SEAL. What do you think?"

"I think most anything you do sounds great to me."

He drew her into another kiss so hot she was surprised the ground didn't have scorch marks beneath her boots. "I love you, Millie Hansen."

"Mmm…" They kissed again. "I love you, Cooper Hansen."

"When we get married," he teased, "are you gonna keep your last name?"

She feigned deep thought. "Being a modern girl, I might go with a hyphen."

"Anyone ever told you you're a sassy little thing?"

The horse heard her name and neighed.

"Uh-oh." Millie laughed. "Looks like I have competition for your affections."

Cooper waved off her concern. "I'm man enough for both of you. So where are the kids? I want to tell them our news."

She gasped. "Oh, no! I totally forgot. Remember Lee's detention? They're both still at school."

After a quick run inside to tell Clint their news, Millie was all too happy to sit alongside Cooper while he broke a few speed laws to get them to Wagon Wheel Elementary in time.

At school, Cooper took Millie's hand, giving her a light squeeze. "Ready?"

"Absolutely. They're going to be so excited."

Since the detention kids still had five more minutes, they found J.J. in the library.

He caught sight of his uncle and rocketed in his direction, colliding into him. "You came back!"

"I love you and your mom and sister too much to stay away." Cooper lifted the boy into his arms for a hug. "I'm sorry I left you for even one night."

"It's okay." J.J. rested his head on his uncle's shoulder. When he closed his teary eyes, his smile was so serene that Millie had to grab a few tissues from the librarian's desk to blot her own eyes.

The happy trio went to find LeeAnn in the cafeteria.

"Uncle Cooper?" She had the same reaction as her little brother, running to hug him.

"I missed you," Cooper said. "Have any pretty dresses?"

"A few. Why?"

Millie couldn't contain her own excitement. "We'll have to get you a new one. That is, if you'll agree to be my maid of honor."

"Wait—are you two getting married?" LeeAnn looked to her mom, then her uncle. "But would that make Uncle Cooper our dad?"

"Your stepdad," he said. "Your real dad should come first in your heart, but I hope you'll save a little room for me."

"Well, yeah, but…" She stopped to cross her arms. "Does this mean you're always going to be around to see if I'm with boys?"

"Yes, ma'am."

She groaned. "Mom, is it too late to call the wedding off?"

"Afraid so." Millie slipped her arm around her daughter's shoulders and laced her fingers with Cooper's. The happiness inside her was indescribable. She'd never dreamed of getting a second chance at love, but here it was, all shiny and new and hers for the taking. All she had to do was get her cowboy SEAL to a preacher. And she planned on accomplishing that pretty darned fast. "I've got my heart set on becoming a June bride."

"Cool!" On their walk to the truck, J.J. took Cooper's hat and set it on his own head. "Can we have wedding cake?"

"You bet," Cooper said.

"And punch?"

He kissed her son's freckled cheek. "All you want."

"Wait a minute," Millie interjected. "Don't drink so much that you get sick. I'm not sure about having to take a sick little boy along on our honeymoon."

"How about if J.J. promises to drink just enough punch that he doesn't get sick, then we all go on a *familymoon?*"

LeeAnn wrinkled her nose. "What's that?"

Cooper opened the back door of the truck. "A *familymoon* will be our very own invention. To celebrate our wedding, I think we should all go somewhere fun."

"The zoo?" J.J. suggested.

"Mount Vesuvius?" LeeAnn tossed out.

"How about Disney World?" Cooper said.

By unanimous decision, the Magic Kingdom was deemed the perfect spot to begin their magical new lives.

Epilogue

To celebrate her and Cooper's first wedding anniversary, Millie had wanted to throw an elegant dinner party in the front yard. She'd dreamed of stringing romantic white lights in the trees and having hundreds of flickering candles.

What she got was a seat on a hard rodeo arena stand, sitting alongside a very pregnant Lynette.

J.J. and LeeAnn were off playing with friends, and Millie jiggled Cooper Junior on her knee. He was already a handful, but just like his father, he was so cute, she didn't much mind.

Cooper's business venture had gone better than even he'd imagined, and his SEAL strength-building and self-protection retreats were already booked into the next year.

"Think they'll win?" Lynette asked when Cooper and Zane were in their respective chutes.

"I don't know," Millie said, "but they sure look good in those red shirts."

While professional team calf ropers got the job done in as little as 3.5 seconds, it took their guys 6.7.

"Sorry we couldn't pull out the win for you." Cooper took his son, sweeping him high in the air.

Millie was next in line for his attention with a leisurely kiss. As handsome as he was, Cooper was a fan favorite on their local rodeo circuit, but Millie was proud to be the only recipient of his kisses.

Clint strode up to shake both men's hands. He'd made a full recovery and had as much fun at rodeos as his son. "Fine ride, boys. You made me proud. You'll pull out a win next time."

"Thanks, Dad." Cooper shifted the baby to his other arm. "Would you mind watching this guy for a minute?"

"Is it time?" Clint asked with an exaggerated wink.

"Time for what?" Millie asked.

"Thanks for keeping a secret, Dad."

Clint grinned while jiggling his grandson. "We didn't tell your momma a thing, did we?"

Cooper drew Millie off into the shadows. "Damn, you look hot."

"Thanks, cowboy." She gave him a kiss. "You're looking mighty fine yourself."

"I appreciate that, ma'am, but tonight, being our first anniversary, I wanted you to know how much I love you, and how this has pretty much been the best year of my life."

"Aw…" Her husband's sweet talk never failed to

make her heart sing. "Thank you, honey. I love you, too."

"Okay, so you know how we pretty much had a budget wedding?"

"I thought our day was beautiful. Marrying you under your mom's rose trellis was the only place I'd have wanted it to be."

"I'm glad," he said, acting all fidgety, "but now that we've finally got a little extra money, I want you to have this. It's high time you had something to really show you're mine."

From his shirt pocket, he withdrew a small, mangled paper sack, and handed it to her.

Hoping she was doing a good job of masking her confusion, she smiled. "Thanks?"

"Go ahead. Open it." He grinned like a kid on Christmas morning.

She unrolled the paper to find a lopsided Oreo. "You got me a cookie?"

His smile only grew. "Eat it."

"Okay?" She started to bite into it, then he drew her hand down. "Not like that. You've got to twist it apart, then lick the icing—only, be careful. I don't want you to get hurt."

"Honey, you're acting strange. Are you sure you didn't get hurt during your run?"

Sighing, he said, "Would you go ahead and lick the damn cookie?"

She laughed. "Sorry. You don't have to get all huffy."

"Then lick, and I won't have to."

Finally doing his bidding, she twisted the top off her favorite treat then gasped. It wouldn't even take one lick to see Cooper had hidden a diamond ring in the icing.

Squealing, she kissed him, licked the ring, gobbled part of the cookie, then kissed him again. "Put it on for me?"

He did. In the process, kissing her hand, then lips.

"This is beyond gorgeous," she said, gazing at the square-cut diamond. "You shouldn't have."

"Want me to take it back?" he teased.

"Just try, and see what happens."

"There you go again with that sass." He drew her tight against him, bowing his head to kiss her good and thorough beneath his wide hat brim.

"Eeew!" J.J. came tearing around the corner with his friend Cayden in tow. "You guys are gross!"

LeeAnn and Kara followed.

LeeAnn asked, "Did you give Mom her ring and the trip?"

He conked his head. "I forgot the trip."

Both kids laughed.

J.J. started jumping. "Show her! Show her!"

From his back pocket, he produced with a flourish a slip of paper. "Since our honeymoon got hijacked, and you're always talking about how much you'd like to see the world, how about a second honeymoon to Machu Picchu?"

"You mean the ruins? In Peru?"

Grinning, he said, "Those would be the ones."

That earned him another kiss!

Millie asked, "Did everyone know I was getting all of this, but me?"

"Pretty much." Her daughter and friend laughed while admiring her bauble.

"Thank you," she said to her husband once the kids

had run off again. "Not just for the ring and trip, but for coming home—for staying home."

"Mill…" He cupped her face with his hands. "Haven't you figured it out? You and the kids are my home. You're my everything."

Millie rested her head on her husband's shoulder while they sauntered hand in hand back into the crowd. What a great night. What a great life. Spying a shooting star, she thanked Jim for sending her his brother—her very own cowboy SEAL.

* * * * *

Since 2006, *New York Times* bestselling author **Cathy McDavid** has been happily penning contemporary Westerns for Harlequin. Every day, she gets to write about handsome cowboys riding the range or busting a bronc. It's a tough job, but she's willing to make the sacrifice. Cathy shares her Arizona home with her own real-life sweetheart and a trio of odd pets. Her grown twins have left to embark on lives of their own, and she couldn't be prouder of their accomplishments.

Books by Cathy McDavid

Harlequin Western Romance

Mustang Valley

Last Chance Cowboy
Her Cowboy's Christmas Wish
Baby's First Homecoming
Cowboy for Keeps
Her Holiday Rancher
Come Home, Cowboy
Having the Rancher's Baby
Rescuing the Cowboy
A Baby for the Deputy
The Cowboy's Twin Surprise

Harlequin American Romance

Reckless, Arizona

More Than a Cowboy
Her Rodeo Man
The Bull Rider's Son

Visit the Author Profile page at Harlequin.com for more titles.

HER RODEO MAN

CATHY McDAVID

To Mike...and the incredible spark you always ignite. Here's to forever, my love.

Chapter 1

The day Ryder Beckett swore would never come had arrived. He'd returned to Reckless, Arizona, and the Easy Money Rodeo Arena. But instead of a hero's welcome, he was slinking home like a scolded puppy with his tail tucked firmly between his legs.

Really slinking. He should be meeting his father in the arena office. In fact, he was five minutes late. Only, Ryder had continued walking. Around the main barn, past the row of outdoor horse stalls, all the way to the horse pastures. There he stopped and forced himself to draw a long breath.

He did want to be here, he told himself. Though, to be honest, he needed to be here. Be somewhere, anyway. Why not Reckless, where he could maybe, possibly, mend a bridge or two? He would if his baby sister, Liberty, had her way. For Ryder, the jury was still out.

Keeping a low profile. Yeah, he decided, that had a better ring to it than slinking. Then again, Ryder possessed a talent for putting a positive spin on things. It was what had propelled him to the top in his field. Stupidity was what led to his downfall.

As he stood at the pasture fence, his leather dress shoes sank deep into the soft dirt. He'd have a chore cleaning them later. At the moment, he didn't care.

When, he absently wondered, was the last time he'd worn a pair of boots? Or ridden a horse, for that matter? The answer came quickly. Five years ago during his last strained visit. He'd sworn then and there he'd never set sight on Reckless again. The aftermath of another falling-out with his mother.

Recent events had altered the circumstance of their enduring disagreement. Liberty, the one most hurt by their mother's lies, had managed to make peace with both their parents. Not so Ryder. His anger at their mother's betrayal hadn't dimmed one bit in the twenty-five years since she'd divorced their father.

Was coming home a mistake? Only time would tell. In any case, he wasn't staying long.

In the pasture, a woman haltered a large black pony and led it slowly toward the gate. Other horses, a half dozen or so pregnant mares, ambled behind, bobbing their heads and swishing their tails. Whatever might be happening, they wanted in on it.

Ryder leaned his forearms on the top fence railing. Even at this distance, he could tell two things: the pony was severely lame, and the woman was spectacularly attractive. Both drew his attention, and, for the moment, his meeting with his father was forgotten.

The two were a study in contrast. While the pony

hobbled painfully, favoring its front left foot, the woman moved with elegance and grace, her long black hair misbehaving in the mild breeze. She stopped frequently to check on the pony and, when she did, rested her hand affectionately on its sleek neck.

Something about her struck a familiar, but elusive, chord with him. Who was she? A memory teased at the fringes of his mind but remained out of reach.

As he watched, the knots of tension residing in his shoulders relaxed. That was until she changed direction and headed toward him. Then, he immediately perked up, and his senses went on high alert.

"Hi," she said as she approached. "Can I help you?"

She was even prettier up close. Large dark eyes analyzed him with unapologetic interest from a model-perfect oval face. Her full mouth stretched into a warm smile impossible not to return. The red T-shirt tucked into a pair of well-worn jeans emphasized her long legs and slim waist.

"I'm meeting someone." He didn't add that he was now ten minutes late or that the someone was, in fact, his father.

"Oh. Okay." She took him in with a glance that said it all. Visitors to the Easy Money didn't usually wear suits and ties.

"Mercer Beckett," Ryder said.

"He's in the office, I think."

"That's what he told me."

At the gate, she paused and tilted her head, her gaze shifting from mild interest to open curiosity. "Can I show you the way?"

"Thanks. I already know it."

"You've been here before?"

"You…could say that. But it's been a while."

"Well, welcome back."

That smile again, familiar but not, and most appealing. It was almost enough to make Ryder break his promise to himself to steer clear of work romances. He'd learned that lesson the hard way and had paid the price with his now defunct career.

Not that he'd be working with this woman exactly. But she was probably a customer of the Becketts, one who boarded her pony at the arena. Close enough.

"You should fire your farrier and find another one." Ryder nodded at the pony. "He or she isn't worth a lick."

The woman's brows arched in surprise and emphasized their elegant shape. "I beg your pardon?"

He indicated the pony's right front hoof. "She has a contracted heel. From incorrect shoeing."

"No offense intended, but you don't exactly strike me as an expert."

"I'm not. But I do have some experience." Living, breathing, eating and sleeping horses for the first half of his life. "You pull that shoe off, and you'll see an immediate improvement."

"Could be laminitis," she countered. "That's common in ponies."

"It's not laminitis."

"You sound sure."

"Remove the shoe, and you'll see." When she hesitated, he added, "What could it hurt?"

"I'll ask one of the hands." She slid the latch and opened the gate.

"I can do it for you. Remove the shoe."

"In those clothes?"

"What's a little dirt?"

She laughed, a low, sexy sound he quite liked. "We'll see."

Was he crazy? Flirting with a potential customer. A woman who could be married with three kids, for all he knew.

She started through the gate, leading the pony. The horses behind her also wanted out and began shoving their way into the narrow opening. A bottleneck formed, with the more aggressive of the horses squealing and nipping at their neighbors.

"Back now." The woman waved a hand, which had almost no effect.

Ryder stepped forward. If the horses succeeded in getting loose, the Easy Money hands would be in for a merry chase.

"I'll help."

Before she could object, he positioned himself between her and the brood mares, blocking their escape. Once she and the pony were on the other side, he swung the gate shut.

"Thank you," she said when he turned around.

"Good thing I happened by. You'd have had a stampede to contend with."

"My hero." Her teasing tone matched the twinkle in her eyes.

"Let me remove that too-small shoe, and I'll really be your hero."

"What about your meeting with Mercer?"

"It can wait."

A small exaggeration. Ryder's father had little patience with people who kept him waiting. Even so, Ryder didn't change his mind.

They began a slow, painful procession toward the

barn. If possible, Ryder would have carried the pony. Fortunately, before long, they reached an empty stall.

"I'll get a rasp and a pair of hoof clippers."

"I'll show you where they're kept."

"Not necessary."

The curiosity was back in her eyes. "I suppose you know where the tack room is, too."

"Center aisle."

"You have been here before."

Feeling her stare following him, he grinned and strode down the aisle toward the tack room. The next instant, he remembered his hard-learned lesson and sobered.

Voluntarily resigned. In order to join his family's business.

That was what his letter to Madison-Monroe Concepts had cited, though there was nothing voluntary about Ryder's termination. He'd quit his job as senior marketing executive rather than be involved in a messy lawsuit with him named as the defendant. At his lawyer's suggestion, he'd left Phoenix the second the ink was dry on the settlement agreement and before his former boss changed his mind.

Which, technically, made him four days early, not late to his meeting with his father.

No one in his family knew the details of his termination. As far as they were concerned, Ryder had undergone a change of heart, prompted by his father's insistence the Easy Money needed a top-notch marketing expert to guide their rapidly growing bucking stock business and a wish to better know his much younger sister, Liberty.

There it was again, *massaging* the truth to obtain a positive slant. In this case, Ryder had his reasons.

By the time he returned to the stall, the woman had tied the pony to a metal pole by the door. Ryder removed his suit jacket and draped it over the stall wall. He'd been warm anyway. September in Arizona was a lot like summer in other states. Next, he unbuttoned the cuffs on his dress shirt and rolled up the sleeves.

The woman—should he introduce himself in order to learn her name?—worriedly combed her fingers through the pony's long mane. "Are you sure we shouldn't call the vet first? My kids will be devastated if anything happened to Cupcake."

So, he'd been right. She did have children. Which meant there was a father somewhere in the picture. Ryder was almost relieved and promptly dialed down the charm.

"She'll be fine. I promise."

Lifting the pony's sore hoof, he balanced it on his bent knee. Next, he removed the rasp from his back pocket where he'd placed it and began filing down the ends of the nails used to fasten the shoe to the hoof. Once that was done, the shoe could be removed without causing further damage to the hoof. A few good pries with the clippers, and the shoe fell to the stall floor with a dull clink.

Ryder gently released Cupcake's hoof and straightened. He swore the pony let out an audible sigh.

"She'll feel brand-new by morning."

"You won't take offense if I have Mercer look at her?" the woman said. "Just to be on the safe side."

"Not at all." Ryder chuckled. "I wouldn't trust me,

either, if I were you." He brushed at his soiled slacks. "Given the clothes."

She flashed him that gorgeous smile.

Kids. Likely a husband. He had to remember that. She'd be an easy one to fall for, and Ryder had a bad habit of choosing unwisely. Just look at his current situation. Unemployed and returning home all because he'd gotten involved with the wrong person.

"By the way, I'm—"

"Hey, there you are!" Ryder's father walked briskly toward them, his whiskered face alight with joy. "I've been waiting."

"Sorry. Got waylaid." All the tension that had seeped out earlier returned. New knots formed. Sooner or later, he was going to have to tell his father the truth about the real reason he'd quit his job, and he wasn't looking forward to it. "How are you, Dad?" Outside the stall, the two men engaged in a back-thumping hug.

"Good, now that you're here." He held Ryder at arm's length. "Glad to see you, son."

"I was helping…" Ryder turned to the woman, a little taken aback by her startled expression.

"You're Ryder Beckett?" The question hinged on an accusation.

"On my good days."

Only his father laughed. "You should hear what they call him on his bad days."

The woman stared at him. "You weren't supposed to be here till Saturday."

"I got away early." Ryder felt his defenses rising, though he wasn't sure why. And how was it she knew his schedule? That elusive familiarity from earlier returned. "Have we met before?"

"This is Tatum Mayweather," his father said. "You remember her. She's your sister Cassidy's best friend."

Tatum. Of course. The name brought his vague memories into sharp focus. "It's been a lot of years," he said by way of an excuse.

"It has." She removed the halter from Cupcake and shut the stall door behind her. "If you'll excuse me, my lunch hour is over, and I need to get back to work. Your mother's been answering the phone for me in the house."

"Guess I'll see you around, then."

"Sure."

"Bright and early tomorrow morning." His father beamed. "Tatum's our office manager. After I give you a tour of the bucking stock operation, she can go over our contracts with you."

Office manager. That explained her cool reaction to him.

If Ryder accepted his family offer to be the arena's new head of marketing and client relations, he'd be in charge of advertising and promotion, duties currently performed by Tatum.

"Look, it's not…"

What could he say? That he wasn't after her job? Okay, maybe he was, but only parts of it and only temporarily. She, however, didn't know that.

"See you in the morning." She left, her movements no longer graceful but stilted.

Well, at least Ryder didn't have to worry about becoming involved with a coworker. Any chance of that happening was walking away with Ms. Mayweather.

Only after she'd disappeared through a door across from the tack room did Ryder realize she hadn't asked Mercer to check on Cupcake.

* * *

Ryder's father kept up a near constant stream of conversation as they covered the short distance from the barn to the house. "Thanks for coming. It means a lot to me. Your mother, too."

It was no secret Ryder's father still loved his ex-wife and intended to win her back. Ryder had agreed to help and support him with the expansion of the rodeo arena. He didn't, however, understand his father's enduring feelings regarding his mother.

"Hope you're hungry," his father said. "Your mother's fixed enough food for a dozen people."

"I don't want her going to any trouble."

"Your early arrival put her in quite a tizzy. She made an emergency run to the grocery store last night just to have the food you like on hand."

"I'm not picky, Dad."

"Well, this is a big day for her. She's nervous."

She wasn't the only one. Ryder had been fighting anxiety for days now.

Five years was a long time to go without seeing one's mother. They'd spoken on the phone, but only occasionally when he happened to call his sisters. Mostly on birthdays and Christmas. One or the other insisted he talk to their mother, too. He usually relented, solely for his sisters' sakes. Ryder simply couldn't get past what he saw as his mother's betrayal.

His father always defended his mother, saying she was right to divorce him. Ryder didn't see it that way. She cared only about herself and hadn't once considered the effect losing their father would have on her children.

Her selfishness, however, wasn't the only reason his return was difficult. She'd lied. For twenty-five years.

To everyone. And like the divorce, the lies had stolen parts of their lives they could never get back.

"The girls can't wait to see you." His father talked about Ryder's grown sisters as if they were young. Then again, Cassidy had been only ten when their parents divorced, to Ryder's twelve, and Liberty not even born yet. His father probably did think of Ryder's sisters as "girls." "Cassidy's volunteering at Benjie's school this morning," he continued, "and Liberty's in Globe, picking up lumber. That young man of hers is coming to lunch, too."

"You like him?"

"If you're asking me, is he good enough for her, the answer is yes. I like him. Hell, I fixed 'em up."

"That's not the story I heard. You darn near ruined their relationship."

"Water under the bridge."

Ryder's sister obviously possessed a forgiving heart. "What's the lumber for? Fences?"

"Building jumps. We teach English hunter classes now, if you can believe that. Part of our outreach program with the school. We offer riding instruction to students for a discount price. Your mother's on the school board and spearheaded the whole thing."

"I had no idea." What else would Ryder learn about his mother during his stay? Did he care?

"It's good for the arena, and it's good for the community. Gives the students something to do in the afternoons and on weekends. Reckless is a small town without funding for local sports programs. But you know that as well as anyone."

Ryder did. He'd grown up in Reckless until he was fourteen and legally old enough to choose which of his parents he wanted to live with. On the day after his birthday, he'd packed his suitcase. A week later, when nothing his mother said or did and no amount of tears she cried made a difference, Ryder boarded a bus to Kingman where his father had moved.

For a few weeks each summer, he came back. That ended once Ryder graduated high school and left for college, allowing the rift between him and his mother to widen.

Then, a few months ago, Liberty discovered she shared the same biological father as her siblings and made contact, inviting him to Reckless for the purpose of getting acquainted. He did that, along with exercising his right to half ownership of the arena. When Ryder's mother objected, he threatened her with legal action. Having little choice, she eventually caved.

The result, the Becketts were now all in one place, though not reunited. Perhaps that was too much to ask.

His father led Ryder through the spacious backyard with its well-tended lawn. The swings and slide from Ryder's youth were gone, replaced by one of those multicolored modular play sets, he assumed for his nephew, Benjie. Just as well. Ryder sported a three-inch scar on his forearm, proof that the swings and slide had been old and dilapidated even in his day.

His father opened the kitchen door without knocking and called, "Sunny, you here?"

Though his father didn't live at the arena—he rented a small place in town—Ryder suspected he was a frequent visitor to the house. Apparently his mother really was softening toward him.

Her response drifted to them from down the hall. "Be right out."

Ryder paused inside the door.

"Don't just stand there." His father beckoned him with a wave. "It's not like you're a stranger."

Wrong. Ryder was a stranger. He'd lived many more years in Phoenix than Reckless—a mere seventy miles away, yet it might as well have been a million.

He advanced three whole feet before coming to another halt. That was all the distance required to walk from the present straight into the past, and the sensation knocked him off-kilter.

While he stood there, his father went to the fridge and helped himself to a chilled bottled water, further confirming Ryder's suspicions that he was a regular visitor.

"You want one?" He held out a second bottle.

"Thanks." Funny how Ryder's throat had gone completely dry. He accepted the bottle, twisted off the cap and took a long swallow. The cold water restored his balance.

Footsteps warned him of his mother's approach. He had but a few seconds to replace the bottle cap and prepare himself before she appeared.

"Ryder!" Cheeks flushed, she hurried toward him.

He tried to form his mouth into something resembling a smile. He must have succeeded, for she beamed.

"I'm so happy you came."

"It's good to see you, Mom." He uttered the words automatically.

They hugged, his mother clinging to him while Ryder gave her shoulders a perfunctory squeeze. He'd accepted his father and Liberty's invitation, it was his responsibility to deal with the consequences. Beside them, his father grunted with approval.

"Are you hungry?" His mother released him and brushed self-consciously at her hair, which was styled perfectly and in no need of tidying. "I made chili and corn bread."

His favorite meal as a boy. All right, it was still one of his favorite meals. Maybe because it reminded him of the good times, before their lives had imploded.

"Great. Thanks."

After an awkward moment of silence, she said, "I see you got a water."

"I did."

She skimmed her palms down the sides of her jeans. "We could sit in the living room. If you want. Until your sisters get here. Or outside. Though it's hot."

"Anywhere's fine with me," Ryder said. He'd be on edge and defensive regardless of his surroundings.

His father must have taken pity on his mother, for he said, "Let's sit at the kitchen table. Like the old days."

Ryder wasn't sure about the old days, but he reached for a chair. The same one he'd sat in as a child.

Abruptly, he moved his hand to the next chair over. He refused to slip into former habits just because he was back in Reckless, even habits as seemingly harmless as which chair he occupied.

An awkward silence descended. For no reason really, Ryder attempted to fill it with small talk. "How have you been, Mom?"

"All right. Busy. We now have weekly team penning competitions and bull-riding jackpots, monthly roping clinics and have almost doubled the number of riding classes offered. The Wild West Days Rodeo is in a couple of weeks."

As a kid, Ryder had loved Wild West Days. The

week-long, town-wide event included a parade, an outdoor arts-and-crafts festival, food vendors, square dancing and mock gunfights. Cowfolk and tourists alike traveled halfway across the country to participate in both the rodeo at the Easy Money and the other activities.

Ryder's mind went in the direction it always did. "Have you done any promotion?"

"The usual," his mother answered.

"Which is?"

"Tatum updated the website a couple months ago. We've sent out notices, both email and postcards. There are posters and flyers in town."

In Ryder's opinion, posters and flyers in town were a complete waste of resources. There was no need to advertise locally. The goal was to bring outsiders to Reckless.

"Have you considered reciprocating with other rodeo arenas?" he asked.

"What do you mean?"

"Ask them to advertise our rodeo in exchange for advertising theirs."

"Why would our competition do us any favors?" his father asked. "Or us them?" The question wasn't intended to criticize. He appeared genuinely interested.

"It's not competition as long as the rodeos fall in different months."

"Would they go along? The other arenas?"

"We can ask."

His parents exchanged glances, then his father shrugged. "I say yes."

"I think it's a great idea."

To Ryder's ears, his mother's enthusiasm rang false.

He wanted to tell her that she didn't need to endorse his ideas just because she was glad to have him home.

"Tatum can compile a list of potential rodeo arenas in the morning," his father suggested.

His mother readily agreed. "I'll ask her."

"Or Ryder can. They're already meeting."

Yeah. Ryder couldn't help wondering how that would go.

The back door abruptly swung open, and his sister Liberty burst into the kitchen, followed closely by a tall cowboy. Ryder guessed the man to be his future brother-in-law.

He'd barely stood when she threw herself at him. "Ryder!"

Unlike with his mother, the hug he gave his baby sister was filled with affection. "Hey, pip-squeak. How are you?"

She buried her face in the front of his shirt. "Better now."

He leaned back to look at her. "You're not crying, are you?"

"Absolutely not." She sniffed and wiped at her nose.

Ryder pulled her close again, his heart aching. Not spending time with Liberty, not getting to watch her grow up, was one of his biggest regrets about leaving Reckless and his main reason for returning. That, and guilt. She'd suffered the most from their mother's lies. If he could make up for that in some small way, he would.

"I'm really happy you came."

Would she say that, love him less, if she knew the other reason for his return?

"After a week, you'll probably be sick of me," he said.

"Not going to happen." Liberty turned to her fiancé. "This is Deacon."

Ryder wasn't the sentimental sort, but the tender way she spoke Deacon's name affected him. He was glad she'd found happiness; she certainly deserved it.

What kind of mother lied to her child about the identity of her father? The same one who thought only of herself and not her children when she unceremoniously tossed their father out and refused to let him back into their lives.

"Nice to finally meet you." Putting thoughts of his mother aside, Ryder shook Deacon's hand. "I've heard good things about you."

"Same here."

In his line of work, Ryder often made snap judgments. Deacon's handshake was firm and offered without hesitation. A good sign. Ryder decided he approved of his sister's choice in husband.

The pleasantries that followed were cut short when Cassidy and, to Ryder's surprise, Tatum Mayweather arrived to join them. Wasn't she supposed to be at work?

For a moment, he and Cassidy simply stared at each other. Once, they'd been inseparable. Then, their parents divorced, and sides were declared. Ryder had chosen their father's, Cassidy their mother's. Growing apart from her was another of his regrets.

He made the first move and opened his arms. She stepped into his embrace, and Ryder swore everyone in the room visibly relaxed.

The hug ended too soon. "Mom," Cassidy said, "I hope you don't mind, I asked Tatum to lunch. She didn't get a chance to eat. Too busy taking care of Cupcake."

"Of course not."

Tatum smiled apologetically. "I hate imposing on your reunion."

"Nonsense. You're like family."

For someone considered to be like family, Tatum looked ready to bolt. Ryder found that interesting. Then again, he found a lot of things about her interesting. Good thing that, as a Beckett employee, she was off-limits.

With everyone pitching in, lunch was soon on the table. Liberty had inherited their father's conversational abilities, and between the two of them, there were no more lulls.

That was, until Cassidy said, "Tatum mentioned you two didn't recognize each other."

"It's true," Ryder admitted.

Tatum echoed his earlier remark. "It's been a while. We've both changed."

"Do you forget all the women you kiss?" Cassidy asked, a teasing lilt to her voice. "Or just the first one?"

"Kiss?" He had forgotten.

In a rush, it all came back to him. The Valentine's Day card. Tatum's desperate look of hope. The casual peck on the cheek he'd given her.

"I'd have bet money you wouldn't remember," Cassidy said.

An undefinable emotion filled Tatum's eyes before she averted her glance. Something told Ryder this had been some sort of test and that he'd failed it.

Chapter 2

It took a full five minutes for Tatum's cheeks to cool. How could Cassidy embarrass her like that? They were best friends. Lifelong best friends.

Worse than embarrassing her, Cassidy had intentionally used that long ago chaste kiss—Tatum had been just twelve and Ryder nearly fourteen—to deliver a dig to her brother. Tatum neither wanted to nor deserved to be dragged into any feud between the siblings.

And, seriously, wasn't it past time they let bygones be bygones? Mercer was sober. He and Sunny were working together running the arena and getting along. For the most part. Business was booming. Liberty had forgiven her mother's duplicity and was making up for lost years with Mercer by spending time with him. Ryder had come home. Cassidy alone refused to let go of the past.

Tatum's anger continued to simmer all during the

lunch. Cassidy should be glad her brother had returned. For her mother's sake, if nothing else. Sunny had hated losing Ryder and longed for a reconciliation with him since the day he left to live with Mercer. As a mother herself, Tatum sympathized. She'd been separated only briefly from her children this past spring, yet it had been the worst four months of her life.

Cassidy was also a mother, though Benjie's father had never been in the picture. Ever. She didn't have to share her child with an ex or contend with a former, impossible to please, mother-in-law. Tatum sighed. Lucky Cassidy.

"Dad, maybe after lunch you can take a look at Tatum's pony."

Her head shot up at hearing Ryder speak her name.

"What's wrong with Cupcake?" Mercer asked, shoveling a large bite of chili into his mouth.

Tatum swallowed before answering. "I, um, thought she might have foundered. Ryder says her limp's due to a poorly fitted shoe."

"One way to find out is remove the shoe."

"He…already did that." What was wrong with her? She couldn't string a simple sentence together without tripping over her words.

Her glance strayed to Ryder, the cause of her unease, though, why, she had no idea. He meant nothing to her, outside of being the recipient of her one-sided childhood crush. The kiss—peck, she corrected herself—while important to her, had meant little to him. She'd presented him with a homemade Valentine's Day card that she'd labored over for days. He read it, then dipped his head and brushed her cheek with his lips. The next week, he'd left to live with Mercer in Kingman, dashing her fragile hopes and dreams.

Over the years, the memory of her first crush changed, from painful to one she viewed with mild amusement and even fondness. Too bad Cassidy had to go and tarnish that for her.

"Is the foot warm?" Mercer asked, still talking about Cupcake.

"No," Ryder replied before Tatum could.

Not that she'd have known if the foot was warm or not. She hadn't checked. Running into Ryder had distracted her.

"Then she probably isn't foundered." Mercer scraped the last of the chili from his bowl. "Ryder has a good eye when it comes to horses."

"I'm sure she'll be fine." Tatum wished the conversation would shift from her to something else. Like Liberty and Deacon's upcoming wedding.

"Where is she?"

"Cupcake? I moved her to the horse barn. In that empty stall next to the gray Percheron."

"I'll take a look at feeding time." Mercer patted his stomach as if to settle his meal.

Tatum felt Ryder's gaze on her and struggled to ignore him. It was impossible. The green-gray color of his eyes was unlike any she'd seen, made more prominent by his strong, masculine features and short cropped brown hair.

To her chagrin, her heart gave a little flutter in return. Good grief. Surely she couldn't be attracted to him. He wasn't her type. More than that, he could well be after her job.

Hoping to hide her reaction, she said, "Thank you,

Mercer. From me and my kids. You know how they love Cupcake."

"How old are they?" Ryder's mouth curved at the corners into a devastatingly charming smile.

Tatum responded by blushing. And all because Cassidy had made Tatum acutely aware of Ryder by mentioning that stupid kiss. When they finished with lunch she was going to give her best friend a well-deserved piece of her mind.

"My daughter's seven, and the boys are four and two."

"Are they in school with Benjie?"

"My daughter is, though not in the same grade. The boys attend day care while I work."

It had been difficult finding reliable and reasonably priced child care in such a small town. The Becketts paid Tatum a fair, even generous, wage. Still, a large chunk of her income went to cover the costs of day care. And rent and food. Making ends meet was a delicate balance. Luckily, her ex paid his child support on time and carried the children as dependents on his health insurance.

If for any reason, that ceased, Tatum would be back to where she was earlier this year. Unable to provide her children with the most basic necessities and at risk of losing them.

The Becketts hadn't just given her a job when Tatum was laid off, they'd saved her family. Her loyalty to them was deep and abiding.

"Tatum's a teacher," Liberty said.

"Was," Tatum corrected.

"You teach art classes."

"Really?" Ryder looked at her with interest.

"Just part-time. Lenny Faust at the Ship-With-Ease Store lets me use the empty space next door. I used to teach third and fourth grade at the elementary school. For seven years." Why had she felt pressured to qualify herself? As if teaching art wasn't good enough.

"Until last December," Cassidy added with disgust. "That's when the school board gave her the boot. Bad decision."

"Now, now," Sunny admonished. "We've been over this before. There are other teachers who've been with the school longer."

"Budget cuts. Right. You were outvoted, and your hands are tied."

"We'll hire Tatum back as soon as we can." Sunny covered the leftover corn bread with a linen napkin. "The board convenes in a few weeks to approve the new budget."

Tatum didn't want to get her hopes up, but she couldn't help herself. She loved teaching. Other than her own children, nothing gave her greater satisfaction or enjoyment, and she missed it terribly.

To her vast relief, talk turned to the upcoming Wild West Days Rodeo and the arena's record number of entries.

"Ryder has some notion about…what did you call it?"

"Reciprocal advertising," Ryder said, then went on to explain the concept.

Tatum thought the idea innovative, though her experience with marketing was limited to her job at the arena and what Sunny had taught her.

Cassidy shrugged. "We've always done well enough without having to swap advertising with other rodeo arenas."

"We could do better," Ryder said.

"What if it backfires and we lose business?"

"Nothing ventured, nothing gained. Look at what Dad's done with the bulls he purchased. He told me revenue's increased over fifteen percent in two months."

"Because of the weekly bull-riding jackpots and team penning."

"It's just an idea, Cassidy. I'm not married to it."

Ryder's response was casual, as if he couldn't care less. A stillness of his hand and tension in his jaw gave Tatum the impression he cared very much and didn't like his methods being questioned.

The Beckett family dynamics were certainly interesting and, at times, bewildering and frustrating. Did none of them realize this was the first time in who knew how many years they were all together? Couldn't they play nice this once?

Excusing herself, Tatum said, "Duty calls. My voicemail box has probably reached its limit and is ready to self-destruct."

"And I have a meeting with a client." Deacon pushed back from the table. "Thank you for lunch, Sunny."

"I'll walk you to your truck." Before joining Deacon, Liberty bent and gave Ryder a quick kiss on the cheek. "I'm really glad you're home. Let's have dinner soon."

"How about tomorrow night? I need someone to show me around town. A lot's changed."

"Great! Deacon and I will pick you up at seven."

A smile spread across Ryder's face, and Tatum was momentarily disarmed by his handsomeness. It was amazing, really, that, at thirty-six, he remained a bachelor. Women no doubt pursued him in droves.

One by one, everyone left the kitchen. Cassidy had

to supervise preparations for the roping practice later that afternoon. Once Liberty saw Deacon off, she'd recruit a couple of the wranglers to help her unload the lumber she'd bought. Mercer was taking Ryder to his place to settle in.

Sunny started clearing the table.

Though she'd been the one to suggest leaving, Tatum offered, "I can stay and help, if you want."

"Thanks. Then I'll go with you to the office. There's a pile of paperwork calling my name."

Ryder paused on his way to the door, stopping Tatum as she carted an armload of dishes to the sink. "See you in the morning?"

"Right."

He didn't move. "Look, I'm sorry."

"For what?"

"Not remembering. The kiss." Those compelling eyes roved her face, then lingered on her mouth. "That wouldn't happen now, I guarantee it."

The next instant, he was gone. Thank goodness! One second longer, and he'd have heard her sharp intake of breath.

Tatum tried to tell herself that Ryder was in marketing. Essentially a salesman. Winning people over, even flirting a little, was part of the job and second nature to him. Yet, a thrill wound slowly through her, confirming just how susceptible she was to him. She simultaneously dreaded the coming morning and couldn't wait for it.

Cassidy sat at the front desk when Ryder entered the ranch office. "Hi. Tatum's not here yet."

Her tone wasn't exactly welcoming, but neither was it distant. Did she consider him an interloper rather than an asset to the business? She still treated his father that way at times.

"I came early to see you."

It had been easy enough to learn from his father that Cassidy made a habit of visiting the office ahead of Tatum, who had to drop off her sons at day care. She liked to review the day's schedule and answer emails. According to their father, it was the only break she'd have all day.

"I didn't come empty-handed." He produced two paper cups of steaming coffee. Sitting in the visitor chair across from her, he passed her the cup with caramel latte scrawled in black marker on the side.

After a pause, she accepted it. "Dad tell you this is my favorite?"

"I've been picking his brain."

"You actually stood in line twenty minutes for coffee?" Cassidy sipped tentatively through a hole in the plastic lid.

"I got up early and beat the morning rush. Who'd've guessed? Reckless has a gourmet coffee shop."

She eyed him from over the brim of her cup. "Things change."

He eyed her back. "They do."

"Is this a peace offering or a bribe?"

"I don't want to fight, Cassidy."

She set down the coffee. "We're not fighting."

"You embarrassed Tatum yesterday just to get at me."

"I do owe her an apology."

"If I didn't know better, I'd think you're sorry I came home."

"Why wouldn't I be glad? Really. Mom's ready to

burst with happiness. And Liberty's so excited, she's downright annoying. The whole family's reunited at last, yadda, yadda, yadda."

"What about you?"

"Depends."

"On?"

"Mom, for one. You broke her heart when you left. I don't want you to do it again."

"The only promise I made Dad and Liberty when I agreed to come here was that I'd try."

"An honest effort is all I ask."

Did she think he'd give anything less? "Mom and I have a lot of bridges to mend. It won't be easy."

"It's going to be as easy or difficult as you make it."

Interesting comment for someone who was starting out by making things difficult. But, his sister was probably right. "Let's stick to the reason I waited twenty minutes in line for overpriced coffee."

"I thought you said you beat the rush."

"A slight exaggeration."

Cassidy laughed. It wasn't much of a laugh. More like a dry chuckle. Still, it beat the heck out of their mother's forced cheerfulness at lunch the day before.

"Why are you really mad at me?" he asked.

"Tatum. She needs this job, Ryder. And you're a threat to it."

"Not as much as you think."

"Dad has other ideas."

Ryder considered leveling with Cassidy about this being a temporary stay until he landed another position. Gut instinct made him hesitate. "I'm not a threat to Tatum."

"When she lost her job at the school, she also lost custody of her kids."

"Wow! You're kidding."

"Temporarily lost custody. But she fell apart."

"What happened?"

"Tatum's good with money. But the divorce left her without any kind of nest egg. And you know what teachers make, especially in Reckless. Squat. She had no savings to fall back on when the school board laid her off last December. The extra money she makes off of her art classes is barely enough to put groceries on the table."

"Couldn't she find another teaching job outside of Reckless?"

"That takes time. She also had her house to consider. She didn't want to move if she could help it."

If anyone understood the difficulty of finding a good job and dwindling resources, it was Ryder. The past two months of searching had produced no results other than draining his bank account. Though what hindered his job search had less to do with lack of available employment and more to do with the bad reputation he'd created for himself at Madison-Monroe Concepts.

His stomach involuntarily tightened. He'd live down his mistake. Eventually. Come hell or high water.

"We gave her a job as office manager," Cassidy continued, "and that took a lot of arm-twisting. Tatum is proud and refused what she called a pity job."

"Dad says she's pretty good at what she does."

"She is. Which is why it's not a pity job. But then the bank foreclosed on her house anyway when she couldn't keep up with the payments. She and the kids moved in with us. Rent free. That *was* charity, and she struggled to accept it."

"Seven people. Four bedrooms. It must have been crowded."

"We didn't care. But her ex-mother-in-law got wind of the situation and convinced her son to hire an attorney, claiming Tatum couldn't provide adequately for the kids."

"He sued for custody?" Ryder was appalled. "Why didn't he help her make her mortgage payments? They're his children, too."

"It didn't go that far. Luckily. Tatum compromised. She turned over care of the kids to her mother-in-law. Just until she saved enough money working for us to rent an apartment. It was a rough period for her. The kids, too. They missed Tatum and hated living with their grandmother."

"Did she mistreat them?"

"No, no. She's not the warm, cookie-baking kind of grandmother, but that wasn't the problem. She lives in Glendale. A four-hour round trip. Tatum only saw the kids once a week at most. The day she signed the lease on her apartment, she broke down and cried in front of the rental agent."

"She's lucky to have you and Mom."

"We're lucky to have her. She works hard, even if an office manager isn't her first choice of a job."

"I do remember her drawing a lot. Always walking around with a sketchbook."

Cassidy studied him critically. "So, you didn't forget her entirely."

"No." But he hadn't thought of her in years. A stark contrast to the past twenty-four hours. She'd been on his mind constantly. "You and she barrel raced."

"We did. She met her ex on the circuit, and for a few

years, they traveled from rodeo to rodeo, living in an RV. That wore thin on Tatum. She quit in order to obtain her teaching degree."

"Her husband continued to compete?"

"Nothing would stop him. Tatum did her best to make the marriage work. Full-time job, full-time mom, part-time husband. When she got pregnant for the third time, he left for good, saying something like, 'baby, I just can't be tied down.' She took it hard. I say the jerk didn't deserve her, and she was better off without him."

Ryder tended to agree.

"I'm not gossiping, so don't think that." Cassidy sipped again at her coffee. "I only wanted you to know what Tatum's been through and why this job is important to her." Her voice dropped. "Don't mess it up for her."

"I won't. I promise."

Cassidy looked skeptical.

"My plan is to create and implement a sound marketing strategy for the arena." One Tatum or his mother could manage after he was gone.

Funny. He hadn't realized until this moment how similar his and Tatum's situations were. Both of them working interim jobs while hoping for a better one. Both of them resisting to take what they considered charity.

Okay, maybe that wasn't so funny.

"What exactly is going on with Mom and Dad?" Ryder didn't want to talk about Tatum anymore. "Do you think they'll get back together?"

"God, I hope not." Cassidy turned away from him to stare out the window.

It wasn't eight in the morning, yet the ranch was alive with activity. Hands cleaning stalls. Customers exercising their horses. The carpenters Liberty had hired to construct the horse jumps were making a ruckus behind the barn, banging hammers and running the chain saw. Mercer conferred with a rep from the grain dealer.

"For once I agree with you."

Her head swung back around. "Why do I think there's a catch?"

"No catch. Mom threw him out. Abandoned him in his hour of need. Lied to him about being Liberty's father. He'd be a fool to get involved again."

"She had every right to throw him out," Cassidy argued hotly. "He's an alcoholic."

Their parents had purchased the Easy Money before Ryder was born and had taken it from a run-down, dirt-poor arena to the best facility in the southern part of the state. That all changed when Ryder's grandfather died suddenly from a heart attack, and his father began drowning his grief with whiskey. Daily.

In less than a year, the arena went from prospering to the verge of bankruptcy, and Ryder's mother kicked him to the curb. What Ryder knew and his sisters didn't until recently was that their father retained his half ownership of the arena. Their mother had also never paid their father his share of the profits per their settlement agreement. The sum was staggering.

"Reformed alcoholic," Ryder said. "He hasn't touched a drink in over twenty years." He'd stopped shortly after Ryder moved in with him.

"Once an alcoholic, always—"

"Let it go, Cassidy."

"He didn't almost kill you!"

"It was a fender bender. You were fine."

She drew back, her expression one of shock. "What if he'd been going faster?"

One night, their father had picked up Cassidy en route home from the bar. While pulling on to the property, he'd lost control of the truck and rammed into the well house. He'd been sorry. Their mother outraged.

"Mom was justified. He wasn't only a lousy husband, he was a danger to our well-being."

"He's paid for his sins, Cassidy. We all have. Mom divorced him and told everyone some cowboy passing through was Liberty's father. Our little sister deserved to know the truth. Mom had no right denying either her or Dad."

"She had her reasons. Good ones."

"Two wrongs don't make a right."

"In this case, they do."

"She didn't just reject him." Ryder's anger rose, its grip like a vise around his chest. "She tore our family apart. Took our father away from us. That wasn't fair."

"She's not the only one to tear our family apart." Tears welled in Cassidy's eyes.

"What are you saying?"

"You left. And you hardly ever visited. You're only here now because you quit your job. You don't love us or want us. We're just your last resort."

Ryder sat in stunned silence. She thought *he'd* rejected *them*?

Before he could say more, Tatum entered the office. One glance at them, and she pulled up short. "Sorry. Am I interrupting?"

Chapter 3

Both Ryder and Cassidy insisted that Tatum hadn't inadvertently walked in on a private and sensitive conversation. She didn't believe them. Ryder had stood so fast, he almost upended the visitor chair. Cassidy averted her gaze but not before Tatum spied the look of utter distress on her friend's face.

Old wounds. When the Becketts weren't hiding them, they were poking them with sharp sticks.

"Why don't we start with a tour of the place?" Ryder suggested, depositing his empty coffee cup into the wastebasket near Tatum's desk. That put him in close proximity to Cassidy, and she noticeably tensed. "If you're free," he added.

He must have visited the Dawn to Dusk Coffee shop on his way in this morning. Cassidy wouldn't have gone despite her penchant for caramel lattes. "I shouldn't leave the office unattended," Tatum said. Lunch yesterday had been an exception. Usually Sunny relieved her.

"It's okay," Cassidy volunteered. "I'll watch the phones."

"Are you sure?" Tatum was about to suggest that Cassidy give her brother the tour when he cut her short.

"Come on." He motioned toward the door.

"Let me put my things away first."

"Meet you in the barn." The next instant, he was gone.

Wow. Whatever had happened between him and his sister must have been worse than Tatum thought. She stowed her lunch in the small countertop refrigerator and her purse in the desk drawer.

"You okay?" she asked Cassidy in a whisper, though Ryder was well beyond earshot.

"I'm sorry about yesterday. I shouldn't have mentioned the kiss."

"We were kids." Tatum straightened, her previous anger at her friend dissipating.

"Yeah, but it was a big deal for you. At the time."

"Forget about it, okay?" On impulse, Tatum gave her friend's shoulders a quick squeeze.

"What was that for?"

"Do I need a reason?"

"I guess not." Cassidy's face relaxed. "Go on, get out of here. I need my daily dose of Facebook."

Tatum laughed. It was a joke the two frequently shared. Both were borderline workaholics and wouldn't ever wile away the hours surfing the net.

In the barn, she met up with Ryder. "Where do you want to start?"

"How's Cupcake?"

They strolled the long aisle. "I haven't had a chance to check on her this morning."

"Let's start there."

"She's better," Tatum had to admit after they took the pony on a short walk around the wash bays.

"When's the farrier due next?"

"Unless there's an emergency, he's here every Thursday."

"She'll be okay until then. If you do take her out for a ride, put a hoof boot on her."

"Thank you. I probably shouldn't have doubted you."

"It was the clothes." He smiled.

Tatum had to stop herself from ogling. Today he wore jeans, a Western-cut shirt that molded nicely to his broad shoulders and a cowboy hat that was scuffed in all the right places. He looked as if he'd never left the ranch.

"What made you give up rodeoing?" She recalled Sunny bragging on her son, who'd won several junior rodeo championships before abandoning a promising pro career.

"College."

"Not enough time to do both?"

"Not enough money. Finances were tight. I had to make a choice."

Tatum was familiar with that dilemma. She lived it on a daily basis.

They returned Cupcake to her stall, hung the halter on a nearby peg and continued their tour of the grounds. He was careful to take her arm when they walked over a hole or navigated an obstacle. Tatum didn't need the assistance. She liked it, nonetheless.

"I always figured I'd wind up like my dad and make rodeo my life," he said.

"You're more like your mother than you realize. She's really savvy when it comes to business."

Lines appeared on Ryder's brow. "I hadn't thought of that before."

"It's not a bad thing."

He avoided commenting by asking, "Besides the bulls, what else is new?"

"Not much. Tom Pratt gives monthly roping clinics."

They wandered toward the bull pens, which were located on the other side of the arena, far from the horses. The two didn't always mix, and it was best to maintain a healthy distance between them.

"He was smart to do that. Nothing will grow the arena faster than good bucking stock."

"We can hardly keep up with the requests."

In addition to providing bucking stock for their four annual rodeos, the Easy Money leased horses and now bulls to other rodeos. It was their single highest source of revenue. Tatum had felt guilty when the Becketts first hired her, thinking they were giving her a job solely because she was a close family friend. That opinion soon changed. With the increase in business, she was earning her keep and then some.

What more could Ryder do to grow the business than Mercer already had? It seemed to Tatum they were at their capacity for bucking stock contracts. Unless the Becketts purchased more bulls. Or Ryder assumed even more of Tatum's duties. Then she really would be a charity case.

A pair of lone riders were making use of the arena. Tatum and Ryder stopped at the fence to observe them.

"Dad mentioned the after-school program," he said.

"That's going well. So well, your dad's considering building a second practice ring just for the students."

"But rodeo events are where the real money is."

"Lessons and horse boarding more than pay for themselves."

"I wasn't insinuating Mom and my sisters' contribution weren't an important part of the arena. There's room for both."

As they started for the office, Liberty passed them, riding one horse and leading a second. She stopped to say good morning and to remind Ryder of their dinner plans that evening.

"What are you up to?" Ryder asked her.

"Endurance training. This is a client's horse." She indicated the tall gelding behind her prancing nervously in place. Pulling on the lead rope, she groaned in frustration. "He's raring to go. I'll catch up with you later."

Ryder stared after her. "I wouldn't have guessed she'd be the one to take after Dad. Then again, none of us knew she was related to him."

Tatum and Cassidy had shared many a long discussion about her parents. Tatum understood Sunny's motives for lying to Liberty—she didn't want to give a raging alcoholic any reason to remain part of their lives. But Tatum wasn't sure she'd do the same thing in Sunny's shoes, if only because of the wedge it had driven between Sunny and Ryder. Losing her children for a mere four months had been unbearable. Sunny lost Ryder for twenty-two years, and she still didn't have him back.

"Ready?" she asked.

"Where to now?"

"The outdoor stalls and back pastures," she suggested.

They went in the same direction as Liberty. Ryder, Tatum noticed, slowed his steps to keep pace with her shorter strides. He was tall. Her chin barely reached his shoulder. He must have grown six inches after he left. If he kissed her now, he'd have to dip his head considerably further.

Stop it!

The mental reprimand was useless. How could she not think of Ryder when he walked beside her, near enough to touch if she extended her hand a mere three inches to the right?

What had they been talking about? Oh, yeah, lessons and boarding.

"Liberty's also in charge of the trail rides," Tatum said. "There's usually one every weekend when we don't have a rodeo."

"Just one?"

"We don't have enough requests for more than that on weekends."

"Are they profitable?"

"Actually, yes."

"What's the margin?"

"I'd say about the same as riding lessons."

"How do we advertise the rides? And don't tell me on the website and posters in town."

"Okay, I won't. But that's what we do."

He muttered under his breath.

"There are tourists in town," she protested. "They see the posters."

"What about the marina at Roosevelt Lake? Do we have a poster in their window?"

"No."

"We should."

Did he notice he was talking in the plural? "Is that more of your reciprocal advertising?"

"You catch on fast."

"I'll call them and ask if we can deliver a poster."

"I'll do it. In fact, I'll just take one over this afternoon. That way, I can bring back one of theirs."

"Good idea." She supposed a face-to-face meeting was better than a phone call. Harder to say no.

Twenty minutes later they were through with the tour. Approaching the office from the outside entrance rather than the barn, they climbed the three steps to the awning-covered porch. Cassidy still sat at Tatum's desk. Sunny wasn't there. Tatum could see her empty office through the open connecting door.

Was she avoiding Ryder? Had Cassidy told her mother about her fight, or whatever it was, with Ryder?

"You're back." Cassidy quickly closed the webpage she had open on the computer and stood.

"Stay longer if you aren't done," Tatum offered.

"It's all right. I have to make a run into Globe for supplies."

"Didn't Liberty do that yesterday?" Ryder asked.

"She bought lumber. I'm getting vet supplies. Dewormer and penicillin. There's been three cases of strangles reported this month in the Mesa area. We don't want to be caught with a low supply if it should move to Reckless."

"That's serious."

Tatum concurred. She'd seen a strangles epidemic before. The highly contagious infection attacked the lymph nodes between a horse's jaw or in its throat and caused flu-like symptoms lasting weeks, if not months. Should the Becketts' bucking stock or boarded horses succumb, their entire business would be in jeopardy.

"It is serious," Cassidy said. "So, if you'll excuse me."

"We can order penicillin online, and for a lot cheaper, with a prescription."

"I've already thought of that." Cassidy lifted her chin. "Doctor Spence is coming tomorrow."

Ryder softened his voice. "I wasn't questioning your abilities."

"See you later."

"That went well," he said after Cassidy left.

Tatum ignored him and sat at her desk.

"Did I say something wrong?"

"Look." She leveled her stare at him. "If you weren't questioning her abilities, you were questioning something."

"You're right." He dropped down into the visitor chair. "I'm sorry to involve you in our squabble."

"Squabble?" That hardly described their longstanding clash.

"This big reconciliation Liberty and Dad are hoping for may not happen."

"It definitely won't happen if you don't try and get along."

"We argued about Mom. And," he admitted, "the way I've acted in recent years."

Big surprise. Not. "How about we institute a new rule? No discussion regarding family at work, unless it relates to work. I'll tell Cassidy and Sunny. You tell Liberty and Mercer." She felt as if she was refereeing a fight between her children.

He considered for a moment, then relented with a shrug. "All right."

"That's what I like to see. Progress." She rolled her chair over to the lateral file cabinet by her desk, deciding they should start the office part of Ryder's orientation with the current bucking stock contracts. She opened the drawer and removed a dozen manila folders. "I probably shouldn't point this out…"

"But you will."

"Your resentment toward your mother. It mirrors Cassidy's toward your father."

"Are you saying we'll never find a common ground?"

"I'm saying there's more common ground than you think." She slapped the folders on to the desk, the impact making a loud noise. "Let's start on these."

Ryder stopped to refuel his truck on the way into Reckless. Based on the number of things he'd accomplished, it had been a productive day. He'd spent the morning with Tatum, interfering with her work but also gaining an understanding of how the office ran, including an overview of the accounting system and record keeping. He and his father had had lunch at the Flat Iron Restaurant with one of the arena's oldest clients.

After that, Ryder had headed to the marina at Roosevelt Lake, posters and flyers on the seat beside him. The marina manager, a crusty old guy who could have played an extra in a *Pirates of the Caribbean* movie, was agreeable to Ryder's suggestion that they help each other out.

On impulse, he'd driven to the outskirts of Globe and the mining company offices. After being passed from one person to the next, he'd finally been granted a meeting with the personnel manager's secretary. The middle-aged woman had listened patiently to his pitch—the Easy Money Rodeo Arena would be a great place for employee parties or retreats. She'd agreed to give the material Ryder left with her to her boss and thanked him for his time.

Productive day. No question about it. But nothing a trained monkey couldn't do. Ryder had been a senior marketing executive in charge of several multimillion-dollar accounts. And here he was, delivering posters and flyers and trolling for business. Something he could have done in high school.

Running errands. Sleeping on the trundle bed in his dad's spare room. Fighting with his sister. He might as well be in high school again.

"Ryder Beckett," someone shouted. "Buddy, is that you?"

He glanced up to see a hefty young man approaching, a friendly grin splitting his full face.

"It is you. Son of a gun!"

"Guilty as charged." Ryder hoped the man's name would come to him without having to ask. "How are you…?" At the last second, his brain kicked in. "Tank."

"Dandy as a pig with slop." They shook hands. "I heard you were back and working for the family."

He'd said *for* the family, not *with* the family. To Ryder, there was a large distinction. Did everyone in town think like Tank, that Ryder had been given a job as opposed to being made a part of the business?

Then again, did he care? He was leaving soon.

Once more, Ryder questioned his motives for returning. He could have chosen somewhere else to lay low. Eventually found temporary employment. But he'd allowed loyalty to his father and Liberty's heartfelt pleas to sway him.

"What happened to that fancy job you had in Phoenix?" Tank asked. "Your mom was always telling everyone what a big shot you were and how much money you made. This must be a step down."

Damned if Tank could hit below the belt.

"Dad asked for my help, and here I am. Family comes first."

"Sure. Course." Tank may or may not have believed Ryder, but he didn't dispute him. "Got me a family of my own now. A wife and little boy."

"Congratulations."

"Heard about your divorce. Sorry, man." Tank didn't sound particularly remorseful or sympathetic.

"It was a long time ago."

Ryder did the math. Thirteen years.

He'd met Sasha, a woman eight years his senior, right out of college, and she was like no one he'd ever known. Confident, sexy and adventurous, in and out of bed. Unfortunately, they fell out of love as quickly as they'd fallen in and spent the next year making each other miserable before coming to their senses.

The only good part about the marriage had been Sasha's little girls. Ryder had liked them and frequently spent more time with them than their own mother did, especially near the end. They, in turn, adored him. Leaving them behind had hurt.

One short-lived relationship after another had him swearing off any commitments for the foreseeable future. This last debacle with his coworker had only reinforced it.

"One of these days, you'll meet the right person," Tank said.

"I guess."

Beside him, the gas nozzle clicked loudly. Ryder reached for it. "Nice seeing you, Tank. You ever bring your family around the Easy Money?"

"We're coming to the Wild West Days Rodeo. Already bought our tickets."

"Good. Looking forward to seeing you there."

They shook hands again, and Ryder climbed into his truck. Starting the engine, he heard Tank's words again—*working for your family*—then slammed the heels of both hands on the steering wheel. He wasn't mad at Tank; he was mad at himself.

Enough was enough. He'd let this happen, he thought, and he could remedy it. Pulling out his smartphone, he went through his saved emails. There! He found it. The one from a friend giving Ryder the name of a head-hunter. He dialed the number and set the phone down. The next second, his Bluetooth kicked in, and he could hear ringing through the speaker on his dash. When the receptionist answered, he asked to be put through to Myra Solomon.

"This is Myra."

Ryder introduced himself, giving the name of his friend. "He suggested I give you a call."

"I'm glad you did. Tell me a little about yourself and what kind of job you're looking for."

Ryder talked as he drove, casting his termination in the best possible light. When he finished, Myra groaned tiredly.

"Cut the B.S., Ryder. If we're going to work together,

you have to be straight with me. Save the sugarcoated version for prospective employers."

"I quit."

"I know that. I'm interested in why."

"My boss and I didn't share the same visions."

"Whatever happened, we'll work around it," Myra said. "But in order to help you, I have to know what really went down. If not, you're wasting both our time."

Ryder swallowed. He'd been through this before with another headhunter. "I quit rather than be sued."

"For what?"

"Inappropriate conduct."

Myra whistled. "How inappropriate?"

"Not at all."

"Then, why?"

Now it was Ryder's turn to groan. "I was dating a woman at work. One of my subordinates. A member of my team, actually. And before you ask, there was no company policy against employees fraternizing."

"Did you advise HR? Sign any kind of agreement?"

"Yes, we advised HR, and there was no agreement for us to sign. When the relationship ended, I advised HR of that, as well."

"Then, where does the inappropriate conduct come in?"

"We dated for four months. She wanted more, to move in together, and I didn't. Rather than string her along, I ended things."

"That's it?"

"Not entirely. She didn't take the breakup well. She'd call me at all hours and corner me in the office. A couple of our discussions got a little heated. About a week later, one of the other team members received a promotion she was also in line for. She believed I black-balled her."

"And did you?"

"Absolutely not. I was asked for my input on both candidates and gave them both good recommendations. No favoritism. The next day she filed a complaint."

"You just said you showed no favoritism. What were her grounds?"

"During one of those heated discussions, she got carried away. I tried calming her by putting my hand on her arm. She later claimed that I touched her inappropriately."

"Were there any witnesses?"

"A few. They reported seeing me touch her but not where. They weren't close enough."

"Excuse me for stating the obvious, Ryder, but that was stupid. You should have avoided this woman at all costs. Especially after she started calling you. In fact, you should have alerted HR that she was harassing you."

"Live and learn."

"Is any of this in your personnel records?"

"No. That was part of the deal we reached. She dropped the suit, and I quit."

"Well, that's one good thing."

"Not really. Advertising is a small world, and it's filled with big mouths. Even though I did nothing wrong, a lot of companies are reluctant to hire me. She got what she wanted after all."

"Then you move out of state," Myra said matter-of-factly.

"I'm considering it."

"Okay, here's what we're going to do. I'll email you our representation contract. Once you send it back, we'll set up a meeting. Wear your best tie. My assistant will film a short interview with standard questions. We should be able to generate some interest with that. We'll also polish your résumé and rehearse answers to potentially difficult questions. What's your email address?"

They discussed a few more details before disconnecting. Ryder felt both better—he was being proactive and taking steps—and discouraged. How could he have screwed up this badly? Getting involved with a coworker? Worse, a subordinate. He should have his head examined.

Pulling into the arena, he parked by the office and got out. Still plagued by the conversation with the headhunter and not quite ready to face anyone, he went instead to the barn. Without quite realizing where he was going, he found himself standing in front of Cupcake's stall.

The pony snickered and came over for a petting. Ryder automatically gave her a scratch between her short, stubby ears. The next minute, he was in the stall, examining her sore hoof.

"I think you'll live."

Cupcake investigated him, snorting lustily when she encountered his hair.

"Quit it, will you?" Ryder laughed and dropped her hoof.

He and Cassidy once had a pony a lot like this one when they were young. A sorrel named Flame. With two parents involved in rodeo, they'd learned to ride at a very young age.

Suddenly, Ryder missed being on a horse. He'd remedy that this weekend, he decided.

"Hey! What are you doing to our pony?" The annoyed voice belonged to a pint-size girl who, given her long black hair, could only be Tatum's daughter. She stood in the open stall door, hands fisted and planted at her sides.

"Checking her foot."

"I don't know you." The girl backed away and gave Ryder a very suspicious once-over.

"I work here. With your mother."

"Then, why haven't I seen you before?"

"I'm new."

"I'm going to tell my mom."

He expected her to take off running. She didn't. Instead, she opened her mouth and screamed at the top of her lungs.

"Mom!"

"Hey, it's all right. You don't have to—"

She screamed again.

The next second, Tatum came charging up the aisle, one boy in tow, the other, younger one bouncing on her hip. "What's wrong?"

"Nothing," Ryder said.

The girl pointed accusingly at him. "This man is trying to hurt Cupcake."

Chapter 4

"Sorry about that." Tatum suppressed a grin. "I don't know what got into her."

"No harm done. You got here before the police were called."

She walked beside Ryder, carrying her youngest, Adam, because he'd pitched a fit when she tried to put him down. He got that way sometimes after day care, clingy and insecure. The mother in her was patient and understanding of his separation anxiety. The teacher in her wanted him to be more independent. "Gretchen is leery of strangers."

"I noticed."

"She's gotten worse since…" Tatum almost said, since she'd left the kids with her former mother-in-law. Fortunately, she caught herself before having to explain those dark and difficult months. "Lately."

"Who needs a watchdog with Gretchen?"

Tatum took the half smile Ryder offered as an indication he wasn't offended. Not that her daughter had done anything all that awful, other than accuse him of hurting Cupcake. At the top of her lungs.

"She isn't here every day. Cassidy picked up her and Benjie from school, then swung by and got the boys from day care, which is right down the road. We do that a lot. Share driving responsibilities."

"Sounds like a good system."

It was. Two single moms helping each other out. They also swapped turns running errands and babysitting. Not that either of them needed a babysitter much. For dates, at least. Tatum was acutely aware of how a woman in her midthirties with three children, ages seven and under, sent most guys running straight for the hills.

Ryder was among that group. According to Sunny, he was a confirmed, born-again bachelor who put his career first. Not wanting children could be one of his reasons. Or, he might want his own, not a ready-made family.

She'd heard that particular excuse more than once when, last year on a whim, she'd tried internet dating. What a mistake. There was only so much rejection a gal could take.

"How did your visit to the marina go?" she asked.

"We now have a poster in their window." Ryder went on to tell her about his stop at the mining company offices.

She was impressed. No one in the Beckett family had ever reached out to a large corporation before. "If you give me the secretary's name, I'll follow up in a week. Or you can make the call."

"I think that's a good idea. You're probably less pushy than me," he added with a chuckle.

"I was thinking more like she'd listen better to another woman."

His chuckle increased to a laugh. "You've missed your calling, Tatum Mayweather. You'd make a good marketing exec."

"I love my job."

"Which one?"

"Both. Teaching and working here." She did love her job at the ranch, in her way. "Where else can I bring my children with me when we're not busy?"

Gretchen and Drew, her oldest boy, walked ahead of them, Gretchen leading Cupcake and Drew batting stones out of their path with a stick. The pony's limp had completely diminished, and Tatum wasn't worried about letting the children ride her.

To that end, they'd stopped first at the tack room. Rather than leave, Ryder had insisted on saddling and bridling the pony, though Tatum was more than capable of doing it herself.

"Where to now?"

She pointed at the round pen across from the outdoor stalls. "We usually ride there. Cupcake's small. Less chance of being trampled by bigger, faster-moving horses."

He started ahead.

She had to walk fast in order to keep pace. "Seriously Ryder, I don't want to keep you. I'm sure you have somewhere else to be."

"I've missed working with horses." He opened the gate to the pen and swung it wide.

"A pony ride can't be what you had in mind."

"I'm free until dinner tonight with Liberty and Deacon. Might as well spend the time with you."

Her heart skipped, and, all at once, she was twelve years old again and deep in the throes of a crush. Tatum had grown up with the two older Beckett siblings, she and Cassidy becoming friends in first grade. Funny, Tatum hadn't noticed Ryder much until that last year before he left. She blamed puberty for her heart flutters then. She couldn't say the same thing now.

"Me, first." Drew abandoned his stick the moment they entered the pen.

"My turn. I'm oldest." Gretchen pushed past Drew, grabbing the saddle horn and trying to hoist herself up. She lacked the extra foot in height to manage it on her own.

"Now, now." Tatum set Adam on the ground, but he instantly wrapped his arms around her leg and stuck his thumb in his mouth, a habit he'd mostly given up months ago. Had something happened at day care to prompt this worse-than-usual insecurity? She'd ask in the morning when she dropped him off. "No need to fight. You and Drew can ride Cupcake together."

Their combined weight was easy enough for the sturdy pony to handle.

"I'm not riding with him." If looks could vaporize, Gretchen's younger brother would be no more than a puff of smoke.

"All right," Tatum said evenly. "Then Drew can go first."

"Not fair!" Gretchen shrieked.

Who were these incorrigible monsters? Sure, her children could act up with the best of them. But why today and why in front of Ryder?

"That's enough, young lady. Lower your voice, please."

"But I'm outside."

The argument wasn't entirely illogical. Tatum often chastised her offspring for yelling in the house and cautioned them to "use their inside voices."

"How about you ride Cupcake," Ryder suggested, "and I'll give Drew a piggyback ride?"

Not quite sure she'd heard him right, Tatum stared. She wasn't the only one. Gretchen and Drew did, too, their small mouths slack-jawed.

"You're spoiling them," Tatum insisted.

Without waiting for an answer, Ryder lifted Gretchen on to Cupcake's back and settled her in the saddle. Next, he grabbed Drew by the arms and swung him around on to his back. Drew had to hold tight or he'd have fallen.

Gretchen gave Cupcake a nudge with her heels and jiggled the reins. "Giddyup."

Drew did the same to Ryder, though instead of reins, he tugged on Ryder's shirt collar. Cupcake started out, making a circle of the pen. Ryder followed, with Drew laughing and Gretchen pouting because, in her mind, she'd been trumped by her brother.

"Anyone ever tell you you're a good sport?" Tatum said to Ryder as he passed.

"I need the exercise after driving all day."

Right. If there was an ounce of fat on him, it was buried beneath layers of muscles. The guy was built.

Gripping Adam's hand, she moved to the corner of the pen and watched Ryder play with Drew. The same charm that had won her over yesterday, before she knew who he was, worked its magic on her now. Tatum could hardly catch her breath. Looks and confidence were definitely sexy, but, to her, nothing made a man more attractive than being good with children. Stronger even than a powerful love potion.

During his next pass, his gaze sought hers. Tatum glanced quickly away, afraid her expression would reveal too much.

This beautiful, crazy arrangement lasted five whole minutes. Just long enough for Tatum to fall a little further under his spell. It might have continued longer if Adam didn't suddenly start wailing.

"Wanna ride. Wanna ride."

"Your turn next, sweetie."

"Now!" He let his legs go limp and flung himself to the ground, nearly jerking Tatum's arm from its socket. When she didn't let go, he twisted from side to side. She had ten seconds at most before he succumbed to a complete meltdown. Wouldn't that be icing on the cake?

"Enough, Adam," Tatum said sharply.

In the classroom, be it school or art, and with other people's children, Tatum never lost control or raised her voice. She couldn't make that claim when it came to her own brood, especially when they were testing the limits of her patience like today.

"Ride," Adam howled.

Ryder came over, and Tatum felt her cheeks burn. "Honey, please, stop."

He did. But not because of anything Tatum said or did. Ryder had scooped up the boy and held him close to his chest.

"You really don't have to do this." She wanted to tell

Ryder that giving in to Adam's tantrum was teaching him the wrong lesson. She didn't. The boys' giggles were too hard to resist.

"My dad used to cart me and Cassidy around when we were his age."

Tatum had to wonder if her best friend remembered any of the good times with Mercer like her brother obviously did.

"Hey." Gretchen reined Cupcake to a stop in front of them and glared. "Mom says we're not supposed to roughhouse around the horses."

Tatum *did* say that and was frequently ignored. Gretchen likely wanted in on the fun her brothers were having but refused to ask. Next best was ruining their fun.

"It's okay." Drew hugged Ryder's neck harder. "We have an adult present."

Tatum's throat closed. She ached for her children, who missed their father and moments like this. Monty had come around only a few times since their divorce, though his work as an installation foreman for a national auto parts chain brought him to the Phoenix area at least every other month from his home in Flagstaff. Gretchen, old enough and smart enough to figure out that her father didn't want to see her, was especially hurt.

"She's got you there," Tatum told Ryder. "You might spook Cupcake, and Gretchen could fall."

"Aw, no, Mom," Drew threw his head back and wailed.

"Noooo," Adam echoed.

Without missing a beat, Ryder turned toward the

gate. "Come on, boys. We've got bigger pastures to ride."

While Gretchen continued circling the pen with Cupcake, an activity that had lost a lot of its appeal, Ryder and the boys frolicked outside the round pen. Before long, Gretchen reached her fill of being excluded and pronounced, "It's Drew's turn."

"Okay." Tatum didn't think either of her sons would abandon Ryder in favor of Cupcake.

Even so, she helped her daughter dismount, then looped Cupcake's reins over a fence railing. "Your turn," Tatum said to Drew upon leaving the pen.

"I don't want to ride."

Of course he didn't. "You need to give Mr. Beckett a rest. He must be tired."

"How about I go with you?" Ryder offered.

Drew bestowed a Christmas-morning smile on him. "All right!"

"Wanna ride," Adam said, refusing to be left out.

"If it's okay with your brother."

"Okay." Drew's joy visibly dimmed. He didn't want to share his new best pal with his brother, but he'd rather share than miss out entirely.

Using one hand, Ryder lifted Drew off his back, then lowered Adam to the ground. He didn't resume sucking his thumb, but he did grab Ryder's leg.

"Daddy!"

Uh-oh. Tatum's stomach dropped to her knees. Could her children not go fifteen minutes without embarrassing her? "Honey, he's not—"

"You stupid dork!" Gretchen shoved her little brother, nearly knocking him over. "He's not our daddy."

"Gretchen! No name-calling. You know better."

Adam burst into sobs. Drew looked ready to cry but held himself in check. Tatum wished for the ground to open up and swallow her and her children whole.

"I'm not your daddy." Ryder lowered himself so that he was eye level with both boys. "I am your friend, though. And that's good enough. Now, let's ride Cupcake."

Like a miracle, Adam's tears dried, and Drew's smile reappeared. Gretchen, however, was another story, and she remained aloof.

The boys rode Cupcake a full twenty minutes before tiring. Ryder stood in the center of the pen, giving them instruction. Correction, giving Drew instruction. Adam sat behind his brother, holding on. Tatum couldn't resist and took several pictures with her phone. All right, she admitted it. She took a few shots just of Ryder. Who could resist?

"Time to get home, boys." Tatum scanned the area for Gretchen. Her daughter had found twin sisters to play with, children of Liberty's client. Confident her daughter was fine and adequately supervised, she returned her attention to Ryder.

"Let's unsaddle this steed." Ryder lifted first Adam, then Drew, off Cupcake.

"What's a steed?" Drew asked.

"A powerful horse."

"Cupcake's not powerful."

"Says who?"

While they were taking Cupcake to the barn, Mercer hailed Ryder. "There you are."

"You go on," Tatum said "I can unsaddle Cupcake."

He waved to his father and kept walking. "Be right there, Dad."

"Are you stalling?" She didn't intend to be blunt; the question had simply slipped out.

"A little."

"Is something wrong?"

"No." He took her arm as if to hurry her.

Under different circumstances, she'd have appreciated the sensation of his fingers firmly pressing into her flesh. Instead, her hackles rose. The past forty minutes had been simply a ruse.

"You don't have to use me, use the kids, as an excuse to avoid your family."

"Is that what you think?" Ryder asked.

Tatum's chin went up. "Frankly, yes."

They stopped outside the tack room. Drew held Cupcake's reins out of reach while Adam jumped up and down in place, crying, "Me, me, me."

"Okay, it's true. I am avoiding my family." Before she could offer a retort, he reached up and cupped her cheek. He didn't stop there and brushed the pad of his thumb along her bottom lip. "But I can't think of a better diversion."

Oh, to lean into his hand. Better yet, stand on her tiptoes and press her lips to his incredible mouth.

Steeling her resolve, she resisted. "Thank you. The boys appreciate it."

"I wasn't talking about them."

"Ryder." Her voice almost failed her.

"You're right." He let his hand drop. "Much as I'd like to explore possibilities, I can't. It wouldn't be fair."

"Because I work for your family?"

"That's one reason."

"I might not be an Easy Money employee for much longer if the school board approves the new budget."

"Let's see what happens." He patted Drew's head. "Come on, you two. I need help unsaddling this steed."

Tatum fought off the pain. Ryder hadn't exactly jumped for joy when she mentioned the possibility of returning to teaching. Why hadn't she kept her mouth shut? He might still be cupping her cheek.

Ryder and his father sat in the rickety wooden stands. Third row. They were the sole spectators. The arena at the Lost Dutchman Rodeo Company in Apache Junction wasn't set up to accommodate official rodeo events. These stands were reserved strictly for customers, such as the Becketts, in order to observe the available bucking stock in action.

And they were getting a lot of action this morning. The five bulls they'd seen so far were all prize-winning and in their prime. No one could fault their quality or potential.

The final bull scheduled to view was, at that moment, being herded from the narrow runway into the bucking chute. He was a tough-looking Brahma cross-breed with a large dark patch on his hind end that, if one used imagination, resembled the shape of a closed fist. Ryder wondered if that was any indication of the bull's bucking abilities.

Slowly, the cowboy lowered himself onto the bull's back, his spotter straddling the wall beside him and ready to pull the flat braided rope that would tighten the cowboy's grip. Two other Lost Dutchman hands stood nearby, their boots on the bottom rung of the fence, arms slung over the top rail. If necessary, they'd jump in and pull the cowboy off, should, for any reason, the bull become agitated or threatening.

"Watch." Ryder's father nodded in the direction of the chute. "That brute will dive left the second he breaks free."

"You're wrong. He's going to buck."

"See him turning his head? He's setting his course."

"Nope. He's pawing the ground with his back left hoof."

An easy grin spread across his father's face. They'd disagreed like this before. Often. All in good sport. "Winner buys lunch?"

"Get your wallet out."

The wooden floorboard beneath Ryder's feet vibrated, alerting him of Donnie Statler's approach.

Though only in his late fifties, the owner of the Lost Dutchman moved like an eighty-year-old, as if every bone in his body screamed in agony. They probably did. A lifetime of rodeoing was hard on a man.

"What do you think so far?" Donnie slowly lowered himself onto the bleacher seat next to Ryder.

The three had chatted earlier when Ryder and his father arrived that morning. Donnie had taken them around to view the stock and given them a brief rundown on each bull, its history and potential. This was Ryder's first meeting with Donnie, though his father knew the man from back in the day and his many years as a bucking stock contractor. Ryder would have to be deaf and blind not to notice the tension between the two.

They were about the same age and had, from the stories they'd shared earlier, once competed against each other. Heatedly. Both in rodeoing and, as Donnie was quick to point out, for the attention of Ryder's mother—when they were on the circuit and later, after the divorce.

But Ryder didn't think a long-ago rivalry was the cause of the tension. At least for Donnie. Ryder's guess, and he'd bet money on it, was that Donnie didn't appreciate the competition from the Easy Money, which had increased with the recent purchase of their own bucking bulls.

And, yet, here they were, looking at bulls to lease for their Wild West Days Rodeo. Not in competition with the Lost Dutchman at all but as its customer.

Donnie gave Ryder's knee a friendly slap. One with remarkable strength. Apparently he wasn't in as much pain as he appeared. "You can take a spin on that fellow, if you have a hankering."

"Thanks." Ryder chuckled. "Been far too many years for me to try." Fifteen, to be exact.

"Like riding a bicycle, my friend. You never forget."

Ryder had his doubts. "Maybe we can start with something smaller."

"Got us a few young steers in the back."

"I was thinking more of that bike you mentioned."

The men indulged in a good laugh. A moment later, the tension resumed.

"Was a time you leased a whole lot more bulls from me," Donnie said.

Ryder's father was quick with a comeback. "For a while there, we didn't lease any."

That was true. After a bull-goring accident, which left an Easy Money cowboy permanently disabled, Ryder's mother sold off their entire herd. From then on, during the arena's four annual rodeos, she'd lease bulls from Donnie. It had been an agreeable and profitable arrangement for both parties, up until Ryder's father had returned and purchased six new bulls. It was his plan to purchase more.

Donnie chewed thoughtfully on an unlit matchstick. "I've come to count on the income. The loss will cut into my profits."

"That's the way of business."

Hearing his father's retort, Ryder wanted to elbow him in the ribs. The day might come when the Becketts didn't need the Lost Dutchman. Today wasn't it. With entries pouring in for the rodeo, they'd need a lot more than their six bulls. Donnie's were the best around and the least expensive to transport. Angering him would serve no purpose, even if he did seize every opportunity to goad Ryder's father.

"Look, Donnie," Ryder said. "You don't have us over a barrel, but you have us edged up against one. For the moment, we'd like to continue doing business with you."

The other man merely grunted.

Ryder's father smirked. "He's not the only bucking stock contractor in the state."

"I could call my mother," Ryder said. "I know you and she have always been able to come to terms."

Donnie broke out in a wide, gap-toothed grin and slapped Ryder's knee again. "Best idea you've had all day, young man."

His father's piercing glare could have melted titanium. "We can negotiate an agreement just fine without involving Sunny."

That was what Ryder thought all along.

Conversation came to a stop when the chute door opened, and the Brahma bull exploded into the arena, first, two, then, all four hooves off the ground.

Beside him, Ryder's father muttered, "Damn. Would've sworn that fellow'd go left."

Ryder had no time to savor his victory. Beating impossible odds, the cowboy hung on, even spurring the bull to greater heights. The Brahma twisted to the left, to the right, and to the left again before raising his hind feet an easy six feet off the ground.

The display was great while it lasted. An instant before the buzzer went off, the cowboy lost the battle and was launched into the air, sailing high over the bull's head. Having the sense to tuck himself into a ball, he landed well off to the side of the beast, which was quickly chased to the far end of the small arena and out the gate by two more Lost Dutchman hands. The cowboy was up and dusting off his jeans long before the hands reached him.

"*Puño* won't disappoint," Donnie observed.

Spanish for fist, Ryder thought. The mark on the bull's hind quarters. It was an appropriate name. "I don't think any of your stock will."

"Damn straight."

"We could use six more in addition to the ones we've seen, if you have that many available."

"Might." Donnie eyed him, the unlit matchstick bobbing up and down.

"Let's talk." Ryder rose and waited for the other man. Behind him, his father also stood. He half expected Mercer to insist on taking over. That didn't happen. Good. His father was showing some sense.

Ryder hadn't intended to assume control of the negotiations or step on his father's toes. But this was business. Not personal. He had no history with Donnie and wasn't about to lose sight of the bigger goal simply because his ego took a hit.

An hour later, Ryder and his father left the Lost Dutchman with a copy of their newly signed and dated commitment to lease.

"I'm hungry," his father said the moment he was behind the wheel. He'd insisted on driving. "Let's stop at the Flat Iron for that lunch I owe you."

Ryder didn't object and not only because he'd won the bet. Neither of them was much for cooking. If they didn't eat out at least one meal a day, they'd starve.

"You were good back there, son. I'm glad you tagged along."

"I am, too. If only to meet Donnie."

Originally, Ryder had thought he'd stay at the arena. The farrier was due this morning, and he'd wanted to inspect Cupcake. A pony's feet were small and different from a horse's, which no doubt accounted for the ill-fitting shoe in the first place. But Liberty said she'd inspect the farrier's work before paying him. Next to Ryder and his father, she was the best choice and most knowledgeable.

Just as well. Ryder wasn't sure another encounter with Tatum was a good idea under the circumstances. Seemed every time they were together, he either said or did something to give her the wrong impression.

His fault. She'd looked so vulnerable yesterday, he couldn't resist touching her. If only to assure her. Except, he'd done the opposite. She was more confused than ever. He'd be, too, if someone continued giving him mixed signals.

He expelled a long, slow breath. It had been worth it. Her skin was the color of gold and the texture of satin.

He'd wanted to slide his palm from her cheek to her neck, then drive his fingers into that incredible hair. What might it look like fanned across his pillow? Better yet, across his naked chest.

Dangerous thoughts he'd best avoid. Tatum Mayweather's desires were written all over her face. Gold ring, white picket fence and good stepdad to her kids. Ryder would disappoint her, sooner if not later.

"Those terms you negotiated were good," his father said. "Better than our last contract with Donnie."

They were in the truck, heading back to Reckless.

"It was a simple contract, Dad. Tatum could have done just as well."

"She doesn't know the first thing about marketing or promotion. And she sure as heck doesn't know about bucking stock contracts."

"She might surprise you. Have you considered giving her more responsibility?"

"She's quitting and going back to teaching."

What would his father think if he found out that Ryder was working with a headhunter? He wouldn't be happy, that was for sure.

Ryder hadn't promised forever. That didn't mean his father and Liberty believed otherwise. She'd pressured him hard last night at dinner to reconcile with their mother, certain if he did, he'd stay. Ryder hadn't wanted to disappoint her, but he wasn't ready.

Three days home and he'd hardly seen or spoken to his mother, other than the homecoming lunch. She might be giving him time and space to come around. Ryder was choosing the path of least resistance.

"Three months."

"What?" Ryder shook his head to clear it.

"That's my target date," his father said. "To buy more bulls. Enough so that we don't have to lease any from the Lost Dutchman or anyone else. Also some heifers. Within a year, we'll start breeding and raising our own bucking stock."

"Then we *will* be in competition with Donnie."

"There's room enough for both of us. He's strictly a contractor. We have the arena. And he doesn't have your mother."

"Aren't you carrying an old jealousy a bit too far?"

"Not talking about that. Your mom's smart as a whip. She and I, we were unstoppable once. Going to be again."

What his parents did wasn't really any of his business. Still, Ryder felt the need to caution his father. "Can you trust Mom?"

"Are you kidding? She's great with money."

"She threw you out."

"I deserved that. I was a drunk and hell-bent on bankrupting the arena."

"You didn't deserve it, Dad. People make mistakes. You have to quit defending her."

"If I'd have stayed, I might not have gotten sober. Sometimes you just have to cauterize the wound. Hurts like the dickens, but that's the only way it'll heal."

"All right."

"Your mother's not a bad person, son."

Ryder wasn't in the mood to debate. "I'll just shut up now."

"Is that why you haven't married? Because your mother and me couldn't make a go of it?"

"I was married."

"Not for long. And, as far as I can tell, there hasn't

been anyone serious since. Hate thinking it's your mom's and my fault."

Ryder sat back and stared out the windshield. While he'd have liked to dismiss his father's question as nonsense, he couldn't and had asked himself the same thing more than once.

Putting his career first or not finding the right woman were his go-to replies when pressed about his bachelorhood. Could it be he didn't believe in the institution of marriage? Not only had he failed at it, so had his parents. Miserably. Their divorce had wound up dividing his entire family.

With that kind of history, anyone would be scared of commitment, even with a lovely and appealing woman like Tatum Mayweather.

Chapter 5

Tatum wore a skirt today but not because she and Ryder were scheduled to go over the current bucking stock contracts together. Absolutely not. Sometimes, she abandoned her customary jeans in favor of dressier clothes. Like when a representative from the regional office of the PCA visited the arena or during the annual liability insurance audit last month.

She tugged on the front of her skirt as she sat at her desk, making sure the material lay smooth. Right, who was she fooling? She'd totally dressed up for Ryder.

How could she be annoyed at him for sending out mixed signals when she wore an outfit meant to encourage signals? Just as well she hadn't seen much of him the past few days. The upcoming rodeo and the Easy Money's participation in Wild West Days was keeping them both busy. She'd heard from Liberty that he'd inspected Cupcake's new shoeing job and gave the farrier a passing grade.

That was a relief. She really should remember to thank him.

Glancing at the clock on the wall, something she'd been doing all day in anticipation of Ryder's arrival, she smoothed her skirt again. Not that it had wrinkled in the past five minutes.

Luckily, the phone rang, and she was temporarily distracted from stressing over what was nothing more than a work session between two fellow employees. She'd barely hung up when the Federal Express deliveryman arrived with a package. Tatum couldn't wait to see the contents. Placing the large box on her desk, she opened it and rifled through the packing material like a dog digging a hole.

Carefully, she removed the navy banner with its gold trim and silver lettering. It looked good, great even, and she allowed herself a moment's satisfaction.

Tatum had been put in charge of designing and ordering the new banner, the old one being a worn relic. She'd also convinced Sunny that, in order to be properly represented, the arena's logo needed a redesign. If it turned out terrible, Tatum would have borne the responsibility entirely.

But it hadn't, though she couldn't be a hundred percent sure until she saw the banner unfurled. With little room to maneuver, and not wanting to soil the fabric, she draped all eight feet of it across her desk. The ends hung over the sides, distorting the effect. She was just rethinking her approach when Ryder entered the office from the barn door.

"Nice," he commented, taking in the banner.

She could have said the same thing about him. In the week since his arrival, his clothes had gone from having that store-bought newness to casually comfortable. At first glance, he'd easily pass for one of the arena's regular hands. Any better looking and Tatum would do something stupid, like preen or swoon or—heaven forbid—flirt.

"I think so, too." She studied the banner, tapping her lower lip with her finger. "Just wish I could see all of it."

"Here." He grabbed one end and lifted it off her desk. "You get that side."

They stood opposite each other, the banner stretched between them.

"The logo's new." Ryder referred to the silhouette of a bucking horse kicking a dollar sign into the air. "I like it. Your design?"

"Yes." Tatum couldn't resist a grin.

"You're good."

A warm feeling bloomed inside her that had less to do with his praise and more to do with the sexy timbre of his voice. *Stay strong*, she warned herself.

"I was worried it wouldn't get here in time for the parade," she said.

"Mom mentioned we have an entry."

As usual. Participating in the Wild West Days parade was a longstanding Beckett tradition.

"Will you be riding with the family?" Tatum moved toward him, folding the banner as she did.

Ryder did the same. "Doubtful."

"Why not?"

Many of the arena's students would accompany the Beckett family. They'd had to limit the number to the first thirty who'd signed up, the maximum parade regu-

lations allowed. Two of the advanced students, astride
their trustworthy horses, had been chosen to ride at the
front of the group, each carrying one end of the banner. During the rest of the year, it would be used for the
opening and closing ceremonies in their various rodeos
and horse shows.

"We'll see," Ryder hedged.

"It'll be fun."

"Are you riding in the parade?" The tone of his voice
made her think he'd change his mind if she were to
say yes.

"No. But I'm taking my kids to watch. They love it."

"Maybe I'll see you there."

They finished folding and stood together, toe to toe.
A small tingle of awareness climbed Tatum's spine.
"Are you ready to start on the contracts?"

"Where's the best place to sit?"

Good question, and one that caused her awareness
of him to escalate. The other day, he'd occupied a visitor chair, and they'd passed files back and forth over
her desk. That arrangement wouldn't work today; he
needed to see her computer screen. Why hadn't she
thought of this before?

"Well, um…" She went to stand behind her desk, as
if that vantage point would prompt an idea.

He suddenly lifted the visitor chair and carried it
over to the cramped space beside her.

"It's a little tight," she observed.

It was a *lot* tight. Tatum scooted her chair to the right,
creating maybe three extra inches.

"Luckily I showered today," Ryder said in jest before sitting.

Yeah. She'd noticed his crisp, fresh scent earlier.

Lowering herself onto her chair, she strived for control by getting straight to business.

"Did you read the draft letter I emailed you yesterday?" She'd composed a follow-up contract for the secretary at the mining company.

"I did. Well worded."

Again, more praise delivered in that incredible voice of his. How had the female members of his team at the marketing firm been able to concentrate with him as their leader?

"Should I send it to her?"

"Include a discount coupon."

She nodded. "I've also been working on that list of potential companies for reciprocal advertising." She clicked on a document. "These are just for Arizona. I wasn't sure what other states you wanted to try."

"New Mexico, for sure. And southern California."

They'd finished with the list and were reviewing the current client roster when Sunny returned from giving potential new clients a tour of the grounds.

The look of concentration on Sunny's face vanished upon seeing Ryder. "Hi, honey." She came over, bent and kissed the top of his head.

The gesture was sweet and motherly and very much like one Tatum gave her own children. Only they didn't stiffen their jaw muscles.

"Hey, Mom." Ryder's neutral tone was in stark contrast to his mother's warm one.

Sunny's features fell. The next instant she composed herself. "I see you're working. I won't bother you." She headed to her office. Fled was a better description.

Tatum bit her tongue. As bad as she felt for her boss, it wasn't her place to say anything. She also sensed

Ryder wasn't one to be pushed. Any reconciliation would be on his terms.

Still, her heart ached. Ryder and Sunny weren't the only ones affected. All of the Becketts suffered along with mother and son. Did Ryder not see that?

An hour later, he and Tatum were knee deep in the bucking contract files. Where had the afternoon gone? Soon, she'd have to leave to pick up Gretchen from school and the boys from day care. Not Benjie. Cassidy had taken him out of class for a dentist appointment.

Ryder had made copious notes as they'd worked, his bold, strong strokes filling the pages. Several times, Tatum had to stop and answer the phone or deal with a customer. Ryder remained ever patient.

She was just explaining about the Haversons from the Shade Tree Arena in Wickenburg when the phone rang again. Only this time, it was her cell phone from her purse in the lower desk drawer.

Hmm. Most people knew better than to bother her during working hours. This was either a sales call or something important.

"Excuse me." She maneuvered her knees to the side in order to access the drawer. Naturally, that caused them to press against Ryder's. "It's my babysitter," she said, already starting to worry.

"Sorry to bother you," her sitter said in a rush. "It's Drew. He was playing kick ball in the yard with the other kids and hurt his finger."

"How bad is it?" Tatum imagined a cut or sprain.

"Bad. It's sticking straight out at this really weird angle. I'm pretty sure he broke it."

Without thinking, Tatum scrambled to her feet and tried to push past Ryder, shaking badly enough she nearly dropped the phone. She did drop her purse. "I have to go. Drew's hurt."

Ryder blocked her exit. "I'll take you."

"I can't ask that of you."

"You're too upset to think straight, much less drive."

"Gretchen's out at three. She'll be waiting for me at the school."

He took her by the arm, his firm hold silencing any argument. "I'll pick her up after I take you and the boys to the clinic."

"What about Adam's car seat? Your truck—"

"Where's your car parked?"

"Behind the barn."

Over his shoulder he called, "Mom, I'm taking Tatum to pick up Drew. He's been hurt."

Sunny came rushing out. "Do you need anything? Is he all right?"

"A broken finger."

"You'd better hurry."

"I'm so sorry to leave you in a bind." Tatum swallowed a sob.

"Call me later," Sunny said.

"I will. I promise."

Ryder didn't let go of Tatum's arm until they reached her car.

Little by little, she relaxed. It had been a long time since she'd let a capable man take control. She could easily grow accustomed to the change.

First, Ryder delivered Tatum, Drew and Adam to the small medical clinic in town. Then, after Tatum made arrangements with the school, he picked up Gretchen and drove her to the clinic.

They spent exactly ten minutes there. The physician's assistant on duty could do no more for Drew's dislocated pinky finger than immobilize it, secure an ice pack to his hand with an elastic bandage and administer a mild pain reliever.

"You need to see a doctor," she advised. "To set the finger. Preferably an orthopedic surgeon."

At ten past four, they had no choice but to drive into Globe and wait in line at the hospital emergency room—along with countless other sick and injured individuals. Drew couldn't go the entire weekend with a dislocated finger.

Tatum fretted endlessly on the drive to Globe. About Drew, who thought his pinky protruding at a ninety degree angle was cool. About Adam, who fussed and whined because he'd missed his afternoon nap. About inconveniencing Ryder. About leaving abruptly and dumping her work on Sunny. About the costs and whether the health insurance would pay for an emergency-room visit. About whether she should call Monty or just wait.

"Take it easy," Ryder told her and reached across the seat to comfort her. When he would have removed his hand from hers, Tatum gripped his fingers and squeezed as if he alone was responsible for keeping her anchored in place.

He didn't complain and steered the car with his other hand.

"I'm trying." She glanced at Drew in the backseat, bracketed by Adam in the car seat on his right and a very grumpy Gretchen on his left. Apparently she was supposed to go to a friend's house after school. Tatum had admitted to forgetting about it in all the rush. "I should be glad it's relatively minor and something that will heal."

"He'll be fine. I've broken plenty of bones in my life. Survived every one."

"Rodeoing?"

"Most. A couple years ago, I busted my ankle playing second base at a company softball game. We lost anyway."

She offered up a weak smile.

"That's better," he said, wishing he could do more to ease her anxiety.

She released his fingers and rested her hands in her lap.

Damn. That had been nice. Sweet. Gentle. With his former coworker, intimacy had been for one purpose only, as if their relationship was too trivial to sustain any emotional depth. Was that why she'd been so angry at him for calling it off?

The line at the ER was long. Ryder's gaze traveled the entire length of the room, noting the majority of chairs were occupied. A teenaged girl in gym clothes held an ice pack to her collarbone. An elderly man with a crudely bandaged hand cursed the dog that bit him. In every corner of the room, adults and children alike coughed and hacked, fighting off the early flu bug going around.

Ryder guided their small group over outstretched legs to the only available seats. Tatum then read to, cajoled, rocked, and played games with her children in an attempt to keep them from fussing too much. An hour later, a nurse toting a clipboard called Drew's name.

"I want to go with Mommy," Gretchen complained

when the nurse informed them that she and Adam weren't allowed in the examining area. "Not fair."

"I'm sorry to ask this." Tatum gave Ryder a pleading look.

"You just take care of Drew." Certainly, he could handle a two- and seven-year-old for a few minutes.

"You listen to Mr. Beckett, you hear me? Don't give him any trouble."

Adam ignored his mother and attempted to scale Ryder's knee. He had to help the boy the last foot into his lap. Gretchen pouted and plunked herself down on her seat, leaving an empty chair between her and Ryder. She still hadn't forgiven him for…to be honest, he wasn't sure what.

"But I don't want them to fix my finger," Drew moaned as Tatum led him by his good hand. "It's awesome."

They disappeared with the clipboard-carrying nurse though a double door.

"You want to color or something?" Ryder asked Gretchen. "There's some books over there." He had to crank his head sideways to see around Adam, who stood on Ryder's thigh, bouncing in place and talking up a storm in some kind of alien language. Geez, the kid was actually heavy, and his shoes were hard as concrete.

"I'm too old to color." Gretchen stared at the TV hanging on the wall playing an infomercial for a cleaning product. She couldn't possibly be interested in that.

"Okay."

She gave him an entire minute before demanding, "That's it?"

"I guess."

"You're supposed to ask me if I want to read a book or hear a story."

"I don't know any stories." Not any suitable for little girls.

She huffed. "I don't know why my mom likes you."

"She likes me?" Ryder really shouldn't have been so pleased by this revelation. But he was. Immensely. "Did she tell you that?"

Gretchen's response was to fold her arms across her middle, drop her chin to her chest and pout.

"Hungwee," Adam said and flung himself over Ryder's right shoulder.

"Sorry, pal. We're going to have to wait until your mom gets back." Ryder wondered if there was some way he could wrangle Adam off his lap and into the empty chair. The young man sitting across from Ryder and talking on his cell phone didn't look particularly happy about a loud, rambunctious kid in such close proximity.

"Hungwee," Adam shouted.

"There's a vending machine in the hallway." The suggestion came from a woman accompanying her sick friend. "You can probably find something for your son."

"He's not our daddy!" Gretchen turned pink with indignation.

"Oh." The woman drew back. "My mistake."

"No worries." Ryder stood, lifting Adam as he did. "Come on, big guy. You, too," he added when Gretchen didn't move.

"I'm staying."

Given her stubborn streak, he should have anticipated this. "You're not hungry?"

Interest flickered in her eyes.

"Hungwee," Adam bellowed directly into Ryder's ear, nearly deafening him.

Gretchen stood, one painstakingly slow inch at a time.

Finally. Another minute and Ryder's teeth would be ground to nubs.

"I can't eat anything with gluten in it," she announced.

There were exactly three items in the vending machine that met the gluten-free requirement.

"I hate corn nuts," she announced. "And peanuts."

Ryder inserted several dollar bills into the machine and pressed a button. "Corn chips it is."

She accepted them grudgingly.

"Does Adam like corn chips, too?"

"He's not supposed to have junk food."

That left few choices as the vending machine was loaded with junk food. Ryder selected some awful-looking orange crackers with yellow cheese for him.

"Aren't you hungry, too?" Gretchen asked.

Ryder moved to the next machine. "I'm having a soda."

"Mom says sodas are bad for you. They're full of sugar. Can I have a juice?"

The only non-soda selections were plain bottled water and vitamin water. Ryder bought two of the latter and a cola for himself. Hopefully, Tatum would approve of his choice, or at least, cut him some slack, given the circumstances.

When they returned to the waiting area, Gretchen sat next to Ryder—interesting—and ate in silence. Adam gobbled three crackers and drank half his vitamin water, some of which spilled on to his clothes, then promptly fell asleep atop Ryder.

Ten minutes into the nap, Ryder's left arm went numb. He shifted Adam to the other side. The boy, out like a light, didn't so much as twitch an eyelash.

Gretchen had finished her chips. Ryder pretended not to notice when she got up and ambled toward the table in the corner with the coloring books and crayons.

His cell phone rang three times. The first call was from Cassidy, wanting an update. Ryder spoke softly, not wanting to wake up Adam.

"Haven't heard yet. They're back with the doctor."

"Poor Tatum. She doesn't need another problem."

"She seems to be hanging in there."

"What about Gretchen and Adam?"

"She's coloring and he's sleeping." Ryder shifted the boy again, this time laying him across his lap like a rag doll.

"How did you wind up driving them to Globe?"

"Tatum was upset, and I was there."

"Hmm. Well, okay. Seems like you have everything handled." Her tone revealed surprise and—could it be?—a hint of admiration. "Tell Tatum to call me when she has a minute."

The third call came from Myra Solomon. "I've already generated some buzz about you. There's a firm in Denver showing interest."

"That's great." Ryder's enthusiasm was several degrees lower than he'd expected.

"Can you get here now to film that video interview? We'll stay late."

He was supposed to have gone in yesterday for the

video interview but had stalled Myra. He knew his next answer would disappoint her.

"I can't. I'm at the ER with a friend. Her son injured himself playing kick ball."

"Ryder." The headhunter's warning was unmistakable. "You can't put this off any longer."

"First thing, Monday morning. I promise."

"I'd better see your smiling face here by nine a.m. on the dot."

"You will." That gave him two days to come up with an excuse for his absence from the Easy Money. The family was bound to notice.

Finally Tatum and Drew emerged through the door, a different nurse accompanying them. Drew's hand was heavily bandaged, the finger no longer sticking out, and his arm in a sling. His earlier glee had disappeared. In fact, he looked as if he'd been crying. Setting the finger must have hurt.

As they approached, Ryder could hear the young man going over Drew's discharge instructions with Tatum. If her streaked mascara was any indication, she'd been crying, too.

"Read everything carefully. Doctor recommends using over-the-counter liquid children's acetaminophen. If his pain is acute, call this number, and he'll prescribe something stronger. Rest and confinement for the next few days. No strenuous activity for a month."

"Yay!" Drew's glee returned. "I get to stay home from day care," he singsonged.

"We'll see, baby. Mommy still has to work." Tatum accepted the stack of papers from the nurse, and he departed. She took one look at Adam, slung limply across Ryder's lap, and came to a stop. "Oh. Sorry about that."

Ryder shrugged. "Better he's sleeping than crying."

"Was he crying?"

"I gave him orange crackers and vitamin water. If he's sick, it's all my fault."

"He's eaten worse and survived. Once I caught him in the pantry, shoving fistfuls of kitty kibble into his mouth." Tatum brushed at her cheeks.

His heart went out to her. "Was it tough watching the doctor set the finger?"

Ryder remembered a time when he'd fallen from their pony Flame. The cut on his chin had required sixteen stitches. His mother had carried on worse than him. In the end, he'd wound up comforting her.

Why should he remember that now?

"He's so young," was Tatum's only answer.

Gretchen managed to drag herself away from the coloring table. Fists balanced on her hips, she glared at Drew and demanded, "Let me see your cast."

"It's not a cast." He sounded disappointed. "Just a…a…"

"Splint," Tatum said. She turned to Ryder. "He sees the orthopedic surgeon on Monday."

Drew brightened. "Then I get a cast. I want a green one." He stared up at Tatum. "Mommy, I'm hungry."

"Me, too." Gretchen sidled up to Tatum and clutched her free hand.

She smiled apologetically at both her children. "We have to get Drew's medication at the store first, sweetie, then head home. We've taken up enough of Mr. Beckett's time."

Gretchen made a face.

Ryder gently lifted Adam and stood. Without thinking too much about it, he held the still-sleeping boy against his chest. The kid stirred, wrapped his small arms around Ryder's neck, and promptly drifted back to sleep. Ryder absently patted the boy's back.

"There's a drugstore in the shopping center across the street. Also a fast-food chicken place. Everyone like fried chicken?"

"Yes!" Drew raised his good arm in a fist pump.

"I can't have fried chicken," Gretchen said grumpily.

Tatum patted her head. "She's gluten intolerant. There's breading—"

"I heard," Ryder said. "We can go somewhere else."

"It's fine, sweetie. The restaurant has baked chicken, too."

As they were leaving, a nurse came out and called the name of the sick woman. Before her friend left with her, she leaned close to Ryder and said, "You may not be their father, but you'd make a good one."

Tatum obviously heard for a strange look came into her eyes, and she said nothing on their walk to the car.

Chapter 6

Food clearly worked wonders, as far as Tatum's brood was concerned anyway. Adam woke up from his nap in time to demolish a plate of mashed potatoes, a biscuit and carefully cut-up pieces of chicken. Gretchen complained about her lack of gluten-free choices but was pacified with the promise of dessert. Ryder's suggestion, and a good one if he did say so himself.

Drew, Ryder's new best buddy, sat close to him and practically inhaled his food. Tatum rode herd on them all, serving up portions and wiping messy hands and faces with paper napkins.

"Aren't you going to eat?" Ryder asked, noticing she'd hardly touched her food.

"I will." She took a single bite, then became distracted when Adam dropped his straw on to the floor and began to wail. She grimaced. "I'm sorry. Really I am."

"It's okay, Tatum. They're just being kids."

"And you like kids."

"I like yours."

He found her expression difficult to interpret. Was she pleased or irritated with him? The next instant, she turned away.

The thing was, her kids really didn't bother him. The boys were great. A typical rough-and-tumble pair. And Gretchen? Well, she wasn't so bad when she let that damnable guard of hers down. It was to be expected, really. She'd been through a lot in recent years. Her parents divorcing, the family moving—twice—and then being shipped off to her grandmother's for four months. That would put anyone on the defensive.

They made it back to Reckless at about seven-thirty. Tatum had placed several phone calls during the drive. To Drew's father. Her babysitter. Cassidy. And, lastly, her sister in Tucson. Everyone was relieved to hear Drew's dislocation wasn't worse.

Ryder paid extra close attention when she spoke with Monty, listening while pretending not to. He heard resentment and also frustration. Monty, it seemed, wasn't overly concerned that his son was hurt. Only because she'd insisted, he talked to Drew. Tatum handed her phone over the seat and stared out the window during the entire brief conversation.

At the arena, Ryder pulled into a space near the office. He and Tatum exited the car and met up near the rear bumper. Night had fallen during the ride home, but overhead floodlights lit up the arena like a small city while leaving other places in shadows. Such as where Ryder and Tatum stood.

A group of local barrel racers had reserved the arena and were having practice runs. Spectators applauded as a young woman galloped her horse around the course, dirt exploding at each turn.

Ryder didn't see any of his family, but he suspected some of them, if not all, were in the vicinity.

"Thanks again for everything." Tatum lifted her gaze to Ryder's. "You went above and beyond today."

"It was fun."

"Right." She smiled. For the first time all day.

"And different," he conceded.

"That, I'll believe." The corners of her mouth drooped.

"You must be exhausted."

"It has been a long day. And it's not over."

"See you tomorrow?"

"Not likely." She glanced toward the arena and sighed. "It's the weekend. I have art classes all day Saturday. Though sometimes we take Cupcake out for a ride on Sunday afternoons."

He'd forgotten about her not being there on the weekends. Less than a week home, and already he'd fallen into the habit of seeing her on a daily basis. What would happen when he left? Suddenly, he didn't want the evening to end.

"If you need a hand with the kids, just give me a—"

He was rendered speechless by her lips pressing against his cheek. Her touch was both gentle and electrifying. Closing his eyes, he let himself experience the moment.

Don't stop. Not yet.

She must have read his thoughts for she lingered. And lingered.

Her proximity brought with it a heat that invaded his every pore. As did the fragrant scent of her hair. Or was it the lotion she'd used that morning? Not to mention the silky texture of her skin.

Skin? Wait a minute.

Without realizing it, he'd lifted a hand to caress her bare arm.

She made the slightest move to pull away. Ryder would have none of it and drew her close. Closer still. He didn't stop until she was forced to grab hold of his shoulders or risk losing her balance.

"Ryder," was all she got out before he covered her mouth with his, turning a not-quite-innocent peck into a full-blown, make-no-mistake-I-want-you kiss.

She resisted for several seconds before relenting. He groaned low in his throat when she went soft and pliant in his arms.

With very little urging from him, she parted her lips. When his tongue entered her mouth, she answered his bold strokes in kind. Ryder gripped her harder, every one of his senses compelling him to take the kiss further and show her exactly what she did to him. How she made him feel.

It wasn't to be, however. Much, much too soon she withdrew, murmuring, "We can't. The children."

"Okay." He'd forgotten all about them.

Ryder was reluctant to let her go, though he knew he should. Had to. Must.

"That was…" Her voice fell away.

"Don't say a mistake, Tatum. Because it wasn't."

"I'm vulnerable. And you're being sweet."

"I kissed you because it's all I've been thinking of for days."

She sighed. "I'm an overworked single mom with three kids capable of driving a saint to sin. Which, after today, I'm thinking you are."

"Hardly." If she knew the kind of thoughts he was entertaining about her, him and a dark, secluded bedroom, she'd realize just how far he was from being a saint. "You're an incredibly attractive, very sexy lady, who also happens to be a great mother. I admire you, Tatum."

"Mom!" Gretchen stuck her head out the window. "Drew says his finger hurts."

"They're getting restless." Tatum eased away.

Ryder let his hand slide from her arm to her hand. Their fingers linked momentarily before parting for good. He walked out from behind the car and watched her leave. Drew and Adam waved to him through the backseat window. Gretchen simply stared. Had she seen him and her mother kissing?

Tatum also waved, an expression of uncertainty on her face. With good reason. He hadn't given her sufficient reason to expect that theirs was a relationship with a future.

Ryder turned to see his mother approaching. She also wore a look of uncertainty. His hope that she hadn't witnessed him and Tatum kissing was instantly dashed with her next words.

"I couldn't be happier that you're home, Ryder. But not at the expense of hurting that poor girl. She's gone through hell, and I don't want you putting her through any more."

* * *

Ryder's first real conversation with his mother since his return and what was it about? Him defending his actions to her.

She'd requested, insisted, really, that he accompany her to the announcer's booth above the bucking chutes, stating she hadn't locked up for the night. It was an excuse. She wanted them to be alone for the lecture she delivered. Possibly deserved. Nonetheless, his hackles rose.

"I'm not blind, Ryder. That was no kiss between friends."

Denying it would waste his breath and insult his mother's intelligence.

"Tatum doesn't date much, and I'm sure she kisses men even less." His mother flipped switches, powering down the equipment. The floodlights would remain on until the barrel racers were finished with their practice. During the weekends, which included Friday nights, that could last until ten or later. "She likes you. She always has. Which makes her susceptible to misreading your intentions."

"I happen to like her, too."

"In *that* way?"

"I'll be careful not to hurt her." Would he? He hadn't been thus far.

"She's vulnerable, Ryder, and takes matters of the heart very seriously."

He didn't answer right away, his concentration focused on the booth's interior with its large open window and bird's-eye view.

It had been a lot of years since Ryder was here. As little kids, he and Cassidy would pretend they were calling out events for a rodeo. Their mother would turn on the PA system, allowing their voices to carry across the entire property. Often, their father was in the arena, riding a horse or roping a calf.

Good times. He'd forgotten until right now. Another fond memory added to the list of ones he'd pushed aside when his parents divorced.

"She's walking a particularly fine line right now." The censure in his mother's voice returned Ryder to the present. "She had to leave her kids with her ex-mother-in-law for a while after she lost her job at the school and only recently got them back."

"Cassidy told me."

"It was difficult for her."

"I get it, Mom. I won't take advantage of her."

Yet, hadn't he done exactly that? Tatum may have made the first move, but that peck on the cheek was nothing more than a platonic thank-you. He'd taken the kiss to an entirely new level.

And she'd responded. Incredibly. Beautifully. If he closed his eyes, he could still feel her lips on his, her mouth opening in invitation. The gentle slope of her back as he trailed his hand down her spine. Her limbs becoming liquid as their kiss lingered and deepened.

How was it she didn't have droves of suitors beating down her door? And if she did, how would he feel about that?

Angry and territorial, though he'd have no right.

"I wouldn't worry," he said. "I doubt she's interested in me beyond a passing attraction."

"I agree."

Did she? Ryder staved off the blow to his ego.

"Monty wasn't the family-man type. He and Tatum

gave it a go, but as soon as she had Gretchen, the marriage started to fail." She eyed him critically. "You're not the family-man type either."

"How would you know?"

At his brusque tone, she faltered. "You've been single for years. I assumed."

"For the record, you assumed wrong."

She looked stricken. "Sorry. My mistake."

Guilt pricked at him. He supposed it wasn't such a far-fetched conclusion. In the thirteen years since his divorce, he hadn't come anywhere close to settling down.

Not unlike his sister Cassidy. She, more so than him, shunned marriage. Even getting pregnant hadn't changed her mind. She insisted on raising Benjie alone without ever telling the father.

Ryder had long ago decided there were only two reasons for his sister's secrecy. Either the guy was married and she'd had an affair, or he was someone the Becketts would disapprove of.

He'd also decided it wasn't fair of his sister to deny Benjie the right to know his father, or for the father to know his son, whether or not the man was married. Their mother had done the same thing to Liberty—which probably explained why Cassidy believed there was nothing wrong with it. Could his family be more dysfunctional? Amazing, really, that Liberty had found love with a great guy and was headed to the altar. Perhaps she'd forgiven their mother for the lies.

"It's getting late, Mom." He started for the door.

"Wait, Ryder."

"I think we've covered everything we need to."

"If the school board doesn't approve the new budget

and rehire Tatum, she'll be devastated. I'm not sure she can take another personal blow."

"Is there a chance she won't be hired back?"

"The board isn't in agreement on the budget. We meet again the week after next for the official vote."

"You'll keep her on here, won't you?"

"Of course. For as long as she wants."

"She's capable of more. There's nothing I've done this week she couldn't handle with minimal training."

"I disagree. You cut a good deal with Donnie for those bulls. Tatum hasn't ever been involved in contract negotiations."

"She's smart."

"She's also a little shy when she's in unfamiliar circumstances."

"Maybe she can shadow me next time." The idea appealed to Ryder.

His mother hesitated. "I'm not sure your father will go for that."

He'd gotten the same impression when talking to Mercer. "Why doesn't he like her?"

"That's not it at all. He wants you to stay. Training Tatum to do your job makes you dispensable."

"I didn't commit long-term when I agreed to help out."

"He's hoping to change your mind." She moved as if to touch him, then withdrew her hand. "I want you to stay, too."

"Why?"

"You're my son."

"Besides that?"

"The Easy Money is a family business, and you're part of the family."

"If Dad hadn't wormed his way back into the business, would you have still wanted me to be part of it?"

She appeared offended by his question. "Of course."

"You never said so."

"You had your job at Madison-Monroe. I didn't think you'd accept if I'd asked."

She was right about that.

Hand on the doorknob, he paused. There was one question he needed answered before ending this conversation. "Didn't you feel the least bit bad about lying to Liberty, to all of us, for years?"

"I felt terrible."

He chuckled derisively. "Not enough to tell the truth."

"I made a decision. I thought it was the right one at the time. If you're a parent one day, and I truly hope you are, then maybe you'll understand."

"Dad has been sober for twenty-two years. You don't think he proved himself a long time ago?"

"I was afraid."

"It's always about you, isn't it?"

"I did what I had to in order to protect my family."

Cassidy had said almost the exact same thing. Did she and their mother compare notes? Decide what they'd tell him? The thought irritated him. Ryder didn't like being played.

"You should know, I'm in talks with a headhunter."

Her expression instantly fell. "I wish you'd give this, the arena, us, a fair shot before deciding."

"I doubt it would make a difference."

She stiffened. "It certainly won't make a difference with that kind of attitude."

"Good night, Mom." Ryder left the booth and headed

down the stairs. Reaching the bottom he strode briskly toward the barn, his mother's anguished face refusing to leave him.

He'd hurt her with his words. It was, after all, what he'd intended. She'd hurt him, too. Then and now.

The feeling of satisfaction he'd been counting on didn't come. Instead, he wanted to throw something. Or, better, punch a hole in a wall.

He did neither. He left the arena, taking the long way to his father's place.

Chapter 7

Ryder parked his truck along Center Avenue, Reckless's main thoroughfare. As they were every weekend, parking spaces were at a premium. He'd have to walk a quarter mile to reach Tatum's art studio where Benjie was attending Saturday-morning class.

Cassidy had been busy with the barrel racers and unable to get away, their practice heating up in preparation for the upcoming Wild West Days Rodeo. Since he had another errand in town, Ryder had offered to pick up Benjie. After a brief hesitation, and a promise from Ryder that no harm would come to her son, she'd relented.

In truth, he was glad for the chance to have some one-on-one with his nephew. He really didn't know Benjie well and wanted to spend as much time as possible with him before he left.

At the corner, Ryder waited for the light to change and stifled a yawn. The talk with his mother had stayed with him long after it ended, interrupting his sleep. He kept telling himself he was right, his mother wrong. Experience had shown him, however, there were always two sides to every story. He had only to look at his termination from Madison-Monroe for proof of that.

As he strolled through town, he couldn't help noticing the many changes in preparation for the coming week. Wild West Days was a fever the locals had caught.

A white banner with bold red letters announcing the event was draped from one side of the street to the other. Decorations adorned storefronts. Sandwich-board signs outside restaurants advertised specials, such as cowboy steaks and TexMex chili. An area had been cordoned off near the town square for Saturday night square dancing. Carpenters had assembled a wooden judge's stand outside the library. Mock weddings would be performed in front of the judge, and people arrested and charged with outlandish crimes. The wedding license fees and fines would then be donated to the library's book fund.

The summer before Ryder had moved in with his father, he'd been old enough to perform in the "shoot-outs," playing a bandit who was "gunned down" as he tried to escape. He'd milked his role for all it was worth, showing off in front of his pals and, to be honest, a girl or two, with his Oscar-worthy performances.

Reaching the Silver Dollar Pawn Shop, a local establishment founded in the early 1900s that catered to both locals and tourists, he went inside. The store's wares included everything from rare Western antiques to jewelry to the latest electronic gadget. His upcoming video interview at Myra's office had spurred an idea for the arena, one that took hold last night and wouldn't let go. The Silver Dollar seemed a good place to start.

"Howdy!" The elderly woman behind the counter greeted him with a friendly smile. Four feet eleven in her shoes, she looked every bit of her seventy-plus years. "Can I help you with something in particular?" The friendly smile promptly blossomed. "Ryder. Ryder Beckett." She darted around the counter, nimble and chipper as an elf. "My, my, it's good to see you."

"Mrs. Danelli."

"Welcome home." She propelled herself at him, and he enveloped her petite frame in a fond embrace. "How are you?"

"I'm good. Sure is nice to see you."

They exchanged pleasantries for several minutes. Of course, she'd heard about his return. Reckless was still a small town, and news traveled fast. She didn't ask why he'd quit his highfalutin marketing job, but he supposed she was curious like everyone else.

"I actually stopped in for a reason," he said. "Do you, by chance, carry any camcorders?"

"Several. Anything specific in mind?" She led him to an aisle in the store.

"I don't know a lot about them, but I'm looking for something professional and good quality."

"Really good?"

"Depends on the price."

"There was a gentleman who came in a few months ago. Claimed he was a filmmaker. Nature documentaries. Looking for money to finance a project. I wasn't sure I believed him or if I'd even take his equipment. Not much call for the high-end stuff. When he didn't come back to get his equipment out of hock, I doubted his story even more. When I called a few associates in the business, they told me the camcorder was actually one of the better ones on the market for that price range."

She unlocked the cable anchoring the merchandise to the shelf and handed the device to Ryder. It was larger than the handheld models he was used to seeing. A large microphone was attached to the top beside an elongated lens.

"There's a tripod and a case and some other accessories in the storage room. I didn't put them out. If you're interested, I'll find them."

"I'm interested."

Mrs. Danelli reappeared a few minutes later. She dropped the box on the counter, evidently as far as she could carry it. Ryder rifled through the contents while she assisted a newly arrived customer. Luckily, the original owner's manual was still in the case. He quickly scanned it.

"What do you think?" She sidled up next to him, the top of her permed gray hair barely reaching his shoulder.

Ryder replaced the charger he'd been inspecting in the box. "I'll take it."

She gave him a deal, and Ryder thanked her.

"Filming the rodeo this weekend?"

"And the different events around town." Ryder had a friend who was an editing genius and could probably take all the lousy footage he produced and turn it into a decent commercial short. Another friend could supply the voice-over. Perks of being in the marketing business for over a decade. "I'm hoping to make a digital short on the arena. For advertising."

"That's a great idea!"

And right up Ryder's alley. Much more so than delivering posters. Plus, his family could continue to use the digital short long after he left.

Mrs. Danelli sent him off with another hug and motherly peck on the cheek. Outside, he stood a moment and checked the time. Still ten minutes before art class was over. Cassidy had warned Ryder not to show up early. Her son was the class clown, and Ryder's presence would only give Benjie an excuse to cut up.

Hearing a loud clacking, Ryder spun. A riderless horse galloped straight for him, reins flapping and stirrups bouncing with each thunderous stride. Someone screamed. People dived out of the way like pins being knocked down by a bowling ball.

Horses weren't uncommon on the streets of Reckless, especially during Wild West Days. Uncontrolled horses, however, presented a danger.

Ryder didn't stop to think. He set the box with the camcorder on the sidewalk and ran into the street, arms waving and shouting, "Whoa. Whoa there, fellow."

For a split second, he thought the enormous bay gelding might gallop past him. All at once, it gathered its front hooves under it and clamored to a stop, eyes wide, nostrils flaring and flanks heaving.

Ryder gathered the reins and gripped them firmly just beneath the horse's jaw. "Easy does it. That's a good boy."

Whatever had spooked the horse seemed to have passed and, little by little, he calmed. Where was his rider, and was the man or woman all right? Ryder searched the vicinity but saw no one. Eventually, people ventured back on to the streets.

"Anyone know who this guy belongs to?" Ryder called out.

A few folks shook their heads or offered a "No clue," before walking away.

An old-timer wandered over. "That looks like one of Bucky Hendriks's stock. His crew has been in town since early this morning carousing and causing a ruckus. They're a good bunch of boys. Usually. Just get carried away now and then."

"You know where they are?"

"Last I heard, the Reverie."

A bar three blocks over. Strange that the horse's owner hadn't come to fetch him yet. Perhaps he was still inside the bar and unaware.

Ryder checked his watch again. Not enough time to take the horse to the bar and be back to fetch Benjie. But he could hardly abandon the bay, even tied up.

"You have a vehicle?" he asked the old-timer.

"My scooter."

Ryder noticed the motorized chair parked nearby. "You think you can drive it all the way to the Reverie?"

The man snorted with disdain, evidently insulted.

"Let Bucky's crew know I have the horse, and I'll be at the Ship-With-Ease Store. They can find him there."

The old-timer pressed pedal to the metal and took off at a brisk four miles an hour.

The horse perked his ears and stared after the man as if he, too, found the sight amusing.

"Let's go, boy."

Ryder gave the horse's neck a pat, then reached down, retrieved his box and balanced it in the crook of his arm. The horse ambled quietly beside him. They garnered their share of curious glances.

Outside the Ship-With-Ease Store, he stopped and tethered the horse to a wooden column.

Three young mothers stopped, glanced at the store and then Ryder.

"Ladies." He tugged on the brim of his hat, assuming they were parents of Tatum's students.

"Can we pet the horse?" one of them asked.

"Just be careful you don't move too fast."

Ryder heard a sudden bang behind him. Benjie stood at the art studio's large window, both palms and his nose pressed to the glass. Ryder could hear a muffled, "Hi, Uncle Ryder." A moment later, Drew materialized beside Benjie. The two pointed at him and broke into giggles.

Not good, Ryder thought. He could already hear the reprimand from Tatum.

As if on cue, she came up behind the boys. For a second, her gaze connected with his. Before he could mouth the words, *I'm sorry*, she marched the two young troublemakers away.

"Don't worry. She never stays mad for long."

Ryder faced the store owner, who'd come outside. "How you doing, Mr. Faust?"

The two men shook hands. "'Bout time you called me Lenny, I'd say."

For over thirty years, the older man had served as the town's postmaster. Forced into what he'd called an early retirement, he'd opened the Ship-With-Ease Store and proceeded to do a booming business, essentially competing with his former employer.

"Afraid I'm being a distraction," Ryder explained.

"Ah. Breaking the cardinal rule."

"Tatum's a good teacher, I hear."

"Great with them kids. Shame she lost her job at the school. If I have my way, she'll be teaching third grade again starting with the spring quarter."

"You have some sway with the board?"

"I'm one of the members. Serve with your mother. I'll be at the meeting next week."

"She didn't mention it."

"We're up against some strong opposition. Money is tight this year. The school doesn't have a lot to go around. Be a real shame to lose her."

"Do you think the board won't approve the budget increase?"

"Truthfully, I doubt the increase will pass." He sighed expansively. "Sunny and I, we're gonna do our best for that girl. Classrooms are crowded enough as it is. We need good teachers."

Ryder watched Tatum through the window. With the exception of her son and his nephew, every child stared at her with rapt attention. "She has a way with kids," Lenny echoed. "That's for sure. I told her she can use that space as long as she'd like. I'm not doing anything with it. Thought about expanding at one time, just hasn't happened. Don't really care about the extra rent money."

"That's nice of you."

More parents had gathered as they talked, the group swelling to the size of a small crowd. Ryder had a hard time keeping them away from the horse. In hindsight, he probably should have tethered the gelding farther from the art studio.

"I like that gal," Lenny said. "Heart of gold. I'm thinking you like her, too."

Did it show? "She's a good friend of my sister's."

He winked. "If that's what you say."

"I'm just here to pick up my nephew."

"Right."

Ryder was spared further scrutiny when the door to the studio flew open, and the boys tumbled out on to the sidewalk. They were followed by eight or nine other children of similar ages.

"What are you doing with that horse, Uncle Ryder?" Benjie was the image of his mother, looks-wise. Personality-wise, they couldn't be more opposite. Whereas Cassidy was reserved and intense, Benjie was outgoing, boisterous and extremely social.

Was he like his father? Ryder found himself again wondering about the man's identity and why his sister kept it a secret. Did Benjie ever ask? What did she tell him?

"I kind of found him. His owner should be here any second." Ryder ruffled his nephew's already disheveled hair, then turned his attention to Drew. "How's the finger?"

"Mom says I'm brave."

"She's right."

His face fell. "I can't play kick ball. Or go swimming. Not until the cast is off."

"Would ice cream help? I can take you boys to Cascade." The ice cream parlor had been Ryder's favorite place as a kid.

"Yes!" Benjie and Drew exchanged high fives.

"I'll ask my mom." Drew would have darted back inside, but Tatum chose that moment to come out. He practically collided with her. "Mr. Beckett is taking us to Cascade!"

Tatum gave Ryder "the look." "Oh?"

"You're welcome to come with us. In fact, I'd like that."

"I have another class."

"You're on break," Drew said. "You just told us."

"I can watch the horse," Lenny offered.

Ryder grinned. "It's settled, then."

"Well," Tatum hedged.

"Please, Mom," Drew begged.

She pulled out a ring of keys and locked the door, relenting with a sigh.

"We won't be long." Ryder nodded at Lenny.

The older man winked again. "If that's what you say."

Cascade Ice Cream Parlor wasn't far. Just up the street. Tatum ran herd on the boys, which was worse than corralling jackrabbits. They insisted on charging ahead, zigging first in one direction and zagging in the other. Leaving the art studio, even for a half hour, felt a little strange to her. Leaving with Ryder, stranger still. People were surely looking at them. Jumping to conclusions.

"Don't go far," she called after the boys.

They didn't listen.

Ryder walked casually along beside her. "Where are Gretchen and Adam?"

"At home with their grandmother." Tatum's reply was issued through clenched teeth. These days, any discussion of her former mother-in-law set her on edge. "She was going to take Drew, too, but he insisted on coming with me."

She didn't add that Drew pitched a fit when she told

him he'd be spending the entire day with his grandmother. Try as she might, Tatum couldn't convince her oldest son that he'd be returned to her and not forced to live with his grandmother again. When his protests had dissolved into a fit of tears, Tatum had given in.

Her mother-in-law blamed her, of course. Accused her of spoiling Drew. She also blamed Tatum for the dislocated finger. The day care accommodations she'd chosen clearly weren't safe, if a child could suffer such a serious injury.

Tatum tried to tell herself that her mother-in-law's criticisms came from a place of love. She cared deeply for her grandchildren and wanted only the best for them. The problem was, beneath the caring and criticisms were subtle threats.

Mess up again, and you'll be hearing from Monty's attorney.

Not going to happen. Tatum refused to let it. She might not be living in the lap of luxury, but she was hardly an unfit parent.

"Is she visiting?" Ryder asked.

"For the day. It's a compromise."

Her gaze strayed to his profile. What would her mother-in-law think of her having ice cream with a man? A very good-looking one. Or of her kissing him? Tatum still couldn't believe she'd succumbed so easily.

She should tell Drew to say nothing about their trip to the ice cream parlor. Knowing her oldest son, he'd brag to Gretchen the first opportunity. Then, Tatum would have to explain.

Tension lay like a lead ball in the pit of her stomach.

"You and she compromise a lot?"

Glancing at Drew, Tatum assured herself that he and Benjie were occupied and not listening.

"Ruth comes to Reckless one Saturday a month, and I take the kids to see her one Sunday a month. In exchange, she doesn't pressure Monty to file for joint custody. Not that he wants it. He hardly ever visits the kids."

"Then, why?"

"Other than he typically does his mother's bidding?" Tatum swallowed. It did little to alleviate the bitter taste in her mouth. "She...questions my ability to provide adequately for my children."

"Because you lost your job at the school?"

"I went through a difficult financial period. We, um, had to move from a house to a three-bedroom apartment." She skipped over the part where she'd moved to a one-bedroom apartment for several months because that was all she could afford.

"Lots of people live in an apartment."

"Apparently not *her* grandchildren. I'm hoping to find a house to rent soon."

"When you go back to teaching?"

"Yes." And when she finally paid off the bulk of her credit card debt.

"Do teachers earn more than office managers?"

Tatum felt her cheeks flame. As a member of the Beckett family, Ryder had access to payroll information and probably knew her weekly wage. In addition, he and his parents had met several times during the past week to discuss the monthly finances and income projections.

"There are also the benefits to consider," she said. "Retirement. Health insurance. Paid holidays. Your family does the best they can," she quickly amended. "Don't get me wrong."

"I understand. Believe me."

She hadn't stopped to consider until now that he'd probably given up a lot of benefits, too, when he quit his marketing job. Not for the first time, she questioned why he'd left such a good position.

"I realize the school may not rehire me, but I can't help hoping." And praying, she silently added.

"What if you were to be promoted at the Easy Money? You'd get a raise."

"Promoted." She suppressed a laugh. "To what? Sunny is the only other person in the office, and I don't think she's going anywhere."

"You could take on more of the marketing and promotion responsibilities."

"That's your job."

"For the time being." He shrugged. "Who knows what the future holds?"

His careless tone gave her pause. "Are you thinking of leaving the Easy Money?"

"Sooner or later."

It wasn't her place to ask, but she did anyway. "Have you told your family?"

"They know I'm not planning to stay indefinitely."

And they probably didn't like it. Mercer especially. According to Cassidy, Ryder and his mother argued last night. Was that what he meant by "sooner?"

As usual, the Becketts weren't getting along. Nothing cut a visit short like a family feud.

At Cascade's, they perused the many selections. Ryder took a long time deciding. Tatum always had the same thing. A single scoop of fat-free vanilla frozen yogurt. She was definitely a creature of habit.

Then again, she'd broken routine several times this past week. Wearing nice clothes to work. Relying on Ryder's help with Drew's emergency-room visit. Leaving the art studio during her break. Letting him kiss her. Kissing him back.

"What'll you have?" the fresh-faced teenaged clerk asked when the customers ahead of them moved on.

The boys wanted double scoops with two different flavors of ice cream, lots of syrup and sprinkles. Tatum grimaced just thinking about it.

When they were done, Ryder gestured, indicating she should order ahead of him. The words issuing from her mouth surprised her. "A double scoop of chocolate brownie fudge."

"Cone or dish?" the teen asked.

Tatum hesitated. The calories would go straight to her hips and live there forever.

"Don't hold back now," Ryder urged, a twinkle lighting his eyes.

"Cone."

"I'll have the same. And make it those waffle cones dipped in chocolate."

She would surely regret this. "They'll have to roll us out of here."

"What's the point of having ice cream if you don't make a pig of yourself?"

Funny, Tatum couldn't agree more. She might have had her last fat-free frozen yogurt.

The boys were in high spirits. They acted up twice, causing enough of a commotion for customers' heads to swivel in their direction. Tatum cautioned them the first time, using her no-nonsense teacher voice. The boys promptly behaved. For two minutes. A second warning yielded no results.

"That's enough, you two," Ryder scolded.

They immediately quieted. Then, giggling, continued to lick their dripping ice cream. For the moment, peace ensued.

"I'm impressed," Tatum said.

"I'm louder than you."

She wasn't sure about that. Ryder had a way with children. Not just playing with them and being their pal. They also respected him and listened to him.

His former marriage may have been years ago and ended unhappily, but parenting his ex's two daughters, even for a short time, had taught him a lot and allowed his natural tendencies to flourish.

All at once, his cell phone rang. He removed the phone from his pocket and studied the screen, his brows drawing together. Naturally, her curiosity was piqued.

After a moment, he said, "Excuse me," and answered the call.

"No problem." She waved off his concern, then promptly strained to hear his side of the conversation over the din.

"Hi, Myra. Don't tell me, you're working on a Saturday. No, I'm not busy. It's all right." Each sentence was separated by a pause. "Really. Huh. Just a second." He rose from the table and said to Tatum, "Be right back," before stepping away.

Now, her curiosity was more than piqued. It was fired.

"Absolutely." Ryder started for the door, only to be cut off and delayed by a large group of high school students entering the parlor. "I can make it. Nine a.m. sharp. Yeah, I have heard of them. Right. What's the starting salary?"

Starting salary?

"How soon are they looking for someone?" Ryder continued.

Looking for someone? He was talking to this Myra person about a job. He wasn't wasting a moment.

Tatum suffered a sudden emptiness inside.

Finally, Ryder was able to move on and step outside. A few minutes later, he ended the phone call and returned to their table. Even if she hadn't overheard part of his conversation, she'd have guessed that something was up by his guilty expression.

"Sorry about that," he said.

Right. She was the one sorry. His family would be devastated. And, she couldn't tell them. Not without admitting she'd eavesdropped.

"It's all right." She grabbed some napkins from the dispenser and started cleaning up the boys' mess. "We should go. My break is about over."

Drew's "Aw, Mom," was followed by Benjie's "Do we have to?"

"Class starts in five minutes." Tatum was rarely late.

She and Ryder spoke little on the way back.

At the door, they paused. "Looks like the horse's owner came and got him," Ryder said.

Tatum had forgotten all about the runaway.

"Thought for a minute I was going to have to call animal control."

Another pause ensued.

"Thanks for the ice cream," she said. Somehow the thrill of her decadent treat had worn off.

"I'd like to see you later."

Her heart gave a little trill. Was he asking her out? She instantly tamped down the feeling. With an up-coming job interview, probably the first of several, he wouldn't be here much longer.

"To talk," he said.

Oh. About the call she'd overheard. "It isn't neces-sary."

"Tatum." He reached for her, his hand settling on her waist.

She raised her gaze to his, and her breath caught. He was close enough to…

"Mom!"

At the sound of Gretchen's voice, Tatum spun. There stood her mother-in-law with a sour look on her face, a flailing Adam in her arms, Gretchen at her side.

Just when Tatum thought things couldn't get worse, Adam yelled, "Daddy, Daddy."

Like that, the look on her mother-in-law's face went from sour to infuriated.

Chapter 8

Ryder bent over Tatum's desk, his hands braced on the edge. She wasn't escaping this time. "You've been avoiding me all week."

"That's not true." She refused to look at him and instead busied herself with a stack of envelopes. "It's only Thursday."

He glanced at the partially open door leading to his mother's office, which was, fortunately, empty. He and Tatum were alone.

"Is it because Adam called me Daddy again?"

She visibly tensed.

"What did she say?" Ryder didn't specify who. Tatum knew he referred to her former mother-in-law.

"Nothing."

"I don't believe you."

"Excuse me." She pushed back from her desk, the

wheels on her chair squeaking. "I have to get to the mailbox before noon."

"Tatum, I'm sorry."

She closed her eyes and sighed wistfully. "It's not your fault."

"No, it's Monty's fault. If he visited more often, his son wouldn't be calling me Daddy. The guy's a piece of work if you ask me."

"Adam's just two. He's easily confused."

"My point exactly." Ryder straightened. "What's with Monty, anyway? Even when my father was a drunk, he always loved his children and spent time with us."

"He wanted you and your sister and would have wanted Liberty if your mother had been honest with him. Monty wasn't ready for a family."

"That's no excuse," he said.

"I need to be careful. Not give Ruth any more ammunition to use against me."

"Ammunition? What? You're not allowed to date? I'm no attorney, but I'm pretty sure Monty and Ruth can't take your kids away from you because you have a boyfriend."

"You're not my boyfriend," Tatum said hotly.

Okay, he deserved that. He'd led her on not once but twice.

"You're legitimately worried about your mother-in-law interfering in your life. I didn't mean to make light of it. But Monty's the one she should be mad at for his complete lack of parental involvement."

"I don't disagree." Tatum's shoulders slumped, her bluster waning. "That's not the reason I've been avoiding you."

"So, you admit it, then."

She looked around as if concerned they were being overheard. "You put me in an awkward position. How am I supposed to stand by and say nothing to your family while you're out there looking for a new job?"

"I apologize again. I shouldn't have talked to that headhunter in front of you."

Grabbing the envelopes, she huffed in frustration and stood.

"What?"

"Honestly, Ryder, you are really dense sometimes."

He'd have laughed if she wasn't so serious. "You'll get no argument from me."

"I'm not the one you should be talking to about this." She started for the door. "Grab the phone if it rings, will you? I'm going to the mailbox."

"All right." He hated that she was right. "I'll do it."

She paused, her hand on the doorknob. "Do what?"

"You're going to make me say it, aren't you?"

Her eyes narrowed, and she shifted her weight. Ryder had a pretty good idea what it felt like to be a student in her class who'd been caught breaking the rules.

"I'll tell my family I'm actively looking for a new job," he stated flatly.

Tatum's hand fell away from the door. "I feel sorry for them."

"Don't waste your energies just yet."

"Interview the other day not go well?"

He could lie but didn't. "The company wasn't as good a fit as I first thought."

"Oh, well." At least she didn't look smug.

"I want you to come with me."

"Where?"

"I have a meeting with Marshall Whitmen in thirty minutes at the Flat Iron for lunch."

"The head of the Scottsdale Parada del Sol Rodeo?"

"One and the same."

That got a reaction from her. The Parada del Sol was one of Arizona's most prestigious and popular rodeos. Ryder's family had been trying to land the account for years.

"How did that...who set up the meeting?" she asked.

"My father has connections. He heard the bucking stock contractor supplying the horses has pulled out. The distemper virus going around has infected his entire herd."

"That's terrible. But the rodeo is months away. Won't the horses recover by then?"

"Marshall doesn't want to take any chances the bucking stock won't be in top form."

"What possible help can I be at the meeting?"

"It would be a great opportunity for you to see how the negotiations work firsthand."

"Your father and his connections are what got the meeting. He should go with you."

"One of the bulls is acting sick. He's meeting the veterinarian at noon."

Tatum accepted that answer without question. Like everyone at the arena, she was well aware of his father's devotion to the bulls and belief they were the future of the Easy Money.

"Come with me, Tatum," Ryder repeated.

"Because you want someone to take over the marketing and promotion part of your job when you leave."

"Because it will give you the chance to grow your present job skills and increase your earning potential."

"In case the school doesn't hire me back."

"Consider it hedging your bets."

After a lingering hesitation, she smiled. A small, soft one that sent Ryder's pulse soaring. Proof positive she could affect him like none other. He'd promised her he wouldn't compromise her again with touching and kissing. It might be a promise impossible to keep.

She shook her head. "I can't leave the office unattended."

"Let's call my sisters. One of them should be free."

"It's their lunch hour. And they have classes later."

"You're fabricating excuses."

"Not exactly—"

The office door abruptly opened and Ryder's mother entered. She took one look at Tatum and Ryder, then stopped in her tracks. "What's going on?"

"Ryder's..." Tatum faltered.

"I'm trying to convince her to come with me to meet with Marshall Whitmen." He waited for his mother's objection, only she surprised him.

"I think that's a great idea!"

"The phones," Tatum objected.

"I'll watch them."

Ryder allowed himself a huge grin. Round one had gone to him.

"Your mother has an ulterior motive." Tatum sent Ryder an arch look.

"Do tell."

The Flat Iron Restaurant was ten minutes from the arena. Ryder had stretched the drive into fifteen—on purpose, she was convinced. Mostly, he'd talked about Marshall Whitmen and his take on how the meeting would progress. Now that they were nearing the restaurant, she had only a minute at most to speak her mind.

"She's matchmaking."

"You think?" he teased.

"Be serious, Ryder."

"Why would she?"

"She saw us kissing the other night."

He took his time responding. "She told you?"

For a moment, Tatum relived that embarrassing moment. "It's no fun chitchatting with your boss about kissing her son."

"Sorry. I asked her not to."

"You knew she saw us and didn't tell me?" Tatum ground her teeth together in frustration. "A little warning would have been nice."

"She's making something out of nothing."

His observation, delivered nonchalantly, shouldn't have bothered Tatum. She, as much as he, had put the brakes on any potential romance between them. Yet, she was bothered.

"Don't you get it?" Tatum had accused Ryder of being dense earlier, partially in jest. Now, she was less sure. "Your mother is willing to orchestrate a romance between us if it encourages you to stay."

"What if she is? What's the harm? Nothing will come of it."

That word again. Nothing.

Tatum silently fumed. Her anger didn't last, and she put on her best smile. Ryder's reminder that they had no future together was no reason to ruin this very important meeting.

He opened the front door of the restaurant for her, and she preceded him inside. All around them, the restaurant clanked, clattered and bustled with activity. Delicious aromas filled the air. A chalkboard on the wall advertised the day's specials.

Ryder hitched his chin in the direction of a booth. "Marshall's already here."

At his possessive and unexpected grip on her arm, she drew in a sharp breath. Before she could speak, he propelled her ahead of him, his fingers gliding along the inside of her forearm before he released her.

"This way."

She blinked, momentarily disoriented by the delicious sensation his touch evoked.

Marshall Whitmen tossed down his napkin and rose at their approach. He must have been quite early for he'd already ordered an iced tea. His welcoming smile assured Tatum that he didn't object to her presence.

"Good day, Ryder." He tipped his cowboy hat at her. "And who's your lovely companion?"

Hands were shaken. Marshall's grip on hers was strong and that of a man thirty years younger. With his white hair and matching white beard, he could have passed for Colonel Sanders's brother.

"This is Tatum Mayweather," Ryder said. "She's the arena's office manager and has been showing me the ropes. I hope you don't mind that she came along."

A blatant exaggeration. If anything, the complete opposite was true. Ryder was showing *her* the ropes. But she followed his lead, understanding without being told that these types of meetings were a game with established plays.

"Not at all." Marshall's tone dripped honey. "A lovely woman enhances any meal. Even better when she's smart and talented."

Oh, he was a charmer all right. Smooth as silk. Nonetheless, Tatum felt herself soften. "I've admired your work with the Parada del Sol for years," she said. "You have a stellar reputation." He was also well-liked and considered to be fair and honest.

Ryder sent her an approving look. Tatum warmed. She wanted to help the Becketts for all the favors they'd done her. More than that, she wanted to please Ryder and not give him cause to regret his decision to bring her along.

"Do you mind if I take notes?" she asked and withdrew her ever-present spiral notebook from her purse. It was filled with grocery lists, appointment reminders and Gretchen's doodles. But Ryder and Marshall didn't need to know that.

"Good idea." Marshall beamed. "These days I can't trust this old memory of mine."

Ryder motioned for her to slide into the booth. She scooted all the way to the wall to make room for him. Still, it was cramped. Bumping body parts was inevitable—and distracting.

They didn't talk business until their lunch orders were placed. Ryder, Tatum noticed, waited, taking his lead from Marshall. Once the subject was broached, he pitched the Easy Money's bucking stock with the confidence of someone who'd been a member of the family business his entire life.

"You know the quality of our horses, Marshall. There are none better in Arizona."

"Absolutely. Wouldn't be here today if I didn't."

"Every one of our head has been vet-checked this past week. No signs of distemper. We'll continue our diligence up until the rodeo and provide health certificates upon delivery of the stock, dated no later than one day before the rodeo. That's a guarantee."

Marshall nodded thoughtfully. "Sounds fair."

Negotiations ceased when the food arrived. Evidently, Marshall didn't conduct business while eating. The men started on their burgers. Tatum resisted devouring her salad. Eating out was a real treat for her. It beat her brown bag lunch any day of the week.

"I know a Mayweather," Marshall said to Tatum. "Monty Mayweather. Former bull rider. Any relation to you?"

"My ex-husband."

"Apologies if I brought up a sore subject."

"None needed. Monty and I are on good terms." Interesting how the slight fib slipped easily off her tongue. This wasn't the place or time to admit her lousy ex-husband cared more about his freedom than his three children.

"His loss." Marshall sent Ryder a look that, if Tatum interpreted it correctly, meant Ryder's gain.

"Tatum's also an art instructor. She has a studio in town."

She wanted to kick Ryder under the table. Why had he brought that up?

"Do tell." Marshall studied her with interest. "I dabble a bit with oils myself."

"Really?" Now it was her turn to show interest.

"A hobby. Mostly."

"Some of Marshall's paintings are hanging in the lobby at the Scottsdale Civic Center." Ryder angled his head away from the rodeo promoter and winked at Tatum.

She felt foolish. There had been a reason for him

to mention her studio. She and Marshall shared a love of art.

"That's wonderful," she said with heartfelt enthusiasm. "You must be very talented."

He shrugged off the compliment. "I wouldn't say that. My wife, being a member of the chamber of commerce for twenty-plus years, might have more to do with it."

Talk turned to the upcoming Wild West Days. The waitress had hardly removed their empty plates when Ryder said, "We'd love to have you and your family as our guests at the rodeo finals on Sunday afternoon."

"Why, thank you. It's much appreciated."

Tatum picked up her pad and pen. "I'll have passes delivered to your office tomorrow. VIP section." She didn't ask Ryder's permission before making the offer, confident he wouldn't object. "Is four enough? Or six?"

"Four's plenty. Leena and I will bring the grandkids."

"Looking forward to meeting them." Ryder confidently eased into the rest of his pitch. "That'll give you a chance to observe our bucking stock up close."

"The Lost Dutchman has also approached me."

Ryder nodded. "Donnie's stock is top-notch."

"It must be, or you wouldn't use him yourself."

"For bulls," Ryder was quick to clarify. "For now."

"You buying more?"

"My father's in the process."

The waitress returned and refilled their iced tea glasses. Talk continued, eventually getting down to the nitty-gritty. Tatum's pen made scratching noises as she jotted down numbers and dates and dollar amounts. Working for the Becketts, she'd typed, revised and filed enough contracts to know these terms were good, each party giving up something but getting something better in return.

Ryder demonstrated a real knack for negotiating, impressing Tatum. If he stayed in Reckless, he could do a lot to take the Easy Money to the next level. Like his father had back in the days before he started drinking. Then again, Ryder's talents were perhaps wasted in a small town. He was used to greater challenges and a faster-paced environment.

"As much as I enjoyed this, I have to get back to the office." Marshall reached for the hat he'd set on the seat beside him. "Write up a letter of intent and email it to me. We'll go from there."

"I'll have it for you tomorrow." Ryder tossed several bills on to the table for a tip.

He'd also picked up the lunch tab. It was Tatum's guess Marshall was frequently treated to meals by bucking stock contractors vying for his business. Even so, he'd thanked Ryder graciously.

"I'm looking forward to working with you," Ryder said at the door. They'd stopped just outside the restaurant before parting ways.

"Tell your parents hello for me." Marshall adjusted his hat, pushing down on the crown. "Have to say, I was a little surprised to hear Mercer had returned to the Beckett fold. Your mama was dead set against him for years."

"You aren't the only one surprised."

"Then again, you've returned, too."

Ryder grinned pleasantly. "Things change."

"That, they do." Marshall gave a small wave as he strolled away. "Including the outfits that supply bucking stock for the Parada del Sol."

Excitement coursed through Tatum. The signatures had yet to be signed on the dotted line, but it appeared the Becketts had just landed a lucrative new client. She was thrilled to have contributed in her small way.

"Nicely done," she said to Ryder when they were alone.

"I like Marshall. He made it easy."

"There's nothing easy about negotiating a contract."

"Beats pleading with store owners to put our posters in their windows." He showered her with a breathtaking smile. "You were good. I think you should attend every meeting."

She laughed as they crossed the parking lot to his truck. The sun beat down on them, unusually warm for late September. In the distance, the mountains shimmered, their foliage more brown than green this time of year.

"Sure," she said. "But only when the client also happens to be an artist."

"First rule of any sales meeting. Find common ground and make a connection."

"I think the free passes were more of an inducement than the fact Marshall and I both like to paint."

Ryder shook his head. "Free passes were just added insurance."

The truck was hot when they climbed in, and the leather seat burned the backs of Tatum's legs even through the fabric of her slacks. "Why are you doing this, Ryder?" She fastened her seat belt. "And don't tell me it's because you could be leaving."

He inserted his key and started the engine. The truck, a one-ton diesel, roared to life. "You're smart and tal-

ented and capable of doing more than managing an office."

"Right. And you don't feel the least bit guilty about
my former mother-in-law giving me grief because
Adam called you Daddy."

"I'm not that noble, Tatum. Though, I'd like you to
think that if it raises your opinion of me."

"Quit joking."

He drove for several more minutes before answering. "When I picked up Benjie the other day at the studio, Lenny Faust mentioned being on the school board
with my mother."

"Yes." She let the single syllable word trail.

"He didn't sound optimistic about the board voting
in the new budget."

"Ryder, I—"

He cut her off. "It's like the passes we're giving Marshall. You learning to negotiate contracts is added insurance. Make yourself indispensable to my parents,
Tatum."

She chewed on that for a moment. With more to contribute, she'd feel less like a charity case. And if she
had any chance of affording a larger place to rent, one
that met with her mother-in-law's approval, she'd need
to boost her income. If she didn't get her old teaching
job back, elevating her earning potential at the arena
might be her only solution.

To accomplish that, Ryder would have to leave town
and vacate his job. That would devastate his family.

It would also, she realized, devastate her.

Chapter 9

Only one night remained before the start of the Wild West Days Rodeo. Fridays were traditionally the first round of competition and always important. Points earned went a long way toward participants qualifying for the final round on Sunday.

Which meant Thursday evening was the last chance for riders to practice. The Easy Money parking area was packed with vehicles and trailers. The stands held family and friends, there to support and encourage. Every available pen was teeming with activity. Every available hand toiled laboriously. Ryder's family scurried around like the proverbial chickens with their heads cut off. Ryder included.

The livestock, however, rested. They had a lot of work ahead of them and needed to be in tip-top shape. The Lost Dutchman bulls had arrived that morning, fit and full of themselves. Mercer had spent the day inspecting each one from horns to tail, pronouncing them raring to go.

In lieu of calves, ropers were using a Heel-O-Matic to hone their skills. The mechanical device consisted of a heavy-duty fake calf mounted on to a three-wheeled dolly. Tonight, the dolly was pulled by one of the wranglers driving an ATV. Cowboys exploded from behind the barrier and, if their aim was true, roped the head of the fake calf. It didn't exactly mimic the real thing, but it came close enough.

The barrel racers had finished thirty minutes ago, after an intense two-hour practice session, and turned the arena over to the ropers. Bull and bronc riders, if they weren't competing in other events, took the night off and, like the bulls and horses, rested up for tomorrow.

"On deck, Ryder," Cassidy called. She stood near the box, calling off the names of cowboys in the order they'd signed up.

What in the world had possessed Ryder to think he could rope after all these years? Even a fake calf attached to a three-wheeled dolly exceeded his abilities.

The idea had come to him an hour ago. When Tatum and her family arrived, to be specific. She'd taken the kids to the pizza parlor in town for dinner, then returned to the arena to assist if needed. Mostly, they were watching the ropers practice.

Drew, so Ryder had been told, was going a little stir-crazy at the day care, what with not being able to play outside because of his cast. Tatum had thought spending an evening with Ryder's nephew, Benjie, would take some of the edge off. Benjie was doing his best to corrupt Drew and entice him into playing when he should be sitting quietly.

Ryder sympathized. He felt a little stir-crazy himself, which could explain his present circumstances.

He and his mother were talking, but only when they couldn't avoid it. Cassidy blamed him for upsetting their mother and had let him know in no uncertain terms. Mercer had gotten wind of his job interview—Ryder's fault for leaving his contract with Myra on his dresser. As a result, his father and Liberty were constantly needling Ryder to stay. Then, there was Tatum. To protect them both, he was maintaining a strictly professional relationship with her.

That didn't stop him from wanting to pull her in his arms every time he got within ten feet of her. And those wounded expressions she continually wore made it all the harder.

Tightening his grip on the lariat hanging by his side, he forced himself to relax. He'd wanted Tatum to see he could still compete with the best of them despite years of working in an office. Instead, he was about to humiliate himself.

"Let's go, Ryder," Cassidy called, then spoke into a handheld radio. She'd been giving instructions to the young man driving the ATV since practice started. He reversed direction and lined up the Heel-O-Matic, backing the fake calf into place.

Ryder jogged his horse to the box and got in position. This wasn't his first outing on the young gelding. Twice he'd gone for a short ride, the last time with Liberty. He'd also found a spare hour to throw a few tosses with a lariat. The hay bale he'd used for a target didn't lope across the arena like a live calf or bump along like the Heel-O-Matic.

Something told him he'd need a lot more practice riding and roping if he expected to impress Tatum.

When he was ready, one hand gripping the reins, the other on his lariat, he nodded to his sister and said, "Go."

She signaled the young man driving the ATV. At once, Ryder and the fake calf were off and running.

The gelding responded immediately and perfectly to Ryder's cues, going from a standstill to a full gallop in the blink of an eye. Ryder's hat flew off, but he didn't pay attention.

Instincts he'd been certain were gone for good suddenly kicked in, and he let them guide him. Arm in the air, high over his head, he twirled the rope. As the gelding thundered across the arena floor in pursuit of the fake calf, Ryder took aim and let the rope fly.

He watched it stretch out in front him, steady and true. Elation filled him. God, he'd missed this. The thrill. The rush. The excitement. He may not have made rodeoing his career, but there was no reason he couldn't make a hobby of it. Especially if he stayed in Reckless.

And, just like that, the noose missed the fake calf's head by a good foot. The rope fell to the ground, limp and lifeless as a cut clothesline. The gelding, sensing there would be no battle with the calf, slowed to a trot before coming to an abrupt halt and snorting—in disgust, Ryder thought.

"That makes two of us, boy." He patted the gelding's neck.

One of the wranglers ran over and returned Ryder's hat. "Good try, partner."

Ryder thanked him and reeled in his rope, his gaze searching the stands. Great. There was Tatum and the kids. All of them watching. She waved. He raised his hat in response before plunking it down on his head.

He should have known better than to try and show off. What was he? Fifteen again?

Behind the bucking chutes, he dismounted. His ploy to be alone with his shame didn't work.

"Tough luck, son."

At least his father didn't patronize him. "I'm a little rusty."

"The good news is you can always improve."

"Need help with anything?"

His father chuckled. "Looking for an excuse not to embarrass yourself again?"

"Guess those practice sessions behind the barn didn't pay off."

"You picked the right horse, anyway."

"Good thing. He alone saved me from complete humiliation."

Most competitors brought their own riding stock to a rodeo. The Becketts maintained a few head in reserve for cowboys whose horses sustained an injury or suffered an illness that knocked them from the competition. This gelding was one of the reserve stock.

"If you have a minute," his father said, "I want to run an idea by you."

"I'm all ears." Ryder continued walking the horse, letting him cool down. His father fell into step beside him.

"I got a call earlier today. Do you remember Harlo Billings?"

"The stock contractor from Waco?"

"One and the same. He's retiring a month from now and looking to sell his bucking stock."

Ryder didn't need a map to see where this conversation was going. "How many bulls?"

"More than we need or can afford. I have my eye on ten bulls and three championship producing heifers. Two of the bulls are high-dollar earners."

"Impressive. But that's a lot of stock for a single purchase."

"He's willing to let them go for a good price."

When his father named the amount, Ryder released a low whistle. "You weren't kidding."

"He's more interested in the bulls finding the right home where they can reach their full potential than making a killer profit."

Ryder debated stating the obvious. The partnership agreement between his parents, written when they'd divorced—and kept secret from their children until recently—didn't allow one of the partners to contribute assets or make purchases without the consent of the other. That clause had caused a heated disagreement when Ryder's father bought the first six bulls.

"What does Mom think of the idea?" he asked.

"I haven't told her yet."

Figured. "Do you even have the money?"

"Enough for a down payment. Harlo's agreed to carry the remaining balance over the next five years at an interest rate better than the banks are offering."

"Very generous of him."

"He knows what these bulls are capable of and their earning potential. It's a safe investment for him."

"You planning a trip to Waco to inspect the bulls?"

"I've seen them. Just this past summer at the Crosby Fair and Rodeo."

"You'll have to convince Mom. Any financial note needs to be signed by the two of you."

"I am. I will." His father sent him a sly grin. "I was hoping you'd be there when I raise the subject."

Ah. To act as a buffer "I should let you face her alone."

"You think I'm afraid?"

Ryder grinned despite himself. "If you're smart, you will be. She's pretty formidable when she's riled."

They reached the barn. Ryder led the gelding down the aisle toward the tack room. While his father watched, he unsaddled and brushed the gelding, then returned him to his stall. His last task was to bring a bucket of oats. The horse would need his energy for the upcoming weekend.

"With that many bulls, we may have to hire a handler," Ryder mused aloud.

"I already have someone in mind. Shane Westcott."

"Don't think I know him."

They strolled to the arena and watched the practice continue.

"Shane's been around a long time," his father said. "Came into his own a couple years after you left the circuit. Retired a champion after walking away from a fall that should have killed him."

"Is he in the market for a job?"

"No. But I'm not letting a little thing like that stop me."

Ryder didn't doubt his father's abilities. With the exception of his mother, Mercer Beckett could sweet-talk *any*one into almost *any*thing. Hadn't he convinced Ryder to return when it was the last thing he wanted?

"You need to buy the bulls and heifers first."

"Timing is everything. I'm going to wait until after Wild West Days to tell your mother."

"Tell her what?"

Both men spun to find Cassidy staring at them, hands planted on her hips. Ryder was instantly reminded of the day Gretchen had caught him in the stall with Cupcake. He half expected Cassidy to scream for their mother at the top of her lungs.

"Nothing." Their father leaned an arm on the arena fence as if all was right with the world. "Just talking arena business."

"Liar," she spat. "You haven't changed at all. You're still the same deceitful SOB Mom threw out of the house."

Their father jerked as if she'd backhanded him.

"Cassidy." Ryder stepped forward. "That's enough."

"It's okay." Their father pushed off the fence. "She's right. I was lying."

Cassidy pivoted.

Before she could leave, their father hooked her by the arm. "Wait. Honey, please."

"Let go of me."

"I'm considering buying some additional bulls and three heifers."

"You can't. Not without Mom's approval."

"That's what Ryder was saying. And I told him I was waiting until after this weekend. There's no big secret."

"Then why lie to me?" Her eyes sparked with accusation.

"I shouldn't have. I just wanted to avoid a huge fight right before the rodeo."

"Because you know Mom doesn't want to buy any more bulls."

Ryder had thought to let things play out between his father and sister. Her attitude changed his mind. "You can't speak for her, Cassidy. And the fact is, none of us, you, me or Liberty, has any say in the running of the arena."

"I thought this was a family-owned business." She visibly bristled. "Doesn't my opinion count?"

"Nothing's been decided," their father said. "And nothing will be without a family meeting. But I'm going to be honest with you, that won't take place until after I speak to your mother."

Ryder's father wisely omitted the part where he'd asked Ryder to be in on that discussion.

Cassidy stared at them both for several seconds. When she spoke, it was through clenched teeth. "You're only saying that because I overheard you."

"Cassidy." Ryder had had his fill of his sister's dramatics. "You're being unreasonable."

"You always did side with Dad."

"And you've always sided with Mom."

Cassidy opened her mouth to speak. The next instant, she clamped it shut and stormed off. But not before Ryder noticed tears gleaming in her eyes.

"That didn't go exactly as planned," his father said.

The casual remark irked Ryder. "She has a point. You did lie to her, now and in the past."

"Now, wait a damn minute."

"Mom lied, too." Ryder's gaze traveled the entire arena grounds. For one surreal moment, the place looked strange to him. As if he'd never seen it before. "Why am I here? Why do I even bother?"

"What are you talking about?"

"Everyone wants me to reconcile with Mom, but what about you refusing to get along with Cassidy?"

"It isn't that simple."

"None of this is." Ryder didn't care who saw them and vented his anger. "I've always blamed Mom for dividing this family when she threw you out, and lying to you about being Liberty's dad. But you're doing the same thing. Splitting us right down the middle."

"Be patient, son."

"You know something, Dad? I didn't quit my last job. Not unless you count leaving rather than being fired as quitting. And you know why I was going to be fired? Because I screwed up by allowing my personal life to affect my professional one. From that little display I just witnessed between you and Cassidy, I'd say you're guilty of the same thing."

He stormed ahead, leaving his father behind.

Come Monday, Ryder would call Myra and do whatever she advised. Go on interviews. Career coaching. Refresher classes. Get a new haircut and buy a new suit if the headhunter thought it would make a difference. Anything to get the hell out of Reckless.

"You're under arrest," the sheriff said and aimed his pistol at the bank robber's chest.

"You'll never take me alive." The dirty, ragged man squirmed in an attempt to break free of the two deputies pinning his arms.

"This day's been a long time coming, Johnny Waco."

"You might have killed old Lazy Eye Joe, but you

ain't got me yet." All at once, the bank robber broke free and made a run for it down the center of the street.

The sheriff raised his pistol and fired. Smoke exploded from the tip of the gun but no bullet. Even so, the bank robber threw up his arms and face-planted in the street, then writhed melodramatically as if his last breath were leaving his body. The crowd gasped in shock and fear.

"You got him, Sheriff," one of the deputies said, awe and respect in his voice.

The sheriff holstered his pistol. "That scum and his good-for-nothing partner will never bother the decent and upstanding people of Reckless again."

The crowd broke into applause. As if touched by a magic wand, Johnny Waco and his partner, Lazy Eye Joe, sprang to their feet, fully restored. The second deputy, a teenager no older than Ryder had been when he'd performed in the Wild West Days shoot-outs, distributed flyers.

"Next show's at one o'clock," the sheriff announced. "Then at three and five. Deputy Maynard here is handing out the schedule." The sheriff wagged a warning finger. "Remember, you ne'er do wells and troublemakers. At any time, any place, you could be apprehended. Criminals will be thrown in jail. And for you men taking advantage of our lovely, innocent ladies, pay special heed. There's been more than one shotgun wedding in these parts." He winked. "All fines and fees will be donated to the local public library. So, if you are apprehended, be generous."

Lively conversation erupted around Ryder while residents of Reckless, and tourists settled in for the parade, due to start shortly.

He'd left the lineup on the north side of town where he'd been helping his family ready the Easy Money Vaqueros. The arena's students were the tenth entry in the parade. His parents were riding along with the students, as well as Cassidy and her son Benjie.

Liberty and her fiancé, Deacon, would be watching from the sidelines. Ryder had left in search of Tatum and her children, hoping to join them.

No sense making excuses, he'd decided. At least to himself. He wanted to see her. She was the safe harbor in a storm, and he'd been in the midst of an emotional hurricane since Thursday evening when he'd argued with Cassidy and their father. Luckily, he supposed, they'd all been busy with the rodeo and hadn't talked much to each other. When they did, it was all business.

The sidewalks were packed. Every few feet, Ryder bumped into someone and offered an apology. People had made miniature camps in front of storefronts, using folding chairs, stools and even ice chests as seats. Food vendors, in their trucks and carts, were stationed at every corner, reminding Ryder that it had been years since he'd last eaten a corn dog or fry bread.

He had no idea where Tatum was; they, too, hadn't spoken since yesterday. Was she frustrated with the latest Beckett squabble and letting him know?

Instinct guided him in the direction of the Ship-With-Ease Store and her art studio. A few minutes later, his guess paid off. She perched on a lawn chair with Adam in her lap. Beside her, Gretchen and Drew moved their matching child-size lawn chairs into place.

Pleasure brought a smile to his face and a spring to his step. The next instant, he came to a grinding halt, and his spirits sank. Her former mother-in-law, Ruth, sat beside the kids and looked decidedly displeased to see him.

Bad timing. The worst. Tatum must have invited her to the parade, since it wasn't her usual day to visit.

Before he could turn around and leave, Tatum glanced in his direction. His name issued softly from her lips. "Ryder."

Escape became impossible when Drew looked over and spotted him. "Mr. Beckett!" The next instant, the boy was out of his chair and running.

"Drew," Tatum called. "Come back."

Ryder's legs took the brunt of Drew's impact. "Hey, buddy. How you doing?"

Holding on to Ryder's waist, he stared up with huge eyes. "Will you watch the parade with us?"

"I'm not sure…"

"Daddy!" Arms waving, Adam struggled to free himself from Tatum's grasp.

"Adam, that's not your father," Tatum said but not fast enough.

"Haven't you corrected him yet?" Ruth asked icily.

"Several times." Tatum tried to restrain Adam. "He hasn't caught on."

"If Daddy was here," Gretchen said, "Adam wouldn't be confused."

Everyone stared at her. From the mouths of babes, Ryder thought.

"That's enough from you, young lady," her grandmother scolded.

Gretchen's bottom lip began to tremble.

"It's all right, sweet pea," Tatum soothed and opened her free arm.

The girl jumped from her chair in order to snuggle with her mother.

"I'll catch up with you later." Ryder touched the brim of his cowboy hat and addressed the older woman. "Ma'am."

"No!"

Tatum's outburst halted him.

"Please," she implored. "Join us."

He understood then. She didn't want to be alone with her mother-in-law. And while he normally avoided other people's family drama—he had plenty of his own—he stayed. Because Tatum had asked.

"You can have my seat," Drew offered.

"I think it might be a bit too small for me. I'll stand."

"Here." The elderly gentleman next to them pushed a plastic crate over.

"If you're sure."

"We're not using it."

"Thank you." Ryder placed the crate next to Tatum's chair and sat. Leaning forward, he peered around her. "Nice to see you again, Mrs. Mayweather. Hope you're enjoying Wild West Days."

"I am. Thank you." Her mouth barely moved when she talked.

Okay, Ryder admitted it. He was purposely trying to push her buttons.

"We saw the shoot-out." Drew squeezed himself between Ryder's knees.

Adam squealed and doubled his efforts to get down. "Daddy! Wanna see Daddy."

"Here." Mrs. Mayweather reached across the two small folding chairs. "I'll take him," she insisted.

Adam wasn't happy being denied, and Tatum made

her point by taking her ever-loving time relinquishing her son to his grandmother.

Good for you, Ryder thought.

Gretchen stole the spot in her mother's lap that her baby brother had vacated. They were still sitting that way, the two children's chairs empty, when the sound of clip-clopping hooves signaled the start of the parade.

The mayor and grand marshal came first, seated atop a replica stagecoach drawn by four horses. A pair of colorfully dressed clowns came after the stagecoach. Carrying scoop shovels, they were accompanied by a third clown pushing a wheelbarrow. The trio joked with the crowd, pantomiming for laughs. Their real job was to clean up any "accidents" the horses might have, clearing the way for the next entrant.

After the clowns came the grade-school marching band and the Future Farmers of America. Their float, a flatbed trailer covered with streamers, was pulled by a tractor. The marina also had an entry—a boat on wheels—as did the mining company.

"That reminds me." Tatum leaned close to Ryder. "I heard back from the mining company secretary yesterday. Sorry I forgot to tell you."

"And?"

"She sounded interested. Said she'd give us a call at the end of January."

Three months away. "That's something, I suppose."

"I mentioned our ability to accommodate team-building activities."

"Can we do that?"

"We could by the end of January."

Ryder grinned, glad their former camaraderie had returned. "Always thinking, Tatum. I like that."

"I can't take all the credit. We practice team-building exercises in school."

They continued watching the parade, periodically conversing over the children's chatter. The Easy Money Vaqueros earned a loud round of applause from the spectators. When the Shriners passed by, throwing candy and small trinkets onto the sidewalks, children fell on the prizes like starving dogs with a bone.

"I had some upsetting news yesterday," Tatum said. "Lenny's considering renting my space out at the first of the year."

That took Ryder aback. "Why?"

"He got a notice from his landlord. His lease is coming up for renewal, and they want to raise the rent."

"What about your classes?"

"It won't matter if I get my teaching job back."

"I thought you wanted to keep up the art classes even if you did."

"No. Yes." She gave a one-shoulder shrug. "I have this sort of crazy idea. A new career if the school doesn't rehire me."

"Tell me."

"It's stupid, really. I don't have the money needed to start a business."

Ryder was intrigued. "What kind of business?"

She glanced quickly at Ruth, who was preoccupied with her grandchildren. Tatum spoke in a hushed voice. "A craft store. I'd also stock art and teaching supplies, so my teacher friends wouldn't have to drive into Globe." She smiled. "Of course, I'd devote an entire section of the store to my art classes."

"I think it's a great idea."

"Be serious." She blushed prettily. "A craft store in Reckless? Arizona's most Western town?"

"All right, I admit to being supportive of any new business venture. But what you've described makes sense. The people in this town have a need, and you've developed a business to fill it. Plus, it's something you'd be good at."

"Now, if I could just win the lottery."

"Get a small business loan."

"Let's be honest." She sighed. "My credit history isn't the best."

She was talking about losing her house. "There were mitigating circumstances. What counts is that you got yourself back on your feet. And quickly, too."

"Not sure I'm fully back on my feet yet."

"I could help you. I happen to be good at managing money." Ryder had spent most of his professional career developing budgets for clients and working within those budgets.

"If you're still here. Cassidy mentioned you took off yesterday morning, and were gone for a few hours."

Evidently his second consultation with Myra hadn't gone unnoticed. "Did she tell you we argued?"

"The way she put it, she argued with your father, and you got involved."

"Frankly, it was a free-for-all. Dad and I had words, too, after she left."

"I'm sorry."

Ryder reassured himself that Ruth was still not listening before confessing, "I did meet with the head-hunter."

Tatum gave him an I-told-you-so look. Because he couldn't think of a comeback, he said nothing.

They watched the remaining parade in relative silence, commenting now and then on something of interest. Thirty minutes later, the parade came to an end. Almost immediately, the crowd began to disperse. Ryder thought the time had come for him to take his leave.

"See you at the rodeo tonight."

"Don't go," Drew whined and hurried over.

Tatum didn't second her son's plea. If her mother-in-law wasn't there, he'd question her. Was she mad because he might leave Reckless still at odds with his family or mad because he might leave her?

"Thanks for the use of the crate." Ryder pushed it toward the elderly gentleman. When he straightened, he found himself face-to-face with Tatum. She'd been tying Drew's shoelace.

For a long moment, they simply stared at each other.

"What's going on?" her mother-in-law asked.

Ryder and Tatum instantly sprang apart.

Drew just couldn't keep quiet. "Mom and Mr. Beckett like each other," he singsonged.

Tatum inhaled sharply. "Drew!"

Before Ryder could offer an explanation, he was grabbed from behind, his arms anchored by the strong grip of one of the deputies.

"Just come with me, sir. If you know what's good for you."

"Wait a minute," Ryder protested.

"It'll go easier for you if you don't make a fuss. This young lady's father insists you do right by her."

"What?" Ryder twisted to see over his shoulder. Another deputy had a hold of Tatum.

"This way, sir."

"My father's in Michigan." Tatum's objection also fell on deaf ears.

The two of them were escorted across the street to the judge's stand in front of the library.

Donnie Statler sat behind the table, wearing a black judge's robe and spectacles. "You're in a lot of trouble, young man."

"How much do I owe, your honor?" Ryder was more than happy to make a donation.

"Not so fast. We're far from done here."

Ryder turned to Tatum, his brows raised.

She shook her head in bewilderment.

Donnie banged his gavel. "I need two volunteers to witness the union between this man and this woman."

Chapter 10

Tatum didn't know who was responsible for this...
this...stunt—she'd put her money on Sunny—but when
she found out, they were going to get a very large piece
of her mind. Forced into a mock wedding ceremony with
Ryder! Of all the nerve. Thank goodness her mother-in-
law had been nearby and able to watch the kids.

Her mother-in-law! Oh, my God. What must she be
thinking? She already didn't like Ryder just because
Adam called him Daddy. Which he wouldn't do if he
saw more of Monty.

Could her day get any worse?

Even though the young deputy holding her was bigger and stronger, she tried wrenching free. He held fast.

"Now, now. Your pa will have my hide if I let you
get away."

"My pa!" she sputtered and whirled on him, then gasped with shock. Her eyes narrowed. "I know you."

He averted his head.

"You're Kenny's cousin." Kenny was a teenager who worked part-time at the arena.

No doubt remained. Sunny had to be behind this. Damn her blasted matchmaking scheme.

"First order of business," the judge continued in a booming voice, "is the marriage license fee. Customary amount is ten dollars but we'll gladly accept more. And my clerk over there takes credit cards." He motioned to a young woman with a scanner attached to her smart phone.

My, how times had changed.

Ryder, also closely guarded by a deputy, reached into his back pocket and withdrew his wallet.

"You don't have to do that," Tatum said.

Ryder spared her a sideways glance, then withdrew two twenties. Quadruple the fee. Well, that was nice of him, and the amount would buy a lot of books for the library.

Her earlier irritation toward him evaporated. He really was a generous guy. All he'd done was offer to help her with a craft store business that would likely never see the light of day, and all she'd done was chastise him, then practically ignore him.

"Let's get this over with," he grumbled.

She immediately retracted all her good and kind thoughts about him and snapped, "You aren't the only one being put on the spot."

"Shall we proceed with the vows?" The judge indicated the man guarding Ryder. "Do you have the rings, Deputy?"

The man fished two items from his shirt front pocket. "Right here, your honor." He gave one to Ryder and the other to Tatum.

She reluctantly accepted the dime store plastic ring. Green? Really? Who had a green wedding ring? Ryder's, she noticed, was blue.

"Do you, Tatum Mayweather, take Ryder Beckett as your lawfully wedded husband? To have and to hold until death do you part?"

She rolled her eyes.

"Hurry up, miss." The judge glared at her. "Yours isn't the only ceremony I have scheduled today."

In that moment, she recognized him. Donnie Statler from the Lost Dutchman Rodeo Company and a friend of the Becketts. The robe and slicked-back hair had thrown her off. Sunny was certainly calling in the favors.

"Fine." Tatum ground out.

"I believe the correct response is, I do."

"Okay. I do." She caught sight of Ryder, and her breath abruptly stilled. He didn't look nearly as perturbed as she felt.

"Your turn," the judge—make that, Donnie—said to Ryder. "Do you, Ryder Beckett, take Tatum Mayweather as your lawfully wedded wife? To have and to hold until death do you part?"

Ryder didn't hesitate. He captured both of Tatum's hands in his and gazed deeply into her eyes. "I do."

He did? He would? Her knees weakened even as her heart beat wildly with the anticipation of a bride on her wedding day.

Wait, wait, wait. This wasn't real. She and Ryder weren't getting married. And, yet, a part of her, the part that held her true feelings for him in a small, secret place, wanted to believe it.

"Now for the rings," Donnie said. "Tatum, repeat after me. With this ring, I thee wed."

She heard the pretend judge through a haze and, despite her impaired senses, repeated the words. With trembling fingers, she placed the green ring on Ryder's finger. It slid easily over his knuckle, fitting as if custom-made. She stared at the ring for several seconds, mesmerized.

Taking her hand, Ryder slipped the blue ring onto her left finger. It, too, fit perfectly. "With this ring, I thee wed."

Tears stung Tatum's eyes. She couldn't be crying. Not here, not now. Blinking, she fought to bring her spiraling emotions under control.

Donnie banged his gavel again, giving her a start. "I now pronounce you man and wife. Young man, you may kiss your bride."

A kiss! She'd forgotten about that part.

Tatum had no time to prepare herself before Ryder's mouth claimed hers with a possessiveness that was every bit as wonderful as she might have wished for.

He didn't break away, even when one of the deputies cleared his throat. Neither did she. His arms, firm and strong, circled her waist and drew her closer. Tatum had no choice but to go up on her tiptoes.

Actually, technically, she did have another option. But she wasn't about to end this incredible, impossible moment.

"Setting the bar kind of high for the rest of us, aren't you?" The remark came from a man in the audience.

Audience! She'd somehow forgotten they weren't

alone. Quickly, she pulled away. When Ryder didn't stop her, she scrambled down the platform steps and plunged into the crowd.

Where were her children? Her glance darted from one end of the street to the other. Back at the store? They must be.

She hadn't gone far when Ryder caught up with her. "Wait."

"Please. Not now."

He kept up with her frantic scurrying. "I'm sorry," he said. "I took things too far."

"It wasn't your fault." She'd participated fully. Willingly. "I think your mother set us up." She scanned nearby faces, furtively searching for those of her children.

"She may have. But the kiss was my idea and mine alone."

"Ryder, it's okay."

"I won't bother you again."

"Bother?" She stopped short.

"Bad choice of words," he said.

"No kidding."

Knocking back his cowboy hat, he chuckled dryly. "How is it I can never say or do the right thing around you?"

"And that's funny?" She reached for her purse, only to realize she'd left it behind on her lawn chair. So much for phoning her mother-in-law.

"That was a self-deprecating laugh."

"Mommy!" Gretchen's cry carried over the crowd. "We're here."

Relief flooded Tatum. She started forward, only to have Ryder block her path.

"I have an appointment early next week in Globe with a potential new client. I want you to come along and shadow me."

"No."

"We're a good team. We proved that with Marshall Whitmen."

"Your father—"

"I already cleared it with him."

She studied his expression. "What's really going on?"

He hesitated before answering. "Nothing."

"I don't believe you."

"Nothing yet."

"You have another interview."

"The less said, the better. I refuse to put you in a position where you have to lie for me."

Dammit. He was being obstinate.

"Mommy!" Gretchen's call sounded closer and more urgent.

"Goodbye, Ryder."

Tatum left him standing there. As she hurried toward her children, she held her left hand out in front of her.

The cheap blue ring gathered the sun's rays and, for a split second, glinted brightly, more dazzling than any gold wedding band.

Sadly, the effect didn't linger. Like Ryder's affection for her, it was only fleeting.

Ryder needed to return to Phoenix to wrap up some loose ends. That, at least, was the excuse he'd given his family. Tatum heard it from Sunny. Not him. Truthfully, he'd kept scarce since the Wild West Days Rodeo.

It was for the best, she insisted. Their pretend wedding may have been a farce, but her emotional reaction to it was real and, frankly, alarming.

A busy schedule had made avoiding Ryder, and protecting her heart, easy. The only time they'd talked was when he mentioned the meeting in Globe tomorrow with the potential new client. He was determined she accompany him and—what had he called it?—shadow him. She'd refused and assumed the subject was closed. Then, this morning, he'd sent her an email.

Groaning in frustration, Tatum pushed thoughts of Ryder from her mind. She had a lot of work piled on her desk, typical after a big rodeo. Final attendance numbers needed to be run. Contract laborers paid. Remaining funds deposited in the bank. Follow-up phone calls placed and photos uploaded to the website.

She welcomed the distraction. The school board was convening tomorrow and deciding on the new budget. Sunny had promised to inform Tatum of the voting outcome right away. She kept reminding herself it wasn't the end of the world if the school didn't rehire her. Her job at the arena wasn't unpleasant. More importantly, it enabled her to put a decent roof over her children's heads, albeit a small one.

So what if they didn't have a backyard to play in or the latest electronic learning devices? The wolf wasn't howling at their door anymore. And there were her art classes.

For the time being, that was. Until Lenny leased out her space. Perhaps she could find a new one...

Longing to teach full-time returned, an ever-growing void deep inside her. Managing an office, even a busy one, didn't give her the same satisfaction as standing in front of a classroom filled with bright, eager students ready to learn.

Maybe someday she'd teach again. *Yes*, someday, she promised herself. In Reckless or elsewhere. No reason she had to remain. Especially if Ryder left.

Hold on a minute! What did she care if he stayed or went? It had no bearing on her plans.

She cared because Ryder was important to the Becketts, and *they* mattered to her.

Returning to her computer, Tatum opened the spreadsheet she'd started earlier that day and began making entries. Mercer wanted to see how the various bucking stock performed based on the competitors' scores. Together, they'd designed a report that would give him the information in a concise, easy-to-read format. It was a task right up Sunny's alley, but Tatum was the one Mercer had asked for assistance.

Sunny said she was fine with it. Tatum thought otherwise.

As much as she loved the Becketts, she'd grown weary of their ceaseless squabbling. They sure knew how to make things hard on each other. Cassidy had told Tatum about Mercer's desire to purchase additional bulls. Sunny, of course, objected and, as usual, the three siblings were taking sides and forming alliances. Though they were attempting to be civilized, tensions simmered just beneath the surface, and they were no fun to be around.

Then again, who was Tatum to talk? The Mayweathers were no better. She and Ruth hadn't spoken since Saturday. Monty, however, had called last night after two weeks of "radio silence." He'd asked about Drew's dislocated pinky, then pumped her for information on her personal life. Awkward!

Ruth must have put him up to it, and Monty went along. That he should take an interest only because another man was in the picture irked Tatum to no end. Weren't their children important enough on their own?

She winced as a headache chose that moment to make its presence known. Frankly, she didn't blame Ryder for his unexpected trip to Phoenix, if that was indeed where he'd gone. He could have flown out for the day to L.A. or even Denver to interview. She envied his ability leave all this stress behind.

She was just entering the last batch of numbers into the spreadsheet when the intercom rang. A quick check of the display confirmed her suspicions. Sunny was calling from the extension in the house. She often went there during lunch. Though, come to think of it, Tatum hadn't seen her boss all morning. Another Beckett mysteriously absent.

Picking up the receiver, she said, "Hi, Sunny."

"Hey, are you busy?"

"Not too bad. The phone's quieted down." It had been ringing off the hook most of the morning.

"Can you spare a few minutes?"

"Absolutely."

"Meet me in the house."

That was a strange request. "There's no one to cover the office."

"Put the phone on answering machine and lock the door."

Only someone who knew Sunny well would detect the strain in her voice. "Is something wrong?"

"Just come."

Her stomach in knots, Tatum did as requested. Her sense of doom increased as she crossed the backyard to the house.

"Hi," Tatum called, knocking as she entered the kitchen.

"We're in the living room."

We? Tatum passed through the connecting archway and had her answer. Lenny sat on the couch alongside Sunny. He stood at Tatum's approach.

"How you doing?" he asked, his tone kind.

Surprise rendered her speechless. Then, all at once, she knew. He was on the board with Sunny. This had something to do with her teaching job.

"Sit down." Sunny indicated an empty seat.

Moving in slow motion, Tatum managed to make it to the side chair and sit without falling to pieces.

"A conflict arose in the schedule," Sunny started. "The board decided to move up the budget meeting to today."

"You didn't tell me," Tatum murmured, annoyed at herself for missing the notices.

"We thought it best to wait."

Until the vote was taken, she silently finished for them. Because the majority of members didn't support allocating additional funds to hire more teachers.

"I'm sorry," Lenny said. "We fought as hard as we could."

"It's all right." Tatum swallowed. "I know you did."

"There'll be another budget meeting this spring." Sunny reached over and gave Tatum's hand a sympathetic squeeze.

Six months. It felt closer to a lifetime.

"A lot can happen between now and then," Lenny said.

"And, of course, you have your job here."

Her pity job, thanks to the Becketts' charity.

"Plus," Lenny added, "I'll talk to my landlord. See if he's willing to cut me a deal on the new lease."

They were being nice. And supportive. Not to acknowledge that would make Tatum appear unappreciative. Right now, at this juncture in her life, she needed the kindness of friends.

"Thank you." She stood, grabbing the chair arm for support. "You have both done so much for me."

"We love you, Tatum," Sunny said.

"If you'll excuse me, I'd like some time alone."

Sunny walked her to the kitchen door. "Take the rest of the day off if you want."

Tatum shook her head. "No. I'd rather work."

"I understand."

Sunny didn't. She probably figured Tatum wanted to keep busy so as not to dwell on the disappointing news. She was wrong.

Tatum's agenda for the afternoon had changed. Rather than catch up on the post-rodeo paperwork, she was calling Ryder and telling him she'd be going with him to the meeting tomorrow in Globe.

Chapter 11

Being early made no difference. The restaurant Lynda Spencer had chosen for their lunch meeting was packed. After a five-minute wait spent sitting on a bench squeezed between a pair of elderly men and a trio of rowdy teenagers, they were led to a table.

"Is the entire population of Globe here today?" Tatum asked, half in jest, half serious.

"The food is supposed to be good."

She picked up the menu, intending to peruse it. Except, she was distracted. "Maybe not the best place for a meeting. It's pretty loud."

"Lynda raved about the barbeque pork."

Okay. Tatum was fast learning. If the client wanted to meet in a busy, crowded, noisy restaurant, then that was where they met.

Ryder checked his watch. "She won't be here until twelve-fifteen."

"Then why the rush?"

He'd insisted they hit the road, urging her to hurry when she wanted to finish updating the weekly calendar.

"I need to talk to you before Lynda gets here."

"About what?" Tatum's anxiety shot through the roof. She was already a wreck, fretting about the meeting all last evening and convincing herself the whole thing was a mistake. She was no sales person.

"I'd like you to take the lead today," Ryder said.

"What? No!"

"You conduct the meeting. I'll be your wing man."

She sat back, stunned. "I have zero experience. Repeat, zero."

"You've been helping me since I came home. With the secretary from the mining company and with Marshall Whitmen. Not to mention returning my messages, composing my correspondence and making cold calls to other rodeo arenas about reciprocal advertising."

"Not the same," she insisted.

"You'll do fine."

Tatum rubbed her damp palms along her skirt. "I can't possibly—"

"You can. You will."

"Why not tell me this on the drive over?" she snapped. Or yesterday, when she called him to say she'd changed her mind?

"Because I knew you'd be nervous."

"I am."

"And say no."

"Loud and clear, in case you haven't heard me yet."

"Tatum, listen to me." He waited for her to look at him, which she did reluctantly. "I went on an interview yesterday."

"I figured as much."

"The company is headquartered in Vegas with branches all over the country. Their HR team was in town recruiting, along with the VP of marketing."

She let that sink in. "Are you taking the job?"

"I might. If they offer it to me."

"Have you told your family yet?" She groaned. "You must think me a nag."

He ignored her question. "I heard about the school board vote. I'm sorry."

"Me, too. But what can I do except move on?" She shrugged. "Which is why I'm here with you today."

"I agree, and this meeting with Lynda is your chance to prove your worth to my parents. I have faith in you."

"I need more experience."

"I'll be right next to you the entire time. If you flounder, I'll step in. If you veer in the wrong direction, I'll steer you back on track. Just take your cues from me."

She shook her head vehemently.

"This is your chance, Tatum. Think about your kids. Wouldn't you like to be earning five thousand dollars a year more? That's what I'll tell my parents you're worth."

"Your dad won't pay it."

"We stand to make almost that much money on this contract alone if we land it. If *you* land it."

Tatum had her doubts. Mercer was beginning to warm up to her, it was true—they'd worked closely together this past week—but give her a five thousand dollar raise? Not happening.

"Once they see how well you do, they'll be on board."

Tatum drew in a deep breath. "I'm scared," she admitted.

"Of what? Failing or succeeding?"

"I want to be a teacher."

"Are you worried you'll find a career you like better than that?"

"That's not it. I'm afraid of…of…change."

He chuckled mirthlessly. "That Monty is a piece of work."

"What does he have to do with this?"

"He took all the fight out of you. The girl I remember was brave and strong and willing to go after what she wanted."

Like giving an older boy a homemade Valentine card?

"The divorce was hard." And what had happened since.

"Don't let it define you."

Her spine straightened. "I don't."

"Really?" Ryder's tone rang with challenge.

"I'll have you know I've bounced back from some pretty dire circumstances."

A slow grin spread across his face. "That's my girl. You'll be amazing."

She gawked at him. "You did that on purpose. Goaded me."

"Consider it a pep talk."

"I ought to…"

He silenced her with a subtle wave. "Save it for later. Here comes Lynda."

Tatum's resolve faltered. But only momentarily. Like yesterday right after Sunny delivered the news about the school board vote, it returned with a vengeance and filled her with determination.

She could do this. Better herself for her children's sakes. Tatum was good with people. And smart. Creative. And, like Ryder said, he'd be right there, stepping in if need be.

When Lynda Spencer reached their table, Tatum rose first to greet the smartly dressed woman and held out her hand. "Ms. Spencer. It's a real pleasure to meet you. I'm Tatum Mayweather with the Easy Money."

Tatum left the restaurant walking on air. Oh, she'd flubbed up during the meeting. More than once. Not terribly, though. And as promised, Ryder had jumped in to rescue her. She couldn't say she'd led the meeting, but she'd contributed. Greatly. The final contract terms had been her suggestion, further encouraged by Ryder's imperceptible nod of approval.

Lynda—she and Tatum were on a first-name basis now—hadn't even asked for a formal letter of intent. Rather, she'd told Tatum to forward the completed contract at her earliest convenience.

No wonder Ryder loved his job. She, too, could get used to this amazing elation at the close of every deal. It wasn't the same sense of satisfaction that teaching gave her. Far different, in fact. It was, however, rewarding and fulfilling. She'd missed the feeling.

"Nice grin," Ryder said as they wove through the parking lot toward his truck.

She had the humility to look chagrined. "Sorry."

"Don't be." He went around and opened the passenger door for her. "You have every right to gloat. Heck, I'd be gloating, too, if I were you."

"I can honestly say you taught me everything I know."

"I'm recommending my folks give you a bonus when Lynda returns the signed contract."

"That's not necessary."

"No guarantee. But they need to know how well you did."

She paused. The words she'd intended to utter died on her lips when she realized she was caught between Ryder and the truck's interior. Not trapped exactly but... contained, his strong arms bracketing her sides.

A sudden warmth pooled in her middle. She would have attributed it to the warm afternoon if not for the light-headedness that increased the closer he got.

Struggling to bring a calm to the abrupt storm of emotions, she said, "I'll run the draft contract by you before giving it to Mercer."

"I'm sure it'll be fine." He dipped his head. Only a fraction of an inch but enough to ignite a delicious thrill.

Was he going to kiss her? A small, silent voice inside her pleaded, *yes*, *yes*.

"I hope you don't mind," he said, his voice trailing off.

"What?" Take her to dinner? Take her home? Take her in his arms?

"I have a stop to make on the way out of town."

"A stop?" She leaned involuntarily toward him.

Ryder did the same and reached behind her. Only instead of pulling her against him, he removed the portfolio he'd left on the seat and dropped it to the floor.

"The hardware store. I told Dad I'd pick up some lightbulbs and salt pellets for the water softener. He's helping Mom with chores at the house."

So much for spontaneous romantic gestures. Ryder backed away, and, when she climbed onto the truck seat, he closed the door behind her.

Good grief. She was such an idiot, reading meaning into a meaningless comment. What had she been thinking? That he wanted to stop for flowers and a bottle of wine? Hardly.

With all the casualness she could muster, Tatum continued the conversation, as if Sunny's honey-do list was absolutely riveting. "Chores for your mom?"

"Yeah. Dad's trying to get in her good graces." Ryder sent her a wry look. "He's hell-bent on remarrying her."

"Cassidy told me." She'd talked Tatum's ear off one night well into the wee hours. Tatum had listened and given what counsel she could.

"She's not happy about it," Ryder observed, "but Liberty's overjoyed."

"What about you?"

"My parents' love life is none of my business."

The three Beckett siblings divided, as always. Was he, like Cassidy, not in favor of a reconciliation? Tatum could see both sides. Sunny and Mercer were a great team, even if they did disagree from time to time. Plus, they had a long history together, not all of it unhappy.

On the flip side, Sunny had lied to her entire family about Mercer being Liberty's father. It was a lot to sweep under the carpet. A lot to forgive.

Ryder turned the truck into a small plaza. She had been there more times than she could count. A couple doors down from the hardware store was a hobby shop with its gaily painted windows advertising specials. Before the school had laid her off, she'd made a monthly trek to the hobby shop in search of classroom and art supplies.

"Come on." Ryder beckoned when Tatum hesitated. "It's too hot to sit in the truck."

He was right.

Groaning to herself, she flung open the passenger door and got out. Did she have to continually turn a good time into a bad time simply because she'd misinterpreted something Ryder said?

"Tatum. Hi."

At the familiar voice behind her, she spun. "Maggie. Hello." She stopped to speak to her friend. "Don't you have class this afternoon?"

"There's an assembly next week, and I volunteered to make a supply run." Maggie carried a large sack with the hobby shop's trademark logo in each hand.

"Looks like you bought out the entire store."

"I figured I'd make the gas count." She eyed Ryder with curiosity. "Hello, have we met before?"

"Ryder Beckett." He smiled.

"Of course. I should have guessed. You look like your father." Her smile widened to include Tatum. "Are all the Beckett men heartbreakers?"

Tatum forced herself not to react. Inside, she worried that her attraction to Ryder was obvious to anyone who bothered to look closely.

The three of them visited for several minutes. Before leaving, Maggie told Tatum, "We miss you at the school."

"I miss everyone there, too."

"I'd best get going." She switched both bags to one hand in order to give Tatum a hug. "It's a long drive home, and I have supper to get on the table."

In the hardware store Tatum followed Ryder from aisle to aisle, still feeling a little uncomfortable and put out. At the truck, he loaded his purchases into the bed, the heavy bag of salt pellets landing with a thud.

"If you opened your store," he said, "your friends wouldn't have to drive into Globe."

"There's no chance of that happening."

"Not with you doing as great as you did today."

She'd been thinking more about a lack of finances.

They didn't talk much after that, and Tatum let her gaze aimlessly travel the streets of town. Ryder's sharp right turn startled her out of her reverie.

"Where are we going?"

"The marina," he answered without preamble.

"To take down our rodeo poster from their window?"

"They don't need us for that."

"Then, what?"

He clammed up. Tatum was just beginning to get annoyed when he entered the marina lot. Instead of parking near the quaint, nautical-style building with its life preservers hanging from the roof eaves, he drove to the north edge and the lakeshore.

"Ryder."

"I thought we'd play hooky for a bit." He opened his door and stepped out. "Come on, Tatum. Walk with me. It's beautiful out."

It was. Bright afternoon sun reflected off the rippling water, splintering into a million flickering diamonds.

When she hesitated, he said, "I want to explain. About what happened at my old job and why I really need to find another one."

That, she decided, was worth playing hooky for.

Chapter 12

Revealing the biggest blunder of one's life wasn't easy. Revealing it to a woman you cared about took it to the next level.

In the parking lot of the hardware store, Ryder had nearly kissed Tatum. Would have kissed her if given the chance. Fortunately, he'd stopped himself in the nick of time, before heaping mistake upon mistake.

His mother was right; Tatum had been through a lot and was practically raising her three children alone. She needed her job at the arena. More so now that the board had voted against rehiring her. He couldn't mess things up for her by getting personally involved. There was too much at stake.

Beneath their feet, the pontoon dock swayed and creaked like the moving floor of a carnival fun house. When it appeared Tatum might lose her balance, Ryder grabbed her elbow and steadied her.

"These aren't the best shoes for a dock."

He glanced down at the delicate black sandals, her painted toenails peeking out from beneath the straps. Feminine and very sexy and about as far removed from cowboy boots as possible. He wondered what her feet would look like bare and nestled next to his.

"I like your shoes," he said.

A bench was anchored to the end of the dock, large enough for two adults if they sat elbow to elbow.

Ryder gestured, and Tatum gratefully wobbled over to it.

She pulled the folds of her frilly skirt tight to her legs before sitting. It was also feminine and very sexy.

Ryder gave a low moan. Tatum could break down every one of his defenses just with the clothes she wore.

He sat beside her. The bench rocked sharply before settling. In the distance, a speed boat zoomed past. At the marina store, a group of fishermen ambled inside, poles and tackle boxes clasped in their hands. Water birds flew overhead, clustered together in a small flock. The next instant, they changed direction and drifted to the lake's surface in a graceful, seemingly choreographed, dance. Touching down, they dunked their heads completely under water in search of a meal.

"It's beautiful." Tatum's eyes widened as she took in the sights. "I can't remember my last trip to the lake. It's not far. I should bring the kids here more often."

She was rambling, his suggestion that they talk obviously unnerving her. Well, she had nothing on him. Ryder's mouth was bone dry, and the air felt too thin to breathe.

"I didn't quit Madison-Monroe," he finally said.

"Okay, I did quit, but only because if I refused, I'd have been fired."

"Fired?" She studied him with interest, not judgment.

"And slapped with a lawsuit."

"What happened?"

"I was accused of inappropriate conduct." He swallowed again. "By one of my female team members."

"I don't believe it."

He'd been expecting her to recoil. Find him repulsive. Certainly be shocked. Instead, she'd defended him. That wouldn't last when she heard the details.

"Within the span of a week, I went from being head marketing exec of a large ad agency to being out of a job and pretty much unemployable."

"That's a serious charge. Why would she accuse you?" Trust Tatum to bypass the superficial and get to the crux of the matter.

"I did touch her. On the arm. It could have been construed as inappropriate."

"Was it inappropriate?"

"We dated. When I ended things, she became angry."

Tatum listened quietly as Ryder explained the details of his office romance, the messy breakup and messier aftermath. He tried to be as honest as possible and not paint himself as the victim, though that was how he felt.

"I screwed up," he concluded.

"You did."

Apparently, she was through defending him.

"You shouldn't have touched her arm. Not at the office and not in front of other people. Other than that…" She exhaled slowly. "There's always risk in crossing professional boundaries. The school has a strict no-fraternizing policy. I suppose with good reason."

"Which is why I wanted to talk to you," he said.

"About the school's policies?"

"About us. This attraction we have." He waited until her gaze met his. It was guarded. "We work together. Seeing each other, engaging in any relationship other than platonic, is not a good idea."

She pondered for several moments before answering. "The arena is different from most work places. It's impossible to separate personal relationships from professional ones. The owners are former husband and wife. Their three children work for them. Cassidy and I are best friends. Your mom is like a second mother to me. Liberty is marrying a former employee, who also happens to be the arena's legal counsel. I don't think it's possible to cross more professional boundaries than those."

"Are you saying you think it's all right for us to date?"

"No, I'm not. But for different reasons."

He took a stab in the not so dark. "Because I'm leaving."

A flash of anguish shone in her eyes. "I've already been abandoned by one man."

"I wouldn't hurt you, Tatum. Not intentionally and not if I could help it."

"I believe you." She offered up a tentative smile. "And I appreciate you telling me what really happened at Madison-Monroe."

"I thought you should know."

It did explain a lot.

Tatum glanced over her shoulder at the parking lot. "We should probably get going."

"That's right. You have to pick up the kids."

"Actually, it's Cassidy's turn. She's dropping Gretchen off at the boys' day care for me. One of the other children is having a birthday, and they're throwing a small party. I'm free until seven-thirty."

"What are you going to do with all that extra time?"

"I'm not sure. Maybe sit down and have an uninterrupted dinner for once. Read a book." She sounded almost gleeful. "Watch a grown-up TV show."

Ryder was both glad and relieved that they were back on an even keel. Perhaps they could remain friends after all.

At the arena, they each returned to work. Tatum hit the office, and Ryder reported the good news about Lynda Spencer and the new contract to his father.

"Tatum did well today," he said.

"Taking notes again?"

"Actually, she led the meeting." Tatum might disagree, but Ryder believed differently.

"You put her in charge?" Frown lines creased his father's brow. "This could be an important new client."

"Tatum negotiated the terms. Lynda agreed to them. She's expecting a contract ASAP and committed to signing it. Tatum's drawing up the paperwork now."

"You're coaching her?"

"*Mentoring* her is a better word."

"Why bother?"

His father set the rake aside. He'd been cleaning horse stalls in the main barn. It was a task normally performed by one of the hands, typically the lowest on the totem pole. But Mercer Beckett wasn't above helping out in any capacity when needed, and, at the moment, they were shorthanded.

"She has potential. And I won't be available for long. She could fill in for me."

"You find a new job yet?"

Here was a perfect opening if Ryder ever saw one. "I've been approached by a couple of companies looking for an account exec."

"Is this because of the argument we had last week?"

"I'm glad to be home, Dad. I appreciate everything you've done for me. But let's be honest. You've created a position where there wasn't one. A position that, between you and Tatum, isn't entirely necessary."

"We're growing. Every week. I may have created the position, but it won't be long before we can't run this place without you."

"You're cleaning stalls, Dad. Hire another wrangler and you're going to have plenty of time to do my job."

"I called Harlo Billings this morning and put in an offer on those bulls and heifers."

"Mom agreed?"

"She didn't disagree."

It occurred to Ryder that his father may have another agenda. "I don't want your half of the arena."

"What are you talking about?"

"Cassidy and Liberty will take over the Easy Money when you and Mom retire. Not me. You can't dangle part ownership like a carrot on a string and expect me to bite."

"That's a crock of horse crap if I ever heard one."

"It isn't, and you know it." Ryder tried a different approach, one that would strike a chord with his father. "You're paying me a good wage. Think how much livestock you could buy instead."

"We could increase to five rodeos a year. Generate more revenue."

"Come on. Be reasonable."

His father grunted.

"I took this job only until I got my feet under me," Ryder said. "And to make you happy."

"I don't want you to leave."

That was closer to the truth. "Whatever happens, Dad, I won't stay away like before. I'm committed to reuniting this family and returning often. Besides, I haven't said yes to anyone yet."

Ryder's father pulled him into a fierce and unexpected hug. "I reckon you have to do what's best for you. Much as I'd like the Easy Money to be your calling, it obviously isn't."

"I love this place. I always have. But I want to, need to, work for a company where I can make a real difference. Where my contributions are valued. Where I *earn* my keep."

"You can do that here, son."

Ryder wasn't convinced. "You're the driving force behind the changes and growth. I'm just riding your coattails."

"I don't see it that way."

But Ryder did, and, in the end, that was what counted.

Later that afternoon, he returned to the office to find it empty. His mother was helping Liberty set up for the team penning practice starting at five. Tatum had already left for the day.

Using the computer at her desk, Ryder checked his emails, answering the urgent ones and leaving the remainder until tomorrow. Next, he returned a half dozen phone calls. During the last one, his cell phone rang. It was Myra.

"Good news," she announced in a chipper voice. "The head of HR from Velocity Concepts called. They've made you an offer."

The company Ryder had interviewed with yesterday. "That was fast."

"Apparently you were heads and tails above the other candidates."

Unlike the interview last week, this job was a good fit. Velocity Concepts had been formed fewer than three years ago. The founders were young, aggressive and innovative. He'd get in mostly on the ground floor.

"Which branch office?" The recruiter had mentioned several.

"Here's the best part," Myra said. "They want you for the northwest Phoenix location."

Not next door to Reckless but less than a two-hour drive, depending on traffic. Very doable, Ryder decided.

For what? Keeping his promise to his father that he wouldn't stay away like before? Getting to know Liberty and Benjie better. Dating Tatum?

Why not? He and Tatum would no longer be coworkers, and she could feel assured he wasn't going away. Excitement coursed through him.

Myra's mention of the offered salary jolted Ryder from his mental wanderings. He asked her to repeat the amount.

"That's not as much as I'd hoped."

"We can always ask for more. But, considering your circumstances and the current job market, it's doubtful you'll be able to get as much as you were earning at Madison-Monroe."

Ryder read between the lines. His "little mistake" had cost him dearly and was forcing him to start lower on the pay-scale ladder. Being prepared for such an outcome didn't lessen the sting.

"Look at the pluses." Myra continued selling the company by listing the many positive aspects.

"Email me the offer," he said. "I'll look at it tonight." And likely accept it, he told himself.

"I'm sending it as we speak."

"Thanks, Myra, for believing in me." He'd needed someone in his corner, and she'd been there.

"They want an answer within forty-eight hours."

Ryder was already heading toward the office door. "I'll call you by nine tomorrow."

He'd long left the arena and was driving in the direction of town before admitting to himself his destination.

Tatum's apartment was easy to find. He'd looked up her address a few days ago. At his loud knock, she called, "Coming," and a moment later, opened the door.

His jaw literally dropped. She'd changed from her work clothes into teeny shorts and a snug T-shirt that outlined every curve of her hourglass figure.

"Is something wrong?" she asked.

"Something's right." He scanned her face, wanting to see her reaction.

"What?"

"Invite me in, Tatum. I have news."

Out of habit, Tatum searched the small living room for her children. Then, she remembered. They were at the birthday party and would be for—she checked the wall clock—two more hours.

"What news?" She shifted uncomfortably. There

was no reason for her to feel incredibly nervous and vulnerable.

Yet, she did. For she was truly alone with Ryder. For the first time since they were young. Possibly ever.

She trusted him. Of course she did. His kisses hadn't been inappropriate. It was herself she didn't trust. Not when his sexy smile melted her resolve and caused her heart rate to quicken.

"The company I told you about, they came back with a formal offer," he said. "A decent one."

She went over to the couch and sat, trying not to think of what this meant for her and what a good opportunity it could be for him. A chance to rebuild his career, which was important to him.

Still, shock rippled through her like a small quake. He'd be leaving any day. She was bereft already.

"Where?" she asked, amazed at her composure.

"Velocity Concepts."

Removing his cowboy hat and setting it on the coffee table, he joined her on the couch—which usually felt plenty big, even with her entire brood piled upon it. Ryder, however, took up most of the available space. Not crowding her but making her acutely aware of his presence. Her body responded despite her mind's strict instruction to remain indifferent.

"I'm not familiar with them." Frankly, she wasn't familiar with any marketing company.

"They're relatively new but with an impressive portfolio of clients."

She'd wanted to know where the company was located, not their name. Perhaps it was best that he'd misunderstood her. Then he wouldn't see the depths of her disappointment at his leaving.

"Well, good luck." What else was there to say?

"This is a positive thing, Tatum."

Was it? Probably. She'd secretly pined after Ryder since his return. But despite their passionate kisses, she doubted he really wanted her. Not in the way she craved to be wanted. Desire differed from love or even genuine affection. Desire didn't demand a commitment.

Perhaps the story about his coworker was simply an excuse, one he'd given to let her down easy rather than admit he wasn't emotionally available.

"How did your family react?"

"I haven't told them yet. I came here first. I figure I'll break it to them at our staff meeting on Friday morning. After I've formally accepted the offer. I did tell Dad I was looking for a job."

She would beg off the meeting, she decided. Better than having to sit through the news a second time. Sunny, she was sure, would be watching her for any response.

"Your mom and sisters will be upset." At his leaving, of course. But Sunny had also been hoping for, counting on, a reconciliation.

"I promised Dad I'd come back often. It won't be like before."

"I'm glad for you," she said with all the sincerity she could muster. She'd seen this coming. Ryder had warned her repeatedly. Nonetheless, it hurt.

"You could be glad for *us*."

"Us?"

He slid closer, the cushions dipping beneath his weight. If she wasn't mistaken, his eyes darkened as they fastened on her. The vulnerability she'd felt earlier gave way to awareness.

"We won't be coworkers anymore," he said, his gaze intense. "We can see each other without crossing any of those boundaries you mentioned."

"See each other?" She felt like a parrot, repeating everything he said.

"Date. I want to go out with you, Tatum."

She turned away, fearing her expression reflected too much of her feelings. How was it Ryder could disarm her simply with a look?

"You'll be far away. I can't handle a long-distance relationship."

"Phoenix isn't that far."

She stared at him in amazement. "The job's local?"

"Local enough. Off the 101 and the 17."

Tatum was familiar with the area, having driven past it dozens of times on her way to her ex-mother-in-law's house in Glendale.

"I won't leave you, Tatum," he stated. "Not like Monty did."

For a moment, she dreamed. Until reality returned. "You can't make that kind of promise. Truthfully, we don't know each other well. You've only been home a few weeks."

He rested an arm on the back of the couch, his fingers finding and sifting through the long strands of her hair. "That's the purpose of dating. To get better acquainted."

She should ask for time to think about it. "How soon? Until you take the job at Velocity?"

"I'm requesting two weeks. That should give me enough time to teach you more about my job and to convince Mom and Dad that you deserve a raise. You'll get that bigger place to live, Tatum."

A sudden thought unraveled her. "You're not doing this for me, are you? Taking the job? Because I won't—"

"I'm not. But neither am I ignoring the benefits. For both of us."

Wasn't this what she'd always hoped for? A chance to be with Ryder *and* the ability to earn more income? What in the world was holding her back? She should be throwing herself at him.

"I'm high maintenance. You'll probably regret getting involved with me."

He laughed. "Not possible."

"Seriously. I have three children. You haven't begun to see them at their worst. And a nosy, interfering ex-mother-in-law."

"I happen to like your kids. And your mother-in-law doesn't scare me."

"But are you ready for a family? I don't think so," she answered before he could. "And I don't date casually."

"Okay."

"Really? Because there's no other way I'll consider going out with you. Not saying I need a gold ring, but I do need a serious commitment."

If she'd thought to dissuade him, she thought wrong.

Reaching over, he pulled her into an embrace. "I want that, too, sweetheart."

She was desperate to believe him. Nothing would make her happier.

"Two weeks." He leaned in and brushed his lips across her cheek. "Let's date until I leave for my new job. It'll be like a test run."

She resisted. "You're not a car I'm thinking about buying."

His lips moved to her mouth. "Take a chance, Tatum,"

Ryder said against her lips before covering them in a crushing kiss.

The compelling evidence of his desire pressed into her leg as he eased her backward onto the couch cushions, his mouth tasting the sensitive skin of her neck. Softly uttered endearments filled her ears.

Gorgeous. Sexy. Incredible. She hadn't felt any of those things in a long, long time.

Wait. That wasn't true. She'd felt them and more each time Ryder had kissed her. He'd told her with his lips and words and touch that she was much more than an overworked, dowdy mother and office employee. With him, she was a sultry and sensuous beauty.

"Have dinner with me on Friday." His breath was warm, and his masculine scent filled her senses.

"The kids." She opened her eyes, momentarily disorientated.

"Ask Cassidy to watch them."

"All right." How could she say no? Impossible with him tugging her earlobe into his mouth.

Another deep, incredible kiss left her limbs boneless. Oh, dear. What would making love with him be like? Tatum had an overwhelming urge to find out.

"I'll pick you up at seven," he said. "There's a new band playing at the Hole in the Wall."

"You dance?" She hadn't been in years.

"I won't embarrass you."

"You could never do that." She thought of being in his arms, gliding across the dance floor to the strains of a slow song. Suddenly, she couldn't wait.

"Unless you want to go into Globe instead. Then, — let's make it six-thirty."

"I don't care." She didn't. "The Hole in the Wall is fine."

All she wanted was to be with Ryder. Experience the heaven he could take her to in three seconds flat. To that end, she arched against him, expecting another kiss and perhaps a hand exploring the parts of her body left too long unattended. Instead, he pushed away from her and practically jumped to his feet.

"Ryder?" She blinked, stupidly she was sure. "What's wrong?"

"I should go." Something akin to desperation filled his eyes. Or, was it frustration?

She took the hand he offered and rose. "So soon? The kids won't be home for a while."

Heat seemed to radiate off him. "If I stay, I'm going to want to do more than kiss you, Tatum."

His words poured over her and ignited a thrill. "What if I want you to stay?"

The heat intensified. "Think about what you're saying."

"I am."

"I won't ruin what we have by moving too fast."

He made perfect sense. Tatum didn't want to ruin what they had, either. But neither did she want him to go.

"I've been simply existing for years now. Making it through every day as best I can." She looped her arms around his shoulders and lifted her face to his. "You make me feel special, Ryder. You've opened doors for me. Shown me that there's a life out there waiting to be lived."

He lowered his head until their lips were a hairsbreadth apart. "You need to be absolutely sure. I won't take you to bed any other way."

"Who knows what tomorrow will bring? This could be the start of an amazing future or just the best two weeks of my life. Regardless, I'm going to enjoy the time we have without regrets."

When Ryder moved to kiss her again, she retreated. His look of question turned to raw hunger when she clasped his hand and led him down the hall to her bedroom.

Chapter 13

Ryder's hands on her naked body. Strong. Firm. Possessive. Eliciting seductive moans and tiny shudders from her, then an exhilarating climax. Without being told, he'd understood where to touch her, how much pressure to apply and that kisses and nibbles along the base of her neck drove her absolutely crazy.

Tatum had imagined this, being with Ryder. She was human, after all, and a woman. But even her best fantasies hadn't come close to the real thing.

Before undressing her, he'd produced a condom. She didn't ask why he carried one in his wallet. She was just glad he'd brought one. After pleasuring her expertly and thoroughly with his mouth and hands, he'd placed the condom over his impressive erection.

She'd done that to him, she thought with no small

degree of satisfaction. Brought him to a fully aroused state with nothing more than her utter abandon.

Ryder, she'd learned, liked watching the results of his efforts. His eyes had remained riveted on her face in the semidarkness as he'd coaxed one exquisite response after the other from her. Tatum discovered that she, too, liked watching. Seeing his eyes fill with desire. His jaw muscles tense and flex from the strain of holding back. His chest rise and fall in rhythm to her own rapid breathing.

She intended to return the favor when he finished with the condom. He no sooner collapsed onto the pillows than she slung a leg over his hips and straddled him.

"Baby," was all he got out before she wrapped her fingers around him and guided him inside her. After that, he communicated only in groans and deep exhalations.

"Tell me," she demanded. "How does it feel?"

His response was to grab hold of her waist and bury himself inside her.

"Tell me," she repeated.

"Like nothing else. Smooth. Slick. Intense." He punctuated the last word with a desperate sound from someplace low in his throat.

Tatum smiled. She wanted this experience to be like nothing else. Whatever happened between them, and she vowed to be a realist, this night, this moment would be one of a kind. For both of them.

Leaning forward, she brought her breasts to his mouth. He suckled each one, the pressure he applied building as did the power of his thrusts. When she could take no more, she pulled away, denying him. He swore under his breath, then released an anguished hiss when she reached between their bodies and let her fingers play. Ryder lasted only a few seconds longer before his release crashed down on the both of them with startling force. Even before the last tremor subsided, he pulled her down to meet his mouth in a searing kiss that went on and on and on.

"You're amazing." He cradled her face in his hands.

"You're not so bad yourself."

"I was worried."

"About what?"

"Pleasing you."

No one had ever pleased her more. "Couldn't you tell?"

"I thought so. I admit to getting a bit lost for a while there."

Love talk. Tatum started to think she'd missed it, then wondered if she'd ever really engaged in it before. No, not like this.

Several seconds passed before either of them moved or spoke again. Eventually, Tatum eased herself off Ryder and stretched out next to him, their legs entwined and her head resting on his shoulder. Perfect and peaceful. Too bad it couldn't last.

"I hate to break up the party." She trailed her fingers through his thick chest hair and down his belly, enjoying his sharp intake of breath. "But the kids will be home soon."

"I'll leave."

She propped herself up on one elbow to stare at him. "Get dressed, at least. I can come up with a reason for you being here. Not for us frolicking with our pants down."

He didn't immediately spring from bed. "I need you to know something, Tatum."

"All right." The seriousness of his tone worried her.

"Whatever you may think of my past, I don't take sex lightly." He tucked a lock of her hair behind her ear. "You're important to me. Very. More than you can imagine."

"Good." She let herself relax. "Because you're important to me, too."

"I won't say anything to anyone about tonight. You can trust me."

"I'm not ashamed."

"Neither am I, but I don't want people getting the wrong impression."

His argument had merit. "I think we should tell your parents we're dating. We both work for them, after all. For the time being."

He swung his legs onto the floor and stood. She couldn't resist and took a moment to admire his toned, athletic build. Ryder may work as a marketing executive, but he had the hard, sculpted body of a man who earned his living outdoors.

"I'll leave that to you," he said solemnly.

"Are you uncomfortable with telling them?"

He yanked her to her feet and into his arms. "I couldn't be prouder. Or happier."

"Maybe we can tell them together."

"I'd like that." He smiled, and her heart dissolved into a puddle of mush.

It was a fact of life. While undressing and making love had been natural and easy, dressing was somehow a little awkward. Particularly when she turned on the light in order for them to locate their clothes.

Tatum slipped on her shorts from earlier. Certain her face shone beet-red, she averted her gaze. A moment later, Ryder came up behind her. Wrapping his arms around her waist, he rested his chin on the top of her head.

"Can I call you later?" he asked.

"Tonight?"

"Yes, tonight." He nuzzled her ear. "And tomorrow when you wake up."

Hearing Ryder's voice first thing in the morning? Just like that, the awkwardness perhaps only she'd been feeling evaporated.

"Okay." More than okay. It was wonderful.

She walked him to the door. Ignoring the neighbor who'd come out to dispose of her trash in the communal Dumpster, Ryder kissed Tatum. It was less intimate, less sensuous than when they'd been making love, yet a languid sigh escaped her. If only it could be like this always.

"See you tomorrow, sweetheart."

Sweetheart. She liked the rich timbre of his voice when he spoke the endearment.

Ryder wasn't gone five minutes when Cassidy showed up with all four children. Tatum went from quietly indulging herself in memories to fending off a friendly assault of hugs and kisses, accompanied by cries of "Mommy, can I watch TV?" and "Drew hit me in the arm with his cast."

A pile of inexpensive trinkets, bounty from the birthday party, appeared in the middle of the living room floor.

"How were they?" she asked Cassidy.

Her friend stopped dead in her tracks and gave

Tatum a long and thorough once-over. "What happened to you?"

"Nothing?"

"You are so lying."

"I swear. I'm fine."

"I can see that. You're glowing."

Was she? Tatum grinned.

"Tell me," Cassidy insisted.

"Kids, clean up this mess. Then, get ready for a shower."

The three older children emitted cries of disappointment as they reluctantly gathered up the strewn trinkets. Adam crawled on to the couch and flopped over in the exact spot Ryder had been sitting when he first kissed Tatum. Right before she'd asked him to stay.

"How come Benjie doesn't have to take a shower?" Drew complained.

"I'm sure he does. At home."

Cassidy completely ignored Tatum's subtle hint that it was time to go. "Was Ryder here?"

"What makes you say that?" Tatum answered, a bit too quickly and too defensively.

"He wasn't at the arena. Dad says he's been AWOL for a while now and won't answer his phone."

"Maybe he had an appointment."

Good thing the older kids had disappeared into the bedrooms and Adam was half-asleep, because Cassidy refused to cease her interrogation.

"I thought I was your friend. Your *best* friend."

"You are."

"Then come clean. It's obvious you're happy. If that glow is Ryder's responsibility…well, he's my brother. I think I have a right to know."

Tatum looked around again, making sure no one seven years of age and under was listening. "He was here."

"And?"

"We're going out. This weekend. To the Hole in the Wall."

Cassidy nodded mutely.

"Does that bother you?"

"No. Yes."

"What's wrong, Cassidy?"

"He's not a relationship kind of guy."

"Maybe he's changed. He was married once."

"And done nothing but dated casually since. Every phone call I'd ask, and he'd answer the same. There was no one special. I'd hate to see you hurt."

"Rest assured, I'm going into this with my eyes wide open." Of course, Tatum was hoping, not so secretly, that Ryder was becoming more and more a relationship kind of guy. "It's just a date. Let's not get carried away."

"What date?"

Both Tatum and Cassidy whirled to see Gretchen standing not ten feet away.

"I'll explain later, sweet pea."

"Tell me now."

"Don't you have spelling words to study?" When her daughter refused to budge, Tatum said, "We'll talk after Cassidy and Benjie leave."

"Is Mr. Beckett your new boyfriend?"

Tatum made a practice of being painfully honest with her children when possible, something their father wasn't. Now, however, she chose to massage the truth.

"He and I are just going out. It's too soon to call him my boyfriend."

Anger distorted Gretchen's features as she cried out and bolted straight to her bedroom. The next thing Tatum heard was the door slamming.

"Oh, dear," Cassidy said.

All the joy Tatum felt the past hour left her in a rush. "I should go to her."

"I'll get out of your hair." She cupped her hands around her mouth and hollered, "Benjie. Let's get a move on."

Benjie dragged his feet. Eventually, mother and son were headed toward the door.

Cassidy hugged Tatum. "Call me if you need anything."

"She'll be okay."

"Mom dating is a big adjustment."

Cassidy spoke as if she knew, which was funny, considering she never dated.

"You okay?" Tatum opened Gretchen's bedroom door and stuck her head inside.

Her daughter lay on her twin bed, a stuffed bear clutched in her arms. As Tatum advanced into the room, Gretchen rolled over and faced the wall.

Sitting on the edge of the bed, Tatum said, "Please, don't be mad at me. I was going to tell you." She rubbed Gretchen's back, a leftover gesture from when her daughter was a tiny baby.

"Do you like him?" Gretchen's voice sounded small and uncertain.

"Yes, I do. And he likes you. Drew and Adam, too. I'm hoping you'll give him a chance. He's a very nice man."

Gretchen squeezed the stuffed bear tighter. "Is he going to be my new daddy?"

"Absolutely not. No one will ever replace Daddy."

"Lisa Anne's mommy has a new boyfriend."

Her playmate from school. Tatum heard the name often.

"And then her daddy went away."

"That won't happen."

"It might. If Mr. Beckett becomes your boyfriend."

"Your daddy loves you." Even as Tatum said the words, she doubted them. Monty was the slowly disappearing parent, and it had nothing to do with Ryder.

"I hate him."

"Don't say that! Daddy may not see you often—"

"Not him. I hate Mr. Beckett."

At her daughter's pitiful outcry, Tatum's heart broke. Gretchen's anger and resentment at Ryder had nothing to do with him and everything to do with her poor excuse for a father. She was simply too young to understand the difference. Unfortunately, Tatum's relationship with Ryder could—and probably would—suffer because of it. She didn't want that to happen, but family came first.

"We'll call Daddy tonight, okay? Find out when he's coming to Phoenix next and where he's staying, then drive over to see him."

"Promise?" Gretchen's eyes glistened with unshed tears.

"Absolutely."

Tatum refused to think about what would happen if Monty came up with his usual bunch of excuses.

"What's wrong?"

At Ryder's sudden appearance, Tatum involuntarily jerked and banged her knee on the open cabinet drawer.

She hadn't heard him come into the office. That was what she got for letting her thoughts consume her.

"Why do you think something's wrong?"

"You've been hiding all day."

"I have not." She closed the cabinet drawer and faced him. "We talked this morning. Twice."

Ryder had called her shortly after her alarm went off and again on her way to the arena after she'd dropped the kids at school and day care. His timing had been good, which showed he paid attention to the small details of her life. It was flattering and sweet. And the kind of thing a boyfriend would do.

She'd cut him short. Both times.

Gretchen's tearful outburst resounded in Tatum's head. Her poor little daughter had gone to bed unhappy when their call to Monty went unanswered and the voice-mail message they'd left unreturned.

"I looked for you at lunch," Ryder said.

"I had some errands to run."

"You left? I didn't notice."

"Cassidy and I drove together."

He studied her critically. "What's really bothering you?"

"I'm just busy." She started for her desk. Luckily, the office was empty and no one was listening. Unluckily, Tatum couldn't use unwanted eyes and ears as an excuse to have this conversation later.

"Tatum, sweetheart. Tell me. What chance do we have if you won't communicate?"

The tender look in his eyes was her undoing.

"Gretchen's worried that, because of you, Monty will stop coming around. She doesn't want to lose her father."

"Monty stopped coming around long before I entered the picture."

"She's young. She has trouble comprehending a complicated situation."

"What can I do to make it better?" He lifted his hand to her cheek.

Tatum closed her eyes and abandoned herself to the sensation his caress evoked. "Be patient."

"We are still going out this weekend."

Her eyes snapped open. "About that…"

"Don't say you've reconsidered."

"I have to think of my children."

"The boys like me. We're pals."

"Gretchen's sensitive. She's the oldest and misses Monty the most."

"I get it. It was the same for me when my dad left."

Not entirely. His mother had insisted his father leave. And it was a well-known fact Mercer would have visited his children much more frequently if Sunny had allowed it. Monty, on the other hand, had been the one to do the leaving. And he'd rather be anywhere else besides Reckless.

"I won't take no for an answer," Ryder said. "I'm picking you up at seven on Friday."

Her defenses rose. She didn't like being put in a difficult position. "Please, don't make me choose."

"Don't use Gretchen as an excuse."

She drew back, astounded. "I beg your pardon."

"If you're having doubts about us, Tatum, say so. Don't make Gretchen the scapegoat."

"I'm not." She pressed a hand to her forehead. "Okay, maybe I am having a few doubts."

"That's better." A small smile lifted the corners of his mouth.

"How is that better?"

"We can deal with doubts. Overcome them. As long as you're honest."

"This is new for me. Dating post-divorce and with children who are heartsick because their father can't bother with them and scared that I'm trying to replace him."

She went to her desk and plopped down into her chair. Exhaustion, emotional and physical, overwhelmed her.

Ryder leaned his back against the lateral file cabinet. "What about his mother? Have you called her?"

"To tattle on him? I doubt he'd appreciate that."

"She might have some influence on him."

"Ruth and my relationship is tricky at best." Tatum shook her head. "She already suspects something between you and me. She might jump to the wrong conclusion."

"How could asking for her help in convincing Monty to visit his kids be misconstrued? It's to their benefit. And his. And hers, really."

"You're right." A less pleasant thought occurred to Tatum. "She might ask me to bring the kids to her house more often. Monty does visit her when he's in town." But not his own children. Tatum just didn't understand.

"Great," Ryder said. "Especially since I'll be moving to that same area."

"They might not like it. They're still afraid I'm going to leave them with her again. Drew wouldn't go with her the day of the parade."

"What would it hurt to initiate a conversation with her?"

"Nothing, I suppose." Tatum conceded she could be making a mountain out of a molehill. "I'll call her tonight." She suddenly noticed a printout of the contract for Lynda Spencer on the corner of her desk and reached for it. "I finished drawing this up. It's ready for you and your father's review."

He took the contract, gave it a cursory once-over, then, grabbing the pen off her desk, signed on the bottom of the third page.

"You didn't even read it," she accused.

"Don't need to."

"Ryder. I'd feel a whole lot better if you and Mercer both looked at it."

"I was there when we, when you, negotiated the contract with Lynda. I'm well aware of the terms."

That was true. "Still."

"Send it." He promptly stood. "I have a meeting with Joe Blackwater. He's on his way here."

The rodeo promoter was one of the Becketts' oldest clients. He'd also been instrumental in helping to clear Deacon's name when he was falsely accused of causing a bull goring accident eleven years ago.

Tatum walked Ryder to the door. "See you later?"

"Depends on how long Joe wants to shoot the breeze and when you leave to pick up the kids."

"I'll call you after I talk to my mother-in-law."

"You'd better."

Hauling her into his arms, he planted a kiss on her mouth that sent a tingle clear to her toes.

She swayed unsteadily when he released her. "Wow. What was that for?"

"Putting those doubts of yours to rest."

His grin could be considered confident. Cocky, even. On him, it looked good.

She stood at the window after he left and watched him saunter across the open area to meet Joe Blackwater.

Ryder's kiss hadn't erased her doubts. Tatum was too practical for that. It had, however, lessened them. Ryder did have that effect on her.

Should she be worried? Probably. Tatum could easily lose her head around him, as she'd proven more than once.

Chapter 14

Ryder and his father stopped at the Flat Iron for breakfast on their way to the arena. He shoveled his food into his mouth, only half listening to Mercer, his thoughts constantly straying to Tatum.

They were going out tonight. On a date. To Tony's Pizza Parlor for dinner, followed by dancing at the Hole in the Wall Saloon. Local spots where they were bound to be seen and recognized. Eventually, everyone would know they were dating, and Ryder had no problem with that.

Being with her, getting to know her, looking into her eyes and hanging on her every word, that was the important part. If their good-night kiss turned into more and they had a repeat of the other night, who was he to object? If not, that was okay with him. Ryder intended to take this relationship seriously and to make the most of it.

Her call to Ruth had netted some results. Monty phoned the kids, and, according to Tatum, they'd talked for a record-breaking thirty minutes. No plans, however, to visit. One step at a time, Ryder supposed.

Only when his father mentioned the bulls did Ryder perk up and pay attention.

"Mom finally caved?"

"I prefer to say she appreciates a deal when it comes along. That and we made a good haul on the Wild West Days Rodeo. Better than expected. We're going to the loan office today to sign the papers."

"Wow. That was fast."

"I told you, Harlo wasn't going to wait forever. I'm lucky he waited as long as he did." His father drained the last of his coffee. "If we want those bulls to pay for themselves, we're going to have to promote the heck out of the arena. You'll have your work cut out for you."

Ryder had planned to tell his family about Velocity Concept at the staff meeting this morning. Maybe it couldn't wait.

"Dad. I have some news."

"You're not still thinking of leaving." It wasn't a question.

"I've accepted a job at an ad agency in northwest Phoenix."

The explosion Ryder anticipated didn't happen. Instead, his father calmly asked, "How soon?"

"I told them I needed two weeks to wrap things up here before I could leave. That was yesterday."

There was a long, heavy pause. "Dammit, Ryder. Why?"

"I told you from the start my coming back was only temporary."

"A few weeks isn't temporary. It's a vacation. We need you."

"Tatum can help. She'd make a great assistant to you." He considered mentioning dating Tatum, then thought better of it.

"She's not family."

"Close enough." Ryder pushed his empty plate away. He had a lot to accomplish before the staff meeting at eleven. "We should probably get going."

"We aren't done talking about this. Just wait till your mother hears."

He was probably wasting his breath, but he tried anyway. "Dad. The decision's made."

His father shook his head. "It was our dream to—"

"Your dream. Not mine."

"Rodeoing's in your blood."

"But not in my heart."

"I'll give you a raise."

"Give Tatum the raise. She's going to deserve it before long. You'll see."

"Why do you keep pushing her?"

"What do you have against her?"

"She's an art teacher, for crying out loud. She'll quit us the first chance she gets."

Like me. His father didn't have to say it.

"She won't quit if you give her a reason to stay."

"It didn't work for you."

Ryder ignored the bite in his father's voice. "Give it a rest, will you?"

"Is this because you and your mother still aren't getting along?"

Would it make a difference if they were? "In all honesty, no."

"Don't you think it's time the two of you made up? The reasons for your anger at her aren't valid anymore."

"She didn't take you back, Dad. You had to wrangle your way in. To a business that was half yours to begin with. Forget the astronomical amount of money she owed you. Still owes you."

"I don't care about the money."

Ryder didn't let go. "If not for Liberty tracking you down, neither of us would be here. Just because we are doesn't excuse what she did."

"What if I asked you to make peace with her? For me."

Saying no to his father had never been easy for Ryder. "I'll think about it."

"That's all I ask." His father grabbed his key ring and wallet off the table. "I'll get the tab."

At the arena, the two of them separated. While his father went to the office—it was his habit to tackle paperwork early—Ryder took his camcorder to the bull pens. Whenever he had a few spare minutes, he'd been taking footage and was almost ready to forward it to his friend for editing. Hopefully, the final digital short would be ready in time to promote their next rodeo. It would be something special to leave his family.

He was almost done when his name was spoken softly behind him, in a way he hadn't heard in years. Shutting off the camcorder, he turned and faced his mother. Honestly, he'd been half expecting her. News traveled quickly among his family. His father had probably gone straight to Sunny after their heated exchange.

Ryder didn't mince words. "I take it Dad told you about the job."

"He did."

"If you're here to try and change my mind, don't bother."

She didn't so much as flinch at his harsh tone. "I understood why you left when you were a boy. You and Mercer were close as could be. Had the kind of father-son relationship every mother hopes for, and you missed him terribly. Blamed me for the divorce. I was certain after a few months, or maybe even a year, that you'd tire of your father's drinking, miss me and Cassidy, your friends, and come home. Only you didn't. Other than those few summers during high school." She searched his face, her expression pensive. "Why, Ryder?"

"I might have. If you'd have shown even the slightest decency to Dad. He did stop drinking. Right after I moved in with him."

"Yes, but there were no guarantees he wouldn't start again, and I couldn't take the chance. I loved him too much."

"Loved him? You had a funny way of showing it."

"I knew as long as he and I remained married, he wouldn't change. In large part because I enabled him. I thought, hoped, that by divorcing him, the shock would force him to get sober. Maybe even before we actually went through with it. Losing me sobered him up once before."

"What do you mean, before?"

"Your father was a wild one when we first dated. I thought he just liked to party with the boys and drink too much. I might have been young and inexperienced, but, after a while, even I could see that he had a drinking problem. I insisted he stop or we were through."

"And he did?"

"Didn't touch a single drop." Her eyes filled with sadness. "Then, he started again at your grandfather's wake and, this time, didn't stop. Nothing I said or did made a difference. Eventually, alcohol replaced everything important in his life. His job, his family, his friends. Me."

"I'm sorry, Mom, but I just don't remember any of that."

"Oh, he was an expert at hiding it from you and Cassidy. When you two were anywhere near, he was the epitome of a fun and happy dad, even if he was tanked. When you weren't, he became bitter and morose and angry. Really angry. The fights were the worst."

"With you?"

"With everyone. Sometimes, it was like a switch was flipped. One minute, he was laughing and joking. The next, he was accusing whomever of some invented infraction that generally resulted in a brawl. Three times in three months I was called to the clinic when he was hurt. Twice, I had to bail him out of jail."

Jail? Ryder hadn't heard these stories before. "Did he ever hurt you?"

"Not physically," she assured him. "Not ever."

"I didn't know."

"I didn't want you to know. Or your sister."

"I might have been able to help."

"I doubt that." She gave him a sad smile. "There were nights he didn't come home, and I'm not kidding when I tell you I was glad for the reprieve. I had my hands full as it was, taking care of you kids and running the arena. I didn't need a drunk to nurse on top of that."

"Did you ever try to get him help? AA. Counseling."

"Countless times. That's the thing about an addict, no one can help them if they won't help themselves. All I could do was try my best to keep the business from going under and to provide for the family."

Ryder realized with more than a little guilt that he hadn't ever considered how hard it must have been for his mother. Hadn't cared enough to ask. He'd been too busy being angry at her.

"I might have stuck it out a whole lot longer, even when he lost all that money on a herd of sick calves." Her voice shook. "It was the accident with Cassidy that convinced me he had to leave. I couldn't forgive him for that. Or take the chance that something worse might happen the next time. My children came first. Even at the expense of my husband and marriage. I know that's difficult for you to comprehend."

"Not as much as you'd think."

Before coming home to Reckless, Ryder wouldn't have given his mother's argument much weight. Meeting Tatum, seeing her relentless devotion to her children, had altered his perspective. Like his mother, she'd endured hardship and sacrificed greatly for the sake of her kids. Also like his mother, she was dealing with a daughter who sorely missed her father and didn't understand why he had to go away.

If Ryder could be understanding and sympathetic to her, could he not grant his mother some of the same understanding and sympathy? It was something to consider.

"You free later?" He held up the camcorder. "I'll be done here in about fifteen minutes."

She hesitated, perhaps unsure why he was asking. "I have to run to the bank before the staff meeting."

"Later, then? I'd like to continue this conversation." A delighted smile illuminated her face. "I'd like that, too."

"We still have a lot of ground to cover, Mom."

"One step at a time, sweetheart."

He gave her a one-armed hug that was filled with far more emotion than the full embrace they'd shared his first day home.

She reached up to pat his cheek. "I can't help myself," she said by way of apology.

"I don't mind." And he didn't.

"See you." She left, a spring to her step he hadn't seen before today. Ryder chuckled. They hadn't mended all their broken bridges, but they'd made a start. And it felt good.

He was just finishing filming when his cell phone chimed. He read the display and groaned. His father? Really? The man couldn't walk out and find him?

"What's up, Dad?"

"I need to see you right away. I'm in the office."

The curt demand rubbed Ryder the wrong way. He felt six rather than thirty-six. "I'll be done in about fifteen minutes."

"Now, Ryder. It's important. You need to see this."

"All right. Fine." He powered down the camcorder and returned it to the case.

Tatum was sitting at her desk when he entered. He'd have liked to give her a kiss, but that would be entirely inappropriate, and he'd had enough trouble in the past with something far less provocative than a kiss.

"Morning." He flashed her a smile as he passed her desk.

"Hey." The smile she gave him in return was ripe with promise for the coming evening.

Ryder suppressed a groan. Surviving the long day wasn't going to be easy. He'd be counting the minutes until he picked her up tonight.

"Shut the door," his father said upon seeing him, his tone brusque.

Ryder drew up short. "What's wrong?"

"Now."

He did as his father insisted, his defenses rising.

"Sit." When Ryder complied, his father handed him a thin sheaf of papers.

He scanned the first page of the contract for Lynda Spencer. "Yeah?" He started to hand the papers back.

"Dammit to hell, Ryder."

"What's wrong?"

"How could you agree to these terms?"

"They're good."

"They're ridiculous."

Ryder flipped to the second page where the terms were outlined and read. "Wait," he muttered. "These aren't right."

"You can say that again."

"There must be a mistake." He saw it then, a transposition—numbers reversed—and his blood ran cold.

"You said Tatum handled the meeting and negotiated the terms."

"She did, but this isn't what we agreed to."

"I spoke to Lynda Spencer before I called you.

Frankly, she's pretty happy, which is why she signed the contract and returned it so fast."

"She can't expect us to uphold these terms."

"It's a done deal."

"We'll go back to her–"

"Forget it. That's not how your mother and I do business. We have a reputation to uphold, and honor our contracts even when we've screwed up."

"I understand that, Dad."

"We can't have an employee working for us who makes mistakes that cost us thousands of dollars."

"You're not firing Tatum."

"She sure isn't getting any promotion."

"This is my fault entirely. She asked me to review the contract. Even handed it to me, in fact. I signed it without looking and instructed her to send it."

His father stared at him as if he'd just announced his intentions to run for president. "What in God's name is the matter with you? You let a complete novice negotiate a contract with an important new client and then send it out unreviewed. I can't believe what I'm hearing. How did you ever make it to head marketing executive?"

The verbal lashing was harsh. And deserved.

Ryder's head pounded. He'd been here before. Not with his father but in a meeting at Madison-Monroe. Then, his boss had asked almost the identical question. Ryder hadn't had a good answer that time, either.

Blurring the boundary between business and personal. Hadn't he learned his lesson already?

"I'll call Lynda," Ryder said. "Explain the situation. Make it right."

"Weren't you listening? This contract is signed

by both parties. Legal and binding. We are officially screwed."

"Take the money out of my salary."

His father continued as if he hadn't heard Ryder. "There go the funds for transporting the new bulls."

"I'll run by the bank in town and withdraw the money now." He could borrow against his credit card.

"Don't you think instead you should stay here and clean up this mess?"

"I said I'll pay you back."

"I don't want your money."

"No, you just want to control me. Use what happened to strong-arm me into staying." It was the same tactic his father had employed on Liberty, Cassidy and their mother. They'd resisted. And despite being in the wrong, Ryder was resisting, too.

"You're missing the point," his father said. "You have an obligation to your family."

"I have an obligation to rectify my wrongs. And I will. But I'm still taking that job, Dad." He stood. "And leaving Reckless."

His father's features darkened. "Send Tatum in on your way out."

"You aren't talking to her without Mom present."

"I'm her boss."

"You're angry at me. Don't take it out on her."

"I'm just going to talk to her."

"It was a typo. One I should have caught when I reviewed the contract—which I didn't. She followed instructions."

"A typo, as you call it, is a careless oversight. She should have double-checked her work before giving it to you."

"And that's what you're going to talk to her about," Ryder stated. "Double-checking her work. With Mom present," he reiterated.

"She's gone. Won't be back until the staff meeting. This can't wait."

"Then you talk to Tatum with me present."

"You're making more out of this than you need to."

"You shouldn't be alone with Tatum. It's bad policy."

"Policy?"

"You want to avoid any misunderstandings. It's less likely to happen with a third person in the room." If only Ryder had heeded his own advice.

His father frowned. "Are you saying she could accuse me of something I didn't do?"

"Or something you didn't say. People often react badly when they're being reprimanded. They're upset. Not listening. Misinterpreting. Better to wait for Mom."

He didn't believe Tatum was like his former coworker, exaggerating a situation for her own personal agenda. His suggestion was also to protect Tatum. She needed an advocate, and his mother would fill that role.

"Okay." His father leaned back in his chair. "I'll wait."

Ryder expelled a long breath. He wanted to be in on the meeting. He also knew from experience that wasn't wise.

"You and I aren't through," his father added.

They would talk again, and when they did, Ryder would be handing his father the money this mistake had cost the arena.

"I'll be back in an hour."

His father's gaze pinned him in place. "Don't say

a word to her. You hear me? I know you two have a thing."

"I won't."

As much as Ryder wanted to give Tatum a heads-up, he'd keep his mouth shut. Every move he made, every step he took, from this moment on had to be carefully executed. He wouldn't endanger Tatum's job any more than it already was.

In the outer office, he paused at her desk.

"Everything okay?" she asked.

"Great."

"Ryder."

"I'll catch you later." Because she needed reassurance, he squeezed her shoulder.

"Okay. But I'm—"

"I promise you, everything will be fine."

It would be, too. He'd move heaven and earth if necessary to safeguard her. And if his father dared to fire her, he'd help her fight it tooth and nail.

Once outside, Ryder went straight to his truck. How could he be so stupid? Twice in three months he'd made a colossal error. Twice he'd let his feelings for a woman affect his better judgment.

Only this time, he wasn't the only one to suffer the consequences. He'd cost his family a sizeable amount of money and brought the woman he truly cared about under unnecessary scrutiny.

Tatum didn't phone Ryder after her meeting with Mercer and Sunny. Instead, she placed a call to a temporary agency she'd applied to right after losing her teaching job. The Becketts had come through with the office manager position, so she hadn't followed up with the agency. She did this afternoon.

They had a position open at a preschool in Mesa. She could start next week as soon as she passed the background check and completed the application process. Tatum requested twenty-four hours to think about it. There were the Becketts to consider; she owed them a reasonable notice. And there were her art classes. Her students' parents deserved reasonable notice, too, and any refunds due.

The meeting with Sunny and Mercer had been her worst nightmare come true. For two hours after Ryder left, she'd fretted and stewed, sensing something had happened between him and his father. Or, that he'd told his family about the job offer, and there'd been a falling-out.

Never in her wildest imagination had she thought she'd made an error in the Spencer contract or that she would be receiving a stern reprimand.

Sunny had assured her the oversight was an honest one and that ultimate responsibility lay with Ryder. Tatum took only a small amount of consolation from that. Yes, he should have reviewed the contract. She'd asked him to do it. But the actual transposition was her carelessness.

She wasn't normally like that. Tatum took pride in her work, always did her best. She was organized and diligent and paid attention to details. Except for the Lynda Spencer contract.

Then, she'd allowed blind determination and Ryder's overconfidence in her abilities to cloud her judgment. She should have refused his directive and not sent out the contract until it was reviewed. By Mercer if not

Ryder. But she'd been pleased and flattered and lulled by the pretty picture of the future Ryder had painted and a desire to be worthy of his affections. Such a fool!

God, what would her mother-in-law say when she found out? Tatum's stomach twisted into an uncomfortable knot. Ruth would probably try and gain custody of the kids through Monty, claiming Tatum wasn't in a financially secure enough position to adequately provide for them. She might be right, considering that Tatum had been in this exact same position six short months ago.

Knowing Sunny and Cassidy were having dinner right about now, Tatum pulled into the driveway and unloaded her kids from the car. With Adam balanced on her hip and the other two in tow, she knocked on the Becketts' back door. Cassidy answered it.

"Hi. You're a little early."

The plan had been for Cassidy and Sunny to watch the kids while Tatum and Ryder went on their date. She'd explained the change in plans to her children on the drive over. They weren't happy to be missing out on playtime with their friend.

What would Ryder think when he showed up at her place and she wasn't there? What would he think when he called her cell and she didn't answer because she'd purposefully left it in the car? Doubtless he'd be unhappy, too.

"Sorry to interrupt you at dinnertime," Tatum said, "but do you have a minute?"

Concern clouded Cassidy's features. The door swung wide. "Sure, sure. Of course."

Drew tumbled in first. "Where's Benjie?"

"Watching TV with my mom." Cassidy gave him a gentle nudge. "Go on, if you want."

He tore across the kitchen and around the corner. Gretchen also went, at a considerably more sedate pace. Adam, evidently having another one of his "off days"—that, or he'd picked up on Tatum's state of mind—clung to her and whined softly.

She watched until both older children disappeared, thinking Drew's hair was in dire need of a cut. She should have taken him to the barber last weekend, only she'd been too preoccupied with Ryder and the mock wedding. A lot of things had gone unattended recently, and she was paying for it now. Well, after tonight, she'd be able to catch up.

"Can I talk to your mom, too?" Tatum asked. "I won't take long."

In response, Cassidy turned off the oven and lowered the heat beneath a simmering pot. "Be right back."

She took the same route as Drew and Gretchen. A minute later, she returned with Sunny. The two must have exchanged words, for Sunny wore the same worried expression as Cassidy.

"Honey, about today," Sunny said, "I know you're upset. Mercer was much too hard on you."

"He wasn't. He was doing his job." Tatum squared her shoulders as much as possible with Adam in her arms. "I came here tonight to tender my resignation."

"No!" Cassidy rushed forward. "You are not quitting. It was a stupid little whoops. I make them all the time."

"It's not just the Spencer contract and the numbers mix-up. It's the reason I made the mistake in the first place." Ignoring the painful lump in her throat, she shifted Adam to her other hip. "I let my personal life interfere with my job. Affect my judgment. That's unprofessional and unacceptable."

"This is about Ryder, then," Cassidy said, her voice flat.

"It's about me. I love you both, even more because you came through for me and the kids when I really needed it. But we all know teaching and art are my first loves, and I'm not an office manager."

"You're a great office manager."

"I'm competent. Good on my best days. But I'm no administrative assistant, and I'm certainly no marketing or promotion person."

"You don't have to be," Sunny insisted.

"The customers adore you," Cassidy added.

"And I like them. Interacting with customers has been the best part of working here."

"Then, stay."

Tatum wanted Sunny and Cassidy to understand and did her best to explain. "All the years I spent teaching, I was careful to never cross the line. And it was difficult sometimes, believe you me. The students with issues, the parents who didn't care, I often wished I could put those lines aside, but I didn't. Four months on this job and I not only do that, I cost you a substantial amount of money."

"We'll recover," Sunny assured her. "We have before. From much worse."

"Please reconsider," Cassidy pleaded. "Mom's right. A few thousand dollars isn't that big of a deal."

A few thousand dollars? Tatum thought about what she could do with that sum. Put a deposit down on a rental house. Finally get those new tires for her car. Start a college fund for her children.

"It's for the best," she said. "I can't continue working here with Ryder."

"He's leaving." Cassidy sounded as if she'd been expecting her brother's departure all along.

"I heard."

"Then, why quit?"

"You've been good to me. Better than I deserve. I refuse to be a hindrance."

Funny, Ryder said essentially the same thing about his job with the arena only on a temporary basis. Were they both taking advantage of their loved ones? She hadn't understood his reasons for seeking a different job before. Now, they were crystal clear.

"You are not a hindrance," Sunny insisted.

"I went from living with my parents to living with Monty. Other than the twenty months since the divorce, and not counting the two months we stayed here with you, I haven't lived on my own. I wouldn't be now if not for you. It's time I grew up. Stopped depending on others to carry my load."

"Tatum." Sunny looked as if her heart was breaking.

"It's obvious I can't rely on Monty, other than for child support. Even when his children were at risk of losing the only home they'd ever known, he didn't step up. I have to make it on my own, or as much as I can."

"What are you going to do?" Cassidy asked, tears threatening to fall.

Adam had begun to drift off. Tatum patted his back while rocking from side to side. "I have a potential teaching job in Mesa. At a preschool. Temporary to start, but it could work into a permanent position. I'd have to begin next week. I know it's short notice…"

"No worries," Sunny insisted. "We'll manage."

"What about the art classes?" Cassidy asked. "Can you turn those into something full-time?"

"I doubt it. There aren't enough children in Reckless interested in learning to paint."

"I'll speak to the board members," Sunny offered. "Maybe we can shift some money around. Or, you could substitute teach."

"Don't bother. You'd be wasting your time." Tatum had no expectations that the board would change their position. Not without a new source of revenue.

"Have you told Ryder yet?" Sunny asked. Both she and Cassidy knew about his and Tatum's date.

"I will."

"When?"

"I'm not sure. Maybe tonight."

"He feels terrible." Sunny said. "And blames himself."

Ah, so he'd talked with Sunny, not just Mercer. Tatum admitted to being curious how that conversation went.

"He shouldn't."

"Yes, he should." Cassidy huffed with indignation. "It was his responsibility to review that contract before you sent it out."

Sadness filled Tatum. "You're always so hard on him. And Mercer. They're family, and you only get one."

Cassidy looked chagrined. "You're right."

Tatum thought of Monty and Ruth. Was she too hard on them, as well? They were still family. Her children's father and grandmother. Perhaps Tatum should heed her own advice.

All at once, Benjie appeared in the kitchen. Sliding to a stop in his stockinged feet, he announced that he was starving. Tatum took her cue to leave.

"Come on, kids," she hollered. "Time to hit the road."

Her small troupe responded, heads hanging as if leaving was the worst punishment ever rendered in the entire history of the world.

Tatum checked her phone after getting into the car. Three missed calls from Ryder. A small icon appeared at the top of her phone's display, alerting her she had a voice-mail message. Maybe more than one.

She didn't call Ryder on the drive home, preferring privacy when they spoke. Holding her breath in anticipation, she pulled into her parking space at her apartment complex. Would he be there waiting for her? As it turned out, he wasn't. She was both relieved and disappointed.

Thirty minutes later, she answered his next phone call.

He didn't bother with hello. "Are you okay?"

"I'm fine. Adam, though, is sick. I think he's running a fever. Sorry, I should have phoned."

A fib, yes. But Tatum just couldn't face Ryder tonight. Not after the day she'd had.

"Can I help?"

"I'm just putting him to bed now." That much was true. "Sorry about tonight."

"I could come over."

The tenderness in his voice tore at her already vulnerable heart. "It's not a good time. I'm tired." Another truth.

"Okay. I'll call you in the morning." The tenderness had vanished. He'd figured out she was blowing him off.

She hated herself in this moment. She'd hate herself worse when they finally did talk, and she told him about her decision to quit the arena and leave Reckless.

Ryder would probably hate her, too.

Chapter 15

Ryder found Tatum in the Ship-With-Ease Store, speaking with Lenny Faust. He'd tracked her there after learning that she'd given her notice.

Her notice! What the heck was she thinking, quitting the Easy Money and moving? The anger he felt, at himself, his family, his father especially, at her even, was overshadowed by his fear that she might actually leave Reckless, going who knew where, and it was all his fault.

Cassidy had let the news slip earlier, assuming Tatum had already told him about her termination. Later, he'd have to apologize to his sister for his outburst. At the moment, finding Tatum and convincing her not to quit took precedence. Clearly, she'd had a knee-jerk reaction to the reprimand she'd received and wasn't looking at the long term.

A buzzer announced his arrival at the store. Tatum stood at the counter, Lenny on the other side facing her. They both turned to stare at him. Lenny winked. Tatum remained stoic. Ryder cut a direct path to Tatum. "Can we talk?"

"Give me a few minutes." She held herself rigid.

"Take your time," Lenny said and hooked his thumb over his shoulder. "I've got some cartons in the storeroom to unpack."

Ryder barely waited for the other man to leave. "You *quit*."

"We are *not* having this discussion here."

"I agree."

He took her by the arm and, ignoring her small gasp of protest, led her to the art studio next door. Lenny might be in the storeroom, but the walls weren't soundproof, and Ryder wanted to keep his and Tatum's conversation away from prying ears.

"You can't," he said the instant they were behind the closed door. "You need this job."

"I have another one lined up."

"What? Where?"

She raised her chin a notch. "It's not really any of your business."

"The hell it isn't. We're dating."

"Technically, we haven't been on even one date."

Her remark hit him in the gut, stronger than any fist. "Did the other night mean that little to you?"

Her features crumpled. "It meant more to me than you can know."

"Not enough, apparently, because you're hightailing it out of here the second we hit a bump in the road."

"This is more than a bump, Ryder."

"You were reprimanded. For a mistake that wasn't your fault. Big deal. It happens all the time. You learn, make changes and have it out with your boss if necessary. Hardly a reason to blow off your job and pull up stakes. Move your entire family."

Now it was her turn to react. "It is a big deal. I cost the Easy Money a lot of money."

"I cost them the money. I'm trying to repay it, but, so far, my parents won't let me. I'm thinking of just depositing the money directly into the arena bank account."

"I won't let you! It's, it's—"

"My decision. And I'd do a lot more than that if it stopped you from leaving. You love living in Reckless. And you like your job at the arena."

"You can't simply buy your way out of this."

"I'm making recompense for my error."

"Not your error. Mine."

He was growing weary of her stubbornness. "We can argue this point until we're both blue in the face. It's not the real issue. Your quitting is. You're upset and you're also embarrassed."

Her blush confirmed it.

"Take a day and calm down."

The blush morphed into a flush of anger. "You just don't get it. How come you can quit your job and move away when you screw up but not me?"

"My mistake was a lot bigger. And could have cost my employer considerably more than a few thousand dollars. Yours was a typo."

"It's *exactly* the same. I allowed my relationship with a coworker to affect my judgment and cost the company. The amount is irrelevant."

He wasn't ready to concede. "I was pressured into

resigning rather than face a potential lawsuit, and your employer wants you to stay. In fact, they're heartbroken you quit." He recalled Cassidy's sobs when she'd told him about Tatum's notice.

"Not your father."

"He likes you."

"I'm not his first choice for an office manager, and he sure as heck doesn't want me handling any of the marketing or promotion. With good reason."

Frankly, she baffled Ryder sometimes with her mulishness. "You're still stuck on the notion that my family is giving you charity."

"They have. Do you think somebody else would get a mere slap on the wrist? I've been treated differently from the beginning."

"Me, too. And my sisters. We're family."

"Dammit, Ryder. You aren't making this easy."

"I'm trying not to."

She groaned with frustration. "It's time for me to grow up. Other than going to college and obtaining my teaching degree, I haven't done one responsible adult thing on my own. When Monty left me, I mismanaged my finances and lost my house."

"He should have helped you. He had a responsibility."

"Maybe. Or maybe I simply messed up. I may resent my mother-in-law, but without her, I'm not sure what I would have done. Now, I've messed up again. I want to learn my lessons, handle my problems, and I can't do that if I continually let other people rescue me."

The part of his brain that remained rational saw the logic behind her argument. It gave him pause and cleared his head.

"Okay. Fine. Quit the arena. But that's no reason to leave Reckless."

"I need a job. There aren't many in town for the taking. Not that would enable me to earn a decent living."

He asked the question in a much more reasonable tone. "Where are you going?"

"Mesa."

His shoulders slumped, the fight going out of him. All this anger and frustration for nothing. Mesa was an hour at most from north Phoenix where he'd be located. In fact, now that he thought about it, the distance was more doable than her living in Reckless. He'd been wrong to jump to conclusions. To come in with both guns blazing. Really wrong.

"I'll help you move," he said.

"I beg your pardon."

"We can do it together. Look for new places. Buy furniture. I've got a bunch of stuff in storage." An idea occurred to him. A good one. "Let's rent a place together. Halfway between our two jobs. There'd be some driving for both of us, but later we could buy a house, and you could look for a closer job."

"What the heck are you doing?" She glared at him, furious. "I'm not moving in with you."

"Why?" The idea made complete sense to him.

"Weren't you listening to me? Because I need to grow up, Ryder."

"This isn't charity. It's two people in a relationship planning a life together. A future."

"I have to think of my children."

"They like me."

"Not Gretchen."

"She'll come around."

"How well you get along with them isn't the problem. I'm just not ready to make any kind of commitment. Not until I figure out my life."

The slam to the gut Ryder received earlier was nothing compared to this. He felt pummeled, as if he'd been run over by a convoy of tanks.

He could love Tatum. Might already be in love with her. Yet, she was tossing him aside like yesterday's garbage.

How wrong he'd been, and how right she'd been when she'd said she wasn't ready for a relationship.

"Look." As if sensing his anguish, she made an appeal. "We can still see each other."

At that, Ryder laughed. A loud, short burst that had her taking a step back. "See each other?" He'd stupidly believed he meant more to her than that.

"I wasn't being funny."

"No, you weren't."

He was vaguely aware that his remarks had wounded her, but he didn't care. She'd shot her share of arrows without thought or concern.

"And now that I want to take our relationship to the next level, you're the one putting on the brakes. Tell me that isn't funny."

Sweeping her hair over her shoulder with a jerk of her hand, she started for the door. "I think I should go."

Ryder didn't stop her, which seemed to give her second thoughts because she hesitated at the door leading to the store, her hand on the knob, a perplexed expression on her face.

"That's it?" she asked.

"What else is there?" He didn't try to mask the bitterness in his voice. "You've decided. Any arguments I make will fall on deaf ears."

Pain ravaged her face. "This isn't how I wanted it to end."

"At least you're admitting you wanted it to end."

"Not true," she protested. "You're twisting my words."

"Am I? Or, are you finally being completely honest, with yourself and me?"

At that, she turned the doorknob and left, walking out of the studio and out of his life forever. He waited a full two minutes before letting the emotional weight of what had just transpired push him down into the depths of emotional despair.

How he made it to his truck he wasn't sure. Where he was heading, he had no idea.

At the street light, he stopped and let the truck idle, not proceeding even when the light turned green until the driver behind him laid on the horn.

Just as well he was leaving Reckless. After today, there was no reason for him to stay.

"You're wrong."

Ryder cranked his head in the direction of his father's voice. "About what?" Frankly, he could take his pick of accusations.

"With Tatum."

He'd expected his mother to be the one giving him grief, not his father—who'd often treated Tatum with ambivalence. Yet, there Mercer stood at the door to the guest bedroom Ryder had occupied since returning to Reckless, a disgusted scowl on his whiskered face.

"Your mother called." His father didn't wait for an

invitation, not that Ryder would have issued one, and entered the bedroom. "She said Tatum is upset."

"That was some reprimand you gave her. She did quit."

"Damn woman is overly sensitive, if you ask me." His father grumbled something unintelligible under his breath. "But that's not why she's leaving Reckless."

"She told me differently." Five days ago, to be specific.

"You disappointed her."

Ryder turned from the window he'd been staring out of, mentally reviewing his list of regrets. "How exactly did I do that? By wanting to date?"

"You pushed her into taking a responsibility she wasn't ready for and didn't want."

"No kidding." His father had some nerve. "I seem to remember telling you the exact same thing before you decided to reprimand her and not me."

At that moment, Ryder felt the need to haul his suitcase out of the closet and start packing. He was heading to Phoenix this weekend in search of an apartment near his new job.

His father stared at the suitcase. "I thought you were giving us two weeks' notice."

"I figured since I'm such a washout, you'd have no objections to me cutting that short."

"You're wrong."

Ryder shook his head and threw the suitcase on to the bed with enough force, the headboard banged the wall.

"Fix this," his father said.

"The wall?"

"Don't be stupid. You know what I'm talking about. Convince Tatum to stay."

"I thought you wanted her gone."

"Hell, no, I don't want her gone. And not just because it would break your mother's heart and quite possibly cost me my relationship with Cassidy."

"Then, why?"

"I didn't want her doing your job, making it easier for you to leave. She was, is, a fine office manager."

"You keep forgetting, I never intended to stay permanently."

"Because you don't like taking handouts from your family?"

That sounded a lot like Tatum's complaint. Why had he insisted she wasn't taking charity from his family and shouldn't resent their help when he felt the same way? If he examined his reasons more closely, he probably wouldn't like what he found. He'd been out for himself and willing to use Tatum and her personal plight to get what he wanted.

She was right to toss him aside. He didn't deserve her.

Come to think of it, he didn't deserve his family, either. They'd been nothing but good to him these past weeks. Best to make a clean break, painful though it might be.

"Look, I like working at the arena. But the fact is, I have more potential. Greater ambitions. And you're overpaying me."

"Well." Despite them being the same height, his father managed to look down his nose at Ryder. "Didn't realize we were such a step down for you."

"That didn't come out right."

"No? Somehow I think it came out exactly how you intended."

"You're right." Ryder should apologize.

Rather than lash out in anger, his father sat on the footlocker at the end of the bed. "I did the same thing when I left all those years ago. I pretty much hated myself and figured other people felt the same. If they didn't, I was bound and determined they would by the time I left. Worked hard at it, too. Like you're doing."

Ryder really didn't appreciate how well his father knew him.

"Let's say, for the sake of argument, you're capable of more than the Easy Money has to offer. When did you get so all-fire full of yourself that you stopped having to make the most of a job and have everything handed to you on a silver platter?"

The remark struck Ryder like a blast of cold water. He'd worked his butt off for the first dozen years of his career, turning a sometimes mediocre position into an exciting and rewarding one. Had the fiasco at Madison-Monroe altered him? Taken the wind from his sails? The thought that it had rankled him.

"I might not have given this job a fair shake."

"How 'bout that?" His father chuckled dryly. "Your old man isn't as dumb as you thought."

"I never said you were dumb." The suitcase remained open and empty on the bed. Ryder had yet to throw any clothes in it.

"Can't say the same about you." Mercer shook his head.

"Because I'm leaving?" Why did they have to argue the same point over and over?

"Because you're letting that pretty young woman walk out on you."

That hit a nerve. "I asked her to stay. Suggested we rent a place together."

"Moving a little fast, aren't you?"

"Doesn't matter. She won't listen to reason."

"Maybe the problem is you're not being reasonable. Women think differently than men."

"Like you're an expert on women," Ryder scoffed.

"Trust me, I'm the furthest thing from an expert. But I don't need to be one to know you should go after Tatum. Fight for her. I didn't when your mother divorced me. Took me twenty-five years to come to my senses. Even then, I needed Liberty to show me the error of my ways. I'm trying to save you the trouble."

"Dad—"

"Not sure what went wrong at that last job of yours and, frankly, I don't care. But whatever happened changed you. You're not the same man I knew a few months ago. You're whipped."

Whipped? Ryder hated the sound of that. It too closely resembled what he'd been thinking himself.

"I got involved with a coworker. It didn't end well. She made trouble for me. A lot of trouble. She did it because I let her."

"Doesn't sound like anything Tatum would do."

"No, I'm the one who made trouble for her."

"Look." His father stood and put himself between Ryder and the suitcase on the bed. "You can fix this. There's still time."

"And I presume you're going to tell me how."

"Chase Tatum down. Convince her you love her and will do anything for her and those kids of hers. Who desperately need a father, from what I can tell. Make her stay. Propose if you have to."

"Propose? Didn't you just say it was too soon to move in together? Now you're suggesting I propose?"

"Women want a commitment. Living together is a token effort at best. No wonder she turned you down."

Hard to believe but his father did make sense. Ryder had known all along Tatum was the marrying kind, not the date-then-live-together kind.

"You could do worse than her."

"Truthfully, I'm not sure I could do any better. She's an amazing woman."

"Marriage isn't so bad," his father said. "In fact, I'm considering giving the honorable institution another shot."

Ryder did a double take. "You've met someone?"

"Gawd almighty, you really aren't very bright." Mercer shook his head in disgust. "I'm talking about your mother."

"She know about this?"

"Not yet. I'm waiting for the right moment to pop the question."

Ryder was thinking the right moment might be when hell froze over, given his mother's resistance. But then, she had relented about purchasing the new bulls. And Liberty had told him she'd caught them kissing once outside the arena. Perhaps his father was more persuasive than Ryder gave him credit for.

"You sure you want to live the rest of your life wondering if you made the right decision? Or the wrong one?"

"She's dead set against reconciling. I've tried. She shuts me down every time." The past five days had been difficult for him. A living hell. He wasn't ready to repeat them.

"Charm her."

"Not that easy. She'd have to speak to me first."

"If you can't get her to talk to you, guess you're not the hotshot marketing exec you think you are."

"Not the same thing."

"I disagree. You give that gal your best sales pitch. The most important one you've ever made. See if she doesn't come around."

In a strange way, his father made sense. "And if she says no?"

"What if she says yes?"

Then Ryder would spend the rest of his life making her happy.

His father's next words spurred Ryder into action. "Get after it, son. Daylight's burning."

He left without a backward glance, hopped in his truck and drove to town, taking side roads to shave a few minutes off his time. On the way to Tatum's apartment, he ignored his father's earlier directive and placed a call to Lynda Spencer. The more he thought about it, the more determined he was to see if anything could be done about the contract fiasco.

She answered on the second ring. "Hello, Ryder."

"Do you have a minute?"

"Absolutely."

"About the contract."

"I was wondering when you were going to call me."

"There was a mistake. Numbers transposed."

"I saw that."

"We're going to honor the terms. You can count on us."

Surprise tinged her voice. "I appreciate that. Another contractor wouldn't."

"We both know you're getting a smoking deal."

"I agree. But what do you want, Ryder, if not to ask me to renegotiate the contract?"

He was a little disappointed she didn't offer to make the terms right. They had, after all, reached a verbal agreement. Having no choice, he plowed ahead.

"Give us your next six rodeos. For the same terms we originally agreed to at the restaurant. You owe us that much."

There was a moment of silence before she answered, "That's two years out. We don't normally contract more than a year in advance."

"We just purchased ten new bulls. From Harlo Billings." She'd recognize the name and the stellar reputation attached to it.

There was another lengthy pause. Ryder swore he could hear the wheels in Lynda's mind spinning.

Finally, she answered, "Done. I'll have a letter of intent drawn up and forwarded to your office."

Ryder allowed himself a smile. It would take two rodeos for the Becketts to recover the money they'd lost. The remaining four would be at a respectable profit. And they could use Lynda to promote even more new business.

He disconnected after saying goodbye, satisfaction coursing through him. He'd done his job, maybe for the first time since returning to Reckless. This was why his father had wanted him to work for the family. What he'd meant when he challenged Ryder to turn his position at the arena into all it could be.

Was that what he wanted? To stay in Reckless? Maybe. Yes. But only on the condition he could convince Tatum to stay with him.

Ryder picked up his discarded cell phone and placed another call. This one to Myra. He knew from past experience that he worked best when under pressure and with the right motivation. If he had any chance of changing Tatum's mind, he needed to be sweating bullets.

"Hello, Ryder." Myra sounded glad to hear from him. After he told her the reason for his call, her demeanor noticeably cooled.

"Are you absolutely sure? This is an amazing opportunity."

For her, too. She stood to lose a substantial fee.

"I'm going to stay in Reckless. I haven't given the job with my family a fair shot." He went on to apologize for inconveniencing her and wasting her time. Ryder prided himself on following through with his commitments, and it bothered him to renege on this one.

"I have a couple associates looking for a change," he said. "I'll send them your way."

"Sure. Whatever."

He was offering her scraps at best, and she didn't hide her disappointment. Ryder decided he'd send her the money his parents refused to accept.

In front of Tatum's apartment, he pulled to a stop and parked along the curb. The tidy white triplex gleamed shiny in the afternoon light. Tatum's unit was on the east side. He hadn't noticed the painted flowerpots in the front with their white-and-yellow chrysanthemums when he'd been here the other night. Or the rooster lawn ornaments, frilly curtains visible in the front window and tire swing hanging from a tree in the front yard.

She'd done a lot to make the apartment, such as it was, an attractive home. Imagine what she could do to a real house. Ryder had always lived in a bachelor pad, devoid of a woman's touch. Before now, he hadn't thought he'd missed it. Before now, he hadn't known Tatum.

His brisk knock at her front door went unanswered, as did an insistent ringing of the doorbell. Where was she? When was she returning?

Ryder jogged to his truck. Odds were, she'd driven in to town. Either to pick up the boys from day care or to run errands.

He'd found her once before. He'd do it again. And, this time, he wouldn't let her go. Not until she'd listened to him.

Chapter 16

"Where are we going, Mommy?"

"I have to stop by the store and talk to Mr. Faust."

Tatum dreaded this meeting with Lenny. By her estimation, and after a thorough and discouraging study of her finances the previous night, she could squeak by for about a month. That would give her enough time to finish out the remaining week of her two-week notice at the arena *and* earn enough money for a deposit and first month's rent on an apartment in Mesa.

Her mother-in-law wasn't happy. She wanted Tatum to locate closer to her. Actually, she'd wanted the kids to move back in with her. Just until Tatum was settled. So she said.

Tatum had politely refused. Then, after Ruth had continued pressing, Tatum, for once, stood her ground. It had felt good. Exhilarating. And, this came as a shock, Ruth had backed off. For the moment, Tatum told herself. Her trials with her ex-mother-in-law were probably far from over, but she'd made progress by setting some new ground rules.

"Can we get ice cream?" Gretchen had been asking the same question for the past few weeks, ever since Ryder had taken Tatum and the boys to Cascade's.

"Okay. On the way home."

Tatum relented not because of her daughter's persistence but because, after a difficult meeting with Lenny, she could probably use a little comfort food herself.

Gretchen's smile was short-lived. "Can Lisa Anne visit me in Mesa?"

"Of course. Once we're settled."

Leaving her best school chum was probably going to be the hardest of many adjustments for her daughter. Leaving Benjie would be the worst for Drew. Fortunately, Adam was too young to understand the full implications of his mother taking a new job and moving them—for the third time in less than a year—to a new place. One with a different school, different day care facility, different neighbors.

As she did every hour on the hour, Tatum wondered if she was making the right decision. It had seemed right at the time, now she was less sure. Ryder had called her reaction to Mercer's reprimand knee-jerk and impulsive. Perhaps he was right.

Just thinking his name filled her with regret. But she believed everything she'd said to him during their argument. Tatum couldn't enter into a committed relationship until she'd put her life in order. If not, she'd be depending on him to take care of her and the kids.

She had already been down that road with Monty, and it wasn't a good one.

But, dear Lord, she missed Ryder. The past five days had dragged on forever. They'd seen each other at the arena. That couldn't be helped. Fortunately for her, their conversations were short and polite. Any longer, any more personal or intimate, and she'd surrender to the reconciliation he obviously wanted.

Parking in the small lot behind the store, Tatum and Gretchen entered through the back door. Tatum still had her key, which she intended to return to Lenny, along with an apology. She was leaving him in a bind.

They weren't the only ones in the store. In fact, all of Reckless was a bit busier than usual, probably because school had let out early today. Tatum had debated picking up the boys from day care, then opted not to. They would only distract her, and she needed to stay focused.

Signaling to Lenny that she would be in the art studio, Tatum hurried Gretchen along.

"Can I paint, Mommy?"

"Sure." Tatum quickly busied her daughter with paper and watercolors. She'd rather speak to Lenny alone, and, this way, Gretchen would be occupied and content.

While waiting for the store to empty, Tatum looked around the studio and located some card stock and markers. Sitting at one of the tables, she started creating a sign for the window announcing that the art studio was closing. Last evening, she'd made calls to her students' parents, advising them that classes would be canceled as of this weekend. They all expressed their disappointment and wished her luck in her new endeavors.

Tatum didn't get very far on the sign. By the third word, her eyes filled with tears. She'd miss this place and her classes. Almost as much as she'd miss her friends. She consoled herself with a reminder that she'd be teaching again, if only at a preschool.

During her short cry, the store emptied. "I'll be right back, sweetie pie," she told Gretchen. "You stay here while I talk to Mr. Faust."

Completely absorbed in her painting, Gretchen hardly noticed. Tatum had to smile. She'd been like that once, too, when she was young. Completely and utterly focused on her art.

Lenny offered her a big smile when she walked through the adjoining door. "It's not Saturday. What brings you by?"

"You have a minute?"

"Sounds serious." Lenny's smile didn't waver. He never assumed the worst and was always in good spirits.

Tatum went to the counter and stood across from him. Best to get right to the point. "I'm taking that job in Mesa. I'll be moving sooner than expected."

"How soon?"

"Next week." She could commute to the new job from Reckless, but only for a short time—and only if Cassidy agreed to pick up Gretchen and the boys every day after school. It really was a lot to ask, even of a best friend. Better to find a place quickly. "I'm sorry for having to break my lease early. I promise to have the space cleaned up before I leave, so you can look for a new tenant."

"No problem." Lenny shrugged one shoulder. "Truth is, I may have found another use for it."

"Really?" Interesting, since his rent was going up January first.

"Been talking to the manager at the bank. Interest rates on small business loans are low. Now's as good a time as any for me to borrow money and expand the store."

Tatum was a bit flummoxed. He hadn't ever mentioned expanding the store before. "Is the shipping business that good?"

"It's steady. But I was actually thinking of adding a small office supply store. The pharmacy sells a few things. Envelopes and pens and such. If anyone wants a printer cartridge or masking tape or even paper clips, they have to drive into Globe."

How often had Tatum and her fellow teachers lamented the same thing?

"Might even sell some of that craft stuff you were always needing back when you were teaching."

A craft store. Tatum's silly dream that Ryder had said wasn't silly at all. Did she ever discuss her idea with Lenny? She couldn't remember. She must have. Or, Ryder did.

"Maggie Phillips was in here the other day complaining about needing poster board and markers," he said. "She was hoping to borrow some from you, but you weren't in the studio."

Tatum recalled running into Maggie outside the hardware store in Globe. She'd been on a supply run then, too.

She felt a pang deep in her heart. "I'm jealous of you, Lenny."

"Why?"

"The store. I've wanted to do something like that myself for years now."

Lenny's smile widened. "Come work for me."

"I didn't mean to," she sputtered.

"Can't do it all myself. I'd have to hire someone. Why not you? Unless you're set on that job in Mesa."

Tatum started to tell him yes, she was. The words, however, struck in her throat and refused to budge. She didn't want to move to Mesa. She didn't want to take a temporary position. She wanted to stay in Reckless. Her home.

"How much would the job pay?"

She had to be a realist and not get ahead of herself. Especially after all her talk about needing to grow up and make it on her own.

"Can't afford much to start." Lenny named an hourly wage. "I can see about a raise in a few months."

She could manage on that amount. If she watched her pennies very, very closely.

"Can I continue my art classes?" she asked, already thinking of adding evening classes to the schedule.

"Wouldn't have it any other way."

"Then I accept." She thrust her hand forward, and Lenny shook it gladly.

"Welcome aboard."

The decision felt right, much better than the temporary position at the preschool.

She'd have to call the agency right away. And tell Sunny and Cassidy. They would be glad for her and understand why she wasn't returning to the arena. Running a small office supply and craft store, continuing with her art lessons, was a much better fit for Tatum than working at the Easy Money.

And the kids! They'd be overjoyed. Tatum couldn't wait to tell them. That bigger house wasn't in their immediate plans. It might be if she worked hard and helped Lenny grow the business.

Ryder would be happy for her, too, she was certain. He'd be glad she was staying in Reckless.

Tatum felt another pang in her heart. The new job with Lenny put her one step closer to her goal of better managing her life on her own. But she still wasn't ready for a commitment. Maybe. One day. By then, Ryder would probably have met someone else. He was much too good-looking to go for long without attracting the attention of a woman. And he'd be at a new company, making new contacts on a daily basis.

"I'm meeting with a general contractor on Tuesday," Lenny said.

Tatum cleared her mind of Ryder and what couldn't be and concentrated on Lenny.

"I need a construction estimate to take to the bank before they'll start the loan paperwork. I don't think there needs to be a lot done to the space. Paint and flooring. Some shelves. The ceiling tile is shot. Stocking the merchandise is what'll cost the most."

"Have you ever considered selling teaching supplies? If not selling them, then having catalogues on hand that the teachers can order from? It would be easy enough to have the items shipped to the store."

"I like it." Lenny nodded thoughtfully.

They talked for several more minutes, hammering out details and brainstorming. Tatum forgot about the time.

"Mommy, how much longer?" Gretchen had come into the store.

Tatum went to her, picked her up and swung her in a circle. "Guess what, sweetie pie? We're not moving to Mesa! We're staying here, and Mommy's going to work for Mr. Faust."

Gretchen promptly broke into sobs, hiding her face in Tatum's tummy.

"What's wrong?"

"I can stay in school?"

Tatum stroked her daughter's hair. "Yes, and with all your friends."

Lenny offered them both tissues. It was only then that Tatum realized she, too, was crying. She dabbed Gretchen's cheeks and then her own.

"Let's get your painting," she told Gretchen, "and clean up. I have to pick up your brothers in an hour."

"Can I call Lisa Anne? Please."

Her classmate from school. How could Tatum say no? She handed Gretchen her cell phone. When Lisa Anne's mother offered to take Gretchen with them to the library, Tatum accepted, glad for a chance to continue working uninterrupted.

She and Lenny agreed to meet the following day for coffee and continue their discussion. She'd also attend the meeting he had scheduled with the general contractor.

After Gretchen left with her friend, Tatum made quick work of restoring order to the art studio. With a flourish, she tore up the partially completed sign and threw the bits into the wastebasket. Tomorrow, she'd make new signs. One advertising art classes and the other announcing the store's expansion.

She was just about to leave the studio when the bell above the front door jangled. Expecting to see a parent inquiring about the canceled lessons, or even Maggie needing classroom supplies, Tatum affixed a happy smile on her face and pivoted, ready to spread the good news.

Instead, Ryder walked toward her, his stride long and his expression that of a man with purpose.

"I was just leaving."

Ryder wasn't about to let Tatum off the hook that easily. "I won't keep you long." Just in case she attempted a quick escape, he edged closer.

She studied him up and down. "Are you blocking my way?"

"No." He didn't budge.

"Doesn't matter. I parked in the back."

Damn. He should have realized that when he didn't see her car out front.

"What do you want, Ryder?"

At first, he assumed she was still mad at him. All right, to be expected. He'd said some pretty stupid things to her last week. On second thought, that could be longing in her eyes. Or remorse. Or even uncertainty. Whichever, the fact she didn't demand he leave that instant gave him hope.

"This isn't a good time. Gretchen will be back any second, and I have to pick up the boys."

"Can I come by your apartment later?" he asked.

"We have plans."

Tatum had wavered for an instant before answering, giving Ryder even more hope.

Encouraged, he surged ahead. "I spoke to Lynda

Spencer on the way into town. She committed to using Easy Money bucking stock for her next six rodeos. At the terms we originally agreed on."

Tatum's jaw went momentarily slack. "That's wonderful," she said when she recovered.

"We'll make good money. In the end."

"You have no idea how happy I am to hear that."

"No more than me." He paused. "You don't have to quit now."

"I do."

"This isn't me taking care of you, Tatum. The mistake was mine to fix."

"Actually, I agree." She reached for her purse. "But that changes nothing."

She was leaving. Ryder didn't have much time.

"I turned down the job at Velocity Concepts."

"You did?" She blinked in disbelief.

"I'm staying."

"You are?"

"I'd like to say I had an epiphany. What I had was a serious butt kicking from my dad. Seems he's a lot smarter than I gave him credit for. But don't tell him I said that."

"Your secret's safe with me." A hint of amusement lit her eyes.

For a second, she was the old Tatum. The one before their argument.

"Don't go," he blurted. "Stay in Reckless."

"Oh, Ryder." She was slipping away from him. He could feel it.

"I should have come home years ago," he said.

"Or, maybe you came home at just the right time.

You've reconciled with your mother and joined the family business."

"I found you, too." This time, he didn't hold back his words. "And I shouldn't have let you go. I was wrong. I was stupid. I want a second chance."

"We can't just start over."

"Why not? Mesa isn't far."

"I'm not moving to Mesa."

"Not moving," he echoed dumbly.

"There's been a…a change," Tatum said.

"You're staying?"

Her glance went to the open door dividing the Ship-With-Ease Store from the art studio. Lenny stood behind the counter, assisting a customer. When she returned her gaze to Ryder, a smile pulled at the corners of her mouth.

"Lenny's expanding the store. To include office and craft supplies and even teaching supplies."

"Like you talked about."

Her smile widened, light and lovely. "He needs help and offered me a job assisting him. I'm still going to teach art, and—"

She didn't finish. She couldn't. Ryder left her speechless when he scooped her up in his arms.

"Ryder! Put me down." Her objection was weak at best, so he ignored it.

"Go out with me. Tonight. We'll celebrate. Dinner at the nicest restaurant in Globe."

"I already told you, I'm busy."

"Break your plans."

"Are you crazy?"

"I've been accused of worse."

"Really, Ryder. I'm serious."

He didn't believe her because she was laughing. The sound worked like a magic spell, enabling him to see the future clearly. It included his and Tatum's families joined together for always.

"Put me down." She pushed on his chest with the palms of her hands.

"I will." He gazed down at her. "As soon as you agree to marry me."

Tatum gasped. "You *are* crazy."

"I love you, Tatum." He kissed her then, not caring that customers in the Ship-With-Ease Store were staring at them. When he and Tatum broke apart, her cheeks were flushed. He liked her discombobulated.

"I can't marry you. Absolutely not. It's too soon."

So much for his father's theory that women needed a proposal. Well, at least she hadn't said she didn't love him. And she was still smiling.

"Then we'll date for a while. I think three months should be long enough. In the meantime, we'll find a house. One with four bedrooms. Or five. I can't stay in Dad's spare room any longer."

"Five bedrooms. That's a *huge* house."

"We have a big family." He gave her his best seductive grin. "Who knows? Could be even bigger one day."

She stared at him. "You want children?"

"I want your children. I'll be a good stepdad. And if we have one of our own, all the better."

"You're impossible." Her voice cracked with emotion.

Better than crazy. "I want to marry you, Tatum. When you're ready. When the time is right."

"I love you, too," she said, finally telling him what he desperately needed to hear. "I think I fell for you that first day, when you removed Cupcake's shoe in your dress clothes."

Before he could kiss her again, they were interrupted by Gretchen entering the studio.

She stood staring at them, her lower lip protruding in a severe pout. "I already have a daddy."

Ryder let go of Tatum and went to the girl. Kneeling in front of her, he took her by the shoulders. "I'm not going to take the place of your father. I promise you that. He's your dad and always will be. But I'm hoping we can be friends. Good friends. There isn't anything I want more."

She refused to look at him, so he tucked a finger beneath her chin and tilted her face to his.

"Your brothers like me. Do you think you could learn to like me, too? Even a little?"

"Will you take me to Cascades for ice cream?"

"Every weekend, if that's what you want."

"Okay, then."

Ah, the power of ice cream.

Ryder stood, his chest tight. He'd never been happier.

"Yes," Tatum said.

He looked at her, not sure he understood. "Yes, you'll have dinner tonight?"

"Yes, I'll marry you. When the time is right."

Wrong. He could indeed be happier.

Outside the studio, when Gretchen wasn't watching, he pulled Tatum into his arms and pressed his lips to hers for another satisfying kiss, promising himself that the next wedding in Reckless wouldn't be a pretend one. Theirs would be real and legal and the start of his and Tatum's lives together as husband and wife.

Ryder hadn't merely come home when he returned to Reckless. He'd found his true calling after years of wandering. No one was more surprised than him to discover the confirmed bachelor was really a family man at heart.

* * * * *

SPECIAL EXCERPT FROM

 HARLEQUIN®

SPECIAL EDITION

*Benjamin Graham is a former marine, not a cowboy.
So when he gets a job as a ranch hand, he has a lot
to learn. Luckily, Emily Davis is willing to teach him
everything he needs to know. But as the attraction
between them grows, Graham and Emily will both have
to face their pasts and learn to embrace the future.*

*Read on for a sneak preview of
the final book in the Texas Rescue miniseries,*
How to Train a Cowboy,
by USA TODAY bestselling author
Caro Carson.

She had hopes, high hopes. She wanted to hear him say
he'd taken one look at her and felt the same way she
had: here was someone he wanted to get to know better.
Someone attractive, appealing—even sexy.

But the moment passed. Then another. He studied the
darkness beyond their little pool of light. "You never
leave someone behind in battle. Never."

Not sexy. Kind of grim, actually.

"Were you in the military?" she asked.

"Yes. Were you?"

"No." But there was a compliment in there. It wasn't
sexy, but it was something. "No one's ever asked me that
before. What makes you think I might have served in the
military?"

He didn't answer her.

HSCCEXP50708

She wanted to see his smile again. She nudged him with her shoulder. "Come on, tell me. Was it my fabulous driving skills? Do you think I'd be good at driving a tank, or what?"

His smile returned briefly. "That wasn't your first time off-roading."

"I couldn't call myself a Texan if I'd never taken a truck off-road."

She wanted to touch him. She'd already stood in the warmth of his arms. Heck, he'd already had his hand on her rear end twice, even if both times had been during an escape.

Fortune favors the brave. Those had been the man's own words.

"You want to know why I thought you might be in the military?" She dared to reach up and touch the back of his neck, the clean skin above his collar. She let her fingers comb through the short hair at the back of his head. "It wasn't this haircut. It's short, but not as short as the soldiers from Fort Hood."

"I'm a civilian now. A regulation haircut would be too…unnecessary." He didn't shake her off or step away, but he didn't touch her in return, either, except with his gaze.

She let her hand slip over his shoulder lightly before falling away. "I'll tell you what gave it away. It was the way you ordered me to get back in the truck. Do they teach you to bark out orders in that tone of voice? It's scary as hell."

"It didn't work on you." He grumbled those words, which made her smile.

"I'm stubborn like that, and I already know it's not a good trait. I hear about it from my family all the time."

She pushed away from the door and turned to face him— which meant she stepped over his crossed ankles with one foot and stood in her minidress with her legs a little way apart, his boots between hers. The night air was cold on her inner thighs. "But I didn't bark out any orders like a military man, so what made you think I might have served? Come on, talk to me." She gestured toward the red and blue glow on the horizon. "We can't go anywhere, anyway. Was it my haircut?"

She was joking, of course, but her laughter faded at the intensity of his gaze. She couldn't look away, not even when he turned his attention from her eyes to her hair, somewhere near her temple. Her ear. Slowly, so slowly, his gaze followed the length of her hair as it lay on her shoulder, as it curved over her breast, as it disappeared in the open edge of his coat, near her hip.

She wanted him. He was leaning against his vehicle, arms crossed, ankles crossed, not moving a muscle, setting her on fire with a look.

"There's nothing military about your hair," he said quietly, and he looked back up to her eyes. "It was your head. You keep a cool head."

"A cool head." She breathed in cold air, willing herself to say something, to do something, although her thoughts weren't cool at all. "That's it?"

"That's not all that common." He pushed away from the door and stood before her, a little too close, and not nearly close enough. "You also didn't leave your ex and his friends behind, even though they didn't deserve your help."

Kiss me, kiss me.

But the man didn't move an inch closer. "They were lucky. If I hadn't wanted to dance with you so badly, I would have gotten you out of there before trouble started, and they wouldn't have had you around to bail them out."

Wait—what? To heck with her ex and the fight. "You wanted to dance with me?"

"The second that band played anything remotely resembling a slow song. I ignored the beginnings of that fight, because I wanted to see if the band would play something we could dance to. It's the only way to touch a woman you barely know without being too…"

"Handsy?" Dear God, she sounded breathless. She was breathless.

"That's the word."

He'd wanted to touch her from the start. This insane chemistry was the same for both of them.

He didn't reach for her now. Why didn't he reach for her?

"So dancing is an acceptable way to touch a woman you just met." She kept her voice low in the dark.

"Right."

"And we decided keeping someone warm when it's cold out is allowed."

"True." He didn't move.

"Graham." Emily put her palm on his chest and tilted her face up to his. "It's cold out."

Don't miss
How to Train a Cowboy *by Caro Carson,*
available now wherever
Harlequin® *Special Edition books and ebooks are sold.*

www.Harlequin.com

HARLEQUIN®

SPECIAL EDITION

Life, Love and Family

Save **$1.00**

on the purchase of ANY
Harlequin® Special Edition book.

Available whever books are sold,
including most bookstores, supermarkets,
drugstores and discount stores.

Save **$1.00**

on the purchase of any Harlequin® Special Edition book.

Coupon valid until September 30, 2018.
Redeemable at participating outlets in the U.S. and Canada only.
Limit one coupon per customer.

52615825

Looking for more satisfying love stories
with community and family at their core?

Check out **Harlequin® Special Edition**
and **Love Inspired®** books!

New books available every month!

CONNECT WITH US AT:

Facebook.com/groups/HarlequinConnection

 Facebook.com/HarlequinBooks

Twitter.com/HarlequinBooks

 Instagram.com/HarlequinBooks

Pinterest.com/HarlequinBooks

ReaderService.com

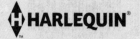

**ROMANCE WHEN
YOU NEED IT**

Looking for inspiration in tales
of hope, faith and heartfelt romance?

Check out **Love Inspired®** and
Love Inspired® Suspense books!

New books available every month!

CONNECT WITH US AT:

Harlequin.com/Community

Facebook.com/HarlequinBooks

Twitter.com/HarlequinBooks

Instagram.com/HarlequinBooks

Pinterest.com/HarlequinBooks

ReaderService.com

Earn points on your purchase of new Harlequin books from participating retailers.

Turn your points into **FREE BOOKS** of your choice!

Join for FREE today at
www.HarlequinMyRewards.com.

Harlequin My Rewards is a free program (no fees) without any commitments or obligations.